KEYS of LIFE

*To Debbie Ilges
this book is about
strong women just
like you !*

Thomas Dorlink

KEYS of LIFE

Book One
Uriel's Justice

Carolyn Schield
Tom Vorbeck

Keys of Life: Uriels's Justice
Copyright © 2014 by Carolyn Schield and Tom Vorbeck

All rights reserved. No part of this book may be used or reproduced in any manner whatsoever including Internet usage, without written permission of the author.

This book is fiction. Names, characters, businesses, organizations, places, events and incidents are the product of the authors' imaginations or are used fictitiously. Any resemblance to actual persons, living or dead, events, or locales is entirely coincidental.

ISBN 10: 0991667018
ISBN 13: 9780991667017

Book design by Maureen Cutajar
www.gopublished.com

For our parents...

ACKNOWLEDGEMENTS

Special thanks to our outstanding copy editor Alexandria Baca, for her incredible patience and great talent. Her tremendous courage was inspirational for this huge project. Pat yourself on the back, Tom and Andrew Aker for this incredible cover. Our families get big thanks for all their support and love. We couldn't have done it without our test readers, so thanks Kevin, Stephanie, Sandra White, Sandra Lovelace, Brad, Julie, Denis Morris, Chuck Schulte, Nancy Cohen, Samantha Koester and Judy Koester. First-time illustrator Kylie Naumann gets a round of applause for the artwork in the book. Our proofreaders get a high-five: Mary Kaarto and Sandra Lovelace. They have hearts of gold. Tom and I have been blessed with wonderful families and friends. Thanks to all of you, we did it.

Contents

Prologue 1
Chapter 1 The Cobra Strikes 3
Chapter 2 Uriel's Fall From Grace 10
Chapter 3 Ash 16
Chapter 4 Uriel the Tour Guide 19
Chapter 5 The Deluge 23
Chapter 6 Ash and Linda's Revealing Photos 27
Chapter 7 Maggie's Project 36
Chapter 8 Eleanor of Aquitaine 39
Chapter 9 Vindija Cave in Croatia (Giants) 42
Chapter 10 Looking for Magdalene 44
Chapter 11 Cordy's Dream 49
Chapter 12 Linda's Gift 51
Chapter 13 Inquisition Hunting the Pure of Heart ... 55
Chapter 14 Marrilac 58
Chapter 15 Linda's Crush 63
Chapter 16 Professor Uriel Continues 76
Chapter 17 The Healer 79
Chapter 18 Secrets Told 82
Chapter 19 The Children of the Nephilim 96
Chapter 20 Ash's Dream 101
Chapter 21 The Light Watchers 109
Chapter 22 The Miraculous Medal Shrine 113

Chapter 23 The Dark Watchers 119
Chapter 24 Chief Saunhac of the Mi'kmaq 123
Chapter 25 Ash the Tomb Robber.. 126
Chapter 26 Life and Death 132
Chapter 27 Chief Saunhac and the Wishing Cup 147
Chapter 28 Chief Saunhac.. 151
Chapter 29 Ash on the Run 153
Chapter 30 Black Belt... 161
Chapter 31 Chief Saunhac's Book 164
Chapter 32 Burnt-out Bob and Uriel the Librarian................. 167
Chapter 33 On the Grid.. 173
Chapter 34 Ash and Dirty Dottie 177
Chapter 35 The Magnetic Poles of Positive and Negative 183
Chapter 36 Magdalene Video Goes Viral............................... 189
Chapter 37 Legend of the Templars 192
Chapter 38 On the Run 197
Chapter 39 De Villiers Restoration Studio 202
Chapter 40 Bob's The Man... 210
Chapter 41 The Nephilim Agenda.. 216
Chapter 42 The Gift 218
Chapter 43 Yes, Ma'am.. 220
Chapter 44 Bill and the Light Watchers................................. 239
Chapter 45 Saint Catherine 241
Chapter 46 A Father's Wisdom 252
Chapter 47 Jerusalem and Meeting an Old Friend 260
Chapter 48 Children of the Nephilim and Ellen's Initiative ... 264
Chapter 49 Cordy Goes to Montreal 266
Chapter 50 Dottie Takes Ash for a Ride................................. 272
Chapter 51 Montreal, Canada 281
Chapter 52 Lunch with Bob..292
Chapter 53 Dinner with Bill... 296
Chapter 54 Ash and the Sweat Lodge 303
Chapter 55 Cordy Meets the Chief... 308
Chapter 56 Ellen Undercover 323
Chapter 57 Jon Lafitte's Promise to Pappa 325

Chapter 58 Pure of Heart Arise..327
Chapter 59 Julia's Dream..352
Chapter 60 Ellen and Bob 354
Chapter 61 The Chief's Funeral...357
Epilogue 360

Prologue

The Mi'kmaq Indians of Nova Scotia have a story passed down by their ancestors about a time when evil and wickedness ruled men. Wicked men killed their brothers and sisters. The sun-god creator was saddened and wept for his children. His tears fell upon the earth, causing a great flood. The people tried to escape the rising waters in their canoes, but only one old man and young maiden survived to populate the earth. They taught their children to respect the gifts of the sun-god creator. Mi'kmaq warriors were taught to be good stewards to the earth and defend it from evil.

Genesis 6:1-8

(1) And it came to pass, when men began to multiply on the face of the earth, and the daughters were born unto them,

(2) That the sons of God saw the daughters of men that they were fair; and took them wives of all which they chose.

(3) And the Lord said, my spirit shall not always strive with men, for that he also is flesh; yet his days shall be an hundred and twenty years.

(4) There were giants on the earth in those days; and also after that, when the sons of God came in unto the daughters of men, and they bare children to them, the same became mighty men which were of old, men renown.

(5) And God saw that wickedness of man was great in the earth, and that every imagination of the thoughts of his heart was only evil continually.

(6) And it repented the Lord that he had made man on the earth, and it grieved him at his heart.

(7) And the Lord said, I will destroy man whom I have created from the face of the earth; both man, and beast, and the creeping thing, and the fowls of the air; for it repenteth me that I have made them.

(8) But Noah found grace in the eyes of the Lord.

The Dead Sea Scrolls were discovered in a cave at Qumran, Israel, in 1946. The Book of Enoch was found among the ancient scrolls, which dated between 408 BCE and 318 CE. The ancient story would last for thousands of years passed down through generations. Archangel Uriel instructed Enoch to write down the lessons taught to him. The sacred knowledge was to reside in the hands of the Pure of Heart. The Book of Enoch was to last until the end of time, and Noah inherited the Book of Enoch from his father. The scroll told of the heavenly trial of the Nephilim, the Watchers, and Nephilim's angry leader, Antar. A Great Flood was to cleanse the earth of the wickedness of mankind. The Archangels and Pure of Heart were the champions of mankind and Earth. They defend against Antar's unquenchable thirst for revenge. The war continues to this day.

Chapter 1

The Cobra Strikes

At Master Wong's Karate School, a slim brunette, her red-gold highlighted hair tied in a ponytail, positioned into a defensive pose. In a white karate uniform with black belt, Cordy McDermott stood focused, her fist moving back and forth, aimed at one point on the wooden board being held tightly by the elderly Master Wong. With lightning speed, she broke the board in half. She swiftly pivoted her body, simultaneously producing a kick with incredible force and accuracy while his younger assistant watched the board he held split in two. Peter Woo, dressed in a black karate uniform embroidered with a cobra, bowed to Cordy. She bowed and resumed her defensive stance.

Peter Woo screamed out, "Hiiiii Ya!" and aimed his fist at Cordy's fearless face. She deftly blocked his arm and counterpunched to his chest. He tried again to hit her with his leg kick, but she moved and dodged it. Cordy kept her balance instinctively.

This fighting dance went on for ten minutes of punch and counterpunch. Woo, getting frustrated, decided to make a daring move

Keys of Life

of running at her. She grabbed his attack arm after skillfully avoiding a blow with his fist and pulled his weight against her, forcing him to become unsteady.

Cordy seized the moment, taking advantage of Woo's aggressiveness and his loss of balance. She took his weight and grabbed his arm, flipping him to the floor and finishing him with a final punch. Everyone in the room sat mesmerized at the battle of the two black belts. Woo smiled from the floor and yelled, "Enough!" Cordy's face changed from fearless determination to bear a radiant beaming smile. Her hand reached out and pulled him up. Master Wong patted Cordy on the shoulder and said, "Well done, Cordy."

He explained, "You handled his frustration perfectly, and your patience won out. You are learning total calm under pressure."

She smiled at the compliment. "Thank you, Master Wong." She looked at her watch and moaned, "Oh no, I'm going to be late."

Woo laughed, "She's focused when she is fighting me but forgets the time."

Cordy playfully rapped him on the head and quickly ran out the door.

Cordy drove her car onto the main street and into bumper-to-bumper traffic. She mumbled, "The traffic is awful today. Let's take the short cut." She turned right and a row of brick houses with well-kept lawns flew by. An older woman walked her Doberman and tiny poodle down the sidewalk. Children were playing on the front-yard lawns. Cordy turned on the radio, and a singer crooned, "I need an angel like you" while the rock-and-roll tune blared.

Out of nowhere, a screaming, half-naked woman in her twenties ran in front of the car ahead of Cordy's. Cordy slammed on the brakes to avoid hitting the stopped car. She watched as the surreal scene played out before her.

The young woman screamed and pleaded to the driver of the car, banging on his shut window, "He is going to kill me. Help me!"

The Cobra Strikes

The terrified driver of the car swerved around and sped past her. Cordy grabbed her cell phone and called emergency services.

"A woman is in distress on Hobby Lane. Send the police. The woman looks like she has been attacked," she said to the operator.

Somewhere in the back of her mind, Cordy knew the police were going to be too late, and this woman needed help immediately. She accelerated and pulled the car up to the crying woman and rolled the window down. "Get in!"

The bruised and battered woman jumped in and closed the door. She looked behind her through the back window and saw her hunter running toward them.

She screamed, "Oh my God, here he comes!"

The girl's dirty hair was filled with tangles. Her face was bleeding and bruised, like she had been beaten, and her voice had a Middle Eastern accent. The terrified girl looked at Cordy and yelled, "Drive as fast as you can. He is going to kill us!"

Cordy saw in her mirror a six-foot-tall bald, muscular man with tattoos on his arms running down the street toward them. He pointed his gun and started to shoot at Cordy's car.

He screamed at them with a heavy eastern European accent. "You lying witch. I'm going to kill you. No one escapes from me!"

"Oh, we'll see about that," Cordy yelled back.

She pushed the car's gas pedal to the floor, the wheels screeching as it raced away. He aimed his gun straight at Cordy's head.

"Get down!" Cordy yelled.

He opened fire, and one bullet shattered her outside mirror. Cordy raced up the road in a zigzag pattern trying to gain some distance. She swerved as her car almost hit oncoming traffic, which honked at her.

Cordy looked in her rearview mirror as the man aimed to shoot again. The Doberman and tiny poodle had escaped their elderly owner. The dogs, sensing the danger, had pulled their leashes away from their owner and attacked the huge man. They charged at him from behind and knocked him down to the ground. The dogs' owner screamed for the children to run home.

The poodle ferociously bit his hand holding the gun, while the Doberman chomped down on his balls. The man screamed in pain and kicked at the Doberman with his boot. The Doberman retreated, stunned by the blow for a few seconds. The tattooed man freed himself and ran, while being chased by the growling and snapping Doberman. He climbed over a tall fence to avoid them. The black Doberman and tiny white poodle barked at the fence as the man fled for his life.

The battered girl in Cordy's car was hysterical and crying. Cordy weaved through traffic at racecar speed. She drove down the street to Holy Angels Hospital and pulled up to the Emergency Room door. Cordy jumped out of the car and grabbed the crying girl from the other side. She tenderly held the trembling girl and yelled through the emergency automatic open door.

"I need some help out here, now!"

Paramedics saw Cordy and rushed to help. One young male EMT picked the screaming girl up and carried her into a room, placing her gently on a stretcher. Cordy grabbed a blanket and covered the girl, who looked like she was going into shock.

With tears streaming down her face, she grabbed Cordy's hand. "You saved my life. Thank you!"

Cordy tried to calm the girl down because she was shaking all over. The nurses and doctor started an intravenous line of normal saline. Sirens could be heard outside, and police ran into the emergency room. The doctor knew who they were looking for, yelling, "She is in here."

The doctor shined the pen light in the girl's eyes. "What's your name?"

The girl looked confused and begged Cordy, "You must call my father. He will be worried about me."

The girl moaned and tightened her grip on Cordy's other hand. "Don't leave me," she cried.

Cordy replied, "I won't leave you."

The Cobra Strikes

The girl squeezed Cordy's hand. "My name is Minah, daughter of Prince Hamanai."

"Are you allergic to any medicines, Minah? Are you hurt anywhere?" the doctor asked. The policeman answered, "We think we know who she is, and her father is on his way. She has been missing for five days. Minah was kidnapped. The FBI is on their way, too, and she is to have a 24-hour guard."

The female doctor had a syringe in her hand. "Now, Minah, I'm going to give you something to help you sleep."

The girl's eyes closed slowly, and she drifted off to sleep.

"I'm going to check her body for internal injuries. We need to order a MRI, stat. Unfortunately, I think social services needs to call in a psychiatric consult, and we need to check to see if there is any evidence of rape," the doctor said to the nurse.

Cordy looked at Minah's blood pressure and oxygen pulse oximeter.

"How's she looking, Doc?"

The doctor shook her head, "She looks like she has been beaten and heaven knows what else. Her neuro checks and vital signs are good. I think she's going to make it — thanks to you."

A young guy in his thirties wearing a gray suit flashed his badge. "I'm Detective Jacob Washington. Can I ask you some questions, miss?"

Minah's tight grip slowly relaxed while Cordy held her hand. He placed his hand over Cordy's and said, "She is going to sleep for quite a while."

"I don't want to leave her," Cordy whispered.

"That guy is still out there," Washington gently reminded her.

Cordy let go of her limp hand, and a policeman handed her a cup of coffee. The detective showed her a picture of the guy who shot at her car.

"Is that him?"

Cordy nodded her head.

"He is a Bosnian. Pretty brutal guy, he runs a prostitution ring with sex slaves. Minah was kidnapped from college. Ramone

Bossa is his name. He hit the jackpot with Minah. She is the daughter of a very wealthy man. Bossa decided to ask for ransom. Minah is a pretty brave girl. I have no idea how she escaped. Most of his girls do not escape and are brutally killed when they are of no more use to him."

Tears welled up in Cordy's eyes when she realized what a miracle it was that Minah escaped. Cordy looked at her watch. "I am really going to be late now. I have to get going. I have a seven-year-old to pick up."

A tall well-built young policeman smiled, "I'll get you there on time."

Detective Washington nodded, "I need to keep your car for a little while. They're doing a ballistics check on your mirror. Let Officer Thomson drive you where you need to go, and we'll bring you back to get your car later."

She thanked Detective Washington, shaking his hand, and followed Officer Thomson. Cordy jumped into the police car with sirens blazing. She was on time after all.

The police car pulled up to the schoolyard at Saint Mary Magdalene Catholic School. Cindy McGregor, a petite 30-year-old with a shapely figure and a wicked smile on her face, sauntered up to the window of the car.

"What'd she do now, officer?"

Officer Thomson smiled, "Nothing, miss, except be a hero."

Surprised, Cindy instinctively put her arms around Cordy's shoulders. "Girl, you look like you need a big hug," she said.

Tears welled up in Cordy's eyes as she realized the dangerous events that took place and how lucky she was to be alive. She laughed, "You can be the nicest but goofiest friend sometimes."

Cindy giggled, "What did you do, rescue a cat out of a tree? Where's your car?"

"Ballistics is checking it out," Officer Thomson chimed in.

Cindy's eyes widened.

"Ballistics!"

Chapter 2

Uriel's Fall From Grace

At the London Art Museum, walking through the galleries, a tour guide with his back to a group of high schools students is looking at Leonardo da Vinci's painting *Virgin on the Rocks*. He explained, "The painting consisted of four characters: Mary, John the Baptist, Jesus, and the Archangel Uriel in a cave of rocks next to a stream of water. It depicted a legend about Archangel Uriel rescuing John the Baptist's family and bringing them to Egypt to join his cousin Jesus's family to escape the evil King Herod. Da Vinci paints Uriel without a halo. Uriel's fall from grace came at the same time as the Merovingian king's fall.

"Merovingian King Childeric III was a puppet king and under Pope Zachary's complete control. In these times, the Pope did not just control Rome but had become a kingmaker. In 747 AD, Pepin the Short asked the Pope, 'Who rules, the one with power or the one with the bloodline?' The Pope answered, 'The one wielding the power should be king.'

"In 751 AD, King Childeric was powerless and his crown was

Uriel's Fall From Grace

removed by the Pope, who was brought to the monastery of Saint Bertin. The young Merovingian Childeric had his long hair cut by the monks on orders of the Pope. The long hair represented the magical power and royal rights of Merovingian kingship. The Merovingian resembled Samson the Nazarite, whose power came from his hair. Their rulers were called the sorcerer-kings, and legends talked about their long hair being the source of their power, including the ability to heal people."

A long-haired young man popped a bubble from his chewing gum and whispered to his girlfriend. "The long-haired dudes had super powers, magic wands, and crystal balls."

The docent answered calmly back, "You will see the crystal ball and scepter in their paintings. Crystal balls have been found in some of their graves. Yes, legends tell many stories of their special powers. Good observation, long-haired Daniel."

The students looked at each other in a surprised hush and then laughed at the tour guide's joke. The tour guide knew the young man asking the question was named Daniel even though his back had been turned the whole time to look at the painting. It was like he had eyes behind his head.

"A book is being passed around the group with a picture of the latest possible lost da Vinci called the *Salvator Mundi*. What you see is a picture of the long-haired Jesus of Nazarene holding a crystal ball. It is an interesting coincidence." The students looked at the book's picture as it was passed around.

"The deposed and short-haired Childeric was placed in a monastery near St. Omer. Pope Zachary's work was not done for he was to show the power of the papacy over kings and heaven. Uriel the archangel was in the early church, one of the four revered archangels. The archangels represented the four cardinal points of north, south, east, and west on a compass. "Michael and Gabriel were named in the Book of Daniel. Raphael was named in the Book of Tobit. Uriel was named in the Book of Enoch and Second Book of Esdras. Uriel was known as the angel of justice and repentance. Pope Zachary believed a cult to Saint

Uriel was taking hold throughout the church. He decided that images of archangel Uriel would be removed in the churches, and so his face was erased from church walls. He was removed from veneration with a stroke of the Pope's pen. It was one of the first times a Pope would decide which angels Catholics could pray to. The Pope's hope was that Uriel would disappear from man's memories.

"An archangel is not an easy one to outsmart, especially the archangel of justice. Followers in the church hid their devotion to Uriel by using the symbols of the eagle angel, bull angel, lion angel, and man angel. The official version given to the people was that these symbols represented the four authors of the New Testament, and the angels were placed at the four cardinal points inside the church. They represent the constellations Taurus the bull angel (vernal equinox), Leo the lion angel (summer solstice), Scorpio the eagle angel (autumnal equinox), and Aquarius the man angel (winter solstice).

"Pope Zachary removed Uriel and Childeric III, thus demonstrating the supreme power of the Pope over heavenly and earthly kingdoms. In 745, Pope Zachary removed the two books that mentioned Uriel from the canon. The Book of Enoch and the Book of Esdras became apocryphal books. Other churches, such as the Anglican, Coptic, and Eastern Orthodox churches, would respect Uriel in the future, and some Catholics did not abide by Pope Zachary's decree. The Celtic Church held Uriel in reverence and placed him in their Book of Kells."

A young girl spoke up from the back. "He looks like a she to me," she said, pointing to the girlish looking angel in the painting *Virgin on the Rocks*.

The guide answered her back, "Excellent point! You are right, to some the angel does look like a girl. Da Vinci may have thought angels came in both male and female forms. He liked to paint androgynous-looking subjects. Perhaps he was giving the viewer the choice to pick."

The young girl asked, "Do angels walk on Earth?"

Uriel's Fall From Grace

The guide smiled, "Da Vinci would answer that question with a yes and use for evidence the Bible stories where angels appear and visit people such as Abraham, Mary Magdalene, and Lot to name a few witnesses.

The museum guide pointed to the painting above. "It seems Leonardo may have been a fan of Uriel even though it was forbidden," he said. "In the painting, da Vinci placed archangel Uriel sitting with the Holy family in exile. John the Baptist was an elder male child and would have been killed in the Massacre of Innocents decreed by Herod. Herod issued an order for all first-born males to be killed.

"Da Vinci portrayed two versions of this story in the *Virgin of the Rocks*, including one where Mary, John, Jesus, and the archangel were not wearing halos. You will see that painting at the Louvre in Paris. Da Vinci's second version, which you see before you, shows Mary, John and Jesus with halos but the archangel sitting does not have one. Da Vinci placed Uriel in the painting to show his devotion in protecting the Holy family. His fall from grace from the Pope's decree is reflected by his lack of a halo."

"Leonardo da Vinci was a visionary who could see into the future. In his sketchbooks, he had pictures of machines that man would invent later in history, such as the helicopter, tank, and solar power. He wrote about a prophetic dream of a great deluge that would wipe out mankind. The *Virgin of the Rocks* could also have been a prophetic work by da Vinci. Some say the story shown in the *Virgin of the Rocks* happened on February 11, 1917, to Saint Bernadette, who had a vision of Our Lady of Lourdes near a grotto in Lourdes, France. In da Vinci's *Virgin of the Rocks*, water plays an important role. John the Baptist and Jesus gave the sacrament of baptism to mankind. They knew the healing powers of water and about it being the key ingredient for life. Water is seen at the bottom of the painting. In Lourdes, Saint Bernadette made the point that the water from the spring there would have no power unless one believes. The power of believing one can be cured is powerful medicine of which modern science is starting to realize with their research on what is called the 'placebo effect.'

"Remember ladies and gentlemen, the Pure of Heart will survive even through great cataclysms. The vision of Our Lady of Fatima in 1917 revealed three prophecies to shepherd children. The third secret prophecy was withheld from the public until 2000. In the prophecy, the angel with the flaming sword stood with Our Lady and cried, "Penance, Penance, Penance," foretelling a great disaster to the church and world in the future. The unnamed angel with the flaming sword in the prophecy is not venerated by the Catholic Church. His name is Uriel, who guards the Tree of Life at the gate of Eden. The *Virgin of the Rocks* reveals Uriel as the angel who guards the children of Adam and the Pure of Heart. Leonardo must have believed a day would come for the Pure of Heart's return and those who look on his painting would remember this message, found in Matthew 5:8, "Blessed are the pure in heart: for they shall see God."

The tour guide turned around and smiled, "You may proceed downstairs for lunch, and thank you." The students walked toward the stairs. The museum tour guide, dressed in a suit coat and khakis, was smiling. His name badge read Uriel.

Uriel looked up at the beautiful painting. It was Antar's private joke and a demonstration of his power. The tentacles of the Children of the Nephilim reached even Rome. The Vatican held power over many nations for centuries. Antar's children of the Nephilim were all about power.

Uriel had his friends, too. Many years later, art historians declared it was Gabriel in the *Virgin of the Rocks* because Gabriel was one of the three archangels acknowledged for veneration. The missing halo over the archangel in one version of the painting caused a dilemma with that theory. If it was Gabriel pictured, where was his halo? All the others in the painting have halos, but not the beautiful, protective archangel.

"Da Vinci was one sly and brilliant man for he knew this day would come. Justice is so sweet. Penance, penance, penance is the real message. The time has come for judgment and truth," laughed Uriel as he walked past the painting at the National Gallery in London.

The museums were one of his favorite places when he visited Earth. The four archangels appeared usually only for special errands, but this day he couldn't resist a visit to see the painting. A statue of the Isis holding a baby Horus from Egypt stood near the wall as he departed.

Chapter 3

Ash

All Hell is breaking loose! Chaos reigns the day.
It is October, and all over the Middle East there is great unrest. Egypt's government has fallen. Thousands of people protest outside the presidential palace. Protesters in neighboring countries are taking to the streets.

It is exciting and scary at the same time, but fear of the future is nothing compared to the injustices perpetrated by the Children of the Nephilim. The people have come to realize that death from starvation is worse than dying fighting. The reality in the region is that life must go on, and the driver of Egypt's economy, tourism, must start to flow again like the great Nile or all will be lost.

Already the region has seen cancellations from Christian travelers that some are saying is equal only to the Great Exodus of Moses. Museum treasures are vulnerable, and the Children of the Nephilim have already targeted some of Egypt's priceless artifacts. Military and police are busy keeping the crowds under control, while it's open season for museum thieves in the dark.

Ash

A loud banging noise came from the back of a Toyota 4Runner as Ash, a good looking, tall, muscular man in his mid-thirties, slid a tool box into the rear storage while loading up in front of the Aswan museum. His long hair was streaked blond from the sun, and his skin was tan. The muscles in his arms flexed underneath his dirty white T-shirt as he moved.

To say Ash stood out in a crowd in Egypt was an understatement. His mother was a tribal woman and his father was a German archaeologist so the dark skin was inherited from his Egyptian mother, while the blond hair and blue eyes came from his father. The rippling muscles were a result of a life of working in stone as Ash had taken up his father's profession, archaeology.

Archaeology was the only thing that brought Ash close to his long gone father, whom he had never known. He was an academic with a doctoral degree in archeology from the University of Kiel. Ash's father was in charge of one of the most important digs the Germans had embarked upon. Johan Von Lettow fell in love and married Ash's mother when she was 21, and it caused a lot of controversy with the other German academics on staff at the university.

Ash's mother, Aziza, was something special. She was beautiful, with long, thick black hair and dark brown eyes. Aziza was also brilliant, a gifted healer, and she had intuitive insight, which gave her the ability to sometimes see into the future. She had a photographic memory, so she graduated from college at the early age of 18. Ash's mom was working on her doctorate in Egyptian history when she met the distinguished and handsome Han. Ash's mother's eyes would light up when she talked about him.

Aziza knew that Han was the one for her when their eyes met. He was an honorable man and abided by tradition when courting her. Aziza's father loved him like a son, and they lived happily in Egypt with their little boy.

Aziza knew the region better than anyone. Her last name was Simbel, after all. An honored Egyptian family in the archeology world, her father led the first archeologists to the Abu Simbel

Temples in southern Egypt on the Nile. The temples were on the western bank of Lake Nasser, southwest of Aswan, the city Ash called home.

Ab was the ancient Egyptian name given to the human heart. It was written that the spiritual heart of a baby was formed at conception by a drop of the mother's blood. To the Egyptians, the heart was the seat of the soul.

Egyptians thought the heart was where all emotion, will, and thought resided. Man's life force came from the heart. According to the Egyptian Book of the Dead, the heart gave evidence during the weighing of the heart ceremony. The Egyptian goddess of truth and justice, Ma'at, placed the feather of truth on one scale and on the other placed the heart of the deceased. If the heart outweighed the feather, the soul was devoured by the Egyptian demon Ammit.

Elephantine Island, between the border of Nubia and Egypt, was named Abu, meaning "holy divine father." Abu stood near the Tropic of Cancer, where one could look up at noon and see the sun directly overhead. At the solstices, one would see the sun reverse its direction. Ash grew up surrounded by one ancient majestic playground. As a child, he would bring his staff and set it vertical in the sand on the summer solstice at Abu Simbel, marveling at the loss of any shadow.

Abu was a magical place and had a special connection with the heavens. Ash got ready to photograph a special event.

Chapter 4

Uriel the Tour Guide

> *Book of Enoch*
> *Section III. Chapters LXXII-LXXXII*
> *The Book of the Heavenly Luminaries*
> *[Chapter 72]*
> *1 The book of the courses of the luminaries of the heaven, the relations of each, according to their classes, their dominion and their seasons, according to their names and places of origin, and according to their months, which Uriel, the holy angel, who was with me, who is their guide, showed me; and he showed me all their laws exactly as they are, and how it is with regard to all the years of the world 2 and unto eternity, till the new creation is accomplished which dureth till eternity*

A group of American tourists stood around their tour guide. He was a tall, auburn-haired, handsome man wearing a white California Angels baseball hat and pointing to a picture of the temple of Abu Simbel at the museum in Aswan.

The young Ash stroked his mustache and goatee as he passed by the tour guide only half-listening to him. The guide explained to the interested group, "The Ancient Egyptians created an incredible civilization lasting many centuries. Ancient Egyptian mystery schools produced Moses, Plato, Pythagoras, Solon, Herodotus, and Pliny, some say.

"It was written in the Bible that Jesus' family had fled to Egypt from Israel to escape King Herod's persecution. Jesus was a brilliant child, as seen in the Bible when he was found discussing with the learned rabbis of the Temple. A Jewish population resided and flourished in Alexandria. The Egyptian mystery school's teachings could be found in lands all over the world.

"It was said the great teachings were given to mankind from the heavenly ones who walked the earth with men long ago. The sacred teachings of the ancient mystery schools gave mankind mathematics, astronomy, and the healing arts. They were given only to the worthy. The secret knowledge had been preserved from an ancient civilization long ago.

"Libraries in Alexandria promoted education, and the beautiful female mathematician Hypatia taught there. Hypatia was killed because of jealousy over her brilliance, beauty, and femininity. An educated woman struck fear in the male-dominated society. Queen Cleopatra was a major supporter of the libraries, and her downfall saw the libraries destroyed and scrolls burned. The sacred knowledge from the heavens survived but went underground. The Precession of the Equinoxes lasted approximately 25,800 years, and the Age of Pisces was ending leading into the next Age of Aquarius. The galactic alignment where the earth, sun, and center of the Milky Way align is a rare moment occurring now. It is when the earth's axis is near the galactic equator and points to the galactic center. Had mankind used the sacred knowledge well? It was the end of an age and time for change.

"Sacred knowledge was given only to the initiated ones in the mystery schools of Alexandria. It was passed on from generation to generation. Plato told the story of Atlantis civilization, which had great technology before a cataclysm destroyed it.

"The Pyramid of Giza is an amazing monument to the great building knowledge of the ancient world. Even today, modern

Uriel the Tour Guide

technology would have a difficult time creating the pyramid. The temple's massive structures have survived over the millennium, while civilizations have come and gone. The ancient structures remained even after wars and conflicts. The fight for freedom is a continuous one, even fought today. Please, feel free to tour the museum, and the bus will leave in an hour. My assistant will guide you."

The tour guide watched a busy Ash rush by, intent on his work. He was gathering equipment and loading it on the truck parked near the museum. The guide's name tag read Uriel.

Uriel was familiar with the ancient city of Aswan. He thought back to the trial of the Nephilim and the great deluge. In the old days visits to Earth had been frequent and unrestricted. He was given the job of guarding the Tree of Life with his fiery sword. Who would have predicted that a violation would be committed by a group of heavenly ones named the Nephilim?

The Nephilim came down from the heavens, led by Antar. The crime committed was the Nephilim's taking of Eve's daughters for wives. Enoch was chosen by them to bring forth a petition to the Heavenly Host for mercy and forgiveness. He was favored by the Heavenly Host and was a Pure of Heart.

Enoch's petition failed, and it was judged that a massive extinction event would occur to wipe out the crime of the Nephilim. Enoch wrote about the trial on scrolls and left them to his family for safekeeping.

Uriel remembered how poor Enoch shook with fear in Antar's presence. The Lord of Hosts, commander of the angels showed no forgiveness for Antar and his children. It was then that Antar declared war on the Pure of Heart, vowing to hunt them down and exterminate them. The Nephilim would destroy the Pure of Heart and their children would rule the earth again. It was Uriel who was given the job of protecting Noah and his children from the flood. Antar's arrogance and lust for revenge had to be fought.

Uriel remembered Antar's angry words, "If our children do not survive, then the Pure of Heart shall not." Uriel, unafraid, looked back at Antar, who was once long ago his friend, and answered, "You do your worst, and we will do our best." Uriel smiled at the bright and busy Ash and when no one was looking, promptly disappeared.

Chapter 5

The Deluge

"The Nephilim were on the earth in those days and also afterward when the sons of God went to the daughters of men and had children with them. They were the heroes of old, men of renown." Genesis 6:4-6
In 10:1-3 of the Book of Enoch, the archangel Uriel is dispatched by God to inform Noah of the approaching flood.

Uriel held the ancient scroll, written in Aramaic and called the Book of Enoch. He remembered well the trial of the Nephilim and Antar, their leader. At one time, Antar and he fought side by side, but now they fought against one another.

The Lord of Hosts ordered him to warn Noah of the upcoming extinction event on Earth. Uriel would tell his side of the story and how he placed the ancient scroll, with the sacred secret knowledge of the stars, in Noah's hand. It seemed like only yesterday.

Noah, an older man with beautiful, white hair and an honest face, was tending his sheep. Uriel, wearing white robes and sandals, came from behind him. The shepherd Noah could see this stranger had a heavenly look.

"What is this? A stranger? Let me welcome you to my house for dinner."

Uriel answered, "I have come for no dinner, Noah. I am here to warn you of what disaster awaits the world."

Noah's faced showed surprise and concern. "What disaster?"

Uriel touched his arm gently and guided him to a rock under a palm tree.

"In a few years, by judgment of the heavens, a great deluge will come to this land. It will wipe out all life. You have been chosen because of your great understanding, pure heart, and good life to be saved from this disaster. Extinction of life on Earth must be prevented."

Noah put his hands over his face with a trembling voice asked, "What of my family?"

"All your family will be saved if you follow the directions in this scroll," Uriel softly answered." The scroll contains instruction on how to build an ark. You must hurry, for time is running out. A war has begun in the heavens. I was told to warn you. You are a righteous man, and your heart is pure.

"The Nephilim and Watchers have declared war on Earth. The Lord of Hosts has decided to save your family. The Keys of Life will protect all creation from extinction. You have been chosen for the great honor of protecting the Earth and its children."

Uriel handed Noah the scrolls. He gave Noah a container filled with seeds of plants for the entire world. The container was shaped like a cross with a circle on top. Egyptians would later call it "ankh," the symbol for the key of life.

Uriel looked at Noah.

"Noah, have your children deposit these seeds all over the world. The seeds of life will produce crops and trees for the earth. They have come from the Tree of Life from the Garden of Eden. You will bring this beehive to take with you for the plants will need them."

He pointed above them to a beehive above their heads in the tree. "You have been given honey from the Tree of Knowledge.

The Deluge

The Pure of Heart will taste its sweetness and great knowledge will come when they eat it."

Uriel then handed Noah a crystal ball. "Noah, treasure and protect the light. It has great power and will help guide you. Your families must keep these safe and secret."

Uriel walked away, disappearing behind the tree.

The Great Deluge flooded the Earth thousands of years ago, bringing life in the world close to extinction. Ancient civilizations have recorded stories about the Great Deluge and its destruction. Noah's family was saved from extinction as part of the Pure of Heart.

The bloodlines of his sons Japheth, Ham, and Shem spread throughout the world. Yet the children of the Nephilim were not completely wiped out.

"We saw the Nephilim there (the descendants of Anak come from the Nephilim). We seemed like grasshoppers in our own eyes, and we looked the same to them." Numbers 13:33

Antar's ancient name, Anak, was recorded, and he saw the Nephilim's children had survived. He wondered why they were given a reprieve.

Was it his fierce fighting for his children that changed the Great One's mind? Was it a mistake?

He could hear Uriel's impatience. "You never understood compassion and forgiveness." Antar's face turned to anger, "Forgiveness, compassion, and mercy are for the weak. I know only revenge. Our children's numbers have dwindled and are headed for extinction."

Uriel's flaming sword blazed as he raised his arm to the heavens.

"The truth is revealing itself. You wanted your children to rule, and mankind to be enslaved. Antar, hear my warning. Revenge is not the answer. You will understand when this is over. The lesson is everything is connected. Eve's children are connected to us. We love them and will protect them."

Uriel disappeared and left Antar to wonder what game was being played. His children lived but in fewer numbers. It was thought they would be extinct in a few hundred years. If Antar had his way, all of mankind would have been destroyed, and he would've had his revenge. His children were bigger and stronger, and yet, Adam's children thrived while his died. The Nephilim knew nothing of forgiveness, love, or compassion. They wanted the power to rule over mankind. Antar's revenge would be sweet, indeed.

Chapter 6

Ash and Linda's Revealing Photos

It's early morning, and Ash was finishing packing his truck from the day before. He tossed another piece of equipment into the dusty 4Runner. It was a tripod for the lighting equipment that he was going to use to photograph a semiannual event at Abu Simbel Temple. The assistant curator of the Aswan Museum of Egyptian Artifacts, Roshed Omor, assigned him to the project every time it came up.

Ash grew up around the temples, and he knew them like the back of his hand. He had more experience than some 50-year-old men in the field. Ash was an experienced professional trained by the best.

Rosh stuck his head out of the door of the loading dock. He was an older balding man, with a rotund belly and of average height. He was a loyal friend of Ash's. Rosh knew his family and worked with his dad long ago.

Ash saw him stick out his head and yelled, "There's my taskmaster. Where's my helper you promised me?"

"Oh Ash, I am so sorry," Rosh said, wickedly smiling. He looked at his watch, "I told them to be here on time."

"Yeah, yeah."

Ash pulled his hat off his head. "I've heard that before, Rosh."

Rosh walked over to the truck, finally loaded. "Do you need any help, Ash?"

Ash smiled knowingly at Rosh, "No, your timing is perfect. I just loaded the last piece, and you know that, Rosh."

Rosh started to laugh. "Ash, you know I love you like a son. Sons do all the work, and the old man, he bosses. It's a tradition."

Ash laughed. "You mean, you love the notoriety I bring the museum, and you don't have to lift a finger. What would you do without me, old man?"

Ash poked Rosh's stomach. "You better lay off those bread rolls."

"It is my wife's good cooking," Rosh said, laughing. "You must come to dinner, Ash. She wants to fatten you up."

Ash smiled. "She is a good cook. I'll tell her how you work me so hard, and I don't have time to eat." They both chuckled.

Ash never wanted to be in the limelight, instead preferring to be out in the field. So Rosh took all the credit for Ash's finds and discoveries. You could say Ash was a ghost archeologist. He was very young when his father's dig team came across a major find.

The locals said it was the legendary, cursed star room. Ash's father went missing after a cave collapsed, dropping the room into a shaft with rocks wedging themselves above to close off the entrance.

Despite an extensive search, to this date, no one has been able to find that room again. Han, Ash's dad, was declared missing because his body couldn't be recovered for fear of an even worse collapse. The search team deemed it too dangerous. Nobody was found, and the government declared he died in the collapse of the temple room.

The University of Kiel had insurance on Han, and Ash's mom was able to collect his benefits. That money paid for Ash's education.

Ash and Linda's Revealing Photos

His mother was never one to wallow in pity. All his mother would say is that one day, he was gone. It was never disclosed what they had found in that room. In fact, the whole project was classified in Egyptian and German records.

"Well, if that intern helper doesn't show up soon, I'm going to leave without him," Ash said, putting his baseball cap back on his head.

Rosh started to laugh again, his belly bouncing.

Ash looked at him with a worried look, and it dawned on him.

"You didn't, Rosh, you didn't, I told you no more women!"

Rosh laughed even louder.

Ash shook his head and held his hands up in frustration.

"No, not a woman," Rosh said. "A little girl."

Ash slammed his hat down on the truck. "I quit. It isn't fair!"

Rosh patted Ash on the back. "But Ash, you are great with kids. You remember when I took you out on your first dig at ten?"

Ash smiled. "Well, that is no excuse."

"She is the daughter of a prominent American diplomat and has a great deal of interest in archeology. A summer intern is just following you for a day. The girl has been on six major digs already, and she's only sixteen. She reminds me of you, lots of heart and curiosity. Here she comes now."

"Good morning, Linda." The young girl just held her head down and nodded. Ash, detecting a problem, looked at Rosh with a confused look.

As Ash walked around the back of the 4Runner, Rosh whispered, "I forgot to tell you she has a bad stuttering problem."

Ash put his head near Rosh's. "Oh that's just great, Rosh. My day is off to a great start. I'm babysitting."

Ash jumped in and motioned for Linda to get into the truck. She hopped into the front seat and put on her seat belt.

Ash extended his hand, "Hi, Linda, I'm Ash, and you were late."

Ash wanted her to know that he didn't want this to be a bad

habit. She just nodded again, with her head down. Ash was already losing patience.

"You will look at me when you nod." She looked at him and nodded again but this time he could see her face. Tears were falling down her cheeks, flowing like a river.

Now, Ash felt like an ass. He drove for a while with dead silence in the car. He handed her the scarf from around his neck. Linda nodded and blew her nose on it. Ash had enough of the tears and admitted he was a marshmallow when it came to girls crying.

He pulled the truck over, and softly asked, "What's wrong?"

Linda sniffled. "My-my my parents just ta-ta told me that we have to leave Egypt be-be- because of the unrest. We are ga-ga-going to Ireland. I-la-la-love E-E-Egypt."

Ash nodded. "So do I. When are you leaving?"

"A-a-a week from now." Her chin began to quiver again, and the tears returned. Ash reached over and put his arm around her shoulders. She leaned in, sobbing uncontrollably.

"The-the they're going to-to make me leave my dog here. I-I can't leave Leo to fend for himself on the streets. D-d-do you know what the hungry d-d-do with stray dogs here in Egypt?" Now she was in total meltdown mode.

He had heard people were told to leave the country immediately for their safety. Pets were not included in the evacuations due to limited space. Ash had to think fast but his heart talked faster. He dried her tears with his scarf.

"I'll take Leo and give him the best home ever."

Linda wiped her eyes and came up for air. "You-you would do that? I didn't think you like me."

Ash laughed, "Yes, I do. Now, Linda, stop your crying or the deal is off."

Linda straightened up in her seat and wiped her eyes on her shirt. "De-de-deal."

She smiled, beaming at him. Ash smiled back.

"Just sit back and breathe. I'll promise you the most exciting time you ever had in Egypt today."

Ash and Linda's Revealing Photos

Linda closed her eyes and said, "OK-K-K. For some reason, I- I- believe you."

Ash tried to get her talking.

"Why did you name your dog Leo?"

Linda was like a chameleon, smiling now. "Af-after the movie star, Leonardo. He is m-m-my favorite movie star."

Ash was driving but shaking his head and moaning. "Oh no, not a movie star! I thought it was from Leo the astrological sign in the sky. You know, leo-lion?"

Linda started to close her eyes once more. She might be able to sneak a nap in. Ash drove fast down the dirt road. He had to get there before the sun rose.

They pulled up at Abu Simbel temple and Ash woke up Linda. "We'll have to work fast to get our camera equipment up in time."

The tourists had already started to pack in for the event. Linda nodded. "I will do as yo-yo-you say."

With that, they jumped out of the truck.

Ash was there to photograph a solar phenomenon. The axis of the temple was positioned by the architects of ancient Egypt in such a way that on October 21st and February 21st — 61 days before and 61 days after the Winter Solstice — the rays of the sun would penetrate the sanctuary and illuminate the sculptures on the back wall.

The exception was the statue of Ptah, the god connected with the underworld, who always remained in the dark.

Linda was wonderful. She had a background in photography and made some suggestions to Ash on how to set up the lighting to get the best picture. It made good sense, so Ash took Linda's advice and was impressed with her knowledge.

Ash said, "Linda, did you know that this temple was dedicated to the gods Amon and Re'-Horakhty? Amun, or Amen, is the Egyptian god who later became the great Amen-Ra. Many people will tell you the Egyptian religion was polytheistic. It wasn't. It was monotheistic.

Keys of Life

"Amun was the father-god and creator of everything. Egyptians developed a trinity consisting of Amun, Ra, and Ptah. Ra was connected to Horus, who rode on the solar boat in the sky and in the underworld, where the souls of the dead lived. Ra ruled the winds and Ptah called the world into creation. Ptah spoke and there was the world and universe. It's similar to the story of Genesis; God said, let there be light and there was light."

Linda and Ash looked up at the huge statue of Ramesses II of the 19th dynasty. Ash saluted the statue.

"He represents Osiris, who will be regenerated by the rays of the sun."

Linda pointed to Ash's badge. "I s-s-saw your n-n-name on your museum badge and your l-l-last n-name is Simbel."

Ash nodded. "It's why I get this assignment every year. My mother is rumored to be related to Abu Simbel. He was a young local boy who guided the early archaeologists who discovered the site of the buried temple. Abu had seen the temple from time to time buried in the shifting sands, and they named the complex after him. It's amazing how they moved the temple, rock by rock, because of the Aswan Dam. They even tried to place it exactly in alignment with the sun.

"Linda, follow me. We still have some time before the light is right." Ash looked at his watch. "The only temple that was ever constructed for a woman is here across the way."

He pointed to the temple of Egyptian Queen Nefertari. "This was constructed for Queen Nefertari and the goddess Hathor. When we're done with the photo shoot, I'll take you over there."

Linda smiled. "O-OK. I wo-wo-would like that, Ash."

This was the first time Ash was using the new high-tech digital camera for the shoot. Ash felt eyes staring at him, and an elderly man tapped him on the shoulder.

"You look like you know what you're doing, young pup. Can you explain to my confused wife what this is all about?"

Sam Allen was a typical tourist. He was a chubby, retired man

Ash and Linda's Revealing Photos

loaded with camera equipment. His very patient, plump wife, Brenda, trailed behind him.

Ash smiled, and he had a sneaky feeling Brenda wasn't the confused one.

"Well, the original dates for the event were October 21 and February 21, 61 days before and after the winter solstice. Sunlight would fill the inside of the temple and fall on all the statues, except Ptah, the god connected to the dark underworld. Since the temple was moved, the solar phenomenon happens on October 22 and February 22.

"These days were special, so important events involving the pharaoh, such as his coronation, fell on these days. The Egyptians considered the brightest star in the sky, Sirius, sacred, and October 22 was sacred to Sothis. Sothis was the Egyptian name for Sirius. Its hieroglyph was a five-pointed star, arch, and triangle."

Ash pointed to the stone walls decorated with hieroglyphics. "Sothis was connected to the Egyptian trinity of Isis, Osiris, and Horus, called the dog star. It helped the Egyptians predict the coming of the flooding of the Nile."

Ash moved to his camera and looked at the sun's rays coming up over the horizon. Sam pointed his camera on the statues.

"So, you're saying we're seeing this moment like the ancient Egyptians?"

Ash smiled. "Yep, it's a magical time for the Egyptians, and for us." He positioned himself behind his camera. Linda sat next to him, looking at the horizon.

Ash quietly asked, "Linda, have you always stuttered?"

Linda looked at the ground. "N-n-o, it s-s-started after the accident with m-my grandmother. S-s-she was w-w-watching m-me when I was s-s-six years old and d-d-died of a s-s-stroke. I c-c-can remember h-h-her eyes looking at m-m-mee. I-I've ss-s-stuttered ever since."

Ash looked at her. According to Egyptian tradition, it was a time of magic and miracles. "Who knows, maybe your stuttering will go away?" Ash said while adjusting the camera. Linda

33

smiled. "Maybe that is w-w-why I'm here?"

Ash smiled. "If we get a wish, mighty Ra, then I want my friend Linda here to be cured." The red glowing sun's rays hit the temple, directly illuminating the statues. Ash started taking photos of the gods at the back.

Everyone was in awe of the illuminating effect of the temple. It was always a magical moment for Ash, and he felt the excitement.

© Kylie Naumann

Chapter 7

Maggie's Project

Cindy coyly smiled at the handsome Officer Tim, who was leaning over the window ledge.

"What's your name, officer?"

Officer Tim answered back quickly. "Tim Thomson."

"I'm Cindy McGregor. Thanks for bringing Cordy home," Cindy said as she reached through the open window with her hand out. "Would there be a Mrs. Thomson by chance?" Officer Tim laughed. "No, miss, no Mrs. Thomson."

Cindy's smile got bigger. "Well, that is a shame. Office Tim is home all alone?"

Cordy rolled her eyes at Cindy, and pleaded, "Please excuse me for interrupting, but is Maggie ready?"

Cindy opened the door and pulled Cordy out. "Maggie is doing her homework, and she is in the chapel with Sister Patricia. I'll keep Officer Tim busy while you get her." Cindy plopped in the seat next to the officer.

Cordy leaned over. "Officer, let me go get her. I'm babysitting

Maggie's Project

my friend's daughter. I'll be right back."

"Take your time, Cordy," Cindy said, waving her away with a wink.

Cordy ran over to the church, nicknamed the "rock church" because of its construction from granite blocks. Mary Magdalene was the patron saint of the church.

Sister Patricia was an elder sister in her eighties, and she was showing Maggie, a vivacious little freckled-faced seven-year-old, a wood panel behind the altar. The choir practiced for Sunday Mass, singing Panis Angelicus (Heavenly Bread).

"This panel, Maggie, talks about Magdalene's life, which is based on the French oral tradition."

Sister Patricia was pointing to a wood panel made by the artist Lipinski.

"In this frame, she sees the risen Christ; here she is in a boat landing in Marseilles. And this frame shows her being visited and fed by angels. Magdalene converted many people in France and lived in a cave, praying. Here is a pamphlet explaining the panel."

Maggie saw Cordy. "Cordy, look at all the information Sister Patricia gave me for my homework. I am doing Mary Magdalene for my saint life project."

Cordy smiled at Sister Patricia, who was dressed in her habit. "Hi, Sister Pat, thanks so much for helping Maggie." Sister Patricia walked to the door with them and turned the lights out. "Mary Magdalene is my favorite saint."

Maggie saw the statue of Mary Magdalene in front of the church with flowers around her. "Please, Cordy, can we take her picture?"

Cordy pulled out her cell phone and took a picture of the sad woman kneeling with her hands crossed over her knee.

Cordy whispered to Sister Patricia, "I was taught when I was little that she was a prostitute but some books and movies say she wasn't."

Sister Patricia shook her head. "Old teachings from centuries ago are hard to change. No, Mary Magdalene was only a sickly woman. Jesus cured her, and she became one of his most devout followers. Cordy, I suggest you read the New Testament again, particularly the parts with Mary Magdalene in them."

Cordy smiled. "I guess I better read it for myself. I just never had any time, but I'll make time."

"Maggie, let's go," Cordy yelled. "How would you like a ride in a police car?" Maggie giggled. "Really? Awesome!"

Cordy pointed to the police car. Sister Patricia looked at Cordy with concern, "What's that all about? Is everybody all right?"

Cordy laughed. "I haven't done anything illegal, but trust me, it's a long story. I have to run."

"Well I can't wait to hear all about it," Sister Patricia said. "I told your aunt that I would keep an eye on you."

Sister Patricia waved as the police car drove away with Cordy, Maggie, and Cindy, who had Officer Tim's telephone number tucked in her pocket.

Chapter 8

Eleanor of Aquitaine

The lecture hall was filled with more than a hundred students taking a course on influential women in medieval times. Professor Uriel, a smiling auburn-haired teacher, was a guest professor on the UCLA campus. He was asked to do a lecture series for the university.

Los Angeles was home to the California Angels, and Uriel felt right at home. Professor Uriel started his slideshow with a picture of Eleanor of Aquitaine.

"Ladies and gentlemen, get ready to meet one of the most powerful women of her time — Eleanor of Aquitaine."

"William IX, Duke of Aquitaine and Eleanor's grandfather, was a troubadour. He wrote and sang Occitan poetry. And Duke William's love life was something to sing about."

All the audience chuckled softly. "Fidelity was for monks, not for men. William was not a monk. The Duke was educated in etiquette, a seducer of beautiful women, a crusader knight, and a lover of song. He sang about courtly love. The life of the troubadour was one of freedom. Aquitaine was the land of freedom, where different religions were living together in harmony. Education thrived in the land of Aquitaine, and the country become immensely wealthy.

"William was given a beautiful quartz crystal cup by a Muslim ally. The Muslim told him the cup was called the Magdalene cup, brought by her from Jerusalem. He later bequeathed it to his granddaughter Eleanor."

"At fifteen, Eleanor married the king of France, Louis the VII. Eleanor gave her husband the crystal cup of her grandfather for a wedding present. Her court in Paris was a brilliant talented group of troubadours, poets, and beautiful ladies of court. Chretien of Troyes, a troubadour, came to the court of Eleanor's daughter Marie with songs about the legend of King Arthur and Knights of the Round Table. Chivalry and courtly love influenced the beautiful educated Eleanor, and she listened to the songs about the legend of the Holy Grail."

"Her family came in contact with the Templars during the Crusades, and she granted their operations at La Rochelle exempt from duties in her 1139 charter. The Templars and Eleanor's family were devoted to each other.

"Eleanor was given the rare privilege of seeing one of their prized possessions. Some say it was a wooden box with a golden triangle, which held inside sacred items found underneath Solomon's Temple.

"Eleanor gave King Louis of France two daughters, but the couple fought more often as time passed, and both agreed to ask for an annulment. The annulment was granted, and Eleanor married the young and dashing Henry II of Anjou, later to be the king of England.

"Eleanor and Henry believed the tales of King Arthur. In 1191, a tomb was found at Glastonbury.

"The monk's manuscripts had indicated the grave was of a past military leader in the fifth century. In the grave, the monks found a lead cross, with a message saying 'Here lays King Arthur and his second wife, Guinevere.'

"A monk went to grab the golden long hair of the lady, but it disappeared in his hands. Eleanor and Henry heard of the discovery and oversaw the burial of the large bones of a giant Arthur, and also Guinevere's bones, in chests in a black marble mausoleum. The proper gravesite was destroyed centuries later.

"Eleanor remembered the troubadour songs, and her husband was given the book *Roman de Rou* by the singer Wace. The book tells of the history of Britain and Brutus of Troy. Brutus' genealogy was traced back to Noah's sons Ham and Japheth. It was said that he was to rule over an isle that was inhabited by a few giants named Albion. Albion was an early name for Britain."

Professor Uriel turned on the lights with the flick of his fingers. "Ladies and gentlemen, Eleanor of Aquitaine was Queen of France, Queen of England, and one of the wealthiest and most powerful women of her time. She lived to be eighty-two years old.

"Eleanor of Aquitaine was a woman who ruled bravely in a time when men generally called the shots. We can all take a break for an hour, and when you come back, you'll hear the story of another very brave French queen who followed in her grandmother's shoes." All the students clapped and headed for lunch.

CHAPTER 9
Vindija Cave in Croatia (Giants)

Near the small town of Varaždin in Croatia, a bear cave estimated to be about 60,000 years old is the site of an archeological dig. The cave was home to ancient Homo sapiens and Neanderthals, and their fossils were being collected by archeologists to study the DNA of ancient man. Neanderthals were much larger than Homo sapiens, from the size of their craniums to the width of their chests and arms.

Nathan Sims, an archeologist, emailed his friend with the incredible news of the discovery. He obtained from a laboratory DNA from the fossils by bribing one of the technicians.

Nathan drove his truck to the small hotel where he was staying. He rushed up the stairs, opened the door to his room, and pulled out his worn and banged-up suitcase. The hotel room was scattered with photos from the site. The phone rang.

"Yes, I have it. I've booked a flight out today. It's true — the brain cavity is bigger and the whole body is larger. I was told they found a small percentage of Neanderthal DNA in the human genome of

Europeans and Asians. The skull had small traces of red hair, fair skin, and the second toe was longer than the big one, like Morton's toe. The only possible breeding was done by a male Neanderthal and a female Cro-Magnon. Neanderthal hybridization is now a real possibility. I'm leaving now, and I haven't told anyone except you. It's hard to believe the genocide and the great deluge, but it is true." He hung up the phone and walked out of the hotel. The newspapers reported later that week that Nathan Sims had mysteriously vanished.

At NGenetic Bioengineering Corporation, company president Jeff Henderson received a text message.

"Did you receive the package?"

He typed back to his boss.

"Yes, we received the DNA sample, and analysis has already begun. No loose ends exist. You'll be happy to hear our crops, bioengineered animals, and fish are replacing domestic food sources of all nations, and soon we'll have a monopoly on the world food situation. We know where all the seed repositories are around the world. It'll be easy to destroy them when the time comes. Anything with DNA is open season."

Another typed message came on his screen: "I notice the stock prices are going up and up. I want you to keep me informed on the developments regularly."

Henderson answered quickly, typing, "My purpose is to serve."

CHAPTER 10

Looking for Magdalene

Officer Tim drove and listened while Cindy chattered away about Maggie, Cordy, and herself. Cordy was watching Maggie for Trish, Cordy's old college roommate, a history teacher on a trip to Jefferson City with her class. Maggie couldn't miss school, so Cordy volunteered for the job. Trish's husband had died in Iraq.

"I love kids, don't you, Tim?" Cindy smiled at him.

Officer Tim laughed, "My brother has four kids, and I watched them for him one time. I gave them too much candy and junk food. They all were sick when I dropped them off, and it was my last babysitting gig. I guess I need some practice."

Tim smiled back at a smitten Cindy. Maggie begged Tim, "Can we ride with the siren on? Oh, pretty please."

"Sorry, honey, I only use it for emergencies." Officer Tim looked at her in the back seat. He pulled into the hospital drive, where a camera crew waited. "Oh no, I think we got trouble." Cordy observed the chaos before her. "You girls stay here. I'm going to say goodbye to Minah and get my car."

Looking for Magdalene

"I'll take good care of these girls, Cordy," Officer Tim said in a protective voice. "I'll give you a bit of advice. Don't say too much to the press, and if they ask you something you don't want to talk about, tell them no comment."

"I intend to try avoiding them as much as possible."

Cordy walked over to Detective Washington, who was talking to a forensic and ballistics expert. A woman wearing plastic gloves explained, "It looks like it was a Glock 22. We got lucky the bullet left some marks in the metal. This gun probably came from Europe, I bet." Washington nodded, "I know not to bet against you, Jill."

Cordy turned toward Washington. "Detective, can I get my car back?"

"Yes, the tests are done. Let me introduce Jill Stable, our ballistics expert."

The women shook hands.

"Does this picture look like the gun he had in his hand?" Jill held up a picture of a Glock 22. Cordy looked at it.

"You know, I think that does look like it. I have to admit I was driving away so fast I didn't get a good look at it."

"I guess not. You had other things on your mind." Cordy turned to Washington.

"Did Minah wake up yet?"

Washington shook his head. "No, lets go see her, shall we?"

Washington walked Cordy by the TV crew, where journalist Kate Wilson put her microphone in Washington's face.

"Detective Washington, is this the woman who rescued Miss Minah Hamanai, daughter of Prince Hamanai, the Egyptian ambassador and CEO of Arabian States Oil?"

Washington answered curtly, "Yes, this is the woman."

Kate Wilson pushed the microphone toward Cordy, "Cordy McDermott is the brave woman who saved her. How do you feel, Miss McDermott?"

"I'm just glad I got her to the hospital," Cordy answered shyly. Winston looked at Cordy. "You're pretty brave picking up a strange woman on the road."

Washington grabbed Cordy's arm and pushed his way past Wilson. "That's enough questions." Winston held the microphone to her face, "There you have it, folks, the heroine of the day, Cordy McDermott saves a princess's life."

Cordy walked in where Minah was lying, and an older, bald man, who boasted a dark mustache stood holding Minah's hands. He was well-dressed and behind him, two tall young men in suits stood at attention.

The elderly man crossed the room and shook Cordy's hand. "I believe you are the lady I owe a great debt to for saving my daughter's life. She is a student at the university. Minah is studying to be a neurologist. She refused my bodyguards because she thought they would get in her way. We have been looking for her for two weeks."

His voice cracked with emotion and tears welled in his eyes. "She is my only daughter. I thought we lost her forever. Thank you so very much."

Cordy smiled. "Minah is a very brave girl."

Minah, hearing her name and her father's voice, slowly began to wake up.

"Papa."

"Yes, child, Papa is here," Abu Hamanai said, softly hugging his daughter.

Minah looked over at Cordy. "The other car didn't stop, but you did. You saved me. Thank you." She started weeping and tears rolled off her cheeks. Cordy grabbed Minah's hand. "You're going to be OK. You're safe now. I'll be back to see you. I'm glad you found your family." Washington and Cordy left the father and daughter alone.

Washington gave Cordy her car keys, and she gave him her contact information. The fresh air felt good on her face as she left the hospital. Maggie and Cindy were saying goodbye to Officer Tim. Cordy motioned for them to hurry up. She dropped Cindy off at home.

"Tim is a hunk. He asked me out Saturday night. We're going to the movies."

Looking for Magdalene

Cordy laughed. "Just call me the matchmaker."

Cindy practically skipped to her door. "Maggie, how about a great big pizza for dinner?" Maggie jumped up and down. "Pizza my favorite!"

All night, Cordy helped Maggie with her Magdalene project. Maggie wanted to make a video on the Internet all about Mary Magdalene using the pictures Cordy had taken. The picture of the Magdalene statue at the church was put together with the story of Magdalene. Maggie's story came from the information Sister Patricia gave her from the panel that hung in the church. It showed Magdalene as a devoted disciple of Jesus. She witnessed his crucifixion and burial and was the first to see him at his resurrection. It became more obvious to Cordy as she researched Magdalene that she seemed to be a member of Jesus's family just by the fact of her presence at his crucifixion and burial.

Maggie and Cordy uploaded the video online. Cordy had read in the pamphlet that according to the French oral tradition, Magdalene became a hermit in the French mountains and was fed by angels. Cordy pulled out some pictures she took at another Magdalene church which showed a bull angel, an eagle angel, a lion angel and a man angel. She was curious about what they meant.

Her research showed that the official version was that these symbols represented Mark, Matthew, Luke and John and the fixed star constellations Taurus, Aquarius, Scorpio, and Leo. Maggie had fallen sound asleep by now, and Cordy carried her to bed.

Cordy learned there were four archangels, yet she was only taught about three. Who was Uriel? Uriel, light of God, was in the book of Esdras and book of Enoch. He rescued Saint John the Baptist and Saint Elizabeth from the Massacre of the Innocents.

Leonardo Da Vinci's *Madonna of the Rocks* and *Virgin of the Rocks* paintings came to the front of Cordy's screen.

Uriel warned Noah of the upcoming flood. Cordy was confused and mumbled, "Why didn't I know who he was?"

Uriel was connected to the angel with the flaming sword who guarded the Gate of Eden and the Tree of Life. Cordy wasn't happy when she read of the injustice done to Uriel, just as she felt when she learned Magdalene was given the title of a prostitute when she wasn't. Cordy went to bed troubled and tired. She lay on the bed exhausted. Cordy's thoughts lingered on Minah and the man who shot at them. "All I know is, today, I had an angel watching over me."

Chapter 11

Cordy's Dream

It's a fact that to live, we must dream. It's a beautiful, sunny day, and the trees are a vivid green. She is walking on the sidewalk. She turns and smiles at three auburn-red Irish setters who are being walked by their owner on a leash.

Cordy turns to pet them, but one of the setter's mouths closes gently around her left hand. A man's hand grabs her right wrist. The setter's mouth tightens on her hand in an attempt to keep her on the ground. The force of strength that pulls her up is too great, and the setter releases her.

She is quickly pulled straight up in the air. The setters get smaller and smaller as she looked down at them. Cordy had never flown in her dreams and even in the dream state, she is exhilarated at her weightlessness. The air blowing her hair, and the feeling of joy is incredible. She looks up to see who grabbed her. A young man with reddish hair and a knockout smile is beside her. He had leveled off, and clouds were going by them. Cordy saw a city in the clouds in the distance. The golden city glowed, and Cordy thought they were using solar panels for their energy.

The sun shined, and the glass tower, shaped in a spiral, glowed gold. Amazing and exhilarating, the feelings flashed through her. She looked at the man next to her, dressed in a white linen shirt and loose tan pants with boots. He had no wings but she had no doubt this beautiful man was an angel.

He smiled, his teeth gleaming, and said, "What have you learned?"

As he said it, she was overwhelmed with regret and sadness, and she looked at him with tears in her eyes looking for forgiveness.

"That I am weak," she answered. A great rush of air came, sounding like a tornado. Cordy sat up in her bed and placed her hands over her eyes. What was that all about? She got up and wrote the dream down. She wondered what he meant. "What have you learned?" She made a promise to herself to take his words to heart.

Cordy wondered if she had met archangel Uriel in her dream. She saw how much Minah's father loved her. On one hand, Cordy felt she was all alone. Her parents were dead. But for a second, she learned that maybe she wasn't alone after all. Her journey had started.

Chapter 12

Linda's Gift

Ash could see this was something Linda was born to do. She was a natural, and the excitement in her face reminded him of how much he loved his work.

They packed up the 4Runner and as Ash promised, he took her to the other temple. Ash walked in to the temple with Linda.

"The Temple of Nefertari has the queen's statue the same size as the king's. I believe that the power of women will save the world. They are equal. Yet, they are told by many men that they're inferior.

"Men have written much of history. I often wonder what man is so afraid of. Ramesses II was not afraid but loved his beautiful smart wife. Nefertari, the mother of his sons, ruled with her husband. In Egypt, it was the queen's bloodline that was important," Ash said.

"In Nefertari's tomb was one of the most beautiful Egyptian paintings based on the Egyptian Book of the Dead. The heavenly ceiling represented the dark blue sky and golden five-pointed stars in the heavens. The ceiling was supported by four pillars and in the middle rested a red granite sarcophagus. The golden hall was the place of regeneration. The other walls contained passages from the Book of the Dead to help guide her through the gates and portals of Osiris's kingdom or underworld."

Ash turned and said in a very serious tone, "Linda, do you trust me? Can you open your mind to the possibility that the temple could help your stuttering? The time right now is considered by the Egyptians a magical time."

Linda's innocent eyes looked down at the ground. "I-I have been to every specialist an-and nothing has worked." She looked up at Ash, "O-O-OK, what are you thinking? I'll give it a try if it isn't too weird."

"Lean up against the great wall inside the temple and clear your mind of everything. I told you this day, for the Egyptians, was a magical day."

Linda leaned back against the wall and nodded her head. Ash pulled a tiny Egyptian alabaster jar from his backpack.

"My father found this in one of his archeological digs near Tell Basta, Egypt. As the legend goes, the Holy Family, when leaving Bethlehem from Herod, stopped in Tell Basta. The people of the city did not welcome them so they stayed in a tent outside the city. A spring came from the ground to help provide water for them. The well is sacred, and the water said to have special powers. My mother gave me this to carry with me in case I ever got sick."

Ash placed a sip of the sacred water in the cup. "Do you trust me?" He handed Linda the jar, and she took a sip. It tasted surprisingly sweet. Ash whispered softly, "Linda, close your eyes and take some deep breaths. I want you to feel the incredible energy around you."

Linda felt a tingling flowing from the tips of her toes to the top of her head. An electric impulse vibrated within her. She had never felt anything like it.

After a couple of minutes of silence, Ash whispered, "You can

Linda's Gift

open your eyes now. Time will tell if you experienced a transformation. We can only hope the stars were aligned just for you." What Ash knew was what ancient doctors and the religious community knew long ago and that just recently the scientific community had become aware of — the "placebo effect." It was about the incredible power of the mind, and how, given the right circumstances and belief in a cure, the sick could be cured. Ash created the moment in which Linda believed that she could be possibly cured.

The air had a charge in it. Linda felt the energy course through her body, but the moment was broken by Ash's voice. He was picking up their bags.

"OK, let's get out of here. It'll be after midnight. Your mom and dad will kill me if you don't get home soon."

"Don't worry Ash, I told them I would be late," Linda assured him. "I had the best day of my life. I want to thank you." Ash smiled as she talked clearly.

He sat there, quietly waiting for her to understand. She stopped and whirled around, her eyes as big as saucers and her mouth open. It dawned on Linda that the power of the temple worked. She didn't stutter for the first time that she could remember. She started to cry again. Tears of joy streamed down her cheeks, flooding her face. Ash put his hands up and laughed. "Oh no, you don't. I only allow my students to cry once a day, and you already had your turn today."

Linda wiped her eyes. Ash smiled. "I do have a once-a-day rule."

She reached over and gave Ash a big hug. Linda looked at him in amazement.

"How did you do it?"

Ash laughed, "It's my little secret and now yours. Don't tell anybody!"

"OK."

"Let's get you home."

It wasn't the first time this had happened to Ash. He always had the family gift of healing others. Ash just kept a low profile because he was a loner. He never felt at home with others, except for his mother. To say he kept his distance was an understatement.

Now, for the first time, he was unsure about helping Linda. They had been driving for an hour, and she hadn't shut up. It didn't look like she was going to, either. It was as if Linda had kept all these words bottled up and someone opened the cork. The words flowed out of her like a river.

Chapter 13

Inquisition Hunting the Pure of Heart

Antar, the leader of the Nephilim, remembered the day he became infatuated with Eve's beautiful daughters. He could not resist their beauty and charm. Why should only Adam have children and the love of women?

His army had grown over the years and even Adam's children joined Antar in the fight against Uriel and the Pure of Heart. He looked back in time and saw one of his greatest creations, the Inquisition.

In the year 1244, in Languedoc, France, Antar stood watching the show in his black hooded Inquisition monk's robe, made of the finest wool and rich with gold chains and cross. The Dominican orders of monks were assigned to interrogate possible heretics. Six monks watched as a beautiful young girl, stripped from the waist up, her hands tied behind her back, was whipped. Her once-flawless skin and face were filled with cuts and bruises. A monk named Father John was conducting an interrogation of the witch, named Alix.

Antar knew that her crime was beauty and her refusal to bed Father John. He had gotten so angry with the girl's refusal that he accused her of witchcraft. The Children of the Nephilim had found the perfect home in the Inquisition. Anyone who questioned their orders was tortured and imprisoned.

Antar just watched the brave girl again and again refuse to sign her confession. It was unusual, that Father John could not break her. He wanted to hear her admit her guilt. The witch refused him, and her punishment was more torture. She wasn't attractive anymore, and it was her fault for refusing him.

"Sign, witch. Sign your confession." The monk shouted in the semiconscious girl's ear. Her silence angered him even more, and he beat her relentlessly. Antar gazed at the girl's magnificent eyes, sparkling as tears streamed down her cheeks. Her blue eyes looked like sapphires twinkling in the light, and her golden hair shone. Why were the Pure of Heart so magnificent, so strong, and so brave?

Antar stood transfixed in awe, gazing at the beauty of the Pure of Heart. The Inquisition would hunt down the Pure of Heart, all in the name of Christianity. It was the ultimate revenge for Antar.

The Inquisition demonstrated mankind's cruelty to one another. He witnessed mankind's complete savagery. Antar didn't have to do anything but just watch the Inquisition do his job for him. He looked into the girl's eyes as she stared back at him. He couldn't help getting lost in those exquisite eyes. He whispered to her as he unbound her hands.

"Alix, know this. We never die. Your pain will soon leave you. Be at peace, daughter." She heard his soft, kind voice though nobody else in the room did. She whispered, "Thank you, brother," and looked up at him with those enchanting blue eyes.

Antar thought of the old wisdom, the eyes are the windows to the soul. Alix's soul shined brightly. She fell to the floor in his arms and at that moment, died of shock and blood loss. Father John looked down at her in disgust. "I am disappointed, very disappointed that she died before her burning at the stake. At the very end, she would defy me."

Antar watched him with complete disgust as he covered the girl with a blanket and rose and carried her body to the courtyard. Uriel stepped next to him.

"I'll take her now, Antar."

Uriel grabbed her, and as he did she became brighter and brighter and more brilliant. Antar knew the girl's soul was making the transition. He handed the dead tortured body to an old man, the caretaker. Uriel looked at him, puzzled.

"Why, ole friend, did you comfort her? You have always said you hated the Pure of Heart."

Antar turned his back on them and mumbled, "I find stupidity tiresome and these Inquisitors fall into that category of morons. They grow boring." He turned with his hands outstretched, laughing. "I don't have to lift a finger. The monks do my job for me. I must admit to a fascination with the Pure of Heart. Eve's daughters have always caught my eye." Antar looked back at Uriel carrying the divine girl, now dressed in white. She smiled and waved at him. Antar turned gruffly and felt a familiar warm ache in his chest and then disappeared.

A group of people in France believed in a peaceful existence and disagreed with the fact that the Pope had power over their lives. They were known as the Cathars. Most were destroyed, and genocide ruled the day of the Inquisition. The last of Cathars marched into the fire singing at the battle of Montsegur. Their rich lands were reward for killing the heretics. The Children of the Nephilim grew more and more powerful during the time of the Inquisition. Women were the main targets, for they were the healers and midwives. They were the intuitive ones, considered dangerous. Like Adam, Antar blamed women for his fall.

Chapter 14

Marrilac

Mother Agnes sat in the chapel, praying with her rosary, when Sister Marian rushed in the room, frantic. "Forgive me, Mother, for interrupting you, but I have some urgent news. It is about your niece, Cordelia."

The blood drained from Mother Agnes's face. "What happened?"

Sister Marian quickly explained, "It is on the morning news on TV."

Mother Agnes calmly walked and patted Sister Marian's hands. "Cordy is a blessed child and is protected by the angels. She is all right." Sister Marian shook her head in amazement as she opened the door for Mother Agnes. Mother Superior had an amazing faith and always trusted God. She saw twenty nuns crowded around the television in the visiting room. Their faces showed their great love for their Mother Superior.

"What has Cordy done now?" She had to break up the tension in the room.

"She is a hero! Cordy rescued a young girl from a kidnapper," answered the excited, tiny Sister Catherine.

"Is she all right?"

"Look, Mother Agnes, there she is!" Sister Catherine pointed at the TV. "She looks OK, doesn't she?" Sister Catherine asked the rest of the sisters if they agreed.

"Yes, she does, Sister, and we should give thanks to God that she is." The entire group of sisters made the sign of the cross.

"I'll call her and see if there is anything I can do. Excuse me, and may I say, sisters, thank you so much for your love and concern," Mother Agnes said with calm and assurance. They all smiled and nodded with relief, for they knew Cordy held a special place in her heart. As Mother Agnes walked to her office, she remembered the sweet baby girl born to her loving sister. Cordy was special in more ways than one. She dialed Cordy's cell phone and looked at the smiling angel on her desk. It begins, she thought.

Cordy's cell phone rang, and she ran to her purse. She couldn't find her cell phone. "Where is it?" She pulled out her keys, her comb, her wallet; the phone kept ringing, and she yelled out, "This purse is like a black hole. I put things in, but I can never find them when I need them."

She found the phone and hit the button to answer. Mother Agnes heard the frustration on the other side of the phone. "Oh dear, Cordy, is that you?"

"Oh, Holy Mother," Cordy said as she stuck her hand in some bubble gum that Maggie had given her earlier. Cordy had the stringy stuff all over her hand and the phone. "Hello, Cordy? It's your aunt, and not the Holy Mother."

"Oh, hi, Sister Agnes, how are you?"

There was a pause and then chuckling could be heard in the background, "Dear, are you OK? You sound like you're a bit stressed out. I was wondering about how you were. I saw you on the morning news."

"Oh that, Sister Agnes, it was nothing. I'm OK. Don't worry.

My car got shot at but..." Sister Agnes gasped, "You were shot at? Oh, Cordy!"

"I'm fine, Mother Agnes, just fine," Cordy answered calmly.

"Cordy, I need you to stop by Marillac and pick up a few very important things that your mother gave me."

A silence settled in on the phone, "My mom left me something?" Cordy's mind flashed to her smiling mother holding her when she was five. "Well yes, I'll stop by and see you." "Thanks dear, pencil me in for an hour because there is something very important I have to tell you," answered Mother Agnes.

"OK, well sure. How about tomorrow at about lunchtime?"

"Perfect, dear. I want to hear all about your adventure, too. And for goodness sake, be careful, dear."

"Love ya, Auntie, see you tomorrow."

The memory of her mother brought tears to Cordy's eyes. Cordy started looking at the clock. She yelled out, "Maggie, brush your teeth, and come on down for breakfast."

The cell phone rang again. It was Maggie's mom.

"Hey, lady, how's it going? Yep, Miss Maggie is right here."

She handed the phone to Maggie and whispered, "It's your mom." Maggie jumped for joy. "Hi, Mommy, Cordy is fixing me pancakes. Yes, I did my homework. Yes, I'm being a good girl. Momma, I got to ride in a police car yesterday."

Cordy ran to grab the phone from Maggie and pushed the pancakes at the little girl. "Oh, it's OK. A policeman took us for a ride, that's all. Cindy is going to have a date with him. Good, you're coming home today. That's wonderful. You're going to pick her up after school." She handed the phone back to Maggie. "I love you, mommy, see you soon. Bye."

Maggie was beaming after she talked to her mom. Cordy smiled and her heart took a strange flutter. She realized in that moment how much she missed her mother and father and yet she felt their presence with her every day.

"Maggie, your mom is picking you up after school. Good luck on your school project." Maggie grabbed a blueberry muffin and ran out the door. Cordy grabbed the girl's book bag and ran to the car, putting the bag in the back.

"Maggie, you're going to be late." Maggie laughed and used her muffin to feed some ducks who lived by the pond near Cordy's house. She pulled apart the muffin, setting it on the ground. The ducks were used to looking for food near Cordy's house, and Maggie loved to feed them.

Cordy loaded up the car. "Maggie, c'mon!" Maggie ran to the car and jumped in.

After dropping off Maggie at school, Cordy stopped off at the florist and picked up some flowers for Minah. She walked into the hospital and saw Detective Washington.

"I'm glad to see you again, Miss McDermott."

Cordy nodded. "Please, detective, call me Cordy"

The detective smiled, "I'm glad you could stop by. I have a few questions. Do you remember anything else about the man who shot at you?"

Cordy took a moment to think. "I thought about it, and he had an accent, kinda like Russian. He was very angry and said no one ever escapes him. How is Minah doing?"

"She's pretty traumatized mentally, as well as physically, and barely speaking to us," Washington whispered to Cordy. "You want to see her?"

Cordy nodded. "I want to give her these flowers," she said, holding out some purple Irises. Washington led her to Minah's room, which was guarded by a tall policeman. She walked in and saw a young woman bruised and withdrawn. Cordy smiled.

"Hey, how are you, Minah?" Cordy held her hand gently." I brought you some flowers."

Minah looked at her and the flowers. She recognized Cordy immediately and for the first time in hours, the girl spoke. "Thank you so much for saving my life."

Cordy smiled. "I hear you are studing to be a doctor? I'm a doctor, too." Surprise registered in the girl's eyes as Cordy continued. "Yep, I'm a veterinarian. My specialty is emergency trauma, and I graduated from the University of Missouri's vet school in Columbia. What's your specialty?"

Minah's eyes focused, and she whispered, "Neurology."

"You look like you're a nerd. That's what we called all the neurologists at school." Minah smiled and shot back, "They called the trauma surgeons at my school adrenaline junkies."

"You got me there. I can't deny I love the excitement." Cordy chuckled. "I'm coming to see you again tomorrow, if that's OK. I think after what we went through maybe we were meant to be friends. You take care now."

Minah watched Cordy fly around the room. Cordy picked up the flowers and placed them in a vase by the window with the other flowers. "I'm going to bring you a little surprise. You get some rest now, Minah." Minah smiled for the second time. Cordy made her feel safe. She had a gift.

Minah had seen it before. A doctor she had interned for had an energy around her, nothing scientific, but a gift for healing. Minah had felt it the moment Cordy entered the room. She wasn't the only one who noticed. Her father watched from his chair, amazed at how Cordy got a smile from his daughter.

"See you tomorrow, Minah," Cordy said, waving bye as she walked out the door. Minah's father followed Cordy, and he grabbed her hand. Tears welled up in his eyes.

"Thank you for helping my daughter."

Cordy patted him on the back. "You don't worry. Minah is strong, and she's going to be just fine. I have dealt with abused and traumatized animals. People have many of the same needs. Lots of love, I have found, does the trick." She hugged the surprised man, who was unaccustomed to public signs of affection. As a prince, he had been trained in proper etiquette since he was a child. Cordy walked out of the hospital and headed off to work. He shook his head. "Crazy Americans."

Chapter 15

Linda's Crush

Linda explained to Ash all about the Diplomatic Brat club. It was similar to the Army Brats Club or Air Force Brats Club. It was a secret group of kids whose parents were in the diplomatic corps and who moved all around the world because of it. It was an incredible network and a support group for the kids, largely online.

Once, a boy couldn't take his scooter with him when his parents were assigned to Portugal, so he left it in Chicago for a new girl who was going to use it while she went to school there. Her parents were replacing his parents in the State Department. She left it for him when he returned.

The network was based on trust and secrecy. If one broke the trust, then word got out, and they were banished by the rest of the group. Ash was very impressed by how well it worked out. No one older than 17 was allowed to belong.

Linda told Ash about their private website. The secret code was passed from member to member. None of the parents could understand what was being said, and often just thought it was childish gibberish. Linda was head of the Egyptian chapter. She had to step down because of her family's pending relocation to Ireland.

"What archeology is going on in Ireland? It's Egypt where everything is happening."

Ash tried to cheer her up. "Ireland has New Grange, Linda. It was built in 3200 B.C. You have to go there when the winter solstice lights the chamber. Ireland has a wonderful history which some have connected with Egypt. The legend of the Egyptian princess Scota is one. Read about it. Some believe Scota was a daughter of Akhenaten. They found Egyptian faience beads on a young prince in Ireland. It was like the faience beads on Tutankhamen."

Linda smiled, "Really? Well, I can send you pictures of the archeological digs there." "Linda, please email them to me. I'll be your resource here in Egypt."

"Thanks, Ash."

The Brats had all correspondence go through a spam server so it would be almost impossible for anybody to detect the organization, but Linda trusted Ash completely.

"I could give you my secret password for the online account. They monitor it, but we could talk in code. You know, Ash, the online accounts are being monitored by the government. My dad let me in on that secret."

Ash was surprised. "Really?"

Linda nodded. "I'll give you a copy of how the code works. I trust you, Ash."

It was 11:00 p.m., and they still had one hour to drive, but they could see the lights of Aswan and it was making Linda sad. As Ash drove on the rocky road with his headlights on, he saw a young boy in his teens waving on the side of the road. He recognized the boy, named Mahd.

Mahd and his brother had worked with Ash on another archeology dig. They were well-trained laborers who were essential

Linda's Crush

to the dig. Ash worked alongside them, and they became friends. Ash pulled over, wondering what the heck Mahd was doing out in the middle of the night in the desert by himself.

"You need a lift, Mahd? What're you doing out here at this time of night?"

Mahd laughed. "I was hoping it was you, Mister Ash. Yes, please, sir. I thought you would be coming from the tomb today."

Ash pointed to the back. "Get in, Mahd."

Ash introduced Linda to Mahd. Mahd was sixteen, tall, handsome, and street smart. Mahd could get Ash anything or any tool, and he was a fountain of information. "What mischief did you get yourself into now?"

Ash looked in the rearview mirror. Mahd smiled at Linda, but Linda had eyes only for Ash.

Linda had a crush on Ash. She had been watching his every move all day, including every time he bent over in his tight jeans or took off his shirt in the sun. He was so strong and gorgeous. Linda swore he could be a model for a magazine. He had cured her of her stuttering, and that alone made him the most wonderful man in the world.

Mahd was interrupting her private moment with her hero, and she didn't like it. Mahd answered quickly back, "I am very glad to see you, Mister Ash. I didn't trust some men who hired me. I had a bad feeling about them so I ran off into the desert. They were carrying guns — lots of them. They don't know the desert like I do, so while they weren't looking I made a run for it."

Mahd saw Linda was pretty so he tried to be charming. "You are Ash's pretty assistant, and I, too, helped Ash."

Ash laughed, "Yes, Mahd learned the hard way not to be the first inside a tomb just opened." Mahd laughed.

"I ran out of the tomb faster than I went in."

"Why?" Linda asked.

Ash chuckled. "Cobras were waiting inside, and Mahd found one of them."

Linda smiled because the two guys thought she was thinking

about Mahd's surprise. Instead, Linda was still thinking about the wonderful Ash. She had the nerve to take Ash's bandana when he wasn't looking. It was full of sweat at the time and still damp now. She placed it in her backpack. Ash's sweat had an incredible sweet smell. Maybe it was his aftershave or deodorant. Whatever it was, Linda loved it.

Linda had a crush every other month. Once it was on her handsome math teacher. He broke her heart because he never answered her love letter. She put it on her test paper. Linda did get an A in the class, but her math teacher never answered her or gave her any encouragement.

She smiled, remembering that she did get an A from him, so he probably did like her. Now, Ash was something different. He was making Linda feel things she never felt before. Her heart raced when she watched him. She got hot and weak next to him.

Linda yawned and stretched out her arms. "If it's OK with you guys, I'm going to close my eyes for a bit."

"Good night, Miss Linda," Mahd said, a little disappointed.

Ash was tired too so he understood. "Go ahead, Linda, we still have a ways to go."

She finally got the courage to put her head on Ash's shoulder and then grabbed his forearm. Ash didn't think anything of it. He figured she was just tired from the eventful day.

As the 4Runner bounced around from time to time on the gravel road, her hand would brush up against his leg. Ash was oblivious to what was going on next to him because he wanted to know more about the men with guns from Mahd.

He asked Mahd why he ran off. Mahd was angry about Ali, his neighbor, getting involved with these very strange men. They carried guns and were very secretive. Mahd thought it was a regular job but soon knew they were up to no good. Mahd got scared and ran off. Ali wasn't as worried about them and promised to be quiet while Mahd slipped away in the night. Mahd said Ali was hired by a very wealthy businessman. Ali told him they were going to move some Egyptian artifacts to a safe place.

Linda's Crush

Mahd had figured out they wanted them to steal artifacts, treasures, and books from the tomb museum, which had no security because of the government's collapse. They were taking advantage of the Egyptian riots and unrest. Mahd refused to betray his country so he ran into the desert when they weren't looking. "You're lucky, Mahd, that they didn't kill you," Ash said in a serious voice. "I've been hearing about a dark-force military mercenary group who is stealing and killing through the Egyptian archeology network."

Ash remembered a call from his friend Aziz that they had found something under the pyramid of Giza. "Has Aziz gotten involved with this group?" Ash asked.

Mahd shrugged his shoulders. "Ash, they offer lots of money, and Aziz needs money for his family. I don't know, but he could be." Ash began to worry that private collectors were trying to grab antiquities while they could. He knew they could be very dangerous.

Linda, meanwhile, had an ache that just wouldn't go away, and every time the 4Runner would hit a big bump, it would get worse. The more she brushed up against Ash, the worse it was. The ache got stronger. Linda was gasping for air, and her chest was on fire. She reached down and placed her hand lightly on Ash's thigh.

"What the hell!" Ash screamed. He slammed on the brakes, and he jumped out of the 4Runner. Ash was walking funny. Mahd couldn't figure it out and yelled, "What is wrong, Mister Ash?"

Ash angrily walked around the 4Runner. "Hold on, Mahd, I have to take care of something." In a loud and commanding voice, he shouted at Linda. "Linda, what was that all about?"

Linda yelled out the window. "I love you, Ash!"

Mahd's eyes opened up like silver dollars. "You are a crazy girl!"

Ash stumbled back to the driver's seat. "You are crazy."

Linda leaned towards him, her arms stretched out. "Yes, I admit it. I think you're wonderful, Ash. I think you felt it too, before you stopped."

Ash pointed his finger at her. "What were you thinking Lin-

Keys of Life

da?" he yelled angrily. "Are you trying to kill us? You don't do that to a man while he's driving. I mean, surprise him like that."

Mahd laughed and rolled down the window. "What she do, Ash?"

"Shut up, Mahd!"

Linda turned to Mahd. "Stay out of this. It's between Ash and me." Linda yelled across the truck, "But I love you!"

"Don't talk like that," Ash said. "Your father will kill me. You're just too young for me, Linda."

Linda yelled out again, "But I love you, Ash."

Ash shook his head. "The only place I am taking you is home. I knew this was a bad idea. We're late, and it's getting later. Your parents are probably worried. You get back on your side of the truck or Mahd will drive, and I'll sit in the back."

Mahd yelled out the window, laughing, "Don't worry, Ash, I'll protect you from her." "No touchy Ash while he is driving, or I will bop you one, crazy Linda," Mahd said.

Linda pouted and moved back across the truck with her arms crossed. "OK, and don't worry about my dad. I texted him and told him we were going to be late."

Linda realized they were two guys who had no concept of what love was all about.

Ash got back in and said, "You behave or-or..."

Linda smiled. "Look who's stuttering now."

"That wasn't funny, Linda," Ash said sternly. "You could've killed us, and I'm not ready to die yet."

Linda softly apologized. "I just wanted you to know that I have a crush on you. I'm going to miss you so much."

Ash shook his head and looked to heaven. "Why me, Lord? I suggest you take it slower and with someone your own age."

Mahd started laughing, "I had a crush on a girl in school when I was seven and tried to kiss her. I got my face slapped. At least you didn't get slapped."

"I promise to behave, but I will never stop loving you," Linda solemnly said to Ash.

Linda's Crush

Ash shook his head. "We just met today, and you're too young for me, anyway."

Linda looked at him with teenage adoration. "I believe in love at first sight," she said, letting out a big sigh.

Ash was beside himself by now and not happy. He didn't think it was funny at all. Mahd decided to start trouble in the back.

"How do you know that Mister Ash even likes girls? He might like guys." He winked at Ash. Ash groaned and shook his head. Linda's head shot up, and she had a surprised look on her face. "I didn't think of that. Are you gay, Ash?"

"Linda, you have got to stop talking this way. It's none of your business. And shut up back there, Mahd. You're not helping." Ash was getting mad.

Mahd wouldn't quit and chimed, "Tell her the truth, Ash, and break it to her gently." Linda looked at him softly, "Is it true, Ash?"

Ash turned around and hit Mahd upside the head. "Oww!" Mahd yelled out.

Ash answered back, "No, it's not true. Linda, let's just be friends. I do have some advice for you when you first meet a guy: Take it slower. You scared the hell out of me."

Mahd laughed. "I would not have missed this. I know what this is about, the goddess of love. She likes to trick. You were both in her temple today, weren't you? The legends talk about it. Linda has come under the spell of the love goddess Isis." Linda looked at Mahd.

"We were in the temple of the queen."

Mahd turned very serious. "Isis is the love goddess to my people, and she is known to play tricks. My people believe in the spirits and she is very powerful."

As Ash pulled onto Linda's street, he could tell her family had money. Linda's family lived at one of the nicest hotels. Ash looked at the tall building with its impeccable landscaping.

"Nice hotel."

Keys of Life

"It gets old living in them," Linda sighed. She handed Mahd her email address on a paper. "Will you write me, Mahd? I want to know more about Isis."

Mahd grabbed the paper with a smile. "I will, pretty Linda."

Linda looked sad to be leaving Ash. Ash smiled. "Well, Linda, if I'm not married in 10 years, I'll look you up when you get out of college. Is it a deal?"

Linda reached over to give Ash a hug. Ash was gun shy and backed away and shook her hand. "You bet ya. In a way, we'll be secretly engaged." Linda winked at him. "It will be our secret joke."

Ash laughed jokingly, "Let's keep it just that, our secret joke."

Mahd stuck his head out the window, laughing, "Remember, he is mine first!"

Ash gave him a look that would kill. "Shut up, Mahd!"

Linda smiled. "Well, if you ever need me, just go to my page online and send me a coded message. I'll come running, my dear friend. Mahd may be right, I might have been under the spell of the queen. I do feel kind of dizzy and weak."

"You may be dehydrated. Drink lots of water tonight."

Linda grabbed her backpack. "I will never forget this day as long as I live." She pulled off a silver pin with pentacle on it and handed it to Ash. "May the stars guide you, Ash. You're the Queen of Heaven's knight."

Her parents came through the hotel door with Leo on a leash. "Linda, we were worried about you."

Ash introduced himself and Mahd to her parents. He apologized that it was so late. Her father handed the leash to Ash. "Linda had texted us that Leo was going to get a nice home. Thanks so very much. I made some inquiries and have heard you are an honorable man. Leo is a lucky dog."

Linda hugged Leo and said goodbye with some tears falling down her cheeks. "You be good for Mister Ash, Leo." The lab wagged his tail and barked.

Ash loaded Leo in the 4 Runner, and Mahd petted him. Ash

Linda's Crush

thought to himself, when I see Rosh, I will kill him. Never again will he give me a woman to go on assignment with.

"We had the best day of my life, Mom." Linda's father turned to her, surprised. "Linda, you didn't stutter."

"Mom and Dad, I haven't stuttered all afternoon. It's a miracle. It was at the Temple of the Queen Nefertari. I went in, and when I came out, I was cured. I'll tell you all about it later."

Linda's father shook Ash's hand. "Thank you, Ash, for everything." Ash just smiled. "This morning she barely talked, but now, she hardly shuts up. You tell me how you feel in six months." Linda's father laughed. "I can tell people she takes after her mother."

Linda's mother was a gorgeous blonde, who certainly didn't look her age. She came over and hugged Ash as if he was family. She smiled with a knowing look, whispering in Ash's ear, "Any later, Ash, and we were going to call the troops out after you. Lucky for you, Linda had texted us that you were going to be late. It's wonderful you're taking Leo."

Mother's intuition can't be underestimated, and she knew her daughter. It was good that they were leaving. She could see Ash was a nice guy but a bit naïve about young teenagers. He was also very handsome, something she appreciated.

Ash got the hint. "It's late, and I do apologize for the late hour, but we were able to get all our photos today."

Linda stood next to her dad. Out of the blue, she said, "You will have to tell me what that shiny object was in the left corner of the altar, in the main temple."

Ash looked at her, puzzled. "I didn't see a shiny object."

"Yes, every time you used the flash it would show up," Linda assured him. "You'll see it in the photos, I'm sure. I thought you saw it." Ash look surprised.

"No, I'm going to look for it though."

"Well, you'll see it Ash." Leo stuck his head out and barked. Linda petted him. "You promise, Ash, you will take good care of him."

Ash swore with his hand up. "I guarantee he will have a great home. I've got to get Mahd home."

Ash was only four feet away when he whispered to Mahd, "Well, that didn't go too bad." He jumped in the truck and started the engine. Linda yelled out at the top of her lungs, "I love you, Ash, and please take good care of Leo!"

Ash could hear Linda's mom say, "It is time to go to bed, young lady. We have a big day tomorrow." Ash hit the gas and took off flying out of there.

"Oh God, what a day," he muttered, but it wasn't over yet. "Mahd, hang on, we have to make one more stop." It was near one in the morning when Ash pulled up at Rosh's house. He had a nice garden in the back, and a tall fence surrounded the front and back yard, so you had to ring the bell at the front gate. Ash rang the bell again and yelled out, "Rosh, get your ass down here."

Ash could see the light come on in the window, and then he heard Rosh cussing. He heard him stub his toe and cuss some more. He opened the window and peered through.

"Ash, is that you? What the hell?"

Ash yelled back, "I got something for you, so go ahead an' open the gate." The light went on at the gate. Mahd opened the car door as the gate automatically opened. Leo went running in the yard.

"What is that?" Rosh yelled out.

"That, my friend, is Leo, your new dog."

Rosh rubbed his eyes sleepily. "I'm sorry, did I hear you say my dog?"

Ash pointed to Leo sniffing around Rosh's backyard. "I think he likes it here." Rosh put his hands up in the air. "This can't be, I can't keep a dog."

Ash started moving to his truck. "Oh yes, you can, and you will take real good care of him. He's Linda's dog. You remember Linda from this morning? The girl you put with me, the one that is leaving town today, as we speak?" Rosh smiled.

Linda's Crush

"Oh yeah, how'd it go? You find anything?"

Ash hopped in his 4Runner. "The dog's name is Leo. He loves to play ball, and he also likes to smell them. I got to see that on the way over here. He's checked mine out already." Leo started digging up Rosh's garden. Rosh mouth dropped watching the dog. "He gets fed two times a day, and make sure he has water available." Ash closed the door and stuck his head out the window. Rosh shook his head.

"Oh no, Ash, you can't leave him here."

Ash smiled. "Oh yeah I can. I promised Linda that he was going to have a great home, and yours is much better than mine. You owe me, Rosh."

Ash turned the engine on, and the truck slowly rolled. Rosh ran after Ash. "You can't do this to me, Ash. My wife will kill me."

Ash drove faster, yelling back, "You shouldn't have given me that girl today. As far as I can see, we're even."

Rosh could hear Leo chasing something in the yard, and he was waking the neighbors. Ash could hear Rosh cry out in anguish, "Oh dear God, this can't be happening."

"That's what I said today," Ash shouted. He stepped on the gas and drove away. Ash knew for the first time he had just gotten Rosh back for all the dirty tricks he had given him over the years. He better take good care of Leo, or he'd regret it. Mahd laughed in the back.

"You got him good, Mister Ash. I like Leo. My family loves dogs. I will wait a few days. Mister Rosh will give me Leo and pay me lots of money. I will take good care of Leo, Mister Ash, if Rosh doesn't."

He drove to Mahd's house. His father and mother waited up with the light on. His father opened the door and shouted, "Mahd!"

Mahd opened the door to the truck and yelled back, "Yes, Papa, it is me. Mister Ash gave me a ride home. Go back to bed, Papa."

Mahd's father waved to Ash. He knew Ash and his mother

Keys of Life

well, for he often ate at their house. His father shut the door. Mahd pulled out of his pocket two Egyptian amulets. "Ash, here, take these and keep them for me. I picked them up from the artifacts that those men picked up at the museum." Mahd handed him a lapis lazuli Ibis head stone and a lapis lazuli Heart of Osiris. They were in a little box with the rest of the artifacts.

Ash looked a bit surprised. "The Ibis head is symbol for secret knowledge and the Heart of Osiris is very rare and one of the greatest magic charms of the Egyptians."

"The box had gems all around it with Isis on the top," Mahd whispered. "They were so busy. I opened it up, but just these two pendants were in it. I took them for insurance. Ash, please, will you keep these for me?"

Ash put them in his pocket. "OK, but you're going to have to return them to the museum." Mahd started walking to the house. "I will. Thanks, Mister Ash, for a very interesting ride." And Mahd laughed and waved goodbye.

"Shut up, Mahd, and let's keep this night a secret."

Mahd laughed, "I saw nothing and heard nothing."

Ash drove off into the dark. He was upset that he didn't notice the shiny flash in the photos. He pulled over and stopped the car. He pulled out the camera and was looking at the photos in its memory card. "I'll be damned." Ash couldn't believe his eyes. It was there every time when the flash went off. Something in the left-hand corner of the cracked stone was shiny and reflecting light. A little sparkle shined from inside the rock.

Ash knew that it had to be something metal or glass. It was probably a tourist's beer can. Ash was going to have to shoot the photos over. The photos were no good with the distortion in them. He figured he'd just go back now and retake them in the morning. Ash got half way and started to fall asleep at the wheel. He pulled over and lay on the front hood, which was still warm from driving in the sun.

Ash pulled his jacket over him and looked up into the sky. Stars shined like gems in the sky. The desert cooled off at night and a light breeze whipped through his thick, sandy blonde hair. Ash started to nod off and a smile came to his face as he thought about Linda and how he cured her of her stutter. Leo's face popped in his mind and his wagging tail. Just how big did Leo shit? He let out a chuckle and then dozed off.

Chapter 16

Professor Uriel Continues

The students were back in their seats, and Antar, dressed in black and looking bored, sat in the last row. Professor Uriel nodded to Antar, and the lights dimmed. A cell phone went off, a scary voice saying, "It's the dark one..." and loudly interrupted Uriel's lecture. The student laughed as it played. His face changed as he dropped the phone and it shattered into pieces. The student looked at his broken phone on the ground.

Professor Uriel smiled. "Shall we continue?"

Antar yawned and departed.

"The Duke of Aquitaine title was held by the Counts of Poitiers in France for more than 200 years. Many of the people of Poitiers would migrate to Acadia, known later as Nova Scotia, and they spoke Acadian French. Queen Eleanor often listened to the troubadour songs at her court in Poitiers. The legends of old were passed on by the songs of these minstrels, and the people of Poitiers would take these legends and stories with them. They were the troubadour stories of giants, the wizard Merlin, and the building of Stonehenge.

Professor Uriel Continues

"Queen Eleanor had experienced betrayal by her husband, imprisonment, and the deaths of her children. In 1200, the French and English kings signed a treaty, and King John's sister's daughter and Phillip's heir were married. It was Grandmother Eleanor who chose which daughter would be Queen of France; she chose Blanche of Castile, the younger sister, instead of the 13-year-old Urraca.

"A key part of the decision-making process was evaluation of the astrological charts made for the girls by the court astrologists. The charts predicted both girls would be queens, but Blanche had the more intriguing horoscope. Eleanor also liked Blanche's name better for a French queen.

"Eleanor escorted her granddaughter over the Pyrenees on the way to her wedding. She saw the qualities of a queen in Blanche. The girl was smart and strong, and there was a need for powerful women, especially when men went on the Crusades and left their wives to run their estates. The role of the queen on the chessboard showed that power and flexibility was important to winning any conflict. She was the most powerful piece.

"Women's roles at this time were changing. Eleanor had made inroads on women's place in society, and women's education became important. Noble women were able to read and left illuminated books for their families. The French oral tradition talked of Magdalene's escape from persecution with others in a boat to France. Eleanor taught these stories to Blanche. She understood how powerful stories could be.

"France and England were inundated with stories of the Holy Grail by the troubadours. Eleanor and her eldest daughter, Countess Marie of Champagne, led efforts to educate men about court manners and giving respect to the lovely noblewomen of court. Countess Marie also had the first chapter of Genesis from the Bible translated, as well as other books. Monks made illuminated psalters and Bibles so they could read them. No longer did the Pope determine who should be allowed to read the Bible. The royal houses would read the Holy Book regardless.

"It was at the Council of Troyes in Champagne when the Templars were officially recognized. At the same time in France, heretical religious groups called the Cathars were emerging. Gothic cathedrals were built with the tools of sacred geometry. The masons had a big business building holy temples that had to house the treasures being brought back from the Holy Land. They also brought back the knowledge of how to make stained glass, one of their greatest treasures.

"Eleanor's legacy was her choice of the little Blanche as the next queen of France because Blanche, like her grandmother, was incredibly strong. Eleanor believed women possessed intelligence and a love for learning. The world could change through women's education and a love of reading. And that's how she would've wanted to be remembered."

Uriel left the audience with a picture of Eleanor's grave projected on the screen, her stone effigy showing her reading the Bible. The lights came back on, but Professor Uriel had already left the stage.

Chapter 17

The Healer

Cordy walked through the door of her animal clinic. A little poodle barked, announcing her arrival. A big yellow tabby cat hissed at the poodle to remind him of his manners, and a golden retriever puppy got loose from her owner. The puppy ran toward Cordy.

She swooped up the pup and laughed, "Aren't you cute?"

"Sorry, Cordy," the owner apologized.

"Oh, that's quite alright," she said, as the pup licked her face. "I haven't had my morning kiss yet. I'll be seeing you all in just a few minutes."

The waiting room was full. Cordy slipped her lab coat on and saw her first patient. It was a Sheltie named Mandy, 12-years-old with arthritis in her hips. She wrote a prescription for the dog.

Cordy rubbed her hand over the dog's right hip, and the dog laid still. Marjorie Davis, the owner, smiled.

"Dr. McDermott, you're amazing. Mandy whimpers when I touch her there. You must have a gift because Mandy walks so much better after she sees you. I know she's getting older and her time with us is getting shorter." Tears came to her eyes. "I just want her to be comfortable."

Cordy ran her hands over Mandy's fur. "I understand, and we will keep her comfortable. The X-rays show the arthritis is not getting worse."

Mandy hopped up from the table, her tail wagging, and barked. Cordy smiled and petted her head, "Good ole girl. See you in six months."

The next patient was a guinea pig, carried in a cardboard box by a little blonde-haired girl.

"He isn't eating. Can you make him better, doctor?"

Cordy looked at the black and white furry ball. "Well, what is his name?

"Binkie," the girl said proudly.

"Is Binkie drinking?"

"Yes, lots of water, but he doesn't eat."

Cordy picked up the guinea pig and looked at his eyes. "Let me see if I have something he might like." She opened a drawer and pulled out an alfalfa tablet, while her other hand stroked Binkie."What is your name?" Cordy asked the girl.

"Ashley."

Ashley's mother smiled. "I have to tell you, doc, that you have a great reputation. Everybody says you're wonderful. You're one of the few vets who treat guinea pigs."

The guinea pig started munching on the alfalfa tablet. Ashley squealed. "He is eating, momma. Look!"

"I think Binkie has a vitamin deficiency so I'm going to give you some tablets to feed him and put in his water bottle," Cordy explained. "Some of the food we have nowadays doesn't have the vitamins they should. Binkie will be good as new in a couple days."

One by one, the rest of the animals came in and were seen. Cordy did a couple of surgeries.

"I see your hero status hasn't gone to your head," laughed Pam, an older veterinary technician.

Cordy rolled her eyes. "I could have done without my car getting shot at, that's for sure. The insurance company is having trouble finding where bullet hole damage is covered in my policy." Pam hugged her. "Screw the car. I'm just so glad you're all right. I came in this morning to an answering machine with hundreds of messages asking if you were OK."

"You told them I'm just fine, right?" Pam nodded. "Yes, I told them."

Cordy pulled off her lab coat.

"I'm going to lunch with my aunt." She pointed at the cage where a collie slept. "Pam, be sure to watch Phoebe for a temperature tonight."

Pam was the best assistant Cordy ever had, and she loved animals. Pam was happy to be sleeping overnight in a sitting room on a tiny cot. She and Cordy had agreed they didn't like leaving the animals alone at night.

"I'll watch her," Pam said, waving good-bye as Cordy drove off.

Chapter 18

Secrets Told

Cordy pulled up to the Marillac Mother House, a large white-stone Victorian building surrounded by gardens. A statue of Saint Vincent de Paul stood at the front. Vincent de Paul, with Louise de Marillac, founded the Daughters of Charity.

The Vincentians and the Daughters of Charity were a major influence in 1818, when Thomas Jefferson made the Louisiana Purchase, including Missouri. They dedicated themselves to helping the sick and poor, and educating underprivileged children. They also established a hospital system, which offered care to the poor as well as the rich.

Sister Agnes was a nurse practitioner and Mother Superior at the Marillac Mother House. Cordy loved medicine, and her aunt encouraged her in that passion. Sister Agnes was surprised Cordy went to veterinarian school instead of medical school. If she was disappointed, though, she didn't let Cordy know.

The doors of the suburban St. Louis convent opened to a small sitting room where her elderly, petite aunt opened her arms.

Secrets Told

"Cordelia, my dear."

Cordy loved her hugs but she felt how frail her aunt had gotten since she last visited. Her aunt showed her a picnic basket.

"Are you ready to go on a picnic? The weather is perfect outside."

"What a wonderful idea."

The grounds of Marillac consisted of fifty acres of beautiful forest and gardens. The women walked together for a mile to a white gazebo surrounded by the red, gold, and yellow fall foliage. They sat down on the white bench at a small table under the beautiful gazebo.

Sister Agnes smiled, "Let's see what Sister Catherine packed for us. You want a tuna sandwich or turkey?"

"Tuna."

Sister Agnes handed her the sandwich and opened the thermos filled with ice tea. The elderly nun placed her hand on top of Cordy's hand.

"So, Sister Agnes, what is the news you have to tell me?"

Sister Agnes munched on her sandwich with her other hand.

"It's about how you were born, Cordy, and your family. I'm not going to beat around the bush here, honey. I'm dying of breast cancer, and it's time you knew your family history." Cordy's eyes filled with tears. Of all the people in Cordy's life, Sister Agnes love was always there.

Cordy's voice quivered, "How long?"

Sister smiled and patted her hand gently. "I hope not too long because I miss my family and long to see them. I want you to know dear that I'm always going to be with you, so don't be afraid. The beautiful thing about us is we never really die. We just move on."

Cordy hugged her. "I know, and I will be there with you. You won't be alone."

Sister Agnes smiled and held her hand. "We are never alone, my sweet girl."

The birds were singing, and the sky was blue and cloudless. It was a beautiful day with the sun shining. Sister Agnes handed

Cordy a napkin to dry her eyes. "Cordy, I have to settle some affairs before I die. I want to tell you some things that were kept secret from you. It was for your protection. I hope you understand what I'm going to tell you.

"One is that you were born in Perryville, Missouri, on your grandmother's farm. You know that Perryville is a small town near the Mississippi settled by French, German, Acadian, and Irish settlers. Grandpa staked out Grandma de Grasse's farm when settlers were encouraged to take claim of empty land. Your mother had me deliver you. I was a midwife and nurse practitioner. My watch said it was a minute before midnight on February 11, 1982. The time is important dear. I want you to remember that. You see, there were three people with watches on, and we all had different times.

"Your mother, Mary, and your father, Joseph McDermott, were the happiest couple — so in love with each other. They were so excited, and you were so wonderful. Your father was Canadian, and his mother, Saunhac, came from the Mi'kmaq Indian tribe in Nova Scotia. Your grandfather Bill is a Canadian whose money came originally from the worldwide shipping and fishing company he built called McDermott Shipping. He met your beautiful grandmother in Halifax when she worked as his secretary. Bill fell in love with her and married her. Your father was born shortly afterward.

"Grandmother Saunhac had incredible faith and was a gifted woman. Your grandfather got a terrible skin rash from one of his boats, which carried a very toxic chemical. It was she who ordered water from Lourdes in a last-ditch effort to cure him. Lourdes, France, is known for its miraculous spring water as the place where Our Lady appeared to Saint Bernadette. It cured his rash completely. The doctors were shocked. Grandma Saunhac, poor thing, died when your dad was just a young boy. It came on so suddenly, the illness. Grandpa McDermott was a hard man after that. He loved her so much, and your father was so lost without her.

Secrets Told

"Your father and his father had a very big argument. Your dad left and joined the U.S. Army and became an American citizen. Your mother was my lovely sister, Mary de Grasse, from Perryville, Missouri. She was a nurse at the hospital at Aberdeen Proving Grounds, where your father was stationed. Your father was going to be shipped out but contracted measles. Your mom was his nurse. He ended up working on the base and dated her. After your dad left the army, they married and moved to the family farm in Perryville."

Sister Agnes looked intently at Cordy. "Did your parents say anything about this to you?" Cordy shook her head, "No, it didn't come up. I just knew that I was born in Perryville, and that Dad and his father weren't on good terms."

Sister Agnes sighed, "Upon Grandma de Grasse's death, she willed your mother the family farm. I was in the convent at the time and didn't need it. I had taken a vow of poverty. Your father knew families in St. Genevieve and Perryville that had come from Nova Scotia and Quebec in the Great Expulsion. Many Acadian families settled along the Mississippi River. The Great Expulsion was about the persecution of the French settlers who had their lands confiscated by the British in Nova Scotia. You know the community Bellefontaine was named after a famous Acadian. It's a suburb in the north of St. Louis near the river.

"My sister loved the farm animals and farming. I think you got her gift for healing animals. Your dad became town sheriff to help make ends meet. Joe wanted to keep your birth off the radar. Some people think it was to keep your birth a secret from his father. I think he knew that you were going to be special. He wanted to protect you. We laughed at how you could celebrate two birthdays — one on the eleventh and the other on the twelfth.

"You always wondered why we celebrated your birthday early on February 11. According to my watch, it was your birthday. February 11 is a special holy day related to the Apparition of Our Lady of Lourdes. Saint Bernadette saw one of her visions on February 11, so your mother wanted your middle name to be

Bernadette. Your father remembered the story of his father being cured from the water of Lourdes, and we all agreed. It was a sign."

"You had a special connection with Our Lady."

Sister Agnes smiled, "They snuck you over to the Canadian border and declared you were born in the car. I vouched for them. We obtained your birth certificate soon after."

Cordy was astonished. "Why did you lie? Why?"

Sister Agnes took a deep sigh, "I know this is going to sound very strange, dear, but you remember the story of baby Jesus and the story of Moses? It's a recurring story of how a child is hidden to protect it from evil people who do not want change. I want to show you something."

She pulled out a small book with pictures of illuminated manuscripts.

"St. Louis's Bible had a picture of the Great Geometrician or Architect of the Universe holding a compass in his hand. St. Louis was in the Crusades and his mother, Blanche, was one of his teachers. Their family passed on the sacred knowledge through their Bibles and churches. The compass is an instrument used in geometry. The Freemasons use it in their sacred symbols, and so do the Catholic Church. Sacred geometry goes back to Pythagoras. In the cathedral of Notre Dame at Chartres, France, the zodiac is on the walls and on the stained glass windows. They had a great knowledge of the stars."

Sister Agnes turned to another picture. In Blanche's Castile psalter, a page showed an astrologist looking at the stars with an astrolabe. "They placed a great amount of faith in the stars and so astrology charts were made of certain individuals. They had court astrologists draw up astrological charts to help give them insight on the future. The Magi told Herod of the coming of baby Jesus from the stars. It's the same today. People are looking for what we call the 'Pure of Heart,' specially gifted people whose birthdates and zodiac charts are special.

"I know it sounds crazy, but realize that Herod massacred the children of Bethlehem and the Pharaoh massacred Jewish babies

Secrets Told

to prevent Moses's and Jesus's destinies. It's getting more and more difficult to hide children's birth dates now because of the way everything is computerized. Your parents and I wanted to make your birthday confusing to hide you. It makes databases and large computers so scary, because hiding the Pure of Heart gets harder and harder. Your family belonged to a secret organization that has fought this evil for centuries." Cordy's mouth was open in shock. "I thought astrology was evil, according to the Pope?" Sister Agnes patted her hand. "Rome used the zodiac and even to this day, observes the stars with vigilance. The stars have always influenced man, even in prehistoric times."

Sister Agnes pulled chocolate chip cookies from the picnic basket. She handed them to Cordy.

"Oh! Sister Catherine's homemade cookies are in there. I love them," Cordy said.

Sister smiled, "She made them especially for you. Joseph McDermott, your father, was quite an amazing man. His driving always scared me. I remember jokingly giving him a Miraculous Medal to protect him. You weren't born yet, Cordy, when he was shot in a gun battle in the middle of town.

"A bank robber shot him in the hip, but the Miraculous Medal was on his key chain and saved his life. The bullet ricocheted and ran down his pant leg. His only injury was a burn from the bullet. His femoral artery could have been severed, but it wasn't." Sister Agnes pulled from her pocket the Miraculous Medal. "This is the medal that saved his life and I'm giving it to you. Your mother kept it."

Cordy held the medal in her hand.

"Not a scratch on it. Amazing, isn't it? Dad told me about it when I was seven. I remember you calling me in high school telling me about the airplane crash. I miss them every day."

Cordy pulled out a necklace from under her shirt and showed her aunt. She was wearing a Miraculous Medal. Cordy smiled, "I believe you, Sister. I helped save an older woman's life by doing CPR and just by coincidence, she was wearing a Miraculous

Keys of Life

Medal. It happened at college about four years ago."

Sister Agnes gently touched the necklace. "I'm glad you wear it," she said.

Cordy held her aunt's hand. "I was so lucky that I had you to watch out for me. The Pure of Heart thing, I admit, sounds pretty crazy."

Sister Agnes continued, "Your parents made me your trustee and guardian. I tried to let Our Lady and the angels guide me. I kept you safe and tried to protect you. Your great-grandfather Aughavan fled from Ireland in the revolution. It was said he saw the lights of Our Lady of Knock. He saw them from a distance. A Fenian hedge master doesn't want to attract attention during a revolution so only his friends knew he saw them. It's just a story Grandma de Grasse told us to pass onto our children. I'm just trying to show you, Cordy, that you have a special connection with Our Lady. Your case isn't unusual. I've checked the records.

"I have a connection, too. Louise de Marillac had another name. She was married to Catherine de Medici's secretary, Antoine le Gras. I believe our family may be related to hers in some way. That's why I chose to be a Daughter of Charity. You see, I was already part of the family. Catherine Laboure, who was a Daughter of Charity, had a vision of our Lady and from this, the Miraculous Medal was born. I want you to see how things are connected and keep your eyes open for signs of these connections. Dreams should be taken seriously, such as one I had of you meeting a nice man named Bob who was playing bingo."

Cordy laughed. "Sounds like he is a bit boring."

Sister Agnes smiled, "Who knows what the future brings, but remember your dreams."

Cordy hugged her.

"I thank you so much, Mother Agnes. Your support through college and then in vet school meant so much to me. I was so lucky considering Mom and Dad didn't have very much money. I worked as much as I could but I am very thankful for your support. Mom begged me never to sell the farm if she died."

Secrets Told

Sister Agnes looked out to where two squirrels were eating some nuts. "I miss my little sister. She used to climb on my lap and ask me to read to her. Your mother was so smart and such a fighter. We often talked about how the world would change when women had a voice in government, religion, and economics."

Mother Agnes looked at her niece proudly. "I know she is smiling down on you with pride." She suddenly looked bashful, and a bit timid. "Well, dear, I hope you don't get angry at me, but I have kept one more very big secret from you."

Cordy looked surprised. "What, more secrets? Why would I be angry with you?" The little nun straightened her skirts and looked directly into Cordy's eyes.

"Your grandfather McDermott came to see me. He told me he regretted his mistakes, and he cried in my office telling me how much he loved his son and his granddaughter. It was too late for his son but he wanted his granddaughter to be taken care of. You were in vet school at the time. He saw your picture on my desk, and Bill pulled out a picture of your grandmother. You look very much like her. Bill and I got to be great friends over the years. I told him how you were born. He had great respect for Saint Bernadette and Our Lady of Lourdes, and he felt, like me, that you had a connection with Our Lady. Bill showed me a copy of a yellowed old picture of Lourdes that he kept at his house. We agreed the Lourdes water had curative healing powers but it required faith. Saint Bernadette said without faith, the water loses its power. "Your father knew Bill had a special place in his heart for Our Lady. His eyes were filled with wonder that you were born on February eleventh when Our Lady appeared to Bernadette at Lourdes. I told him I checked the Mother House out of curiosity about the coincidental connections. The church has documentation of similar cases and I showed him the investigation reports that further illustrated you fit the profile of someone with a special connection. People born on one of the days of the visions of Our Lady have a history of coincidences in relation to Our Lady."

Mother Agnes pulled a Miraculous Medal out of her dress pocket and pointed to it. "The Miraculous Medal has a connection with Bernadette and Lourdes. Bernadette was wearing the Miraculous Medal when she saw the vision of Our Lady."

Cordy was having a hard time processing what the Sister was saying. Mother Agnes sighed, "... And then there is me. I am a Daughter of Charity. A child of Vincent de Paul was another coincidence." Cordy tried to interrupt her, but Sister Agnes held her hand up.

"Hold on, let me finish. Your father made me trustee of your estate and guardian. Your grandfather respected your father's wishes that I was to be your guardian instead of him. You are his only heir. Bill wanted to give you some of your inheritance early, but I told him you weren't ready. You were too young for that responsibility. I hope you understand, Cordy. Your father didn't want anything to do with your grandfather. I wanted you to experience a normal life."

Her eyes filled with tears. "I was trustee for the inheritance, but now I'm dying. You are older now and ready. I hope you forgive me dear for waiting so long to tell you."

Cordy was stunned but she hugged her aunt. "Of course, I forgive you Sister Agnes. But why didn't Grandpa Bill come and see me?"

Sister Agnes sighed, "I told him that you weren't ready. I think you are now. Your father warned me about him. He told me how obsessed he got about his money, work, and power. I'm hoping that he is a changed man. It is time for forgiveness and I think you should meet him. Forgiveness and love are the greatest gifts.

"Now, what I'm going to tell you may be hard to believe, so just try keeping an open mind. I know you're spiritual but not in an orthodox way. I feel that you must find your own spiritual way. The Pure of Heart date back to Genesis and Noah. I want you to read up on the Nephilim or the sons of God. Noah and his family were Pure of Hearts. The flood was to destroy the Children of the Nephilim and Noah survived."

Secrets Told

The older woman pulled out a picture of a stained glass window depicting a giant holding a club and a smaller man. "Here, look at this window which was found at Chartres Cathedral in France. It is the Noah window, and it has mystified many historians but they believe it is about Genesis 6:4 which describes the giants or Children of the Nephilim. The sons of God, who came from the heavens and married the daughters of Eve, are in the Bible. This war has been going on for a very long time."

"The Children of the Nephilim survived and want revenge on the Pure of Heart. The Pure of Heart were born during times of conflict and have changed the world by their actions. Joan of Arc is an example of one. Gandhi is another. Leonardo da Vinci, Michelangelo, Galileo, Bernadette, Martin Luther King, Lincoln, and many others are people who are filled with a spiritual fire that changed the world. Unfortunately, certain groups have hunted the Pure of Heart throughout history. The Inquisition burned Joan of Arc at the stake. Lincoln and Gandhi were assassinated. An organization was created to help protect the Pure of Heart. I am part of that organization. Your great-grandfather, Chief Saunhac of the Mi'kmaq, still lives and heads the Protectors of the Pure of Heart."

Cordy's face showed total surprise because she thought her great-grandfather was dead. "Dad told me my great-grandfather was dead. Why did he do that?"

"The chief and your dad had their reasons. Perhaps it had to do with hiding you. Have you had any strange dreams lately?"

Cordy head perked up from looking at her hands. "As a matter of fact, I have."

Her aunt laughed, "Was it about a red-haired angel?"

"How could you have known that?" Cordy said, fumbling with the words.

Her aunt patted her hand. "What did he say?"

"He asked me what I've learned," Cordy said as she looked at the trees.

Her aunt stood up. "It's time you learned the truth, Cordy. Walk with me. You are going to get more visits from angels. I will warn you that some of them are not good. You must trust your heart whenever you deal with them. Joan of Arc was a Pure of Heart, and she reported one of her voices was Michael the Archangel. I know some people thought she was crazy but she did free France from Britain's rule. You make the decisions, remember, and you live with your choice."

They strolled through the oak trees, down a stone path. "Imagine you are a knight going on a quest. You are going to learn more and more things on your journey."

Cordy rubbed her head. "Well, I learned something about Mary Magdalene just the other night. I read the Bible for the first time in a long time. I couldn't find anything about her being a prostitute — only that seven demons were removed from her."

Sister Agnes nodded. "Just like the movies and books talk about. Did you read about the French oral tradition of her going to France with other saints?"

"Yep," Cordy nodded. "Why was I told in school that she was a prostitute? No one told us about the French oral tradition."

Sister Agnes sighed, "You have to find the answer yourself, but I can tell you that Mary Magdalene is very important to the organization that guards the Pure of Heart. She was one of them. Always look for the words 'Magdalene or similar versions of it,' those are the code words for the guardians."

She pulled out copies of paintings from the Internet from her pocket; one was by Poussin called *The Lamentation of Christ*. Cordy looked at it.

"Which woman is Mary Magdalene?"

Sister Agnes smiled. "The viewer has the choice or freedom to see with their own eyes. Art is quite a magical moment between the painter and the viewer. I want you to look at the red-haired cherub and the red-haired child next to each other." Cordy looked carefully. "Are you sure it isn't two cherubs and the other's wings just can't be seen?"

Sister Agnes nodded. "You're right. Many see the painting in that way, but I believe Poussin knew about the Pure of Heart and the child may represent those later who would be killed and would carry on the fight for truth. I have copies of other paintings by Titian, Michelangelo, Rafael, and Bourdon that I want you to look at later when you are alone.

"In Megiddo, Israel, an ancient mosaic floor was found in the oldest Christian church. There, the tiled floor shows a woman named Akeptous, who donated a table in memory of Jesus Christ. Women's role throughout history, the Bible, and now, is a crucial issue. A war has been waged to keep women suppressed and their voices silent. Violence against women has increased. Baby girls in India and China are killed because parents want a son. Magdalene is a symbol for the voices of women that need to be heard.

"I admit for me, the ultimate goal is to have women participate in the decisions of Rome. The time has come for women to have an equal position in the church. In early Christianity, they celebrated the "love feast" on Sunday. In the catacombs, women are shown celebrating the memory of Christ with their children and husbands around the table. It wasn't just a celebration for men. The women of the church dedicated their lives to educate the poor, heal the sick, and help protect women. I want Magdalene to be sitting at da Vinci's Last Supper table with the rest of the Apostles. I think Jesus wanted equality for women in the Church. The sisters have worked on the education of women and the poor, and I am amazed at the changes I have seen over my lifetime. You are a vet and a few decades back, women weren't allowed in college." Cordy put her hand on a tree, staring at the golden forest in the distance. "I found out that the Pope removed an Archangel out of his archangel position. Can he do that?"

Sister explained, "Perhaps that angel you saw in your dream was him? Think about it, and you will find the answer. You need to follow your intuition and your heart, and do what the angel says, search for the truth. Your grandfather and great-grandfather want to see you, and it is time for you to have control of your inheritance."

She pointed at the file sitting at the bottom of the basket. "That file has all the papers, information, and contacts. Your grandfather gave you the first installment of your inheritance to see how you handle it. Remember, Cordy, the money doesn't change who you are. Trust your heart and you will know what to do, but from now on, you will have to be on your guard. Your grandfather will want to see you in about a week. The numbers to reach him are all in there. I believe you're going to see Chief Saunhac, too. It's time for you to understand there is a war going on in the shadows.

"Now there is one more thing, dear. I don't want to scare you. The Pure of Heart have historically been hunted by a secret group called the Children of the Nephilim. The Nephilim's tentacles have reached into governments, secret societies, and religious orders. Word is that you have come up on their radar screen, probably because of that shooting. The girl whose life you saved is a Pure of Heart, probably.

"The Watchers are the ones who keep the balance between the Pure of Heart and the Nephilim. Unfortunately, the Watchers had a split between them long ago. Your grandfather is a leader for the Light Watchers. In your grandfather's defense, the responsibility he has carried on his shoulders for the Light Watchers and mankind is immense.

"The Dark Watchers are the other side, and they have become very powerful. Both use the symbol of the Eye of Ra, or what some call, the All Seeing Eye. You know it as the eye on a dollar bill. It is not just a symbol for the Freemasons. You will see it in churches. The Watchers, too, have ingrained themselves in society."

Cordy looked puzzled. "What, Bill is a Watcher? No wonder Dad got mad at him. Dad never talked about it. I don't know about this, Sister Agnes. I'm sorry, but it sounds crazy."

Sister Agnes sought Cordy's eyes. "You will know when the time comes what needs to be done, but you must heed the good Archangel's advice, Cordy. Your grandfather is a good man, and

Secrets Told

he did everything he could to protect his family. The job is all-consuming, and it is a very lonely job. He needs you." They had reached a statue of an angel carrying a flaming sword surrounded by stones.

"Archangel Uriel is right. You must learn the truth. It will be revealed. I admit you're in danger, so you must be careful. I protected you for as long as I could. You're strong and gifted, but just be on guard. The Order of the Watchers is complicated and one never knows what side they are on. Dark Watchers are usually bloodline families who have a long history of being involved in the long war. I have seen Dark and Light Watchers marry and truces established. You have been protected since birth and hidden by us. I'm just warning you of the intricate alliances that are out there. They are unpredictable for a reason. Sometimes they support the Pure of Heart and other times they sit back and watch them murdered. Their goal is balance and observation. Don't call me at the Mother House. I'm being watched. Any further questions you will need to talk to Grandpa Bill or Chief Saunhac. The chief is an expert on the ancient religions and very wise. Heed his advice."

Cordy was astonished. They had walked to the Mother House, and Cordy realized she was saying goodbye to Sister Agnes. The little nun kissed her cheek and hugged her. "I'm so proud of you and love you so much. I'll call you. Oh, one more thing, dear, go visit the shrine again, you will be in for a surprise when you get there. You will find something very important there. Bye, dear, and be careful."

"You take care of yourself. I'll be OK." Sister Agnes handed her the picnic basket "There are more of Sister Catherine's chocolate cookies. Take them home." She pulled back the cloth covering the file, and their eyes locked on it. Cordy pulled the checkered cloth over the file and took the basket.

"Tell Sister Catherine I'm going to eat every one of them." Cordy drove down the lane, glancing in the rearview mirror as her aunt waved goodbye. She almost wondered if Sister Agnes had gone crazy.

Chapter 19

The Children of the Nephilim

In a towering skyscraper, at the top floor, a group of men and women were sitting around a table in the boardroom. The silver-haired gentleman at the head of the table had his hands crossed.

"What do you have for us, Ken?"

The broad-shouldered, muscular man stood up, and a television screen appeared behind curtains automatically being pulled apart. The television showed riots of thousands of people protesting in the streets of Egypt.

"We think this may be the best time to obtain the powerful Egyptian artifacts that we've been wanting. The riots have allowed us to steal some of King Tut's sacred tablets and his scarab necklace. We need to decide which other objects we should go after."

"Yes, very good, Ken. The perfect time for stealing the treasure and nobody knowing where it went. It worked well in Iraq. Saddam's treasures are now ours. In chaos, we come in and scoop up the archeological treasures. Bravo!" The chairman clapped gently and looked at Ken.

"Thank you, sir. Our support for the rebels has worked perfectly, as we planned. It's cheaper than buying the artifacts, and no one knows we have them." Ken smiled and slightly bowed his head in acknowledgement of the praise the chairman gave him.

A woman wearing a tight black leather dress, who sat next to Ken, looked disturbed. The chairman spotted her.

"Ellen, you look like your thong is too tight. What's the problem, dear?" He spread his arms out toward the table. The girl pulled at her black felt collar as he insulted her. All the people around the table laughed. It was a game. They played the game of master and slave in front of everyone. He insulted her, and she took it. Ellen stood up, showing off her figure "Some of these objects are cursed. I have the report here," she said, picking up a paper off the desk, knowing full well the men at the table had a clear view of her chest peeking out from the low-cut dress. Ellen knew how to control men, and she had their full attention. "It shows the police caught two of the thieves. We hired these bumbling idiots, and they got caught. The police found them talking gibberish to two skulls while lying on the floor. They conveniently died in a local hospital of a mysterious disease."

Ken shifted uncomfortably. "It's a minor issue that the men are dead. The doctors were told to say it was a brain infection from inhaling the mummy dust."

Ellen answered. "You don't get it, Ken. Some of those objects nobody can touch, making them useless to us." Ken glared at her, and she smugly smiled back.

A small voice whispered from the end of the table, "What about a Pure of Heart?"

It was Jason, one of the underlings, who had spoken up, ever so slightly.

"Everybody be quiet." The chairman looked interested. "Well, Jason, please enlighten all of us. We are all ears, my dear boy."

Jason surveyed his papers. "I'm just saying that perhaps a Pure of Heart can wield these objects, even though we can't. If we could make a Pure of Heart obey our commands, then they could help us."

Keys of Life

"Interesting point, Jason, and you demonstrate the need for us to acquire a Pure of Heart for a test."

The chairmen looked intently at all of them. "How is the hunt going?"

Ken turned the lights down, and the screen displayed profiles of seven people. "We just killed Henry Baines, the environmental advocate. He had significant birth charts." We did have a miss on Minah Hassan Hamanai, but she won't be here for long."

The chairman looked intently at Ken. "The Council doesn't like mistakes, Ken. Can you handle this?"

Ellen wickedly smiled. Ken looked determined. "I have one of my top men on it, and Minah is a goner."

Jason softly coughed, "If we kill all of the Pure of Heart, then nobody may be able to handle these sacred objects." The chairman looked at Jason.

"I will discuss this with the Council, but no one is likely to trust the Pure of Heart. The Nephilim's corporations convene next month to give their reports to the appointed members of the Nephilim Council, and I want our chapter to have a stellar report. I want Minah Hassan killed but after that, put the hunters on standby 'til I report to the Council. The Egyptian situation is very delicate and complicated. Minah's father needed to be taught a lesson on obedience. We were going to use her to blackmail him and now she is a loose end that can lead to us." Ken nodded his head. "I live to serve."

Ellen pounced on the moment. "A report is circulating that the Watchers feel the times indicate an increased turbulence coming into Earth's energy field."

The chairman turned his chair so that his back was to his minions. He looked up at the stars in the night sky and the great view of the lighted city. "Ah, they feel it, too. Well, I want everyone on their toes and if the Watchers know something, we need to, also. Knowledge is power."

Ellen pulled on her collar. "I'm on it."

The chairman rose from the table and walked the hall to his

office. The office was filled with ancient artifacts and treasures. Ellen followed him. She shut the door and smiled at him before he slapped her face. The air was hot with anger.

"Can't you keep your pretty mouth shut, my dear?" She refused to show that her face burned and looked at him seductively. Ellen wrapped her arms around him.

She purred and whispered in his ear, "I love it when you play rough. Ken's report was garbage. Why does he get all the fun jobs?" He kissed her softly. "You shouldn't have divulged the Watcher information. You let all of them know you had inside information." Ellen pulled back. "You think there is a Watcher on the committee?"

The punishment came when she misbehaved, and she was ready. He slapped her again and softly said, "Let us hope for your sake that there isn't." His cell phone rang. "It's the Council. Get the hell out of here now." He pointed to the door. Ellen retreated out of the room quickly.

On the phone, Antar's voice could be heard. "Is there any problem? I sense that the Pure of Heart are getting stronger. How is the hunt going?"

The chairman's business-like tone assured Antar. "I have my best men on it. They are vicious and efficient. That's the way you like them." The chairman turned toward his desk, sensing a presence. The chairman had to hold back his fear when he encountered the Father of the Nephilim. One could hide nothing from him.

The handsome man sitting behind the desk swiveled the chair around for the chairman to see. Antar was fitted in a grey Armani business suit. He looked at the chairman with a smile.

"You enjoyed her for a while, but she gets tedious, doesn't she? I must say watching her leave is her best asset."

The chairman sighed, "Ellen is a power-hungry witch. I have to admit, she had most of the men in the room under her spell. I've trained her well since childhood. She's a black widow. She would eat her children and husband for power. She obeys me, and that makes her useful. I can't help it if she's overzealous."

Antar asked, "Do you know how to handle her? Your conditioning has worked so far. She is devious. Be careful you don't succumb to her seductive charms. We do need her to acquire the necessary articles." The chairman nodded in understanding and looked out at the city skyline.

"The Dark Watchers do seem to have found something. We are working on finding out what it is. They have become very powerful in world politics and governments. They hold more key positions of state than the Light Watchers. Who knows, the Dark Watchers and Children of the Nephilim may unite. The future holds many interesting possibilities. As soon as I find out more details, I will get back to you."

"I am so pleased to see Adam's children trained in the ways of the Nephilim," Antar answered. "Man's inhumanity to man is a pleasure to watch. My children were wiped out for fear of their wickedness. Who would have guessed that the Children of the Nephilim would consist of mostly Adam's children? You have done well, my son."

When the chairman turned around, Antar was gone. He knew to fail Antar would mean death.

Chapter 20

Ash's Dream

Any time Ash performed a healing act of kindness, he would become dog-tired. It took only a second for Ash to fall into a deep, heavy sleep. Tonight wasn't any different, but little did he know that this would be the first of many sleepless nights to come.

Ash used to have dreams of being on dig sites that were so real. He would think, "OK, I worked all night in my sleep, so I don't have to go in today." But Ash was dedicated and always showed up. He usually found a rare artifact that morning. Over time, he knew that the dreams were somehow linked to the big find. It was almost like someone was looking over his shoulder, and one of his Irish coworkers would say "Aye, the angels are with this one."

Ash would laugh, "I don't believe in angels. It's all experience and hard work." Somehow in the back of Ash's mind, he knew that when he found an artifact or tomb, it was in the same location as his dream. Ash never told anyone. He knew this ability came from his mother. His mother had this ability all her life, and everyone looked for Ash to carry on in her footsteps with the Elders. The Elders, a group of Egyptian shaman and religious leaders, went back centuries.

Ash was in for a dream of a lifetime. About five minutes after Ash closed his eyes, he slipped into a deep sleep. He was at the temple at Abu Simbel, and the wall was flashing a tiny light in his eyes. It twinkled, and the light called to him.

Ash used to joke about it with his mother. He would laugh, "A dog never forgets where he hides his bones." In this dream, Ash saw a man standing in the temple. He looked familiar, and yet, Ash had never seen him before. When he spoke, though, it was the same voice that guided Ash all these years.

The man said, "I am Atum, the first being and one of the first originators."

Ash mumbled, "You are not. You're the voice in my head who guides me in my dreams." Ash looked around. "I can wake myself up any time I want, and you will be gone."

Atum's voice had the patience of a teacher. "You never saw me in your dreams before because I was always behind you."

Ash shook his finger at him. "No, that's not possible."

"I was behind you, Ash, the idiot," Atum chuckled.

Ash shook his head, trying to wake up, and asked, "Why are you not behind me now?"

"It is time for you to know this to be true, so stop," Atum solemnly answered.

Ash was angry now. "Stop what?"

Atum was losing patience and used his fatherly voice, "Stop trying to wake up. You're going to give yourself whiplash. It is no use. I will let you go when it is time, and you understand. You must relax."

"Who are you?"

"That won't work either, Ash. Yelling will only scare the animals in the desert or wake the dead."

"OK, OK," Ash reluctantly agreed. "What do I need to understand?"

Ash's Dream

Atum explained, "I will give you what you need, a protector and guide. Many will try to kill you and stop you along the way." Ash threw his hands up in frustration. "Great, just great!" Atum calmly answered, "You will have help, Ash. They will seek you out. Dark will turn to light, and light will turn to dark. It is part of who I am."

"OK, you're making more sense because up to now, you were confusing me completely," Ash answered.

Atum smiled, "I was Atum before I was Ra. You were taught Ra is the sun god. Atum can be linked to the words of the Creative Powers and the Creator. I was Atum-Ra in the beginning days. We all knew that we were going to have to leave Eden. A pure bloodline promoted weakness. The genetic code had to be diversified to survive. I came first.

"Some say I was born in the ocean of the universe, but it was the light that created Ra. Atum-Ra was hope and rebirth. I came from the heavens, Ash. It is all about love. What do you love? Men who make decisions based on life and love are always moving to the greater good. Men who look for gold and power are always destroying in the name of greed. Darkness is taking over the light, and it is time for the Pure of Heart to come of age."

"Oh, this is a great dream," Ash complained. He scratched his head. "I'll need a lifetime to understand this dream."

"No," Atum said. "You, my friend, have been preparing your whole life for such a time. You will understand. Now, it is time for the Pure of Heart to emerge. We are at the temple for a reason. You will need the objects of power held by the innocents. Ash, hear me follow the light and open the Altar of Manna. You will know the way. You will have to go early so no one will see.

"Ash, my friend, everything in nature has a fragile balance and Earth's future is in your hands. You will find the one who will give you hope. He will lead you and follow the path. Ash, do not give up. You must trust that you will find another to help guide you along the way. My friend, there will be many hardships and burdens to bear, but love will find you. Ash, you will find the

Keys of Life

keys of life in hidden places all along the journey. You will need to find the garden and the hands that protect the secrets. It is time to share the secrets with the children of Earth," Atum declared.

"Ash, trust your heart, but you remain virtuous until the end."

Ash blushed. "How did you know I was a virgin? I never had time for girls."

Atum laughed. "I have been guiding you ever since you were born, and this is your dream. I am going to give you a protector to be with you. His name is Uriel, regent of the sun. Uriel is the keeper of the mysteries that are deep within the earth, underground and in the hidden depths of the living world. He protected the gates of the promised land of Eden. He kept the Pure of Heart safe from the first cataclysm. I hope you take this piece of advice: whatever you do when you leave the temple, take a different path. Don't hesitate, move quickly, and never go back. They will hunt you down, and if you go back, they will kill you."

Ash's head popped up when he heard the word kill. "This is just a dream, and I could just decide to go home."

"If you don't listen and remain stubborn, then you will die and so goes the world," Atum sighed.

Ash woke up still lying on the hood of his 4Runner. It was still warm, and when he looked at his watch, he saw it had only been twenty minutes. Ash's heart was racing, but he felt the most rested he had been in years. He started to remember the dream.

"Oh, garbage, I need a drink." Ash swung open the front door to the 4Runner and found a fifth of Tennessee Whiskey under the passenger seat. Ash kept the bottle for special occasions with his Irish buddy.

He struggled to get the cap off the bottle as his hands shook. He muttered, "Dreams like that could drive a man to drink." Just as he got the top off a voice came from behind him, "I hope you're not going to drink that bottle alone."

Surprised, Ash bumped his head on the door. "Oh shit!" he yelled.

Ash's Dream

The stranger chuckled, "What a limited vocabulary you have, Ash. I can see this is going to be a challenge."

Ash angrily yelled, "OK, asshole, who are you and what are you doing out here?"

"What are you doing drinking out in the middle of the desert, asshole?" the stranger calmly asked. All of a sudden the truth dawned on Ash.

He pointed to Uriel. "Oh wow, wow, get out. You must be Uriel."

Uriel crossed his arms and smiled. "Not bad for a man with a limited vocabulary. Now what gave me away?" Ash looked around him. It was the middle of the night in the desert, and it was bright as day around him.

Ash was overwhelmed by the light. He covered his eyes with his hands. Uriel strolled toward Ash. "Yes, it's hard to miss me, but it's not as bad in the daytime." He placed sunglasses on Ash's eyes. "Sometimes, it is best to wear sunglasses. The light can hurt your eyes."

Ash took a drink from the bottle and closed his eyes. "I wish this dream would come to an end." Uriel laughed.

"If this is still a dream, then why is your head sore from hitting it on the door?"

Ash rubbed his head and felt the bump. He decided to play along. "So you're my guide?" Ash took another swig of the whiskey, and it warmed his throat. Uriel watched him and then with a powerful hand grabbed the bottle.

"More like a guiding light, asshole!" Uriel took a drink, and chugged it down. "Ah!" Uriel savored it as he swallowed. "It's been a long time." He looked at the bottle. "Tennessee, one of the perks of the job is getting to taste the real stuff."

Uriel started to chuckle. "Ash, you could say I'm the guy who carries the flashlight when you're in the dark." Uriel looked seriously at Ash. "Remember, Ash, you must follow the light. The light of the seven will guide you. Moses had a stutter, but he did know how to listen, save for one time. He paid for it. He listened after that."

Keys of Life

Uriel circled around Ash, inspecting him. "Your limited vocabulary might be a problem, I'm counting on you being a Pure of Heart. You're not the sharpest crayon in the box, are you? I guess someone has to save your ass. I'll be your protector and guide. I accept." Uriel handed over the whiskey bottle. "A piece of advice: when I tell you to move, you better, or this will be the shortest mission both of us has been sent on."

Ash grabbed the bottle. "I don't need a protector. I can take care of myself."

Uriel shook his head, "Again with that limited vocabulary." Uriel rolled his eyes and looked up into the heavens. "Sorry, Ash, no one asked for your opinion, or if you like me. In fact, you only have three more hours before the college grad at the temple turns over his duties to the next shift. Trust me, you want to be out of there before daylight."

Ash rubbed the bump on his head again. "Hey, how did you know where I was going?" Uriel smiled mischievously, "I know everything about you, Ash."

Ash looked surprised. "Everything?" Uriel walked closer to him.

"I know you kissed little Sarah behind the school door when you were seven."

Ash opened his mouth in surprise. Uriel looked up at the stars. "Do you remember anything from your dream?"

Ash looked at the ground. "I'm, I'm still dreaming."

Uriel touched his shoulder. "No, you're not, and you know it."

Ash started to curse again but caught himself. A small sh-sh sound came out before Uriel groaned, "Oh my, you do stutter."

"No, I'm just confused," Ash protested. Uriel started to chuckle again, "OK, let's get this straight, I am talking to an idiot who doesn't know if he is dreaming and has a limited vocabulary." Uriel's frustration began to show. He shook his head and moved closer to Ash's face, waving his car keys in front of him. "Come on Ash, let's get moving. It is still a two-hour drive to the temple. You won't have much time."

Uriel looked directly in Ash's eyes. "Show me you can do it,

Ash's Dream

Ash. It's important. It could save the children of Earth." Uriel headed for the car. "Let's get going. Time is running out."

Ash started to change his mind but remained defiant. "What if I decide to go back home?"

Uriel shrugged his shoulders. "Do you remember anything from the dream? It's your decision but a dangerous one."

Ash thought for a second. Strangely enough, he remembered everything and every detail. He rubbed the bump on his head again. Ash looked up at Uriel, finally realizing this was one of the biggest moments in his life.

Uriel's persuasive voice coaxed him, "Do you really want to go back home?"

Ash's voice was definite. "No, no, if I go back they will kill me." Uriel shouted out to the desert, "Bingo! We have a winner, ladies and gentleman. He's figured it out."

Uriel took another gulp from the Tennessee whiskey bottle. Ash looked at him. "The voice in my head has never been wrong. I trust the voice in my dream." Ash ran to the truck and asked Uriel, "Are you coming?"

Uriel smiled and gazed up to the stars with his hands open. "Amen."

Uriel headed for the 4Runner and calmly explained, "One is disoriented at first when you communicating with a spirit guide. It will get better each time." Uriel walked up to the door. "Ash, drive to Nefetari's temple, and just trust your instincts. Your intuition is a gift so follow it.

"From this time on, you must not tell anyone where you are going, what you are doing and never let them know you were there," Uriel said in a serious tone. "A Pure of Heart is the only one you can trust."

Ash grabbed the Tennessee whiskey bottle from Uriel. "OK, I will go to the temples, and we'll see what happens. I'll just wing it from there."

"Finally, we are leaving," Uriel cheerfully chimed. Ash started the 4Runner as Uriel turned and stepped away.

Ash could see through the window a long, intensely shiny and wide sword hidden in a crisscross leather sheath under Uriel's black trench coat. Almost the entire sword was exposed, and the light that shone from the blade was brilliant. This explained where the intense light was coming from and why Uriel had a great aura around him.

Ash had an hour and forty-five minutes to get to the temple before shifts changed. The car raced down the desert road. Suddenly, the light was gone and the desert was pitch black. Ash slammed on the brakes — he couldn't see a damn thing. He switched the windshield wipers on and checked his headlights to see if they were on. Ash placed his hand up to his head and felt the sunglasses on his face. He ripped the sunglasses off and threw them on the dash. His hand reached over to the passenger side and grabbed the Tennessee whiskey, of which he took a big swig. The 4Runner's tires spun as he headed toward the temple. As he drove away, the tires slid on a big rock in the road, momentarily tipping the truck. "Oh shit!"

Chapter 21

The Light Watchers

Bill McDermott was looking out his penthouse window to the great city of Montreal. He had come a long way from the small fishing fleet. Bill was a billionaire and now one of the most powerful men in Canada. The nights were still long without his wife, Annie.

Annie Saunhac had the sweetest smile, and it flashed through his mind. He met her while fishing near Halifax. Bill never was very smooth with the ladies so instead of asking for her telephone number, he asked if she wanted to be his secretary.

Annie smiled back, "You do need someone to help you get organized. Your office is a disaster." She looked at his stack of papers strewn across the room. Annie organized his office and married him. She was part Mi'kmaq, and he had to ask permission from her father, the chief.

The Mi'kmaq were a Native American tribe from Nova Scotia. They helped the French settlers survive the harsh winters, and later, intermarried. Their families lived peacefully together until the English prevailed during the French and Indian War. The Acadians refused to take an oath accepting the King of England as their sovereign and their church leader and were expelled from Nova Scotia. The Mi'kmaq had no trouble taking the oaths, for they had no respect for the British king. Their gods were of the stars, water, sun, moon, and animal spirits. The Mi'kmaq did not forget their families.

The chief saw how much Bill loved Annie, and he welcomed him to the tribe's family. The men had their love for Annie in common. The chief was proud of his grandson Joseph, and he taught him the stories and rituals of the tribe. Bill held a deep respect for Annie's father. If the chief had it his way, he would have gladly taken the journey home first. Bill and he agreed it was time to see Cordy. She was family. It had been Sister Agnes who had kept her from coming to see them, and he was glad she finally saw the wisdom of telling Cordy they wanted to see her.

"How I wish you were here, Annie, so I don't screw things up. I only have one more chance." Bill said while he gazed at her picture. He picked up the report on his granddaughter Cordelia McDermott. They tried to hide her by having her delivered on the farm by Sister Agnes. His son died in a plane crash along with pretty Mary de Grasse, leaving their only daughter, Cordelia. His granddaughter was an amazing and talented woman. His son, who the Nephilim almost killed in a gun battle, lived for a bit longer before they assassinated him in the plane crash. The agency said it was weather and pilot error, but Bill knew better. He had the reports reviewed by his staff. Someone had tampered with the engine. The Nephilim had targeted his son. He had tried to explain to Joseph how dangerous they were. Joseph just didn't listen to him.

Cordy was top of her class at veterinary school, a black belt in karate, gifted with animals, and above all, courageous as shown when she helped Minah Hamanai escape death. Pure of Hearts had the ability to connect and help one another. Bill held the newspaper with her picture on it in his hand. The headline read,

"Heroine saves woman from sex slave trader." Bill slammed the paper down.

He knew Cordy was showing up on the radars of the Dark Watchers and Children of the Nephilim. He poured a glass of bourbon, the flashbacks of his son's words haunting him, "All you give a damn about is your money." Bill lost his only son the day he stomped off and joined the Army. It wasn't about money, but how could he explain duty to his son? Bill was fighting a war, and he had to make a great sacrifice. He lost his son but he wasn't going to lose Cordelia. He had convinced Mother Agnes to give him another chance.

The cell phone rang.

"Mother Agnes, does she know?"

Sister Agnes answered sadly, "Yes, she knows, but she's a bit shocked. She thought you didn't want to have anything to do with her. I tried to explain that it wasn't true. Cordy will be coming in a few days. I'm counting on you, Bill, to watch out for her." Her voice started to crack. "You and her are all that is left of the family now."

Bill patiently responded, sounding even a bit upbeat, "Don't worry. She'll be just fine. And as for the family, I'm taking her to see her great-grandfather Chief Saunhac. He wants to see her." There was a prolonged silence.

"The chief and I disagree sometimes, but I still have the greatest respect for him. I will keep you in my prayers, Bill. You take good care of her."

"I will, and don't worry. The chief is over ninety years old. What trouble can he get into? Good-bye Mother Agnes, and thank you for everything."

His granddaughter was coming to see him. A painting on the wall had the all-seeing eye of the Egyptian king Amen-Ra. It was the symbol for the Light Watchers. Bill McDermott remembered when he took the oath to serve. He wanted his son to take the oath, too, but he refused. The Light Watchers demanded complete dedication and loyalty. Bill had climbed to one of the highest levels in the organization.

He suddenly felt a presence behind him, combined with a feeling of pure love in his heart. It was an intoxicating feeling. Humans could only tolerate short periods with Uriel, whose presence put people in total bliss and left them craving for more.

Uriel stood there in the shadows. "Well, Bill, are you ready for this? She's going to be put in extreme danger. It's the only way. The Children of the Nephilim have gained too much power. The balance must be maintained. It's time for the Pure of Heart to emerge."

Bill slammed the drink down on the table. "Damn it! Haven't I given enough to the Watchers? My son was right. I should have protected him more. I made a promise to him, and I let him down. Cordy is all I have left." Bill's tears flowed from his eyes and his voice was breaking with emotion.

"Not her please, not her! She is all I have left." His voice trembled, and he wiped his tears. Uriel softly walked up to him and placed his hand on his shoulder.

"I will protect her, but there may be a sacrifice necessary for her protection. Are you willing, Bill?"

Bill smiled with resignation. "I serve the Watchers. Uriel, do what you must but please save her." Uriel looked to reassure Bill and nodded his head, "It will be."

Bill bowed his head, and Uriel disappeared. Uriel was one of the greatest archangels that stood in the presence of the Almighty. Bill knew Uriel would do his best, as would the others. The Children of the Nephilim had a history of inflicting brutal deaths on the Pure of Heart. They had no mercy.

"God help us," Bill whispered.

Chapter 22

The Miraculous Medal Shrine

Cordy had to go on a trip to Perryville and Saint Genevieve, Missouri, to check on some pups belonging to a family friend. It was near the family farm, and she planned on visiting her parent's gravesite on the way.

She was in high school when the principal came and took her to see Sister Agnes, who sat in his office. Mother Agnes told her the news. The plane suffered a mechanical failure and crashed. Her parents died instantly. They were gone, and she was alone. The farm was rented out to the neighbors, and she lived with her best friend and her mother until graduation.

Sister Agnes agreed she should finish high school with her friends, but Cordy was glad to leave town for college. It was the hardest time of her life, and she dove into her studies so she would forget the sorrow she felt. Her pets kept the loneliness at bay. They were the reason why she went into vet school. She found her calling was helping sick animals.

She pulled in at the cemetery near the Miraculous Medal

Shrine in Perryville. Her father had told her that the family had donated land to the shrine and worked there. Many of her relatives were buried there. She placed flowers at her parent's family tombstone, which displayed two hearts carved in the granite.

"I miss you both every day. I wish you would've told me more about what was going on. Maybe I could've helped. I'm going to see Grandpa McDermott and Chief Saunhac. I hope they like me. I'll come see you when I get back."

Turning toward the shrine, Cordy saw a strange man watching her. He was incredibly handsome, almost mesmerizing. Antar had been watching her now for years. She was a typical Pure of Heart — talented, courageous, and naïve. He wore a dark suit and approached her slowly.

"How does it feel to be a Pure of Heart?"

Cordy backed away. "I don't know?"

Antar stepped closer to her. "I'm Antar, and father to the Nephilim. Are you frightened, Pure of Heart?"

Cordy looked him in the eyes. "No, should I be?" Antar got menacingly close.

"You should be terrified." Cordy laughed. "Someone has a very high opinion of himself. Arrogance is a weakness."

"You are not afraid, that's good. We are forbidden to exert power on Holy Ground," Antar said, pointing to her parents' grave. "I have witnessed many courageous men and women die. Some of them were my family. We are similar that way."

"We are not alike. I don't kill innocent people," Cordy said, anger shining in her eyes.

Antar admired her thick chestnut hair, which smelled of vanilla, and her jewel-like eyes. The light she exuded was bright, making his eyes hurt. He thought to himself, why are Eve's daughters so beautiful and desirable?

"I lost children in this war, too." His face was inches from hers.

Cordy's eyes looked bravely into his. "I lost family, too, but revenge doesn't bring them back."

The Miraculous Medal Shrine

Antar looked at her luscious lips as her long hair swayed in the breeze. "Revenge can taste so sweet. You will feel it, Cordy, that emotion of wanting revenge. Revel in it, and let it penetrate your heart. It will make you powerful."

Cordy felt sick as she realized how close she was to wanting revenge for her parent's death. She knew now that the Nephilim were the reason her parents were killed.

Antar gazed at her with intense hypnotic eyes. "I'll be watching you, Pure of Heart. You can join my family any time if you choose."

A plane roared overhead, and Cordy looked up to the sky. When she looked down, Antar was gone. Cordy shook her head. "I'm so messed up."

The small town kept the shrine open most of the day. Cordy enjoyed looking at its beautiful stained glass windows. It had been awhile since she visited the shrine, and no one was in the church. She promised her aunt she'd come here.

One stained glass window showed Saint Bernadette's vision of Our Lady, and the sun shined through it, causing a ray of light to fall on Saint Bernadette's face. No one believed Bernadette when she spoke about her visions, but the healing spring made believers of the people. As a scientist, Cordy was a bit skeptical, but she knew some springs had minerals in them that helped cure diseases. Lourdes spring water was one of them. A few prayers couldn't hurt. Cordy was a believer in the power of prayers. She often prayed for many animals to recover from their surgeries. It couldn't hurt, and the animals felt the love and compassion. She walked farther into the church, named for Saint Mary of the Barrens. The Jesuits and then Vincentian fathers had built a seminary with the support of Bishop Dubourg. The Miraculous Medal shrine was founded in 1818.

The four angels surrounded the main altar. Cordy looked at the Miraculous Medal that her father gave her. It showed Our

Lady with her hands open, light radiating from her palms. The back had a circle of pentacles, interloped with the letter M, and two hearts — one with the crown of thorns around it and the other stabbed with a sword. Cordy thought it might be a symbol for the Pure of Hearts.

A painting on the wall showed Sister Margaret Mary Alacoque in 1673 witnessing the Sacred Heart of Christ. Sister Margaret Mary was born coincidentally on the feast day of Mary Magdalene on July 22, 1647. Another painting on the wall depicted Sister Catherine Laboure, a Daughter of Charity who on the eve of Saint Vincent de Paul feast day had a vision of the Miraculous Medal given to her by Our Lady. Sister Catherine's uncorrupted body lay in Paris in a golden casket to this day.

Cordy walked near the altar of the Miraculous Medal shrine. A circle of white pentacles surrounded Our Lady. A Seal of Solomon was mounted on black and white tiles, arranged like a chessboard. An even bigger white six-pointed star enclosed in a red circle surrounded the seal.

Cordy sat and said a prayer for her parents and Mother Agnes.

She got up to leave when she saw the Passion picture on the wall. It was beautiful and showed Christ on the cross with a young man, probably John the Baptist, standing to his left. A young Mary, holding her hands crossed below her belly, caught Cordy's attention. She felt a shiver up her spine. The woman's hands were in the same symbolic position as the Magdalene statue at the church in St. Louis.

"What the heck is this all about?" She pulled out her camera and took a picture. The altar of Saint Joseph had a winged serpent on the initials. Cordy thought of the twisted DNA strand and how fitting it was to symbolize Joseph's sacred bloodline, which came from David in fulfillment of the Scriptures. Why the winged serpent?

Cordy decided before she left she'd take a stroll to the stone grotto replica of Our Lady of Lourdes. It was quiet and serene. Only the birds singing in the trees could be heard. For a second,

The Miraculous Medal Shrine

the birds stopped singing, and Cordy had the feeling she was being watched. She looked everywhere, but no one was around.

"I need to find out what this is all about," Cordy said to herself as she looked at the statue of Our Lady above her head. She remembered as a child she had hid something there with her mother. She wondered if it was still there.

The rock grotto was made from local stones. Sometimes, during the holidays, Mass was said at the rock altar underneath the grotto. The memory of a little girl placing a beautiful small quartz disk behind a loose rock came to her. The rocks held firmly along the wall except for one big one, loosened with age. Cordy pulled it out and saw the quartz disk, still there after all those years in a small stone box with the words *'call this number'* engraved on it.

Cordy laughed. It looked like a telephone number. The disk shined and sparkled in the sunlight. What in the world was it? She walked past a statue of Our Lady standing on a crescent moon, her foot resting on the head of a serpent whose mouth held an apple. Revelation in the Bible talked about the woman clothed in the sun, proclaiming the end of days. Cordy carried the box in her pocket and walked back to her car. A man in a dark leather jacket watched her from behind two big oak trees. As Cordy left the shrine, his car followed hers.

Cordy headed down the road to the small town of St. Genevieve just a few miles away. Saint Genevieve, a French settlement dating to 1775, was older than Perryville. Saint Genevieve was the patron saint of the city Paris, and settlers came to her town from Canada, France, and Acadia. The British had expelled the Acadians from Nova Scotia.

Cordy pulled up to Saint Genevieve Church, where a statue of the shepherdess looked down upon her and walked in to get a look inside. The church was older, built in the 1800's. Cordy looked up and immediately noticed the symbol of an all-seeing eye within a triangle staring down at her from the stained glass window. She had seen the design on the dollar bill and knew the

Freemasons had used it. But it surprised her to see it in a Catholic church.

The eye was also the symbol of the Watchers, and Cordy then realized the church was Watcher territory. Was she being watched? Cordy wondered if she was just being paranoid. She remembered Antar's point about being on holy ground. Cordy had visited these churches all her life, but now she was seeing them for the first time with a new perspective. She looked at her watch and hurried out to get to her appointment. Cordy had so much to think about between the vision of Antar and finding the box.

The man watched her leave the church. It was forbidden to kill in a church or on holy ground because the Nephilim honored the rule of sanctuary. He would patiently wait for the proper time. Cordy was oblivious to him following her. She had way too many things on her mind to notice.

CHAPTER 23

The Dark Watchers

The Watchers split in to two forces long ago. The Light Watchers supported the Pure of Heart. Their purpose was to keep the balance and protect Earth and her children.

Some of the Watchers didn't have such noble ideas and wanted a share of the power. They looked at the Nephilim as rivals who craved power and dominion over Earth to destroy God's creation. The Dark Watchers were independents who didn't follow the laws of their respective governments. They recognized men's flaws — prostitution, alcohol, drugs, smuggling and gambling. The Dark Watchers were competitors and yet, sometimes partners with the Nephilim. It was a delicate balance. They craved power, and they didn't care how they achieved their goal. Revenge and destruction weren't their major objectives. The real goal was to gain enough power to rule the world, but they didn't want a world government. Governments hindered their businesses, and they saw no need for them. They answered to no one; it was the Light Watchers who carried morals on their shoulders. Light Watchers lived by a code and ran family businesses around the world.

All the secret factions spied on one another. The split happened during the time of Joan of Arc, a Pure of Heart. She had served her purpose by saving France, but the world was not ready for the equality of women. Joan frightened the Dauphin with her popularity among the people. The Dark Watchers saw her as a threat to future balance. They had been stunned at the power of the peasant girl against their armies.

The Dark Watchers profited immensely by selling weapons and starting wars. Joseph de Villiers, a fifty-something man slightly graying at the temples, sat in the chair of his London penthouse contemplating the chain of events.

A box with a golden triangle inlaid on the front was in front of him, obtained during the torture of a Child of the Nephilim. He received the box from a Light Watcher, who was guarding it for the Pure of Heart. Inside the box was an object from an Egyptian tomb of Joseph, son of Jacob, as well as other treasured items.

The object was brought back by the Crusaders and given to St. Louis IX and held in secret. But no one could touch these objects of great power. Anyone who touched them met a swift death or suffered great tragedies. The box had been sitting in the Dark Watcher treasure trove.

Now, it sat on his desk in a special glass container, ensuring that he did not touch it. The box had been studied by scientists, who died later from terrible accidents. They concluded the box emanated a field of energy that had never been seen before. Some called it dark energy, but in the presence of a Pure of Heart, the energy turned into a light energy of intense power. A physicist would say it was similar to matter and antimatter reaction.

It was time for a great swing in the pendulum of power. The Children of the Nephilim were mindless, their only goal, revenge. The Dark Watchers had achieved control of the governments and population. Their symbol was the all-seeing eye, usually accompanied by a darker symbol like a skull and

The Dark Watchers

crossbones. The organization's interest was dominion over mankind and the world. De Villiers had the even greater ambition to be master of the universe and spirit worlds.

The Dark Watchers had formed alliances with the Nephilim over the years. They had reached incredible power. Banks, governments, religious groups, and intelligence agencies were all infiltrated by the Dark Watchers. The chairman of the Children of the Nephilim had concentrated his power into control over corporations. The Dark Watchers were notorious assassins and families with a history of privateering. What Joseph de Villiers needed was the right Pure of Heart to open the box. The head of the Pure of Heart was hiding many priceless treasures, which could change the balance. The precious items were given to the Pure of Heart from heavenly sources, and they were their protectors. Secret agencies all over the world were looking for them.

The Dark Watcher leader ached to possess one item above them all. The Dark Watchers were ready to step up and become the gods they were born to be.

A picture of his pregnant wife, Sheila, smiled at him from his desk. She had committed suicide when he admitted to killing her parents. They stood in his way to her fortune. He also admitted to her and to himself that he never loved her. He enjoyed being cruel to her, and he told her there was no escape. She was his wife and divorce was out of the question until after the baby was born. The psychiatrists labeled her mad, and the state had given him guardianship of her massive fortune. Sheila had no one to protect her, and she was isolated.

Everyone was surprised when she jumped out of their penthouse window. The medication should have kept her lethargic and passive. She was smart enough to hide the fact she was not swallowing her pills. The orderly left her for only a second in a chair on the roof. It was a beautiful day, and he wanted her to have the sunlight. He came back with her lunch and could not find her. The screams of the people below woke the fool up. He looked down and saw a woman dead from a twenty-two-story fall.

Keys of Life

Everything was swept under the rug, and her fortune was his. Shortly after, her attendant suffered a terrible death in a car accident. The one thing Joseph regretted was losing their child. He later found out that he was sterile. The nights troubled him because he would never know if the child was his or another man's. He picked up her picture. "No one escapes me, not even in death!"

CHAPTER 24

Chief Saunhac of the Mi'kmaq

He was in his nineties, and his old bones felt the years. The old man sat on the ground in his teepee, wrapped in a blanket, in Nova Scotia. Chief Saunhac was one of the greatest chiefs of the Mi'kmaq tribe. He was one of the best medicine men and shamans in history. The tribe had great respect and admiration for him. He was a great warrior and fought for the rights of Native Americans.

The Children of the Nephilim had a history of being very cruel to his people. The tribe fought against them and protected him. He was the leader of the Pure of Heart and protector of all the sacred objects. It was time for the Pure of Heart to rise up. In his dreams, the spirit guides came to him and told him that his great-granddaughter, Star Child, must take her place beside him. Star Child was her Mi'kmaq name. Sister Agnes had hidden and protected her long enough. She advised Bill and the chief that they should leave the girl in her care. It was hard to leave Star Child for so many years, but it was time for the family to unite.

Keys of Life

The chief lifted his smoking pipe and inhaled the special blend of herbs. He closed his eyes, and through his gift of remote viewing, he was able to see Star Child grow up. His father had trained him how to walk through walls with the spirits and see far away, even into the future. Cordy held great promise, and he called out to her in his mind. He could see her in his dream.

Cordy sat at a stop sign in her car and picked up the stone box, reading the numbers engraved on it.

"I think that is an international telephone. What the heck, let's dial it and see." Cordy dialed the number. The phone rang in a small white house in Nova Scotia, and the housekeeper answered.

"Hello, Chief Saunhac's residence. Can I help you? The chief is conducting a ceremony right now."

Cordy felt tingles up her arms. "It's Cordelia, his great-granddaughter. Can I talk to him?"

The woman got excited. "Oh yes, hold on!" The woman started to yell for the chief but he was already at the door when she called, as if he knew who was on the line.

Cordy had found the box. He grabbed the phone.

"Star Child, it's about time you called me. Are you coming to visit me?"

Cordy's eyes filled with tears, and her voice shook with emotion, "I love you great-grandpa, and yes, I am coming to see you."

Chief Saunhac laughed, "Do you remember, Star Child, when I sang twinkle twinkle little star to you when you were young?"

Cordy felt the memories of a gentle, loving man singing her a lullaby rush into her mind. "I remember, Chief, I remember."

"I am very glad you're coming to see me, Cordelia, because I have much to tell you about the Saunhac family. They were French knights who fought in the Crusades with Saint Louis. Our families were protectors and guardians of special sacred objects like the one you have just found."

Cordy couldn't believe what she heard. How did he know she found the quartz disk, and then it came to her with his telephone number? "I found it."

Chief Saunhac of the Mi'kmaq

"Good. Bring it with you when you come to see me. It is very important. One of our ancestors, the Templar Grandmaster Saunhac, protected it. It is very old. Eleanor of Aquitaine received it from her son Richard the Lionheart. It ended up with Saint Louis and his mother. It's a family heirloom so don't forget it. I have so much to tell you, Star Child. I will love to see you. I must go now."

"I'll bring it with me, and I can't wait to see you, too," Cordy answered cheerfully. "I love you! Bye."

The chief was thrilled he was going to see his great-granddaughter. He would tell her the story of Eleanor of Aquitaine, Richard the Lionheart, Templar Grandmaster Saunhac, Saint Louis, and Queen Blanche of Castile.

CHAPTER 25

Ash the Tomb Robber

Just before Ash arrived at the temples, he pulled over.

"What am I doing? If I get caught, I could get life in prison for removing artifacts out of a temple. I must be crazy. It must be a full moon. What I need is some clouds."

Just as he said the word "clouds," a large group of clouds passed over the moon, blocking the light. Ash scratched his head. "OK, just call me lucky."

Ash pulled his bag of tools from the backseat. He remembered the dream. *"You will need something special to retrieve the objects."* Ash remembered he kept a telescoping magnet that he used on his truck. In the sand of the desert, dropping a nut or washer would mean it could be lost forever, but the magnet easily found it. Ash reached over to the glove box and started pulling everything out. He called the tool special because it had saved his life many times out in the desert. Ash threw it in his tool bag and off he went.

He was so nervous that when he pulled into a service area used by archeologists for Nefertari's temple, he forgot to put the

Ash the Tomb Robber

truck in park. He got out of the vehicle, and it started to move. Ash let out a series of curse words and jumped back in the truck to put on the brake.

Ash jumped out and ran to the temple. The grad student watching the monitors was studying his book and dosing off and on. Nobody robbed a temple made of stone. One watched so no one destroyed or vandalized the Egyptian artworks. Ash was able to get to the side passage of the temple and enter quietly. He crept in the dark to the burial chamber where his camera picked up the shiny object.

The temple was moved because of Aswan High Dam construction in 1960. The project was a huge undertaking. Every stone was removed as the temple was reconstructed to save it from being flooded. It was surprising that no one noticed the broken slab of granite was cracked and something was in its center. Ash could see from the photo that this block had crumbled in the corner where the shiny object resided. He suddenly remembered that they had installed security cameras in the main rooms two years ago, and now he was on a computer disk somewhere.

Ash crawled under a tilted clay wine jar that had a broken bottom and a solid outer shell. "Perfect." He shuffled and then squatted down, letting the jar sit on the tiled floor. The jar covered his face and helped him blend into the black and white monitors. It was the perfect camouflage, he thought.

He inched his way closer and closer to the wall. Ash had second thoughts. Maybe it was just a bottle cap or something else foolish. He knew one thing: the voice was never wrong. In all his years, the voice in his dream had helped him.

He pulled the wine jar off of himself. He went to the wall where the camera had picked up the shiny object and tried to reach into the open crack. The crack was bigger than he thought, and the hole was wide enough that a man could put his fist through it. Ash was too short, though. The hole was just about a foot higher than he could reach.

Part of the wall hung over the area where the flash of light

Keys of Life

had come from. Ash took off his shirt, but it wasn't long enough to swing over the top ledge of rock and still hold on. Meanwhile, in the monitor room, the grad student started snoring. His head rested on the pages of his book. Ash looked around and saw nothing to help him. "Oh, shit!"

The only thing that might work would be to take off his pants and use the two together. He squatted behind the jar and dropped his pants. It was going to be cold because he didn't wear underwear today. Just his luck, Ash thought. He rolled his eyes. "This is going to be a great video. I can see the headlines now: *Naked Temple Thief Flashes The Mummies.*"

Ash was never big on wearing underwear, and there he stood, in all of his birthday glory. His body was chiseled like the statue of a Greek god, not an ounce of fat on him anywhere. His tan line stopped abruptly at his hips, and his white bottom contrasted with the golden tan found on the rest of his skin.

Ash tied his shirt and pants together and threw the fabric over the stone ledge. He pulled his telescoping magnet out of his tool bag and pulled himself up without any hesitation. He rested one of his feet on the clay wine pot, and his other foot found a small foothold in the stone wall. Ash looked down a crack in the wall toward the back where he could see some stone had crumbled away.

The crumbled stone explained why the light hadn't shown up before. It had blocked the light, but he could see it had fallen away. Ash took his special tool from his mouth and scraped about eight more inches from the seam. He could see the object and started to move it forward with the magnetic tip. It was surprisingly easy to get the object loose.

Ash wanted to grab it, but his strength in the one arm was starting to go. He was going to have to change arms. Ash thought to himself, "OK, on three. One, two, and three!"

With that, he put the tool in his mouth and with all his strength, switched hands. During this maneuver he turned and rotated with his back to the wall and his front to the camera. Now everyone would see Ash in all his glory.

Ash the Tomb Robber

He had both feet on the edges of the clay wine pot. Ash swung back around and reached to grab the end of the object. He let go and fell to his feet. He couldn't believe what he was holding in his hand. It was the Key of Life, a gold ankh of Osiris. It was in all of the carvings of the tomb. Pharaohs used to carry the ankh like a key in their hands, and there was a picture of it near the altar. It dawned on him to look at the altar. The Key of Life was the key. He knew exactly where it was on the altar. Egyptians used the altar to present the goddess Isis with gifts.

He was looking for the symbol of wheat. Ash put his pants and T-shirt on. He ran to the next room, using the shadows of the statues to hide and keeping his back to the cameras. He couldn't believe that he had gotten this far without the guard turning on the alarm. He didn't know that the grad student was soundly snoring in the monitor room.

Ash draped his other plaid shirt over the security camera. He had studied this altar when he was a child and knew exactly where the Key of Life would fit. It had been a mystery for years as to why the altar had a small indentation. Some thought it was simply a wear on the stone over time. Ash never believed that theory. He inserted the Key of Life into the indention. It fit in the center stone perfectly, as if it was made for it. The key went in about three inches, and then Ash turned it to the right.

A small panel moved at the bottom of the altar. Ash looked in the hole with his flashlight. He had learned to never put his hand in a hole without looking. He had seen many workers bit by cobras lurking in the dark. He pushed inside a long metal rod with a small flashlight.

Inside, he saw there was a stone box. Ash emptied his tool bag on the floor and grabbed the stone box, shoving it in his bag. It was the size of a shoebox. He was just about to remove the Key of Life when he remembered that sometimes, one lock could open many doors. Ash turned the key back to center and pushed it in again. He turned it to the left.

A second panel opened at the top, and there was another

stone box inside. Ash picked it up and put it in his bag, which was almost too heavy to carry now. He grabbed his shirt. Ash ran back to the side entrance and peeked his head around the corner. He could hear the guards chuckling in a room. One guard got on the phone and rang the monitor center. "Let's see if Rashid wants to come down and play cards." The grad student's phone rang and woke him up.

"No, Sahni, I'm studying." Rashid rubbed his sleepy eyes and looked at the cameras. There was no reception on camera 10. The screen was black.

"Sahni, check inside the temple and look at camera 10. It's not working." Sahni, a big, heavy guard, got up and told the others not to look at his cards. He took his flashlight as he walked out the door.

Ash hid behind one of the statues of Thoth, a bird. After the guard walked past him, Ash ran toward the truck. He gently laid the bag and key on the front floorboard.

Ash started the truck, leaving the lights off as it was just about dawn, and the first light was starting to peak through the clouds. The guard walked into the altar room and looked at video camera No. 10. A shirt was hanging over its lens.

The guard told Al Shid to pull the alarm, there was an intruder. One of the guards ran outside and spotted Ash's truck heading for him. He fired his revolver twice, and a third time. The front window was hit on the passenger side.

Ash crouched low in his seat and stepped on the gas. Ash flew by the guard. Shots rung out and the side window shattered. The guard kept shooting and finally, one shot blew out the back window.

All the guard could hear as he watched the dust from the truck driving off in the distance was a screaming and swearing Ash. As the sun rose in the east, Ash got to the top of the hill where the road had a fork in it. He knew he couldn't go back to his old life anymore. He knew it wouldn't take long for them to figure out something had been stolen.

Ash the Tomb Robber

One road went back to his house and the other, to the lake. He would have to find a boat so that he could get out of Egypt for a while. He knew the lake was his best and only option. The truck flew down the road heading to the lake. Ash knew his life would never be the same again.

Chapter 26

Life and Death

As Cordy sat at the red light, she could hear sirens behind her. She pulled off to the side of the road onto a gravel shoulder as the ambulance, police cars, and fire truck whizzed by her to an accident up ahead. Looks like a bad one, she thought.

She got back on the road and dialed numbers on her cell phone. Mrs. Johnson answered, "Hello, Cordy."

Cordy apologized, "Mrs. Johnson, it looks like I'm going to be late. I'm in a traffic jam due to an accident ahead of me, and it looks pretty bad."

"You be careful, Cordy. The pups are doing wonderful, so just take your time," Mrs. Johnson said, concerned.

"OK, see you soon."

Cars were lined bumper-to-bumper on the road, and Cordy started thinking about work. She was a veterinarian trained in emergency trauma and critical care. She would get called out on some of the most horrific cases, and in the end had consistent

Life and Death

great outcomes. Her department made more money than any other department in the practice. A lot of money came from customers who donated sometimes three times the amount of their bill because of the great care. They loved Cordy because she realized how important their pets were to them.

"I don't need Grandpa's money. My vet practice is doing well. What I do want is to see Grandpa and especially Chief Saunhac," she muttered under her breath. Cordy was getting hot and pulled off her sweatshirt. She was wearing her college T-shirt underneath, and she felt cooler. It was time to check out what was going on ahead of her.

Cordy waved to the highway patrolman directing traffic.

"Hey officer," she said as she stuck her head out the window. "What happened?"

The patrolman walked up to her. "A truck pulling a horse trailer with a pregnant mare had an accident. They were moving her to a different barn when a tractor-trailer crossed over the line. The driver fell asleep at the wheel. It struck the back corner of the trailer with such force that it swung the pickup truck to the other side of the road. It ended up in a tangled mess going the opposite direction on its side in the ditch. The twisted metal is trapping the mare inside and they don't expect her to last. They were talking about shooting her and putting her out of her misery."

Cordy pulled out her veterinary license. "Officer, I'm a vet. Can you get me up there to assess the situation?"

The officer looked at her credentials and nodded, "Doc, follow me."

In seconds, Cordy was pulling her hair in a ponytail while the officer started his car, waving her to follow. He was driving on the side of the road with his sirens on when they got to the accident site. He pointed for her to walk up to where the emergency crew was standing. He turned around and headed back to direct traffic.

During the day, a man had been following Cordy, but he was stopped from moving any farther by the roadblock. He saw Cordy's car following the police car up to the accident site. The man in the dark jacket was hired by his boss to eliminate the one witness who could identify him in Minah's abduction. He had worked for Bossa for years and had become a member of the Children of the Nephilim. He was a high-priced assassin and expert marksman. The rules for respecting sanctuary and holy ground had been followed, but now she was in the open, among chaos. The police were busy directing traffic, and so he would wait. Bossa had promised him a bonus if he killed her quickly, and time was running out.

The highway patrol officer was directing the cars to a detour road so they could go around the accident. The officer told the man to move but he explained in his Bosnian accent that he would wait. The policeman shrugged. "Suit yourself, but stay clear of the area. I'm warning you the situation is dangerous."

All the cars behind him had turned around and left the scene. The assassin sat on the road alone, watching Cordy. He pulled out his gun to check his scope when no one was looking. He could see her within his crosshairs. Everyone was preoccupied with the accident, and no one noticed him.

She grabbed her bag and ran to the scene of the accident. When Cordy came to the accident, she couldn't believe what the horse trailer looked like. The firemen were trying to cut and pull an opening big enough to see if there was any hope for the animal. Gas was leaking everywhere, and the smell of the fumes filled the air. The fire department applied foam to protect the trailer. Cordy was next to the fireman in seconds.

"You the vet?" one of the highway patrol officers asked. He had his hands on his hip and looked her over. "You don't look like a vet."

Cordy realized that she hadn't put on a bra, and Officer Jim Bob was looking down her low-cut T-shirt. Cordy just shook her head. "In vet school, we called them tits. I can tell what brain you're thinking with, and it's not the one upstairs."

Life and Death

Cordy got to business. "If you don't mind, I've got a lot of work to do here and no time to fart around. So, if you could get my other bag and some rope off my back seat and bring it back to me really quick, you'll be able to get a second look, asshole."

Officer Jim Bob saluted. "Yes, ma'am." He scurried along to her car. Feisty little thing, thought Officer Jim Bob, admitting to himself that he wanted another look.

The head fireman came up to Cordy, shaking his head. "We can only get it open so far, doc, and we'll have to wait for a tow truck to get it upright before you will be able to get inside. We have foam surrounding the trailer to avert any fire, and we are working on the other truck."

Cordy voice was filled with urgency, "It will all be over by then."

The trailer was on its side, and the mare was shrieking with pain and terror. Cordy got up to the trailer and whispered softly, "Whoa, girl, whoa." The mare heard her soft voice and settled down, breathing heavy. Cordy stuck her head and shoulder through the small opening and saw that she could fit, but she knew she couldn't do much good alone.

The mare was still alive but barely. The horse was in labor and in tremendous pain. She stroked the horse, and the men stood amazed as Cordy felt over the horse. If she worked quickly, she could get the foal out before the mare died.

Cordy looked around and saw a tearful young girl who looked about 12 years old. She was small and could get through the opening to assist with the possible delivery. Cordy ran over to the softly crying girl who was being hugged by an elderly man with a logo on his jacket that matched the one on the truck.

"What is your name?" Cordy asked gently.

The tearful girl answered, "Nancy. Is Thunder going to be OK?"

"Is Thunder your horse's name?"

The little girl nodded. "Yes, my daddy gave her to me for a birthday present."

"Is this your father?" Cordy pointed to the older man.

Keys of Life

Nancy shook her head. "No, this is Jimmy, our trainer."

The trainer sadly whispered into Cordy's ear, "We were just getting ready to put her down when we saw your car coming. I told them to wait. You see, that foal was sired by Free Wind, a great racehorse, and is worth over a million dollars. You think we have a chance at getting the foal out?"

Cordy looked alarmed. Talk about raising the stress level, she thought. She bravely looked at him. "We can try."

The little girl pulled on Cordy. "Is Thunder going to be OK?" Cordy grabbed Nancy by the shoulders and dabbed her face with a Kleenex from her pocket.

"My name is Doc Cordy, and Thunder's foal is in trouble. You and I are going to try to help her. You are going to have to be brave and in your heart, know I will not let anything bad happen to you. You need to trust me, Nancy. Can you do that?"

Instantly, as Cordy tenderly held the little girl, a quiet peace fell over Nancy's face. Cordy gently wiped the little girl's tears as she said, "I can help the foal."

"Hold on, what are you talking about?" asked Jimmy, the trainer. Cordy looked at him with great determination.

"Nancy and I are the only two people that can fit in that hole in the trailer, and we are going in to save that baby."

Overhearing Cordy, the highway patrolman shook his head. "It will be your ass, doc." Cordy turned and gave him her black belt battle face, making the patrolman step back. He waved his hands in front of him for protection.

"Do you know who that little girl's daddy is?"

"Life doesn't ask who your daddy is," Cordy fearlessly answered. "It just moves forward. If you look one more time at my tits or ass, you will wish you were somewhere else when I come out of that trailer."

The patrolman stepped out of the Cordy's way. "I warned you. We haven't got the truck safely secure on the side of the road surrounded with foam yet. It could start a fire with the gas leaking everywhere."

Life and Death

Cordy waved the fire chief over. "Is the trailer protected by the foam from fire?"

"Yes, the trailer is secure but the other truck is in danger," the fire chief answered. "It is safe to go in the trailer." He rushed away while yelling orders to his crew.

Jimmy asked, "What can I do? I probably don't have a job anymore anyway."

Cordy looked at Nancy and said, "Are you ready?" She nodded her head yes.

Cordy and Nancy ran down to the trailer. The tow truck pulled the destroyed truck away. They pulled it over to the other side of the road and far away from the trailer. The man in the black jacket watched the destroyed truck rest a few yards away from his car. It would be the perfect cover for him to try to get a shot at her. There was mass confusion. Time was running out for him and Cordy. The driver left the truck by itself. Everyone's attention was focused on the trailer.

Cordy threw the black backpack that held her vet supplies into the trailer. She slipped through the crack but not without difficulty. Once she was in, she reached to help Nancy. Jimmy lifted her up and in she went with no trouble. Nancy looked at Thunder; she could see and smell death hanging in the air.

Somehow Thunder was able to lift her head, as if to say, Nancy please save my baby. Nancy turned to Cordy with composure and bravery and asked, "What do you need me to do?" Cordy pointed, "Come back here." As Nancy crawled to the back, she could see the foal's feet had started to come out.

"Thunder doesn't have enough strength to push her baby out into the world, so we are going to pull and push for her," Cordy said gently.

Cordy yelled out, "Jimmy, we need a rope."

"I already have one," Jimmy said as he threw it into the trailer. Nancy reached over and grabbed it. As Nancy knelt by Thunder's

Keys of Life

head, she gently brushed the side of her horse's face and whispered, "Don't worry, Thunder, we will save your baby."

Cordy whispered to Nancy, "You stay there and keep Thunder calm. We don't have much time."

Nancy handed Cordy the rope and in a second, Cordy had a knot tied around the foal's legs. She passed the end of the rope to Jimmy and told him to go to the back of the trailer.

"Have you ever played tug-of-war before, Nancy?"

She nodded. "Yes."

Cordy prepared her. "This will be ten times harder. On three, Jimmy and I will need to pull with our heart and soul. Jimmy, you got it?"

Jimmy answered, "I'm right behind you, doc." Nancy nodded calmly. "Yes, Thunder's ready."

Cordy counted it down, "1, 2, 3, pull." The foal only moved about an inch. Cordy yelled, "Again, 1, 2, 3, pull!" Three more inches.

This went on for several minutes and then finally, the shoulders and head came out. Nancy got a look at a healthy boy. She yelled out to Thunder, "It's a boy, Thunder!" Thunder was breathing heavy and could only blink her eyes to say thank you. In the trailer, for the first time, Nancy's reserve broke, and a tear ran down her cheek. Cordy wiped off the foal, and the baby squirmed in Cordy's arms. Nancy's chin began to quiver but she pushed it back. She didn't want Thunder to see her cry.

Jimmy was smiling from ear to ear. "Doc, I'll be damned. You did it."

Cordy placed the foal on some straw she laid out. The baby was trying to stand already. Cordy could see Thunder was hemorrhaging, and there was only one thing to do. Cordy calmly looked at Nancy, who was stroking Thunder's head.

"I am going to give Thunder something to take away the pain and let her sleep. Do you understand what I am saying, Nancy?"

Life and Death

Nancy cried softly, "Yes, I understand. It's OK, Thunder had a great life. I enjoyed loving her every day."

"If you want say good bye, it will take a few seconds for it to start working," Cordy said quietly.

Nancy rested her head on Thunder's and whispered, "I promise to take care of your baby, your little man, and spoil him every day."

Cordy injected the horse with a syringe she had in her bag. Thunder took her last breath. She was gone, and so was her pain. Nancy stroked the horse's neck. She tried to brush the tears off her cheeks as she slowly moved down by Cordy, who put her arm around the girl. Cordy looked at the tears running down Nancy's face. "I couldn't have done it without you."

Nancy looked over at Thunder's baby boy. "What do we need to do for Highway Man?" Cordy smiled, "Let's take a good look at him."

They climbed out of the trailer to a clapping audience. The firefighters and highway patrolmen were surprised that the baby survived. After another five minutes, the firemen had the back of the trailer opened and another fire department truck showed up with the Jaws of Life to pull the metal open with ease. Jimmy moved the foal to safety.

Cordy grinned as she looked at Nancy. "So, he already has a name?"

Nancy ran toward the little foal standing unsteadily by Jimmy. Nancy petted him. "Yes, he was born on the highway, and so that's it."

Jimmy smiled and shook Cordy's hand. "It's a damn miracle, that is what it is. Thanks, doc, glad you were around."

Cordy laughed. "Just life and all its surprises." Cordy patted Nancy on the back. "Anything is possible with a brave heart, isn't it, Nancy?"

Nancy nodded, "Yes ma'am, Doctor Cordy."

Keys of Life

The scope moved in on Cordy's head as his finger rested on the trigger. He had moved farther down the road. The assassin was focused on his target. Gas had been dripping from the wrecked truck, forming a small trickle running down the road. A highway patrol car with flashing lights could be seen driving up slowly in the distance from the outside mirror of his car. He swore under his breath. Bossa's man placed the sniper gun down on the floor of his car and pulled out a cigarette, so he would not look conspicuous.

His car was the only one on the road. Perhaps this wasn't the best time to kill her. His lighter came out of his pocket, and he flicked the spark. It took a second before he recognized the smell of gas fumes under his car. He saw the spark light the gas. Out of the corner of his eye, a fireman waved his arms and screamed, "No! Gas!"

Everything was in slow motion, and he saw a man on the hill carrying a flaming sword in his hand. The words whispered in his ear, "Justice comes!"

His car blew up from the leaky gas under the car. The gas trail went the other way and another large explosion came from what used to be a truck. The highway patrolmen looked with shock at the destruction, stopped in time. The fireman grabbed his hat and ran to the fire truck shaking his head. "Who would be so stupid to light a cigarette with gas all around him?"

Everyone was stunned by the fire and explosion. Cordy realized how dangerous it was, and she felt guilty having let Nancy take such a risk. What was she thinking? She owed the little girl big time. Cordy smiled. "Jimmy, if it's all right, I have a courtesy call on the Johnson's farm just two miles down the road. Can I take Nancy with me and then bring her home?"

Jimmy nodded. "Yes ma'am, with what I have seen today I would trust you with my life. Nancy's dad will want her home as soon as possible. I know where Mrs. Johnson's farm is but could you drop Nancy off at her house afterward? It's only five miles farther down. Her father is stuck down the road in traffic. I'll tell

Life and Death

him to meet you at the house. She needs to get out of here. It's too dangerous. I'll take care of Highway Man."

The trailer was off the road and traffic remained chaotic behind them. Jimmy called for another horse trailer for the foal. The firemen were getting the fires under control.

Nancy got in Cordy's truck and off they went. Nancy looked over at Cordy. "You know, I didn't look back at Thunder for a reason, Doctor Cordy."

"It is a normal reaction, Nancy, but why do you think that was?" Cordy knew the importance of talking about what happened to get over trauma.

"When I had my head on Thunder's head, I could feel her heart stop, but then I could feel mine get stronger. You see, Thunder made my heart beat stronger, and it gave me courage. Does that make sense?"

Cordy nodded. "Yes, it makes perfect sense in every way. You both shared a special moment."

"Why are we going to the Johnson's farm?" Nancy asked.

Cordy smiled. "You'll see. I'm making a house call."

Nancy reached in her pocket for her phone and asked Cordy for her cell phone number. Cordy repeated it slowly. Nancy put it in her phone and immediately afterward, Cordy's phone was ringing. Nancy held out her hand, "Give me your phone, doc."

She plugged in the numbers under Highwayman and Brave at Heart. Nancy handed her phone back. "Doctor Cordy, anytime you need someone to help, all you have to do is call me. I will be your helper. I think someday I'll be a vet just like you."

Soon they were pulling in the driveway of the Johnson's farm, which housed a dog kennel specializing in Labrador retrievers. Nancy could see all the dogs running up to the truck. A smiling grey-haired lady came out of the farmhouse and walked up to the door of the truck. She asked, "Cordy, where have you been? The traffic must've been terrible. Oh, and what a surprise, Nancy is with you."

Cordy gave her a wink, "We had a tough morning, Mrs. Johnson. Nancy here is my assistant."

"I helped deliver a foal but lost my mare," Nancy said sadly from the passenger window. Mrs. Johnson walked up to the window and patted her on the arm.

"Yes, child, it is one of the big lessons you learn on a farm. The Lord giveth and the Lord taketh."

Cordy wearily said, "It's a long story. Do you still have that 10-week-old puppy that lost his mother?" Mrs. Johnson smiled. "Yes, I do, and he's eating me out of house and home."

Cordy smiled. "I'm thinking that I'll put that puppy with the foal and see if they'll bond. I heard it works, and I don't have any other options." Cordy pointed to the bouncy lab puppy under the tree. "Nancy, will you go see if that puppy will meet your approval?"

Nancy looked a bit unsure. "Really, my dad is going to kill you. He says that dogs are a distraction to the horses and dangerous. I've been wanting a dog my whole life."

"It's important for the foal. I'll cover for you," Cordy said.

In less than five minutes, Nancy was in the truck with the puppy. Mrs. Johnson brought over a little puppy transport cage.

"He's the best of my litter, just the one you called about. He has papers in the pocket."

"What do I owe you?" Cordy asked.

"Cordy, of all the things you have done for me. Get out of here," Mrs. Johnson said as she walked away and waved.

"You call me when the next litter comes. I have some possible buyers."

Mrs. Johnson answered, "You betchya."

Turning toward Nancy, Cordy asked, "You got a name?"

Nancy smiled. "How about Sunny, because he's already brightened my day."

Cordy smiled and winked, "Gotta go see a baby horse."

They pulled out of the drive, and Mrs. Johnson waved, "Take care, you two."

Life and Death

Nancy's family farm had a large white two-story house surrounded by a white picket fence. Horses were grazing in the field. They pulled into Nancy's driveway, and Cordy let out, "Oh, shit." There were three highway patrol cars in front, one with its light still on.

Cordy smiled sheepishly, "I guess I'm in trouble."

Nancy grinned. "I say more like dead. My dad is the chief of the Missouri Highway Patrol. Sorry, I forgot to tell you."

"Oh, shit," Cordy gasped. Nancy patted Cordy's shoulder.

"It's OK, Doctor Cordy. My dad speaks the same language. He says he's bilingual."

"I'm sorry, Nancy. It just comes out sometimes when I'm stressed."

A tall man wearing a short-sleeved white shirt stormed out of the screen door and flew off the porch in two steps. He ran to the passenger side of Cordy's car and flung open the door. He hugged Nancy and broke down in tears. Cordy had never seen a big man like that cry so uncontrollably.

Nancy hugged her dad. "Dad, it's OK, it's OK, and I'm OK!" she said.

"Nancy," he said as he wiped his tears with a handkerchief. "Baby, I am so sorry to hear about Thunder. I'm so glad you're OK, honey."

Nancy started to explain, "I know, Dad, but we saved Highway Man and when Thunder died, I could feel her heart stir in mine. I could feel her love in my heart, and it beat even stronger. Thunder will always be with me, Dad. I am grateful that with the help of Doc Cordy, I got to say goodbye to her."

Cordy held Sunny on her lap as the puppy tried to wiggle free. Tim Huff had already heard about the wonderful Doctor McDermott from Jimmy. Tim, Nancy's father, looked for the first time at Cordy sitting in the truck. His emotions were conflicted between a sense of thanks and anger. How could she just run off with his daughter like that without telling him? The puppy suddenly wiggled loose and ran over to Nancy's dad, who swooped

Keys of Life

down to get him. He licked Tim on the face. Tim laughed, "Doc, can't you control your dog?"

"He is not Doctor Cordy's dog," Nancy yelled out. "Dad, he is Sunny, my dog."

Nancy's dad took two steps back and looked at the grinning pup. Tim hesitated.

"Now just a minute, young lady, you know our rules about dogs."

Cordy got out of the truck and walked around to introduce herself.

"Dad, he's not for me. He's for Highway Man. You see, Sunny lost his mom and Thunder lost his mom just like I lost my mom when I was little. They need each other."

Cordy was taken back a bit and apologized. "I'm sorry, I didn't know."

Nancy looked at her father. "She died of cancer when I was three."

Nancy's dad held the pup, unconsciously petting him. "It hasn't been easy being a single dad with a young girl. She's like a tomboy, mostly my fault."

Cordy smiled. "You would have been very proud of her, Mr. Huff. She is a pretty brave little girl."

"Oh, you can call me Chief for right now, young lady. You aren't out of the woods yet. I should have you arrested for endangerment of a child, but from what I've heard, it was a miracle the foal lived. That foal is worth a lot of money, but my daughter's safety is the most important thing to me. I knew your father Sheriff McDermott. He was a wonderful man. I was sorry to hear about the accident. Jimmy said you have an unbelievable gift the way you saved that foal. I figure you're level-headed and safe to be around Nancy."

Nancy grabbed her dad's arm with excitement. "Did you see him, Dad? Isn't he something else?"

Cordy grabbed her bag off the seat. "I would like to check him again, if it's OK. You're not going to arrest me then, Chief?"

Life and Death

Tim shook his head. "You come on down to the barn. Jimmy's trying to get him to drink some formula." He set the dog on the ground, and it promptly began to pee. Tim resigned. "I guess you can bring that damn dog with you, too."

Nancy grinned. "Dad, did you know Doc Cordy and you have something in common?"

"Really? I have to hear this one."

"She is bilingual just like you," Nancy said, smiling wickedly. Cordy chuckled, "You didn't have to tell him that, Nancy."

"See, Dad, I told you so," Nancy said as they all started to laugh.

Tim pulled Cordy aside for a second while Nancy watched the puppy. "Doc, I want you to see something that came through from the Feds. The license of the driver whose car blew up at the crash site matched this 'most wanted' picture."

He pulled out his cell phone to show her a mug shot of the dead man, identified as an international criminal from Bosnia. "The FBI said he's connected to another Bosnian who kidnapped an Egyptian ambassador's daughter. Your name came up as having saved the woman's life. I want you to know, Cordy, to be careful and if I can help, you can call on me." Cordy looked surprised as she put two and two together. She realized the man must've been following her. Tim patted her on the back in comfort. "I thought you should know." Cordy nodded. "Thanks." They both walked to the barn to see the foal.

The red barn was in pristine condition and held about seven horse stalls. From the first stall, a little whine could be heard. Jimmy jumped up from cleaning the baby foal. He grinned at Nancy.

"He's beautiful, Nancy, and he's eating like there's no tomorrow." Jimmy held up an empty bottle with a nipple on it. Sunny ran up to Highway Man, who was lying on the ground, and curled up between his legs and started to lick him. Highway Man licked Sunny back. It was a perfect match.

Nancy lay down on the straw and petted them. Cordy could see that they were going to grow up together. Cordy patted Tim on the back. "Well, chief, it looks like everything is going to be OK."

Keys of Life

Nancy's father nodded. "You can call me Tim. I can't thank you for all you've done." Cordy just tipped her ball cap and smiled. "Just doing my job. You'll get the bill." They laughed and Cordy waved as she pulled down the drive.

Cordy got to the end of the drive and stopped her truck. She was going to be late for her dojo's annual awards and demonstration ceremony. Cordy had no time to lose so she pulled out her backpack and started to change. Nancy and her dad could see the silhouette of her body as she frantically put on her uniform and black belt.

Nancy's dad scratched his head. "What a strange woman. I can't wait to pull her over," he said, winking at Nancy.

Nancy laughed. "You don't pull people over any more, Dad."

"Nancy, you are right," he said, grinning. "But I would make an exception in her case." They laughed again. Tim looked down at his daughter and thought this was one of the most traumatic days of his little girl's life. Yet Doctor Cordy had left her laughing and smiling at the end of the day. It was exceptional. He reached down and pulled Nancy close to him.

"I love you, honey."

Nancy pulled him even closer and smiled up at him. "I will teach you to love Sunny." She looked into her father's eyes. "I know you already love Highway Man because he is worth a lot of money, but money isn't everything, Dad."

He squeezed her again but even harder. "You're right, and I learned a big lesson today." Cordy was done changing and put on her turn signal and pulled onto the highway. Nancy and her dad waved one last time. As the pair walked down to the barn to check on Highway Man and Sunny, Nancy said, "Oh, Dad, Doctor Cordy gave me a small sample bag of dog food so we'll need to go to the pet store."

Nancy's dad rolled his eyes. "I guess I have another mouth to feed, that damn dog!"

CHAPTER 27

Chief Saunhac and the Wishing Cup

Chief Saunhac had been the medicine man for the Mi'kmaq tribe for many years. It was said he was a spirit walker, and he was also respected as an elder of the tribe. He had begun to write a book chronicling Saunhac family stories, which he intended to give as a present to his great-granddaughter Cordy.

The Mi'kmaqs had married the French settlers who came to Nova Scotia. The Mi'kmaq tribe had a great oral history and their written words looked very much like Egyptian hieroglyphics. They passed their legends down with each generation through time. It was time to tell the tale of a great warrior Brother Guillaume de Saunhac. He was one of the bravest men who had ever fought in the Crusades.

In 1244 AD, Belcastel, France was home to the Saunhac family. Guillaume joined the Templars and rose to the prestigious position of Preceptor to Aquitaine. He knew of the sacred knowledge brought back from the Holy Land and was keeper of the secrets. Guillaume de Saunhac had proven himself a great asset to the

Templar Order. He was an experienced warrior and excellent swordsman. He was also a highly educated man and helped organize the Templar hierarchy. The Templars were the bankers of Europe and dealt with great sums of money. The Holy Lands were in chaos and constant war, but the Templars had acquired great power and wealth over the years.

Secrets were essential when dealing with different monarchies and with different religious orders. The need for another Crusade was being discussed. Guillaume, as Grandmaster, served as an ambassador, protector of relics and treasures, and military general.

The Templars were given guardianship of many of the relics found in the Holy Land, Constantinople, and Egypt. King Louis IX had used his fortune to procure many of these treasures. Guillaume sent a vial of Christ's holy blood by special courier to King Henry III of England. He thought this would encourage Henry to participate in a future Crusade with money and men. Unfortunately, King Louis IX was not happy that King Henry had obtained such a relic instead of him.

King Louis IX didn't trust the Templars and yet, the King of France had no trouble asking for money from their treasury.

Guillaume had spent some years in Egypt as an emissary to help negotiate trade and peace. He had to partake in some of the mystic Islamic rituals so that he could be trusted. One ritual involved cutting his hand and clasping the hand of one of the leaders of the sultan's army. He was rewarded for his negotiations with a beautiful crystal-clear quartz disk with strange writing found in one of the Egyptian pyramids. A holy man from Alexandria told him that the disk contained great wisdom.

Guillaume de Saunhac was head of the Pure of Heart and his family vowed to protect it.

The sultan gave Saunhac a beautiful alabaster cup inscribed with Egyptian hieroglyphics, called the wishing cup. Guillaume gave the wishing cup to King Louis IX, who was very pleased but worried about the strange pagan pictures on the cup. The king was told the writing came from the same area as Moses and Joseph of Egypt. It

Chief Saunhac and the Wishing Cup

held no interest for King Louis IX, but his mother, Blanche of Castile, found it beautiful. She gave it to the Saunhac family for safekeeping. Guillaume had placed both precious items with his brother's family. Guillaume de Saunhac was elected to be the new Templar Grand Master in 1247.

As a young knight, Guillaume had visited the Holy Sepulcher and carved his cross upon the wall, as did the other Crusader Knights. The crosses on the wall made a mass of interconnected squares that resembled Bouillon's Kingdom of Jerusalem cross. The cross represented Christ's journey, as well as all men's, from birth to death.

He had found that Christianity and the religion of Mohammed, though different, had great similarities. It was announced that King Louis IX would lead a seventh Crusade. Guillaume was in Acre and had brokered a peace deal with the sultan for the strategically important Egyptian city of Damietta. King Louis IX ordered him to stop negotiations for Damietta. Louis IX planned to take the city by force.

Guillaume realized that King Louis IX lusted only for war and bloodshed. It was at that moment that he knew the Crusade under King Louis IX was going to be a dismal failure. Louis never listened to any advice from the experienced Templar Grandmaster. The arrogant Robert of Artois, Louis's brother, never listened to anybody. The Templar Grandmaster wanted to strike Alexandria, a port city of great importance, but it was Robert's advice to Louis that they should attack Cairo. The city Damietta was easily taken. King Louis IX saw it as a sign that God was with them. Guillaume knew they had won just a battle, not a war.

At the Battle of Mansurah, Robert of Artois refused to wait to attack until reinforcements came. He did not heed the Templar Grandmaster's advice or order to wait. The Grandmaster tried to stop the hot-tempered Count of Artois, but his wise words fell on deaf ears.

Robert plunged into attack and forced the Templar Grandmaster to follow. They were annihilated. Guillaume de Saunhac

Keys of Life

survived, as did two other Templars. His fabulous skill as a swordsman amazed everyone around him, even the enemy.

Guillaume had multiple wounds and lost one of his eyes from battle. He lost his brother Gautier Saunhac, who died on February 11 from his injuries. His heart was broken and sadness overwhelmed him, for his brother was very dear to him.

The Templar Grandmaster also had to give the news to King Louis IX that his brother, the Count of Artois, died trapped in a house in the town. The king wept alongside the Grandmaster at the loss of their beloved brothers.

Guillaume would not rest, even when injured. He had fought wounded with one eye and the other covered. He later died in the Battle of Fariskur after losing the other eye in battle. His bravery in battle was renown through history. The story of Guillaume de Saunhac would be remembered in St. Louis IX's biography, by his trusted seneschal Joinville. In Joinville's memoirs, he said arrows shot at the Grandmaster were so many that no ground could be seen.

The crescent moon had risen in the night sky, and the chief placed his pen down. He sighed and tears flowed from his eyes. The price was high, but what they brought back to France from the Holy Land for protection was priceless. The Pure of Heart survived and their prized possessions were safe. Brother Saunhac was brave and a true Pure of Heart.

Throughout history, the Saunhac family was one of great warriors and protectors of the Pure of Heart. The wishing cup had been lost through treachery but it would return to the Saunhacs again. The chief had seen its return in a dream.

CHAPTER 28

Chief Saunhac

The chief continued to fill Cordy's genealogy book with tales of the Saunhac family history. Saunhacs landed in Acadia in early 1603 with the explorer Champlain. Acadia had previously been called Arcadia by the early Portuguese explorer Verrazano. Later, it would be called Nova Scotia.

Saunhac came to this New France to make his fortune. The land was a beautiful, but hostile, environment. He met a beautiful Mi'kmaq woman whose father was chief. A home was made and children born and baptized at Cape Breton.

Saint Anne Mission was named after Jesus's grandmother because grandmothers were held in great respect among the Mi'kmaqs. His wife had been baptized and converted to Christianity. Saunhac later died from consumption, leaving his wife with three sons. Their mother raised them in the Mi'kmaq culture, and they were taught in the Catholic school on the island. Their grandfather taught the children Mi'kmaq writing and stories of the great flood and Glooscap the giant, hunting and fishing, and the magic spells of the great Mi'kmaq medicine.

A war came, and the Acadians had to leave their homes. Britain took their land and sent them away on boats. A few Saunhacs decided to remain with the Mi'kmaq tribe. Mi'kmaq meant family and no matter where they would live, they would always be remembered as family. The stars above would guide them and protect them.

The star symbol had great meaning for the Mi'kmaq, representing Wajok, the Great Father in Heaven. The eight-pointed star was another significant star to the tribe, representing the seven tribes of the Mi'kmaq and peace with Great Britain.

Mi'kmaq legend told of the four colored people who traveled in four different directions, later to return to the center and live in harmony. The Mi'kmaq had signed treaties over their land but the contract was not respected by European nations.

The Acadians set forth on a journey with great hardship and sorrow at leaving their land and family behind. One Acadian family carried a white flag with a red cross on it given to Saunhac by his grandmother. She told the story of great warriors from Europe who brought the flag and the story of Jesus with them.

Crusader knights were guided by the stars and wished to escape from death across the ocean. The Mi'kmaq were the guardians of the great knowledge they brought. It was fitting for them to fly the flag of the red cross on a white field like the Crusaders of old, but they also added their holy star and crescent moon to it. Many Acadians settled in towns along the Mississippi and Louisiana. They brought with them myths and legends from their homeland.

CHAPTER 29

Ash on the Run

Ash didn't have a clue what to do. For the first time in his life, he didn't seem to be in control anymore, and control was something that Ash always needed to feel. Ash needed to do some fast thinking.

He knew that there was no going back the way he came. The police would be stopping everyone at checkpoints along the road. He had experience with how the police caught tomb thieves in the past. Where could he hide? Everyone would have been alerted by now. He knew he was going to have to get rid of the 4Runner, and he couldn't go back home.

Ash had no idea what he had put in his bag. He decided to go back to Aswan, where he could hide out at his mother's place.

He pulled up at a small dock and got out of the 4Runner. The sun was coming up, and there were three small fishing boats tied up at the dock. Ash walked down to the dock and saw an old man with a young boy about the age of 14.

He asked the old man if he could take him to Aswan. The old

man said he promised the boy a day of fishing with his grandfather. The old man explained that he hadn't seen his grandson for about five years, and this was their special day together. He shook his finger at Ash. "No, not today mister."

Ash knew that he didn't have much time before the police alerts came out. He remembered the previous year, after a tomb robbery, it only took 40 minutes for the thieves to be put in hand cuffs.

The old man could tell Ash was very nervous.

"Are you running from the revolutionaries?" he asked.

"Yes," Ash answered the old man.

"Are they close?"

Ash looked at the road. "Very."

"I came here a long time ago to escape," the old man quietly said. "I fell in love and ended up staying in the middle of nowhere. If I were to take you, how would you pay me?"

The old man held his hand out, looking for money.

Ash shook his head. "I will have to pay you later when I get the money. I'm good for it. I promise I'll pay you back."

The old man observed. "I have taken many a dangerous cargo down the river but something tells me you could be the worst and most dangerous of all."

The young boy leaned over and whispered in the old man's ear, and the old man started to smile. He told the boy his father had taught him well.

"What did he say?" Ash asked. The old man pondered. "My grandson said his birthday is coming up and he would look good in that white truck you drive."

Ash knew he was out of time and nodded. "Yes sir, I think your grandson is right. He would look great in that truck. It would be best if he wouldn't drive it for a few years." Ash winked at the little boy.

The old man looked delighted. "Then it is a done deal, as they say in America."

Ash agreed. "Yes, it's a done deal. I'll get my things out, and you can have it."

Ash on the Run

Ash came back with his bag, and the old man pushed a switch on the side of the house. A garage door started to open. A speedboat and BMW sat inside the garage. The young man ran up and grabbed a small tractor that pulled the speedboat out. He took it to the boat launch.

Ash drove the 4Runner in, and the old man shut the door. Ash said to the old man, "It looks like you have taken things up and down the river for some time."

The old man started to laugh, as did Ash. "Things are not always what they seem."

The boy dragged dry branches behind him so that no one could see the tire tracks. Ash jumped in the speedboat. The old man and his grandson let go of the ropes, and they started to go down the river.

Ash thought to himself, now you are a thief, and there's no going back. If you go back you'll die.

Uriel's words came back to him, and he realized how true they were. They had only been going down the river for about 10 minutes when the old man started to drive directly into the wall along the shoreline.

"What are you doing?" Ash yelled.

"You will see," the old man said. At the last minute, he stopped the engine and coasted into a small narrow canyon that doglegged. It couldn't be seen from the water. An overhang kept it from being seen from the air, too. No sooner had they turned into the canyon than a helicopter flew over. They could hear the sirens of approaching speedboats on the lake.

Ash looked at the old man and said, "You are good. You are really good."

The old man pointed to the plane flying above. "You see, stranger, they will be looking for you the next day or two, and what we will do is wait until dark. We will blend in with the other boats in the search and by then, we will go farther and farther away."

Keys of Life

Ash was lucky he had found the old man that day or else he would have been on his way to a prison cell. Punishment for thieves was severe in Egypt. Some thieves didn't go to trial but were found in their cell hanging from the ceiling with a rope around their neck. The official word was that they committed suicide. As for the reason, it was said they were afraid of the punishment that prison guards would inflict. Others believed it was to save the government the time and trouble of a trial.

The young boy asked, "What did you do?"

The old man yelled at the boy, "The first rule is to never ask that question. The only thing we need to know is how much he will pay and where he wants to go. It is to protect him and us."

It felt like forever until the night's blanket of black fell over the river. The crocodiles could be heard splashing as they pursued their prey. The old man decided it was safe to start for Aswan.

A cloud of overwhelming remorse hung over Ash. It was ironic. He had spent his whole life trying to put artifact thieves in jail, and now he was one. He tried making up for his father's shady past, and here he was following in his father's footsteps.

Some rumors had floated around the archeological world that Ash's father raided a rich tomb and then he fled, leaving his wife and son. The university gave his wife a pension despite the rumor, and no evidence of theft was found. The Egyptian police placed the professor on the missing list and after 10 years, declared him officially dead. Some believed that his father might have been killed by a dangerous rebel group, as had happened to another archeologist at the university. Egyptian antiquities were often filled with intrigue due to the fact many coveted the treasures of the Egyptians.

Ash sat back and took some deep breaths. He decided to go below the bow of the speedboat because he knew the police would be using night vision scopes to look for suspect boats.

"Where are you going?" the young man asked.

"I told you never ask about their business," the old man yelled. "You don't want to know. You never ask anyone anything, or you are dead in this business."

Ash on the Run

Ash asked the old man, "What is the biggest mistake most people make when they're on the run?"

The old man sighed. "The first mistake is they ask for help from people they know."

"Oh, that's just great," Ash said to himself. "Here I am going back to my mom's house."

The old man continued, "The second thing is they can't do without their cell phones or computers."

"What do they do then?" Ash asked.

"Like I said," the old man shrugged. "They die because they can't do without them."

Ash wondered. "What would you do?"

The old man shook his finger. "You didn't pay for classes now did you?"

The young man laughed, too. "Come on, Grandpa. What if it was me on the run? You can teach me a lesson or two about getting away."

The old man sighed. "The more you help, the more you care, the more dangerous it becomes." The boy encouraged his grandfather. "Come on, Grandpa. Tell me what you know."

The old man couldn't refuse his grandson and shook his finger at him. "Just this once, you better listen well. I will not repeat it. You should buy new cell phones at least every two days and only use cash."

"What if you don't have cash?" Ash asked.

"Oh, I give this one about two hours on the street, and he will be dead," the old man said, shaking his gray head. "If you're on the run, you can't have morals or a conscious. They will get you killed faster than being just stupid."

Ash laughed. "Sometimes even a stupid man gets lucky." The boy grinned and chuckled. The old man gave stern look at both of them.

"You will have to learn how to break all the rules, steal, and lie. You will become a master of disguise."

"You know what, old man? I'm a dead man, because I live by a code of honor."

The old man and the boy started to laugh. The old man looked intently at Ash. "You have made it this far. You must have been protected by angels to get this far. Most smugglers would've killed you for what is in your bag, but you were lucky my grandson was with me. You would have been dead or caught by now. It is our mercy and compassion for a naïve innocent fool and my grandson needs a nice truck." The old man smiled and bowed his head to Ash. Ash bowed his head and smiled. The old man looked at the river with concern. "Well, your luck is perhaps running out because we are getting close to our destination, and I feel trouble ahead. Something isn't right. It seems there are twice as many boats on the shore than we are used to seeing. You're going to have to swim for the shore because it is too dangerous to take you."

"I can't get my bag wet," Ash said, sounding worried.

The old man smiled. "I guess you will just have to leave it with me."

Ash shook his head. "You know that isn't going to happen."

Ash spotted an old cooler at the back of the boat. "I could use that old cooler, and I'll trade you for it." He pointed to the old green metal cooler. Ash looked at the boy with a smile. The boy asked, "What do you have to trade?"

Ash pulled out a half bottle of Tennessee whiskey from his sack. The boy nodded his head. "It's a deal."

The old man laughed. "I knew a treasure was in that sack. No wonder you were guarding it." The old man gently slapped the boy on his head. "You won't be drinking that whiskey, my little man."

"Well, I know you like whiskey, Grandpa. I was thinking of you." They emptied the drinks and sandwiches out of the cooler. Ash put his tool bag inside, and then he took off his shirt. He stuffed it in the cooler as well. He saw some duct tape next to the throttle. Ash started to run the tape all the way around in both directions so that it would not come open.

The old man whispered, "You better get going. The longer we stay out here off-shore, the more suspicious we become."

Ash on the Run

Ash eased himself into the water, and the young boy handed him the cooler. He shook Ash's hand. "Thanks for the truck, mister. I'll take good care of her. Does she have a name?" Ash chuckled and thought to himself, I don't know why I never named her. He laughed again. "Her name is Linda because when she swerves off the road, she will scare the hell out of you. I once knew a girl named Linda who scared the hell out of me and made me swerve off the road. She damn near killed me. My advice is to be careful and take good care of her."

Ash eased over the side. He pushed off the boat. He could hear the old man whisper, "Don't forget what I told you, and you might see another day."

As Ash drifted down stream, he could feel the cold water. It felt so refreshing. When he drifted through a warm pocket, he would kick his feet so as to stir some cooler water back to the surface. Ash was a proficient swimmer, and the cooler made it easier to stay on top of the water. Ash knew many good swimmers had died swimming in the Nile River at night. If the crocodiles didn't get you, it was the whirlpools that sucked you down.

He didn't have much time to think about it when a boat steered directly toward him. This is great, Ash thought, I didn't even make it a day, and here I thought I was so smart. Just as the boat got close and the spot light shone from side to side, the old man's speedboat pulled between Ash and the other boat.

The old man yelled out to the search boat, "Misters, can you please help me? I am having engine trouble."

The men from the other boat yelled, "Old man, throw us your line, and we will take you ashore. We were wondering what you were doing out in the dark for so long. You don't look like one of the local fishermen."

The old man sighed, "I promised to take my grandson to Aswan for a few days. My engine stalls on me from time to time. I have to get my boat repaired. Do you know of a place close to town?"

The boats headed to shore, and the conversation continued as they towed the old man and the boy. The other two men in the boat wore Egyptian government uniforms. One man with a beard spoke, "We are looking for a tomb robber, and the whole country is on the lookout for him. Old man, have you seen anything suspicious?"

The old man sounded surprised. "It must be a big robbery if all of Egypt is looking for him."

"I ask the questions, old man," the man driving the boat said. "We are going to have to search you and your boat, so we're coming aboard." The only thing the police found was a half-empty bottle of Tennessee whiskey of which they each took a swig. Soon, it was gone. Ash drifter farther down the river as the old man saved his life for the second time.

Chapter 30

Black Belt

Cordy pulled into the full parking lot. She had only five minutes until her exhibition. Her cell phone started to ring and ring as she franticly looked for a parking space. It was her sensei.

Cordy answered the phone and a voice yelled at her from the other end. "Where the hell are you, Cordy?"

Cordy calmly answered, "I am outside in the parking lot looking for somewhere to park." Sensei Woo yelled back, "Just jump the curb and park on the grass. You are on in less than three minutes. Your stack of boards and bricks are ready to go." Click.

Cordy laughed. *Someone is a little bit stressed.* Cordy put down the phone and with that, forced her truck to jump the curb. She put it in park and grabbed her black belt. Cordy ran toward to the building. Just as they were announcing her name, she walked in the arena and bowed to the audience.

She placed herself in position, facing a stack of boards, and in a second, Cordy let out a ferocious yell. Harnessing complete

Keys of Life

focus and an impressive driving force, Cordy snapped every board in front of her, setting a new dojo record. The crowd went wild.

Cordy bowed and then turned to the bricks. With the same intensity as before, she cracked every brick in two. She had learned the power of absolute focus and calm. Cordy told the students, "Karate's main purpose is for your health. It isn't just for physical health but mental health, too. You learn balance and how to defend yourself. It's appropriate to fight someone to defend yourself, but one very seldom attacks others.

"You block the attack and use the attacker's force against him. The energy force of chi pervades all things and uses it properly. My father taught me that Mother Nature presides over all of us. It is all of us who must safeguard the earth. We are the guardians. If you have to fight, you should learn patience and be ready to sacrifice with no hesitation. It is the reason we avoid fighting and try to resolve conflict using peaceful means."

Cordy continued, "Karate is to make the body like iron or like a rock. Your heart should be mighty and bold. It is the one with the greatest heart that wins the battle. It isn't how big you are or strong. I have seen little children fight taller kids and win. Heart is where everything starts." She bowed to all her students. "A teacher learns from her students." The parents and kids gave a big round of applause for Cordy. She bowed and came down off the stage.

Rob, the owner of the school, came running over to Cordy with a big smile on his face. "That was great! More fathers are bringing their kids in for the night classes you teach. The dads loved the show." Rob had a wicked grin on his face. Cordy knew he was up to trouble.

"I know I shouldn't ask why."

Rob chuckled. "It was the way you drove home those two points," he said, chuckling more as he spoke.

Cordy looked puzzled. "When I said, 'you're developing your body like iron and a rock?"

Black Belt

Rob laughed louder. "No, the other two points." Cordy looked confused. Rob pointed to her chest and her clingy uniform. "Did you forget to put anything on today, Miss Cordy?" It dawned on her. She still didn't have a bra on.

She looked down and saw herself saluting. "Oh, you're such a jerk, Rob. Grow up, will you." Rob chuckled some more and put his jacket over her shoulders. Cordy did what any respectable black belt would do.

She stepped into him, grabbing his hand and arm. Rob flipped in the air onto his back in one second. Slam! She sat there with her knee on his chest and his arm twisted. Cordy whispered in his ear, "You could have said something earlier."

It was the first time Cordy had gotten the best of Rob in all of their years sparring. Cordy laughed. "Well, Rob, as a world champion, there goes your undefeated record. Now I know your weakness."

He just nodded. "OK, Cordy, you made your point." Cordy whacked him again.

"Yield," surrendered Rob.

CHAPTER 31
Chief Saunhac's Book

The Chief decided to write another story, handed down by the Saunhacs, for his great-granddaughter Cordy. One story passed from generation to generation was that of Richard the Lionheart, the great warrior king.

Richard the Lionheart was the third son of Eleanor of Aquitaine. His empire stretched from the Pyrenees of France to Ireland. He was more than six feet tall and a giant among men, handsome with reddish-gold hair. He was known by his military success in the Holy Land during the third crusade. Richard was Eleanor's favorite son.

He was a courageous knight, and he had some success during the Crusades against the formidable opponent Saladin. His dream was to be King of Jerusalem. During the Crusades, Richard came in contact with the Templars, who were the guardians of holy relics and sacred knowledge. His mother had told him of a box from Solomon's temple that contained Solomon's ring. It was for the Pure of Heart.

Chief Saunhac's Book

Richard had one prized possession, which he had gained from his association with the Templars. It was Solomon's ring. He had promised to bring it to his mother and show her its power. He came very close to becoming King of Jerusalem but alas, it was not to be. It seems that Richard showed immense possibilities of being a Pure of Heart, but his sins caught up with him. His quick temper and arrogance were his downfall.

Richard was killed by the arrow of a peasant boy. Upon his death, a trusted friend was sent to carry Solomon's ring to his grieving mother. Richard sold the island of Cyprus to the Templars in exchange for the ring. The Shield of David, a compound of two equilateral triangles, was engraved on the ring. Richard used the ring's symbol as magical amulet. It was called the 'Shield of David' or 'Seal of Solomon.'

The name of the God of Israel Yahweh was carved in the middle of the ring, indicated by the letters YHWH. The Seal of Solomon referred to a legend about a magical signet ring, which gave Solomon great magical powers. The Shield of David, or Solomon Seal, was placed over the doors of mosques or churches. It was believed the symbol had protective powers. Richard believed the power of the ring would help him win his battles and give him good fortune. King Richard discovered too late that he was wrong.

The ring poisoned his life at every turn. On his deathbed, Richard realized the Solomon ring was cursed. He was one of the greatest warriors of the Crusades, killed by a little boy. Only the Pure of Heart could handle the power of the ring. Even Solomon, who was the wisest king, went mad later in life because of the ring.

Richard was buried at the Abbey de Fontevraud. His effigy showed his image lying on white linen, painted with a field of more than thirty Shields of David. Inside each Shield of David lay a rose in the center. Richard had no qualms showing the ancient Jewish symbol on his tomb's effigy, despite being a Crusader. He wanted the symbol of the magical Solomon Seal on his grave, which remained for centuries. His long tomb demonstrated his height, and Richard was credited with saying that his family came from an "infernal bloodline" dating back to the days of Noah, Nephilim, and the giants.

The chief wrote, why does this Christian king have the Shield of David on his grave rather than the cross? Legend has that the Saunhacs protected the ring of Solomon, and the lesson here is that only the Pure of Heart can wield the ring.

CHAPTER 32

Burnt-out Bob and Uriel the Librarian

A young man sat in the St. Louis library, bored after reading news about Wall Street. It was raining outside. He was a burnt-out hedge fund manager who took an early retirement. A well-built man in his late thirties turned to the red-haired librarian whose nametag read Uriel and asked if he had a good mystery to read. Uriel smiled. "I have just the thing. Have you read *The Legend of Saint Louis's Lost Treasure*?"

He thought for a second. "I don't think so."

Uriel handed him the book, which was a bit dusty and old. "I think you'll enjoy it, Bob." "How did you know my name was Bob?" the young man asked, surprised. He glanced looked up from the book, and the librarian was gone. He opened the book and began to read.

In November 1226, Blanche was a regent and guardian to her children. King Louis IX was only eleven years old, and the barons immediately challenged Blanche's role. Theobald I the Troubadour Count of Champagne found Queen Blanche attractive,

Keys of Life

mysterious, and brilliant. If a knight was looking for his Guinevere, Blanche was his lady. He composed songs for her, and rumors had it that he had poisoned her husband. He would not betray his lady and did not fall into the baron's plans to depose her. Blanche trusted Theobald and loved him. Many barons whispered that they were lovers.

Blanche used her wiles to outmaneuver the barons. She remembered the advice of her grandmother Eleanor of Aquitaine: A queen is the most powerful piece on the chessboard. The Albigensian Crusade against the Cathars was a genocide sanctioned by Rome during which thousands of French were slaughtered. It was in 1244 that Blanche authorized the attack on Montsegur. The castle of Montsegur looked like a dragon of stone, winding its walls around the mountain. Two hundred Cathar Perfects called the "Pure ones" were burned at Montsegur while the rising sun shined over the hills of the Pyrenees. They had walked peacefully into the fire.

The Inquisition had been born and would haunt mankind for centuries. They would search for the pure ones, and the Nephilim would continue to hunt the the "Pure of Heart." The Inquisitors had the Cathars sew a golden cross on their clothes. The Inquisition had full power to arrest those they thought committed heresy.

Many women were burned as witches, and the Inquisition looked on educated women with the greatest envy and suspicion. A woman's role was to produce more children for the church. Women were considered weak and susceptible to evil and the best place for them was with a husband or in a convent. The convents educated women and took care of the sick and orphans.

Blanche believed in negotiating truces because she had learned more could be gained by this process. War was very expensive. The Cathar threat had been neutralized. Louis looked to the Holy Land for gold to replenish his treasury. Blanche looked on the Crusades as a futile and deadly game being played by the Pope and the kings of Europe.

King Louis IX had decided to take his wife and older children on the Crusades with him. He left France in the capable hands of his mother. Blanche begged him not to go. His devotion to God made him obsessed with getting relics from the Holy Land. Louis told everyone that it was the Holy Land that he wanted, but really, it was Egypt and her promise of riches that dazzled him. He wanted Egypt to fall, for it would make Jerusalem safer. Louis had heard from the monks and Templars that Egypt held mysterious secrets of an ancient religion. The stories of the pyramids fascinated him. He had used his great fortune to buythe crown of thorns from his cousin in Constantinople. He also built the Sainte Chapelle, a great chapel filled with stained glass, to house his relics.

The great pyramids could be seen in Cairo. King Louis IX had sent his mother a beautiful white alabaster cup with strange Egyptian pictures on it. The Grandmaster Saunhac had found it while in the Holy Land as an ambassador. It was called the wishing cup, and Moses brought it from Egypt. Blanche had received word that she lost one son in the fighting; her favorite son Louis was captured and taken hostage. The news left her grief-stricken.

She was older now, but she vowed to protect France as long as she had life in her body. She remembered as a child, her grandmother Eleanor grief-stricken over her Uncle Richard's death. She went all over France gathering the fortune for Louis's release. The barons' strength had increased again, and they were like vultures waiting for their prey. Rumors and messages from the Holy Land could not be trusted. She had already lost one son at Mansoura in the Crusades, and she refused to see Louis die.

Blanche had jewels, gold coins, and other treasures. She managed to get the Cathars to hand over their precious books, which talked about the secret writings of Plato and Pythagoras. Her father had taught her about these "forbidden books" which Rome forbade people to read. In one book, Plato talked about geometry, science, astronomy, and mathematics. The book was a treasure to Blanche. She placed some of these teachings in the family bible so it would be passed down to the children. The Grand Architect, or Geometrician, was the name for God, who held a compass in his hand while designing the Universe. With her son King Louis IX, she helped build the Cathedral of Chartres, which contained this secret sacred knowledge. The monks made the priceless manuscripts into a family bible, with pictures reflecting symbolic and spiritual messages

The Crusaders brought items from Jerusalem, from the Temple Mount excavations, and from Egypt. Blanche also possessed a quartz cup, passed down from her grandmother. Her grandmother told her the story of Magdalene bringing it with her from Jerusalem when she landed in France in a boat. Her grandmother drank the healing waters of the springs from the cup, and it was this to which she attributed to her health and long life. Her Bible would be there for her sons when they returned from this horrible Crusade, and the sacred knowledge within its pages was a treasure.

She was old, weak, and dying and her heart was failing her. The doctors didn't know how long she would live, but she knew she didn't have much time. She had taught her children about Magdalene's cave near Provence, where they would find King Louis IX's treasure. The land where she placed Louis's treasure would be under guardianship of her youngest son Charles. She would place the treasured Magdalene cup, Solomon ring of King Richard, one of the Merovingian king Dagobert's crystal balls, and the wishing cup where her children would know where to find it.

Charles rode to Magdalene's cave with his trusted Franciscan confessor. "It is here, Lord Charles, that Magdalene was said to have retired to pray. Your mother confessed to me the King's treasure is here, protected by spirits of the ring. The cave is said to be haunted, which will keep the curious away. You must allow me to lead the way. The haunting spirits could be a problem, for some of the treasure is theirs."

The Franciscan held his crucifix in front of him and made the sign of the cross as he entered the cave praying and cleansing the way. Charles walked into the cave and the monk lit the candles. The Crusader knights opened one of his mother's treasure boxes.

Charles pulled out the white alabaster cup with Egyptian hieroglyphs on it. "It is the wishing cup!" He took the cup to a small spring, which bubbled up from the cave, and filled the cup.

Charles whispered, "May my spirit live and my eyes see great happiness. I wish to be king and my wife, a queen." He drank from the cup and felt a great shiver down his spine. He replaced the cup in the wooden box while the other box held the Magdalene cup. His knights were sworn to secrecy, and they would keep the cups safe with their lives. One of the knights was a younger brother of the Grandmaster Guillaume Saunhac. The treasure would be there if Louis IX ever returned.

A few days after Charles drank from the wishing cup, Blanche was in Melun and after saying her prayers, she felt faint. Her heart was failing, and she would not look upon her beloved Louis ever again. She fell in and out of conscious, unable to leave Louis a message about his treasure. Blanche could only hope that her stories about Magdalene would lead him to it. Charles was her youngest child, and he was trustworthy. Her son assured her that Louis's treasure was well protected and would be safe on his return. Saint Mary Magdalene would protect him and his family.

The Templars had promised to pay Louis's ransom but they were to hold her treasure for collateral. They took her to Paris by royal carriage, where she died holding her rosary in her hands. Her son Charles would later be King of Sicily, King of Albania, and King of Jerusalem.

King Louis IX visited the Magdalene cave when he returned from the Crusades. He had experienced for himself during his return trip home the miracle of a drowning man calling out for Magdalene to save him. That man lived. Louis vowed to pay homage to Magdalene when he returned from the Crusades. His mother's death brought him tremendous grief.

The Magdalene cave was guarded by spirits, so King Louis IX decided to leave the treasure and close the cave up. Before he closed the cave, a Templar family was assigned by Saint Louis to protect the treasure. Where is the Lost Treasure of Saint Louis? It is said only the Pure of Heart know where.

Bob looked up from the book and the rain had stopped. He thought the mystery was interesting. He looked at his watch and hurried out of the library because he was late for his low-stress waiter job at Bingo's restaurant.

Chapter 33

On the Grid

Ken rushed with files in his arms into the chairman's office. "Someone has come on the grid in Egypt."

The chairman wasn't smiling and looked really ticked off. Ken realized that he had interrupted something. He handed the files to the furious chairman. Ken scanned the room. The room was filled with archeological treasures displayed on glass shelves. The chairman gave Ken an angry look.

"Ken, will you please knock before entering my office? And it better be bloody important," he said. Behind the opened bathroom door, a voluptuous Ellen stood in her black lace corset, black fishnet stockings, and black thong. Her whip in hand and the leather collar around her neck showed she was ready for some afternoon fun with the chairman.

Ken saw his mistake immediately. "I'm sorry, sir. It was important. I didn't know you were busy."

Ken couldn't stop looking at the seductive Ellen. She could feel Ken's eyes stripping her naked. Ellen was enjoying it. She walked over in her spiked high heels, holding her whip, and rubbed Ken's cheek.

"What's the matter, little Kenny? Can't figure out what to do?"

The chairman smiled at Ellen. It was amazing how she got under Ken's skin. As his protégé, Ellen was well trained. He remembered when they brought the little girl to him. He looked at the spellbinding witch before him. The chairman was beaming with pride at his creation.

"Yes, Kenny," the chairman said, placing the file back in his hands. "I think you can deal with a tomb robber. If you think he found something worthwhile, then find it and kill him. It's so simple. I suggest, Ken, that you knock before entering next time. I pay you to handle things, so handle them."

Ken backed away from Ellen and bowed to the chairman. "I can handle it. Yes, sir." He turned and as he left, he closed the door. He could hear Ellen's laugh and the chairman say, "Now, my dear, where did we leave off?"

Ken would get that beguiling siren. He would get them both. Ken paged through the file. The grave robber had to be found and dealt with. The Children of the Nephilim watched carefully the temples of Abu Simbel because of the legend. It was believed an object of power would be found at one of the temples. They had looked for it for centuries with nothing to show for their work.

One temple was for the god Amen Ra and the other, for the goddess Hathor. The temple's location was connected with the sun and the star Sirius. The five-pointed star symbolized of Sirius and the goddesses Isis and Hathor. The sun's rays would illuminate the sanctuary sixty days before and after the winter solstice. A Pure of Heart obtaining a celestial or Atlantean power object would upset the balance in their favor.

Ken's indoctrination and programming started when he was young. His families were loyal children for centuries. Ken's ambition was to replace the chairman, who was getting old and easily manipulated.

On the Grid

Ken called his subordinates into the boardroom. In walked four women and nine men. They wore black suits. They were all loyal to the Children.

"Ladies and gentlemen, please turn your attention to the screen in front of you." A movie screen illuminated at the front of the boardroom.

"We obtained this disturbing video from Aswan, Egypt, at the temple of Abu Simbel. Lights please, Cat." A petite blonde walked over and turned the switch. Immediately, the video showed the temple room of Nefertari, where the motion detectors were triggered and the lights went on in the dark room. The bright lights generated heat and the camera lens was assaulted by a couple of moths. The room was hard to see because of the moths blocking the lens but someone could be seen in the room. A shirt flew up and over camera 10, which confirmed it. Flying moths looking for warmth blocked the cameras. "I know the moths are a problem, but look at camera 9. All of you pay close attention."

The camera showed a naked man climbing the wall. The moth covered his face so all that could be seen was a white butt with a tan line. The girls giggled and one girl whispered, "Nice!" Ken looked over at them and sternly said, "Focus please, ladies. This is important." The next thing they saw was the front of the nude man. The moth again blocked out his face. Cat said in a business-like voice, "Can we please have a close up? Perhaps he has a tattoo?"

Ken zoomed in on the robber's naked butt and found no tattoos. Not once did they see the robber's face during the whole film, which was instead hidden by the moths. "We only have a picture of his butt," Ken said, sitting back in his chair. "We are going to find this guy."

The door opened, and Ellen walked in and sat down. Ken ignored her. She watched the film. Ellen was quite impressed with the tomb robber as he left an impression with the women in the room. He had escaped a guarded facility without anybody able to get a picture of his face. The moths acted almost as if to protect his identity.

"Did the guards get a license plate?" Ellen asked. Ken ran his hand through his hair. "Nope! The dust and dark made it impossible to identify. The police did put out a warrant for any suspicious activity to be reported. They scanned the river for unusual suspects but nothing."

Ken instructed the team, "We need a group to look at the film more carefully and see if we can find anything to help identify this man."

The four girls on the team raised their hands. "We volunteer to get close-ups and look for identifying marks." All of them were grinning. Ellen volunteered, too. "I'm in, and I'll bring the popcorn."

The girls in the room laughed quietly. Jack, who was gay, volunteered, too. "I'm in, and I'll bring dessert. You girls don't get to have all the fun. Plus, I'm good with computers. I'll check the arrests, police reports, airports and transportation hubs."

Ken picked up the file. "Let me know if anybody finds anything. Our people in Egypt are on it. Now let's get to work." Ellen swiveled her chair and slyly looked at Ken. "We and the Watchers will finally get something interesting to watch."

CHAPTER 34

Ash and Dirty Dottie

Ash didn't drift down the river as far as he wanted, but it was starting to get light. Even though he was still close to the search party, it was time to get out of the water because his feet were starting to drag on the bottom. Just like his mom said, it was time to "just get up and do it."

He came out of the water quickly but tried to stay quiet. It wasn't easy holding onto the cooler and maintaining balance. He surprised himself and was soon in the courtyard of a small hotel just off the river shore.

Ash didn't waste time. He pulled at the tape but couldn't get it off. From the dark, a voice with a heavy British accent said, "Well, now, I never expected to see a show like that."

Ash jumped out of his skin and turned to see a woman easily in her early 60s dressed in an evening gown. Ash whispered, "Please ma'am, don't scream."

The woman chuckled. "Young sir, it has been a long time since I have seen a fine looking half-naked man. I usually scream

Keys of Life

when the man is completely naked, and those screams tend to come in succession. I'm not the skittish type, laddie."

Ash looked exasperated. "I need to get my shirt and shoes out of this cooler, but I don't have anything to cut it open with."

The woman opened her sparkling silver-beaded evening bag and pulled out came a six-inch ivory-handled dagger sheathed in gold. "You weren't a boy scout, were you? You know, be prepared. I can help you with that, young man. What is your name, handsome?" She replied slyly.

"Ash," he whispered. As soon as he said it, he thought of how stupid he was. The first person that asked his name, he just told her.

She had blonde hair and did not look her age. She introduced herself, "My name is Dottie but a lot of my friends call me 'Dirty Dottie.'" She gave him a wink.

Ash smiled. "I am glad to meet you, Miss Dottie." Dottie sauntered closer to him, "What a gentleman you are, Ash."

"If you don't mind, I am in a really big hurry," Ash said, holding the cooler in his hand.

"Well," said Dottie. "What young man isn't? Ah, I remember once awhile back in my youth, I had a 19-year-old have two strokes in the valley of love, if you know what I mean." She gave Ash a knowing wink.

"Yes, ma'am. I am in that kind of hurry but even more so."

Dottie's voice took a stern tone. "You can stop with the ma'am. You can start calling me by my real name, Dirty Dottie."

Ash looked apologetic as a "Yes, ma'am" slipped from his lips. She pointed her finger at Ash, "You call me ma'am one more time, I am going in, and my knife goes with me."

Ash started to panic. "Please let me use your knife, Dottie."

Dirty Dottie smiled. "Now that's more like it." Dirty Dottie pulled the knife out of its hard sheath, and even in the dark he could see the silver blade shimmer in the night.

She still had it pointed at him as she moved closer toward Ash, with slow deliberate steps. At the last minute, she turned

Ash and Dirty Dottie

the blade facing up. She pressed her body up against his. She whispered, "My goodness Ash, you're freezing." Dirty Dottie threw one arm around him. She started to rub his muscular shoulder and back. Ash started to back up, but when he felt how warm Dottie was, he leaned in.

He was shivering from the cold air. Ash looked at Dottie. "I really have to go." Dirty Dottie said huskily, "I would rather you stay and let me warm up that incredible body."

Ash let out a nervous chuckle and said, "You are older than my mother."

Dirty Dottie rubbed both her hands around Ash's chest. "Well, we just won't tell her, darling."

Ash looked around for help and tried to move away from Dottie. "You had a bit too much to drink, Dottie, and now I know how you got that name." Without warning, Dirty Dottie reached down with her right hand and cupped and squeezed Ash's left butt cheek.

Ash let out a high-pitched squeal and harder this time, Ash pulled back, pushing her arms away. Ash whispered tensely, "I really have got to go."

Dirty Dottie winked again. "You sure you don't want to come with me instead, sweetheart and I'll warm you up?"

"I've got to go and in a bit of a hurry, Dottie," Ash said, firmly pulling away.

He could see that Dottie's dress was soaking wet, and he realized that thirty years ago, Dottie was probably a looker. Ash apologized, "Now you are cold and wet because of me. I'm sorry, Dottie."

Dirty Dottie seductively whispered, "Ash, I have never been hotter inside."

"You're one heck of a lady, Dottie," Ash admitted.

Ash wasn't wasting any more time as Dottie cut the cooler open. Ash started pulling off the wet duct tape. She handed Ash the knife. She had back-up protection in a small gun in her purse. He didn't scare her, but she scared the hell out of him.

Keys of Life

Ash started to hand her back the knife, and she refused to take it back. She explained. "My fourth husband, Bob, gave that knife to me. He was a marathon runner. You talk about a man with stamina." Dirty Dottie's smile grew bigger as she reminisced, "Darling Ash, when I grabbed your ass today, it was better than my Bobbie's. Ah, my Bobbie's ass, it brings up some wonderful memories."

Dirty Dottie looked up at the moon, and you could see her savor the moment. Ash stood there, dumbfounded at the predicament he found himself in.

Her wicked laugh filled the air as she saw his face. "So, I guess you could say I got to feel the best piece of Asssh I have had in a long time."

Ash started to laugh and Dirty Dottie uncontrollably giggled away. Ash was completely dressed now and had the tool bag out. He looked inside; everything was still dry. Dirty Dottie pointed to the tool bag.

She seductively said, "Oh, my Ash, are you a plumber? It's not too late. You can check my plumbing if I can check yours." She giggled some more. Ash chuckled, "You don't ever stop, do you?"

Dirty Dottie teased. "They don't call me Dirty Dottie for nothing, honey." Ash shook his head. "You're not afraid of me? A strange man swimming up on shore, and you want me to check your plumbing?" Ash wondered aloud, "Where is husband number four?"

Dottie gazed at Ash in appreciation. "Ash, if there is anything I know, it's men. You are a mighty fine specimen, but you are harmless. My Bobbie is long passed away. He was a wonderful man and left me a fortune. I just divorced husband number ten. I was out celebrating and just like a fairy tale, a young hunk of a man washes up on my shoreline."

Ash looked at her intently. "You can say one thing, Dottie, you have loved and lived life to the fullest."

Dottie crossed her arms across her chest. "I have learned one hard lesson. If you live with a man long enough, he will always

Ash and Dirty Dottie

let you down. The best thing Bobbie did was dying. What about you, my hard piece of Ash?

Ash couldn't figure it out, but he felt he could trust Dottie. He smiled sheepishly. "Dottie, believe it or not, I am saving myself for the right woman."

Dirty Dottie almost fell down in shock. "Oh my God, you are a virgin? Well I'll be ... that explains it."

Ash looked puzzled. "Explains what?"

"It explains why you were breathing so hard and got so excited so quick. I thought it was because I hadn't lost my touch. You need to find you a woman. It is you who is missing out on life."

"Well, I hate to run but I've got to go."

Dottie gave Ash a knowing look. "You aren't going anywhere, Ash."

Her expression worried Ash. "What do you mean?"

"They've passed out flyers all over town looking for anybody strange. And there's a reward for any information on a possible tomb robber that leads to an arrest."

Ash stamped his foot, "Damnit!"

"It is more like you're screwed, and it could have been me." She winked at him. "I think that the minute you leave here you're going to be screwed, virgin or not." Dottie was in her element and a light dawned on her face. "Well, I could help you get some transportation out of here."

"How is that possible?" Ash asked.

Dottie whispered, "Well, my door man drives a small moped, and he leaves the keys in it. I could distract him and you could take it."

Ash reluctantly agreed. "I'm game, but how are you going to distract him?"

"Do you really want to know that, my Ash man?" Dottie patted his ass as she headed for the hotel. Ash squealed, "Dottie, stop that!"

Dottie led the way as they went around the front of the hotel. Ash grabbed Dottie by the arm and pulled her back. He kissed her with all the passion he could muster. "Thanks, Dottie. That's for saving my life."

Dottie was breathless. "I thank you for reminding me that the ole girl still has some life left in her." Dirty Dottie walked around Ash. As she passed him, she reached back one last time and grabbed his ass. She smiled one more time for luck, and she slipped something into his back pocket — money.

Dottie scurried away before he could say anything. He could hear her telling the doorman to help her. She had twisted her ankle as she limped along and fell into his arms. The doorman helped her inside, and Ash could see Dottie grabbing his ass. He squealed, "Yes, ma'am!"

Ash ran and put the tool bag in the milk crate resting in the back of the old scooter, and he put on a helmet and goggles. Dottie was right; the keys were in the ignition. The engines started, and off he went. Ash streaked down the drive.

He looked behind him. No one was following him. Dottie and the door manwere busy in her bedroom. Ash rounded the corner. He pulled over by some trees and started to hide Dottie's dagger. He had left it out just in case he needed it. The dagger was engraved, to *my darling wife on her birthday*, with Dottie's name and birth date. Ash just shook his head. Dirty Dottie was 62 years old.

Ash read her name, Dottie Reynolds. Where had he heard that name before? He snapped his fingers. Dottie Reynolds, the famous actress. He watched all her movies. Ash knew it was only a matter of minutes before the scooter would be reported missing. With Dirty Dottie, who knew how long it could be. He laughed and raced down the road.

CHAPTER 35

The Magnetic Poles of Positive and Negative

Ramone Bossa had been running a Bosnian sex-slave ring for more than seven years. The Nephilim found him in a Bosnian orphanage and recruited him. Ramone was filled with anger and hatred. The Nephilim trained him, and he was completely loyal. He had taken the oath, and he wore his tattoo proudly. The Children of the Nephilim's sign was an angel with dark wings. A black dragon with fire coming from its mouth was another of their symbols. On the rooftop of the building across from the hospital, Bossa held binoculars to his face and pointed them to Minah's hospital room window, its drapes open. He rubbed his ear, which held multiple diamond studs.

Minah had been the first girl who had escaped him, and she would be the last. He had not heard from his hired assassin. It troubled him that he had not reported back because it wasn't like him. He was efficient, ruthless, and very reliable.

Bossa was hoping that Cordy was already dead, solving one problem. A nurse came into Minah's room and gave her a sleeping

Keys of Life

pill. His assignment from the Nephilim was to terminate Minah as soon as possible. His cell phone rang and he whispered, "Yes, it will be tonight. I'm personally taking care of it. You must have patience."

The voice from the phone softly said, "We want it done quietly, Bossa." Bossa whispered, "She is sedated, and it will be quick. The hospital staff will be focused on the World Series. I live to serve." The nurse pulled the drapes closed.

"You will sleep, little Minah, you will sleep forever," Bossa whispered in his thick accent.

She had never had to take sleeping pills. The nurse handed her the cup with the sleeping pill. She needed it to stop the nightmares. They were always the same, Bossa was chasing her through the hospital. She grabbed the surgical scissors off the table next to her bed and woke up.

Minah glanced over at the scissors on the tray, lying next to the gauze. The bandages on her arms, where the handcuffs had cut into her skin, were redressed every night. They were healing but still hurt.

"Time to go to sleep, Minah."

Minah yawned, "Yes, I'm ready. Good night." The lights went out, and Minah slept. The nightmare came again. She grabbed the scissors off the tray and ran through the hospital corridors. The jinn, a genie-like spirit, was pointing for her to go to the MRI room.

His face beamed with a bright light, and he was dressed in an Arabian sheik outfit. He assured her calmly, "You will know what to do when the time comes, Minah. Do not forget." He disappeared, and she felt a deep calm sweep over her as she slept. "I won't forget," she whispered in her sleep.

Cordy drove to the hospital and walked into the front door just as the security guard began to close it. "Visiting hours are almost over," he said. "You've got only ten minutes."

Cordy assured him. "I won't be long. Just stopping in to say hi." She carried a little puppy in a pet transport bag and walked down the hall. Cordy participated in the hospital therapy dog program, which allows dogs to visit hospitals, and she had a present for

The Magnetic Poles of Positive and Negative

Minah. Interaction with dogs helped patients recover, and Cordy was going to show her the puppy.

All the nurses were watching the Cardinals baseball game. Cordy asked them, "What's the score?" Two of the nurses yelled back, "No score yet."

It was the World Series, and she couldn't blame them for trying to catch the game. Minah's room was on the wing at the end of the hall. The hall was quiet, and no one was around. Cordy started to feel that something wasn't right.

She saw the empty chair by Minah's hospital door, and wondered where her bodyguard was. In the pet carrier, the puppy barked urgently. Cordy felt it, too, and the puppy barked more and more as they approached the linen closet. Cordy opened the door and saw a policeman lying on the floor.

"What the hell!"

She placed the puppy carrier on the floor and felt for a pulse on the unconscious policeman's neck. He had no pulse.

"Minah Hassan's life is in danger!"

She picked up the broom in the closet, noticing the officer's gun was gone. She saw blood flowing from the stab wound near his heart. Cordy closed the linen closet with the puppy barking inside. Everyone down the hall screamed and cheered as a homerun was hit, drowning out the barking puppy.

Alone, Cordy slowly opened the door to Minah's room. She saw a large man in a white lab coat getting ready to inject something in the sleeping Minah's intravenous line. Cordy recognized the man and slammed the broom over Bossa's head.

The broom splintered apart and fell to the floor. Cordy screamed, "Minah, wake up and run!"

Bossa turned, unfazed at being hit on the head. "You escaped me last time but not this time," he said calmly. "I'm going to enjoy this, and by the way, that hurt."

Cordy assumed her karate stance. "Well, get ready, bozo, 'cause I plan to hurt you some more." She yelled for Minah to wake up.

Keys of Life

"Oh, I know you, little black belt Cordy. I have been watching you, too. You teach the little kids. I know karate too."

He swiftly threw his hand to her face, and she deftly avoided him. He surprised her with his left jab, his hand revealing a dragon tattoo. Bossa had incredible strength, and Cordy fell backward, hitting the wall. He turned to an awakened Minah and started strangling her.

Cordy felt her head for blood and surveyed the room. She noticed the crash cart behind her and dialed up the charge on the paddles to the maximum. Bossa's hands were around Minah's throat when she bit his arm. He released her for a moment from the pain. Cordy pulled the paddles off the defibrillator and laid them on his back. Minah had climbed out of the hospital bed and moved from his reach.

Within seconds, Cordy heard the charge was ready and pushed the shock button. Bossa felt a searing shock through his body and screamed in pain. He crumbled to the floor, stunned from the shock.

Cordy grabbed Minah's arm, and they ran for the door. Minah picked up the surgical scissors off the table on her way with her free arm. Bossa pulled his gun out but it was too late. The girls fled into the hall. Minah, dressed in her hospital nightgown, and Cordy ran for their lives. They climbed up the stairwell. Minah whispered to Cordy, "I know where to go. Follow me."

Bossa pulled himself up and ran after them. His legs tingled from the shock. The hospital staff was cheering for another homerun down the hall. No one had heard the commotion.

As Minah and Cordy hurried through the stairway, Bossa aimed a shot from his silenced gun at them. He missed and hit the concrete wall.

Minah opened the door to the third floor, and a sign pointed to the MRI room. The floor was dark and quiet, and no one was around. Minah and Cordy entered the MRI room, and the big machine sat empty.

Minah set the surgical scissors on the table next to the MRI.

The Magnetic Poles of Positive and Negative

She waved at Cordy to follow her through a door, where the MRI operator controlled the machine. Cordy locked the door and whispered, "Do you know how to operate this thing, Minah?"

Minah pushed the on button and revved up the machine. The lights shone on the command board, and a dial registered that the machine was operational.

"I'm a neurologist remember, Cordy, and I know what I'm doing. Oh no, here he comes."

The girls knelt down and watched Bossa walk into the room with the gun. The MRI monitor showed them everything. Bossa taunted them, "Here little girls, come out and let Bossa kill you."

He put his bald head inside the hole of the MRI. Minah jumped up and pushed the button that placed the magnetic charge at maximum. She whispered on the microphone, and defiantly looked at him through the glass. "Bossa, you're so screwed."

The gun in Bossa's hand flew out of his hand, landing on the MRI. Bossa got ready to look up from the hole in the MRI machine, but as he turned, the metal surgical scissors shot in the air due to the magnetic field activated by Minah. The scissors flew like an arrow and pierced his skull, entering his brain. Bossa looked surprised as the scissors embedded themselves between his eyes. The pierced studs in his earswere ripped out with incredible speed.

Minah never knew how her nightmare ended but now she did. Bossa lay dead on the floor with the scissors in his head. She shut down the MRI, and the police showed up a few minutes later.

Cordy looked with admiration at Minah.

"I guess we are not calling a code." She then hugged the shaking girl.

Minah looked up at Cordy. "I dreamed this, and a red-headed jinn or what you call guardian angel, helped guide me. Cordy, remember to take your dreams seriously."

Cordy nodded her head, "I will, Minah. I will."

Both girls hugged each other again. They walked out of the

Keys of Life

booth and the police asked Minah if she was OK. Minah started telling the officer what happened.

Cordy found Bossa's cell phone on the floor. The last text message read, "Is Minah Hamanai dead?" Cordy suddenly registered that someone wanted Minah Hamanai dead other than Bossa, and it was probably his boss. She memorized the cellphone number and placed it in her pocket.

"Hey Minah, can I talk to you for a sec?" Cordy motioned her over to the door. "Minah, you need to go underground for a while."

Minah looked puzzled. "Why? Bossa is dead."

Cordy showed her the text message. "Call your dad, and go home to Egypt. You can be more undercover, and he can protect you better there than here."

Minah nodded. "I think you're right, Cordy. I'll call my dad. Thanks again for saving my life."

CHAPTER 36

Magdalene Video Goes Viral

Cordy went into her dark apartment. It had been one crazy day. She grabbed a beer from the fridge and sat on the bed with her computer. The quiet of the apartment felt good, and her mind needed to be occupied with other things. The dead body didn't bother her, but the experience of someone trying to kill her hit home. Her instincts came into play, and it was like she had trained all her life for that moment.

She looked through her emails and clicked on one concerning Maggie's video. Apparently, the video about Magdalene had gotten more than a hundred thousand hits online. Cordy checked her email again, noticing one from Oxford professor Dr. Roberts, with the history department at the English university. He was interested in where Cordy found the Magdalene with her hands folded in the strange symbolic way.

Dr. Roberts wrote about the mysteries of the ancient world, and he was well known in his field. He sent her a picture of the Magdalene on the altar at Rennes Chateau, and the hands were exactly the same.

Cordy emailed Cindy and asked her to check on where the school got the statue. Cordy's eyes were getting heavy, and she laid down the laptop, falling asleep.

In the morning, she went to the clinic, and while she was checking on the animals, Cindy walked in.

"I got it! Leslie asked one of the mothers in charge of the fundraiser for the kids at the school and found where the statue was made. It is De Villiers Restoration Art Shop on Lindell. They do most of the statues in St. Louis." Cindy handed the address and the copy of the invoice to her.

Cordy read the invoice, "I think I'll stop in and ask them about the statue."

Cindy teased her. "I won't be able to go with you because I have a date with Mr. Dream Officer Thomson."

Cordy laughed. "You are something, Cindy. I hope you have a great time. Thanks for getting me the information."

Cindy started for the door. "Oh, one more thing Cordy, you better read up on Rennes Chateau 'cause there is a mystery about some hidden treasure there. I would look it up online first before you go in and talk to de Villiers." She waved goodbye and was gone.

Cordy played the video again and looked at the sad, kneeling Magdalene, her folded hands resting on her knee. Her hands weren't proportionate to her body and stood out. It meant something, but what did it have to do with Magdalene?

She watched the video longer, and she saw the wood panel that was behind the altar. It reflected the French story of Magdalene and the other disciples escaping death in the Holy Land by sailing on a boat. Many writers had made movies about Magdalene's life in France. It was definitely a mystery that still held people's attention.

Cordy smiled at the picture of Maggie and her at the end of

the video. She would always remember the fun they had together and how much she learned about Mary Magdalene.

At lunchtime, Cordy drove to De Villiers Restoration Art Studio.

CHAPTER 37

Legend of the Templars

Bob, the man from the St. Louis library, brought the book of mystery with him to work. Bingo's restaurant had slow periods, and he wanted to read more about the Crusades. Anything to get his mind off Wall Street and the stock market. It was hard to let go.

He needed to quit trying to go back into that corrupt world of greed and money. He missed the adrenaline rush of trading the stock market and the excitement. It was like being on a roller coaster ride. He retired, and he needed to get his mind on something else.

Bingo's restaurant business was slow that afternoon, so he sat at the counter reading about the legend of the Templars. He was a retired Navy SEAL, and he could appreciate the loyalty men had in battle.

The tall Godfrey of Bouillon, Duke of Lorraine, knelt before the altar, his sword at his side. The emblem of the Jerusalem cross of the Crusades dangled from the sheath. The cross consisted of four crosses making a square, all connected to each other. The cross would hang next to the sword he wore, displayed at the Holy Sepulcher in Jerusalem in 2012. The symbol meant Christianity would be brought to the four corners of the world. He had done it.

The Kingdom of Jerusalem had been won and he refused the title of king. Godfrey was elected on Mary Magdalene's feast day, July 22, 1099. He remembered the story as a child of the fleeing of Magdalene, Disciples of Christ, and their families from Jerusalem to France, Spain, and Britain. It seemed fitting that he was chosen on her feast day.

The children of the tribe of David had returned home. His title, Defender of the Holy Sepulcher, acknowledged his devotion as protector of Jerusalem. He wore the coat of arms — a yellow cross with four smaller crosses depicting the four cardinal points — on his tunic as well as on his shield. The Crusader cross was placed on the heraldry of all those knights who fought in the Crusades. They came from the four corners of the world to fight for His kingdom. Godfrey had lived to see this day but died shortly after. The Jerusalem cross held great meaning for him and heralded the Kingdom of Jerusalem. He wouldn't die in battle. It was said Godfrey died from eating a poisoned apple, leaving no heir to the Kingdom of Jerusalem, and he was buried with his hands crossed to reflect the Jerusalem Cross.

The Cenacle in Jerusalem was a place of reverence for the Crusaders. The Last Supper occurred on Mount Zion. On the lower level of the Cenacle, they found a tomb believed to be that of King David. A tall King Baldwin II of Jerusalem ruled now, in the year 1118. Count Hugh de Payens of Troyes had arrived on a special mission with his relative Godfrey de Saint Omer. He sought a secret meeting with Baldwin.

A young French knight escorted him through a lovely courtyard. The knight tapped on the door and Baldwin told him to

Keys of Life

come in. The knight announced, "Count Hugh, your highness, wishes an audience."

Baldwin sat in a chair by the fire drinking wine. "Let my old friend enter. I'm anxious for word from home."

Hugh entered and bowed. Baldwin eyed the Count up and down.

Hugh was a dedicated believer, zealous, rich, and educated. A fighter in the First Crusade, he wrote of creating an order of warrior monks who would protect the pilgrims. The other mission of the order was more secretive in nature, thus the need for a private meeting with Baldwin.

Baldwin poured Hugh a cup of wine. "I will grant your request for space at a headquarters at Temple Mount. How many knights do you have, Hugh?"

Hugh looked at him intently. "I hope you do not laugh in my face, but only nine poor knights."

Baldwin tried to suppress his laughter but could not hold it back. "Ha!" Baldwin laughed at the hilarity of Hugh's idea. "You only have nine poor knights defending defenseless pilgrims." Hugh sipped his wine.

"Nine is a powerful number, and we have God on our side. They are nine of the most trusted knights who will obey without question. They will be knights who have pure hearts. We will be looking for relics and Solomon's treasures of the Temple. The Jews have told us that a treasure is located at the Temple Mount. The knights must be pure of heart if they are able to handle them. The poor knights will be looking for it with your permission. We can be the one Order that can be trusted to handle relics with care. We will be called "Poor Knights of Christ and The Temple of Solomon."

Baldwin had heard stories about the secret treasure of Solomon. It was a chance that couldn't be missed. The king stood up as he made his decision. Baldwin shook hands with Hugh.

"You are granted the space, and let us pray that you find the Holy Secrets. I would trust you with my life, Hugh." Hugh stood

Legend of the Templars

up and smiled. "Who knows, we may find Solomon's treasure. The knowledge of the wise Solomon would be the knowledge of the great builders of the Temple."

Baldwin smiled back and said, "You will report to me, Hugh, and no one should know your real purpose, especially not Rome." Hugh nodded and opened the door where his friend Godfrey waited.

"He has granted our wishes, and it begins, my friend."

Temple Mount was the Templar headquarters and below laid the remains of the Temple of Solomon.

The nine brothers dug below, looking for lost treasure within the Holy of Holies. Hugh was sleeping, dreaming of his beautiful wife at home. She kissed him gently. "You will find it, my love." She handed him a beautiful white cup with strange pictures on it, filed with the most delicious wine."

Godfrey shook him gently but Hugh refused to wake, mumbling, "Give us one more kiss, my pet." Godfrey yelled. "Wake up, Hugh," he said, shaking him harder. Hugh snarled, "Be damned, Godfrey, let me be." His lovely wife was gone and just a grinning ugly Godfrey stood there.

"We found something, my Lord, down under the Temple Mount foundations."

Hugh jumped up and climbed down the steps below. "Grandmaster, over here," called Andre de Montbard, pointing to a marble rock with a ring.

Hugh was surprised. "Let us see what is under the rose marble."

Andre, a strong, young Templar, pulled at the ring. Under the rose marble slab was a leather scroll, signet ring with Solomon's seal, a golden triangle, a mesmerizing white two handed Egyptian cup used by Joseph and Moses, 13 scrolls, a diamond carved heart, a map of the world, a crystal ball, a wood stick, and the sword of Moses.

Andre read the Hebrew words attached to the leather scroll, "These treasures are for the Pure of Heart." The Templars placed

Keys of Life

an altar at the spot and an underground church was made at the site. The ancient chamber went further but as the knights approached deeper, a strange feeling of a powerful energy emanated from the rocks. In the dark, the rocks glowed with an eerie light. The men tried to pull the rock from its place, but it was impossible to budge. None of the men had ever seen anything like it.

No one knew exactly what the Templars found under the Temple Mount, not even the Pope. Bernard of Clairvaux soon became their patron when he saw some of the treasures they brought back. The pope sanctioned the Templars, and afterward, recruits came in the hundreds. The Pope granted forgiveness of all sins and a path to heaven if one served or donated to the Templars. They hoped to find more sacred treasures. Wealthy nobility donated lands, money, and goods to the Templars because they were the protectors of the Holy Land. The Templars became the first corporation in Europe. The Templar's power, wealth, and influence increased after their discovery. They were deemed protectors of the relics and courageous warrior knights of the Crusades.

The nine knights left in the place of the treasures a spur, a piece of lance, a small Templar cross, and a major part of a Templar sword. The builders of the Temple of Solomon had left their mathematical formulas within the scrolls. The sacred knowledge of the builders handed down from the time of Enoch was contained in the scrolls. The formula for the magical number of Pi belonged now to the Templars. They had known the knowledge was there from reading the Bible. The secret remained within the brotherhood. The building of the cathedrals and the round Temple Churches would reflect the sacred knowledge of geometry and the great architect of the universe. The legend of the Templars' discovery of Solomon's treasure would be passed on generation after generation.

Bob heard the bell ring on the restaurant door. It meant a customer had come in. He put the book down and went to take her order.

Chapter 38

On the Run

Ash knew that the old man was right. The worst thing he could do was go to his mother's house. But she was the only one who could give him some answers. He decided to pull over and call from a pay phone. Ash knew he had to keep the call short because he figured her phone would be bugged.

He looked in his back pocket and couldn't believe it. Dirty Dottie had put two hundred American dollars in his pocket. Dottie was an angel, though she would disagree with that name.

He ran into a store and put some change in the phone. The phone rang twice, and then she picked up.

"Mom is that you? You sound funny."

She answered hesitantly, her speech guarded, "It has been a hectic couple of days. I'm OK. How are you doing?"

"You know how you told me to trust my visions. I found something, and I need to ask you some questions."

She softly whispered, "What have you done, Ash? Everyone is looking for you. It reminds me of the time you ran away from

Keys of Life

home. You remember when you were 11 years old? I thought I would never find you, but I did. Ash, will you please come home? We will get everything cleared up together as a family."

"Mom, I have to see you, and I will come as soon as I can. I understand everything much better and will see you soon. I love you, Mom, and you be careful."

"You take care of yourself, Ash. I want you to know, no matter what you have done or will do, I will always love you. A mother's love is constant and unconditional," she said, before hanging up.

Ash knew exactly what his mother just told him. The only time she would ever say, "It was a hectic time" was when she had company over. She meant someone was at the house looking for him.

His mom was going to meet him at eleven o'clock tonight at the place where she found Ash hiding. It was the time he ran away from home. It was six blocks away from home, by the bus stop. Ash had gone to get on the bus, but he fell asleep in a shed with latticework around it while waiting for the bus.

It was early in the morning and he still had 12 hours to kill or to be killed. He remembered a small cave at the edge of town that he played in as a kid, but they probably would have talked to his old friends by now. The old man's warning rang in his ears: you must stay away from familiar places.

He knew that the only place where people go and wait a long time was at the emergency room. No one ever questioned who was there or what they were doing there. Ash walked around with the bike helmet on and the visor down. Every time he stopped at a street corner he saw flyers looking for a tomb robber. He picked one up. It had information about the Temple break-in but no picture of him. He might have caught a break.

Ash wasn't taking any chances, so he drove to the emergency room. He parked the moped among a crowd of scooters and mopeds. In Egypt, everyone had a scooter. Police would never be

On the Run

able to find the one he had stolen. He had switched license plates while no one was looking.

The chaos when he went in the door of the hospital was what he hoped. People were told masks were required if you had a cold or flu. Ash quickly took one and put it on. He sat in a corner. Ash was so nervous that he couldn't get comfortable, but exhaustion took its toll. He fell into a deep sleep behind a hospital screen. Thirty people were in the waiting room when he fell asleep and by the time an orderly woke him, it was down to ten.

The orderly asked if he needed to be seen by a doctor. Ash replied, "I am waiting for my girlfriend to get off from work." Ash looked at the clock and could see it was going on nine in the evening and he needed to get started to go meet his mom. He had been sleeping for nine hours straight.

Ash thanked the orderly and said he would wait for her outside. He headed to the emergency room exit and he noticed two police officers looking at the tags on the mopeds. It was too late to use it now. They started to come toward the emergency room door. Ash dropped the tool bag and acted as if he was working on the door. The officers went inside.

Ash mumbled, "Dammit! Now what am I going to do?" He remembered what the old man said: "You will have to beg, borrow, or steal."

He looked quickly in each ambulance to see if the keys were in the ignition. One did. Ash climbed in the front seat. "Well, here we go again."

He turned the key and pushed on the pedal. No one noticed the ambulance pulling out of the emergency drive. Ash's adrenalin was really going now. He was off to meet his mother. Ash started to recognize his old neighborhood.

During Ash's childhood, he often missed his father. His grandfather was a great man in the village and tried to fill those shoes. He told little Ash all the stories of the Egyptian gods and goddesses. Isis, Osiris, and Horus were his favorites. Horus, like him, was raised by his mother. His father, Osiris, was tricked by

Keys of Life

wicked Set. Ash heard stories from his mother and grandfather about how his father was brilliant and so wise. It was the reason why Ash followed his father's footsteps in archeology. The university gave him a free education, but Ash showed everyone that he was worthy of the gift.

He slowed down and parked the ambulance behind some large rocks off to the side of the road. He had decided to walk the last block. He got closer to the shed and he knew it would either be his mother or the police. It was a risk he had to take.

Ash slowly approached the shed door. It was dark, lit only by the stars twinkling above, but it was too quiet. No birds or locusts made a sound. The muscles in his arm tensed ready to strike. The door flew open and surprised him. His petite, ageless mother appeared and threw her arms around him. She gave him a big hug and kiss on the cheek.

"I knew you would understand the message," she whispered. "They were going nuts trying to figure out what I said."

"Mom, how did you get out of the house without them seeing you? You did sneak out without them seeing you?" Ash looked all around. She smiled, "They think I am still taking a bath. I had a dream about you being chased by strange people. I bought one of those rope ladders for getting out of houses with a fire. I climbed out the bathroom window."

"You climbed out the window?" Ash said, surprised.

She nodded proudly, "Yes!" Ash laughed. "You never did like heights, Mom. I'm proud of you for making it. We've got to get going. I will tell you the whole story when we are safe."

Ash's mom shook her head. "No, Ash, not so quick. We have to go by Molly's house and get my things."

"Mom, you're kidding, right? We can't go visiting at this hour."

Ash's mom insisted, "We need to pick up something very important at Molly's house. You have to trust me Ash." She looked at the street. "Now where is your car?"

Ash pointed in the direction at the bushes. "Follow me." They held hands and went up the block to the ambulance. He started pulling the branches off it. His mother looked incredulous. "Oh, Ash, it is an ambulance?"

"Yes, Mom, it is an ambulance. Please don't start in on me. I had to borrow some things to get here." Ash smiled.

"Well, things have a way of working themselves out, don't they?" His mother looked surprised, but Ash just tried to ignore it.

"How far do we have to go to get your things?" She pointed. "It is just up the street. Here Molly comes now."

Molly, a lady in her sixties, was dragging four larger suitcases and three backpacks in a wagon. Ash watched dumbfounded. "How did she know you were leaving?"

Ash's mom ran to meet her and yelled, "I called her on the cell phone just before you showed up." Ash face turned to worry.

"OK, Mom, let's get your bags and go." He was astonished at how heavy the bags were. She had brought everything she owned with her. Ash threw them in the back of the ambulance as fast as he could and asked for his mom's cell phone. She handed it to him. Ash threw it down on the street with all the force he could muster, and it broke into thousands of pieces.

His mom was stunned. "Why did you do that, my son?"

"They are probably already on the way. You know, Mom, they can track you by your cell phone. We are running for our lives and we have to be very careful."

CHAPTER 39

De Villiers Restoration Studio

The store, a brick building dating back to the 1800s, was located in the older part of St. Louis. It still had the cobblestone alley on the side of the studio. The De Villiers studio door had a symbol on the door of a triangle with the Hebrew letters for God in the middle of it. The shop name, De Villiers Religious Art Restoration, rested above the golden triangle with a dark eye in the middle of it. It took a second before Cordy realized this might not be a good idea. The eye was the Watchers symbol. She needed to be on her guard.

Cordy opened the door to the studio and a bell tinkled so that the studio owner knew someone was there. Cordy looked around and saw religious statues all over. Some of the statues were very beautiful, and Cordy recognized many of the saints. Old paintings were lying in the corner, some with torn corners and water stains. Some statues were without heads and holding them or the device that killed them. Stained-glass windows with missing pieces sat on a wooden shelf. The eyes of the statues stared at

De Villiers Restoration Studio

Cordy. She told herself to snap out of it — they were only statues. A black Madonna smiled as she held her son on her arm. One statue stood in the corner with holes in it from the weather.

Cordy heard only silence but she felt eyes staring at her back. She quickly turned to see who was spying on her.

"Hisssss."

A yellow tabby cat assumed a pouncing position on a shelf. Cordy coaxed the cat, "Now, what is wrong, puss? Did I scare away a mouse?"

The cat looked at her fiercely. She stood up on the shelf and limped over a little wooden box with a golden triangle. Cordy noticed the cat had a hurt paw. "I can help you, ol' girl, with that bad leg."

She picked the cat up in one swoop, and the cat purred in her arms. Cordy examined the cat's tender paw, found a piece of wood stuck between the toes, and pulled it out. She set the tabby back on her perch. Immediately the cat walked around on the shelf without a limp. A meow of thanks was heard as she walked away.

Cordy's eyes followed as the cat jumped on the shoulder of an angel statue. She stared at the statue of an angel with a flaming sword and the flashback of her dream came to her.

"He is Uriel, the archangel."

The soft French voice of a distinguished man in his fifties came from behind her. Cordy jumped with surprise.

"I'm sorry, mademoiselle. Don't be frightened. Do you know him?"

She decided to play dumb. Cordy shook her head but her eyes returned to the statue. "No, I haven't heard of him. I only know Michael, Raphael, and Gabriel. Who is he?"

The aristocratic man questioned her. "Ahhh! May I ask? Are you Catholic?"

"I was raised Catholic, yes."

He looked at her through his glasses with a playful look. He walked toward the counter. "Uriel fell into disfavor with Rome.

Keys of Life

The Pope felt the angels were being venerated too much. I have to agree with Pope Zachary. One must remember Michael, the greatest archangel of them all, bowed to Adam. One day, a man will rule the heavens and the angels will do his bidding. The Anglican Church still venerates Uriel, and this statue will go to Saint Uriel Episcopal Church."

Cordy answered with assurance, "I guess Archangel Uriel survived after all."

He nodded, "Yes, he did. St. Louis Cathedral has the unique position of having many of the angels of the Seraphim. They have Uriel up on the ceiling. If you look hard enough, you will find him with his flaming sword on the scales of Justice. Have you been to the St. Louis Basilica?"

"Yes, I have. The mosaics are beautiful. I didn't know Uriel was on the ceiling."

The man looked intently at her. "The Basilica is one of the few that went against the order of Pope Zachary. They don't like to advertise that fact. The hope was even today that he would eventually regain his position but 'tis not to be. The Basilica is in honor of Saint Louis IX, a king who died in the Crusades. He brought many relics back from the Crusades like the Crown of Thorns and some other relics which were lost over time."

Cordy listened to him, but she couldn't take her eyes off the cat's eyes, which were mesmerizing. Cordy looked at the content cat looking down at her. "She is lovely," Cordy said, pointing at the cat.

"I see you have met my spellbinding Isis."

He turned his head to the cat lying on the shelf looking down at them. "Come down, Isis, and meet your friend with the healing touch. Cats were considered sacred in Egypt. I thought Isis was the perfect name for her, and I have fallen under her spell."

The yellow cat jumped down to the counter where the register stood. Cordy reached over and Isis allowed herself to be petted. Purring softly, Isis permitted Cordy to scratch her neck. The elegant elderly man whose tag identified him as studio manager smiled at them.

De Villiers Restoration Studio

"Isis is saying thank you for fixing her paw. She has been timid with it all day. You have a gift with animals."

"I'm a vet. She had a splinter, but she's good as new now."

"I owe you something for helping my sweet Isis. Please pick anything in the studio. It is on the house." Cordy laughed. "Oh thank you, but I don't need anything."

The gray-haired man grabbed her hand. "Please pick anything. I'm in debt to you. I always pay my debts. Isis insists you pick one of my treasures. I will hear not another word."

The store manager stood by the statue of the Archangel Michael with his lance. "How can I help you? Are you looking for a statue, my dear?" Cordy smiled at him.

"No, I was wondering if you could explain something about a statue of Mary Magdalene which was made for Saint Mary Magdalene School on Oakwood Road. Her hands were folded in a very unusual way. I was wondering what it meant or what the symbolism is?"

The solemn man went silent. His eyes were intense on Cordy. He scratched his head. "I don't seem to remember that specific statue. I must be getting old and memory slipping." Cordy's intuition antenna went off. He wasn't going to tell her, and she could tell he was keeping a secret. Cordy probed on, "Her hands are similar to a Magdalene on the altar at Rennes Chateau, France." She showed him pictures of the two Magdalenes with their hands in prayer in the same way.

The statues in the shop seemed to be alive as all eyes stared at Cordy and de Villiers in the studio. Cordy realized how gruesome some of the statues looked. One statue of Saint Denis was holding his cut-off head. A gargoyle menacingly stared at them. She came to realize these statues represented the killing of the Pure of Heart like trophies.

Cordy felt claustrophobic as the faces of the statues closed in on her. The store manager walked from behind the counter. "Rennes Chateau is a place of mystery and poppycock. Treasure hunters have looked for the lost treasure for years, and nothing has been found there. There's a legend that says the treasure of Saint Louis IX is there. I am not interested in treasure hunters."

Cordy laughed. "Oh, I'm not a treasure hunter. Just wondering what the hands meant on Mary Magdalene. Did you make the statue?"

The well-dressed man made a sweeping motion with his hands over the shop. "We restore older statues which come from older churches being closed. It's a great job to find a home for a statue that has lost one. It's sad to see so many churches closing down. It's the sign of the times. No one attends church anymore. Religious art is made to endure centuries. In this day and age, people aren't attending church like they used to." He sighed.

"Religious views change over time like Saint Uriel," he said, pointing to a statue of an angel holding a flaming sword and scales. "One day he's important, the next he's out of fashion. I can't tell you what the hands on the statue of Magdalene mean. It may have meant something long ago now lost in time. Your observation is correct and very astute. It does mean something. I just can't help you.

"Art is the alchemical magic between the artist, artwork, and viewer. It is the ultimate idea of freedom of choice. The viewer has two choices, whether to see with his own eyes or accept what other people tell him he is looking at. If the viewer decides to participate, then he participates in the magical process by deciphering what he or she sees. It is the merging of the conscious and unconscious of the viewer and the artist. It is quite intimate."

He picked up a stained glass window, which contained a light eye with rays of light radiating from it. "It is about the eye of the beholder. The artist doesn't know who will see it but knows how powerful the symbol is on the unconscious. He wants to connect his message with the soul. It goes back to the Egyptians and Buddha. I see it as someone is watching over us, but we have the freedom of choice to choose our path. The Magdalene hands long ago meant something very important to people who understood them. Not all people see the same thing when they view the statue. I guess the question for you is what it means to you.

You are going to have to take the quest of finding that out on your own, my dear."

Silence resumed between Cordy and him. He extended his hand and with a lordly air. "Let me introduce myself. I am Jean Marie de Villiers, and your name, mademoiselle?"

Cordy answered, "I am Cordelia McDermott."

De Villiers opened up his arms. "Fate has brought you here. Do you believe, Miss McDermott, that everything is connected in this universe and there are no coincidences?"

"Well, I have read some Tibetan teachings that refer to everything and everyone as connected, so I guess the answer is yes."

A twinkle came to Mr. de Villiers's eye. "My Isis does not howl and hiss at me anymore. Peace reigns again in my shop. Please, you must choose a gift of my appreciation for healing Isis." He took her arm. "I insist! I will not take no for an answer."

Cordy surveyed the room. It was packed with statues, candles, and religious trinkets. She walked around the room, looking at all the art objects. In the corner of the room, undetected, Uriel and Antar stood, watching her decide.

"Is she the one?"

Antar speculated, "I guess we will see soon enough."

Uriel watched, fascinated. He enjoyed watching the moment a Pure of Heart came into being. It was this decision that would prove if she was the real deal.

De Villiers took her to the glass shelf showing her beautiful jewels and silver chalices. Cordy wasn't interested in jewels. Isis strolled into a corner, circling around an old wood box. She purred loudly while she rubbed her head on the box. Cordy laughed at her new friend.

"OK, Isis, what is it you want to show me?"

Cordy watched the cat in the corner. She reached up to the box, which was hidden behind two statues. Cordy saw a twinkle of light coming from the box just for a second. Isis looked at her with her green eyes. Cordy was mesmerized as she thought she heard Isis say, this is the one, Pure of Heart. The box had an in-

Keys of Life

laid gold triangle, which glimmered when Cordy picked it up. Isis purred in response to her choice.

She looked over at Mr. de Villiers who had moved back behind the counter nervously. It was like he was afraid of the box.

"Can I open it, Mr. de Villiers?"

He answered shakily, "Yes, my dear, but be very careful. It is very old." Cordy opened the box gently and inside was an old Book of Enoch, a small beautiful white cup with two handles and Egyptian hieroglyphs, and a small statue of Mary Magdalene with the hands in the same way as the statue at Magdalene Church. Cordy gasped at how beautiful the cup was because she had never seen anything like it before.

"Is this Egyptian?"

Isis jumped on Cordy's shoulders, looking inside and purring. Mr. de Villiers took a deep breath of relief from behind the counter, where he was hiding. Isis purred more and jumped down to the floor and scurried away. Mr. de Villiers wiped away the beads of sweat on his forehead with a handkerchief.

"I don't know, but it is very old. If I remember, it is from a shop in Jerusalem. Well, my dear, the box is yours. Have you ever read the Book of Enoch?"

Cordy shook her head. "No! I can't take such a wonderful gift." She took the box and pushed it toward him. Mr. de Villiers moved to avoid her and walked over to the door and opened it.

"I suggest you read it. It is very interesting and illuminating. I insist you have it. Isis is very precious to me, and she never makes a mistake. Thank you, my dear, and come again. I'm sorry I couldn't be of more help."

Cordy could take a hint and knew it was time to go or she would wear out her welcome. Mr. de Villiers was literally pushing her out of the shop in a gentle but insisting way.

Antar and Uriel looked at each other. Uriel smiled. "It seems we have a Pure of Heart. What say you, Antar?"

Antar crossed his hands over his chest. "The question is how long does she live? Care to wager, Uriel? She is such a pretty thing but then, they always are attractive." Antar sneered and disappeared.

Cordy expressed her gratitude, "Mr. de Villiers, thank you for everything." She waved goodbye as she walked down the street to her car.

Mr. de Villiers put his hat and coat on as soon as Cordy left. He opened the door. Isis ran out the door with him and scampered away. Mr. de Villiers walked away from the shop, and the yellow tabby jumped up on the fence, waiting for something to happen.

Cordy drove in her car looking at her new gift. The cat watched and waited on the fence. Uriel smiled and petted Isis's furry head.

Two men walked toward the De Villiers Studio door. They picked the lock of the studio door and let themselves in. Isis' eyes watched for a few minutes.

Kaboom!

A massive explosion and fire cloud burst into the air. The De Villiers studio blew up into pieces and was slowly burning to the ground.

"Meow," Isis screeched as she scampered down the alley. The studio fire alarms went off and sirens of fire trucks approached. Uriel looked at the fire. "It begins!"

Chapter 40

Bob's The Man

Cordy was hungry for her favorite hamburger. She decided to go to Bingo's, and she pulled out the envelope her aunt Sister Agnes gave her. The envelope was hidden at the bottom of the basket of food, which Agnes had given her at Marillac. Cordy had been so busy that she hadn't had time to open the envelope until now.

It was her feelings toward her grandfather that had her troubled. Dad didn't trust him, so why should she?

In her mind, though, she admitted he was the only family she had left after Sister Agnes. A man wearing a tilted baseball cap with the Bingo's Hamburgers logo came up to her. "What's your order?"

Cordy looked up at him from the counter. "I'll have the Bingo Special with a chocolate shake."

The waiter looked at her, eyeing her up and down. "You realize that you will be consuming more than 1,500 calories, which goes over the amount of calories recommended for adults for a whole day."

Bob's The Man

Cordy gave him an angry stare. "Yep, that is what I want. By the way, put a slice of bacon on there, too."

The waiter answered with sincerity, "You want me to be honest with you? A salad would be much better for that heart of yours."

"I appreciate your help, but I know what I want."

The guy had an impeccably clean T-shirt with the Bingo's logo. "Do you want everything on it and cheese? I figure that is another 500 calories, but hey, I'm not going to say another word."

Cordy surrendered to his logic. "OK, leave off the cheese and mayo."

"You're not going to regret it." He turned satisfied and yelled, "Bingo Special, hold the mayo and cheese with chocolate shake! We should have that order right up for you."

"Thank you."

The waiter nodded and walked away. He started to put the clean silverware in its bins. Cordy noticed the book on the counter he had been reading. It was titled *The Lost Treasure of St. Louis and the Templars*.

Cordy decided to open up the envelope Sister Agnes gave her. She noticed that she was alone in the restaurant. The first things she saw were two passports, one Canadian and the other American.

Her Canadian passport read Bernadette McDermott, and her American passport read Cordelia McDermott. They had birthdates of February 12th on them, not her real, hidden birthdate.

The envelope also had a letter from her grandfather telling her that he wanted to meet her. He would be sending his private corporate jet to pick her up. She would be flying to Montreal first and then Halifax, Nova Scotia. Her aunt enclosed another letter giving her the inheritance and trust set up by her father and grandfather. It was notarized with her signature.

Cordy pulled out the Stonehenge Money Management report, which stated her assets at seven hundred million dollars. It was a number with lots of zeros, and Cordy felt lightheaded. The waiter saw her getting ready to fall off the bar stool and grabbed her.

"Hey George, bring that chocolate shake pronto!"

Keys of Life

An elderly man with a Bingo's hat ran and gave the waiter the shake.

"Here drink this, and I don't want any argument from you."

Cordy could feel the strength in his arms as he held onto her and his chest was hard. The waiter had no beer belly but the physique of a soldier who was dressed in a Bingo's T-shirt. Cordy spotted it on his bicep. It was a tattoo of two hearts surrounded by stars, a sign for the Pure of Hearts. He placed Cordy back in her chair. The old man handed him a cold rag and looked at him nervously. "Should we call 911, Bob?"

Bob placed the cold rag on her head. Cordy sipped on the milk shake, and the cold rag helped. She held up her hand. "I'm OK, really!"

Bob reassured the elderly cook George. "I think we have a case of low blood sugar, but she's getting her color back." The old man saluted with his spatula and went back to the kitchen.

"Let me introduce myself. I'm Bob Schaefer, and you are, I believe, Dr. McDermott. You don't remember me, but I brought my Chihuahua Freddy for a checkup."

Cordy's head snapped up. "You own Ferocious Freddy, the Chihuahua from hell? At least, that's what my techs call him."

A flashback came of a man bringing in a growling and snapping Chihuahua. Her techs came in, hair tangled and out of place and a mangled glove. Cordy went out to the waiting area listening to the growling and barking. She looked at Freddy and in a firm voice said, "Freddy, behave!" She showed no fear and picked up the Chihuahua by the fur on the back of his neck.

A docile Freddy hung from her hands. Everyone in the waiting room clapped for Cordy.

"Yes, that would be my adorable Freddy. He is a fighter. I like fighters." Bob let her go because she seemed OK as she drank her shake. He brought over her Bingo's Special and some ice water.

"When was the last time you ate today?"

Cordy shook her head. "I don't remember. I just had a bit of a shock just now. I noticed your tattoo of the hearts, and it reminded me of the Miraculous Medal." Cordy showed him hers around her neck. The waiter pulled up his sleeve, "A Navy SEAL is asked to fight under extremely dangerous conditions. The only way you can do it and survive is if you have heart. My mother was very religious and it made her feel better that I had it."

Bob leaned over and saw the Stonehenge logo on Cordy's papers. "Whoa! Stonehenge Money Management is a big hedge fund. Last I heard, veterinarians don't get paid enough to get into that fund." Cordy took a bite into her hamburger. "I hope it wasn't bad news, Doc." Cordy shook her head. "No, it seems I have inherited millions of dollars." Her eyes teared up. "I don't know if I can handle it."

Bob sat down. "Do you mind if I take a look, Doc? I have some experience in this kind of thing."

Cordy looked at the hearts tattoo on his arm and thought of Sister Agnes. She nodded to Bob. "Go ahead and take a look."

He picked up the papers, looking at the accounting and shook his head. "Damn! Doc, most of the companies in this portfolio are mean, vicious, and have questionable ethics. The Craig Company hunts whales and if they keep it up, will send the whales into extinction. Some of the other companies are into arms sales. I suggest you get another fund to run your portfolio. Stonehenge is part of a worldwide organization that runs corrupt corporations. I use to be a hedge fund broker, and I've met the chairman. He is one cold, calculating, vicious bastard, who is power hungry. I got fed up with the Wall Street corruption and retired while I had some morals left."

Cordy asked. "So, Bob, what happened? How did you end up at Bingo's?"

Bob laughed. "It's a long story, but I like you. I went to twenty vets, and none wanted to work with Freddy 'til you, Doc." He pulled off his Bingo's hat. "You're not afraid of anything are you, Doc? Except for seven hundred million. It's scary, and I know plenty of crooks who would love to get a hold of it, too. You have a good heart so I'll tell you my sad Wall Street experience." Cordy ate her hamburger and listened intently.

"Adrenaline junkie is my middle name. I was a Navy SEAL when I was in my early twenties. I was honorably discharged after five years. Wall Street was where the action was, and I went to school for finance. I lived in a penthouse in Manhattan and worked for Golden Hedge Fund. I was young, ambitious, and gifted in the ways of numbers and finance. I have a high IQ, and I graduated from Harvard Business School with all the certifications and credentials to be a top broker. I had one problem though. I was honest, and that is not a good thing to be when working on Wall Street. I stumbled on a massive fraud system concerning derivatives and money laundering. The government was notified, but they didn't do a thing. I decided it was best to just walk away.

"These corporations are powerful and have incredible resources at their fingertips. I just told my bosses I was suffering from massive burn out and they let me go. The tipoff to the government, I made anonymously, so they couldn't track me. Doc, you're stepping into shark-infested waters. I count my blessings every day that I got out alive, 'cause some people don't. "Bingo's is a quiet, peaceful place, and George over there is a buddy of mine."

Cordy looked at him and sighed. "I really don't want to have millions. I don't need it. What am I going to do?"

Bob saw the tears in her eyes. He had seen those tears of desperation before. He handed her a napkin to dry her eyes. "Now, now, stop crying. Maybe I can help you with the money. Bingo's is a bit too quiet for me."

Cordy started smiling at him. "Oh could you, Bob? Maybe we could do some good with it?"

Bob crossed his arms over his chest. "You are not handing me any bullshit. I'll help you but it has to be intended to help the world, not make you richer."

Cordy looked at Bob very intensely. "What if we made the corrupt corporations poorer? If we make them poorer they will get weaker. What if we made a goal to bring the corrupt corporations down?"

Bob's The Man

"You're serious? They don't like losing money."

"You're hired, Bob, so say goodbye to retirement." She pushed the papers toward him. Cordy's relief showed in her face. Bob smiled back at her. "I have to admit, I was missing the hustle and bustle of New York. I'll have to set up an office and hire some staff in New York to handle your portfolio. You need to tell me your favorite charities and causes you support." Cordy thought for a second. "I want some money to be set up for me, so I can hand it out randomly so no one knows where it comes from."

Bob was getting excited. "I'm thinking anonymous gift cards. You could carry them in your pocket, and we could place them all over the world. They're untraceable. I'm your man, Doc."

Cordy stood up and shook his hand. "Bob, thanks. Here's my number. Do you believe in angels, Bob?"

He laughed. "Yes, I believe in angels. When I was in the Navy, there were some weird things I saw that couldn't be explained."

Cordy had a good feeling about him. "How soon can you start?"

"I'll be in New York tomorrow, and we'll be up and running in a week. You email me when you need anything. You have staff now, and you'll need it. I'll give you a hundred million dollar expense account, which you can access at any time. I'll analyze the companies, and you can pick out the ones you want to invest in. You should know I have a gift for making money, so unfortunately, you may get richer. It's a downside to hiring me."

"Just more to give away. Oh, how much do I pay you, Bob?" Bob laughed. "You can pay me what I'm making at Bingo's. I have plenty of money and don't need any more."

Cordy felt like a great weight had been lifted from her. Her grandfather might not approve of her plan, but she knew her aunt and her parents would. She believed in angels and the signs were all there.

CHAPTER 41
The Nephilim Agenda

Nephilim Laboratories was a corporation focused on bioengineering, cloning, and research. The chairman was head of the multibillion-dollar company. The Nephilim had many objectives, one of which was to create a new world. In the future, they would produce animals, food, water, drugs, and human beings. They would own all the patents.

The Nephilim wanted to be the creators. The old creation was to be eliminated. The Nephilim had tampered with the Tree of Life for profit. They had created the first child with a triple-strand DNA, and soon, they would be seeing their super beings replace the children of the earth. The governments could not stop them. Churches warned of greed and the tampering of nature, but the Nephilim's agenda was too strong and powerful. Hybrids were taking over. The chairman grinned at the reports on his desk. They couldn't be stopped.

Watson and Crick had discovered the structure of DNA. Man was taking on the new job of creator. He had already taken the job of destroyer with the atomic bomb.

The chairman realized world domination was within his grasp. Man's knowledge had reached a peak, and now the Nephilim was out to control the masses. Revenge was sweet, and he knew Antar would be pleased. The word was out that they had DNA from an extinct Neanderthal man. The Nephilim had ambitions of altering God's creation again.

Demonstrations all over the world protested the Nephilim's patents but the law protected them. Mankind was going to change, as was Earth. The Nephilim would control food production, energy production, and thus, the populace. Their agenda was destruction and deaths of millions. Extinct animals would be replaced with their patent creations.

The ultimate goal was to manufacture super beings. A child with triple-strand DNA would have incredible powers. The Tree of Life was within their grasp, as was immortality for the worthy. The chairman would not fail.

CHAPTER 42

The Gift

The gas station was busy as people filled their gas tanks, mumbling about the high prices. A young woman wearing a pink scarf over her hair and large sunglasses jumped out of her black hybrid. Its license plate read Sugar Mama. She observed her surroundings, listening to the grumbling from the gas-guzzlers.

A young tearful woman was begging for money. Two small children were looking at her from the window of her 10-year-old, dented car.

"Please, can someone loan me some money to fill my gas tank? I am going to my mother's house. I promise to repay you."

An elderly man yelled, "You need to move your car out of the way so other people can gas up. I hate beggars. Get a job."

The woman with the pink scarf and sunglasses walked in to pay for her gas. She asked the attendant, "What's the deal?" He shrugged.

"Her name is Margaret Fletcher. Lives about 10 miles from here, and she left her husband. Stupid didn't even think about

The Gift

anything except leaving her old man. Her husband is coming to pick her up after work. Don't worry, she's going to get what is coming to her." He winked at her. "You're mighty pretty, even though you drive a hybrid. Hybrids hurt my business, but I'll forgive you because you are so cute."

"Well, Frank Banks, are you the boss of this fine establishment?" the woman said in a steely voice, reading the man's nametag.

He laughed. "No, honey, I just work here."

"I thought so. Perhaps the boss would like a call to let him know how nice you are?" Frank flirted with her and relaxed. "Here ya go, honey, his business card has the number and if you get bored, call me at this number." He handed her a card with both numbers.

"I might just do that, Frank," she said, before she promptly walked out the door. She whispered to herself, "Frank, the moron."

The lady with the pink scarf and sunglasses walked over to the begging woman. "I have a gift card with some money on it, Margaret. It's yours. Fill your tank up and drive as fast as you can to your mother's."

Margaret took the card. "Bless you, and thank you."

The woman calmly got in her hybrid and drove off. Margaret filled her gas tank up and drove to her mother's house. She took the kids to the grocery store to get some food and asked to know the balance on the gift card. The attendant told her $10,500. Margaret started crying.

The newspaper reported numerous stories of a mysterious woman handing out gift cards to poor and desperate families. Everyone wanted to know who the charitable woman was and where she came from. Cordy smiled and placed the newspaper in her purse.

Chapter 43

Yes, Ma'am

Ash drove furiously. "Mom, now is not the time."
"Yes, it is the time, and stop. I said, stop!"

Ash had heard that voice when he was a kid, and he knew enough to stop. He parked outside a small house, where a woman waited for them and motioned for them to come to the door. She was a heavy-set woman with strands of gray mixed in her thick, black hair, and she wore a simple blue Egyptian cotton dress.

The strange woman walked up to Ash and with a puzzled voice asked, "Are you the one?"

"Yes, and I'm sorry I broke your phone," Ash apologized.

Molly's voice became louder, "No, are you the one?" Ash was perplexed.

"Mom, what the hell is she talking about?" His mom smiled. "Well, I kind of told her about your special talents. Her son has been blind for five years after a schoolyard accident in which he hit his head from a fall. Everyone has looked at him and has said it is hopeless."

"Mom, I thought we had a deal. You wouldn't talk about my hidden gifts, and I wouldn't talk about yours."

His mom persisted, "She is helping us, and I couldn't think of a better way to repay her. Molly is risking her life for us."

Ash relented. "Where is the boy? Don't get your hopes up, Molly, but I'll try."

Molly grabbed Ash by the hand and pulled him into the house. Molly's son sat at the kitchen table. He was no longer a young boy, but a young man of about twenty. He turned to the sound coming through the door. He sensed Ash's presence.

"Hello my name is Ash. What's your name?"

"Bernardo or Bernard. My friends call me Ben," Molly's son answered.

Ash scratched his head. "Well, Ben, what have these two crazy moms told you?"

Ben hesitated. "Not much, but they say you have had a gift since you were small. Is that true or are you crazy?" Ben smiled and picked up an orange in a bowl. He started to peel it. Ash admonished them. "Well, they weren't supposed to say anything because it is a secret."

Ash's mom smacked him on his head, and Ash let out a loud, "Ow!" Ash's mom had her arms crossed over her chest in anger. "Don't call me crazy! Ash, you may have moved out years ago but I haven't lost my touch. You give me some respect, young man. It wasn't easy bringing up a boy alone."

Ash started again, "Mom, I am not a little boy anymore."

His mom gave him a stern look, "Well, start acting like it."

Ash's mom smacked his head again, and Ash yelled even louder, "Ow!"

"You get my point!" His mother's anger showed.

Ash rubbed his head, ready to dodge her, and said, "Yes, ma'am."

Ash became serious and approached the young man calmly eating his orange.

"Ben, we don't have much time. So someone turn off the lights," he said. Molly quickly flipped the light switch. It was almost pitch

Keys of Life

black, as there were no windows in the kitchen. He pulled the alabaster cup from his backpack and placed the sacred water into it.

Ash gently explained, "Ben, this sacred cup was found in the holy city where the Holy family fled from Herod. The healing water is from the sacred well. Many people have been cured because of their faith in its healing power."

"We need the darkness for your eyes. The eyes have been in darkness for five years so they will need to adjust."

Ben nodded, "I understand. Darkness and I have become friends over the years. I'm not afraid."

"You will need to keep your eyes closed for at least 10 minutes after we leave and then only dim light for the next day," Ash said calmly. He dipped his fingers in the cup and placed two drops on each of Ben's eyes. Molly reassured them, "I will see to it."

Ash placed his hand over Ben's eyes, and Ash's mom could see the silhouette of Ash's head drop. He became rigid for a few seconds and then relaxed.

Ash was drained from the experience. "It will be."

"Will he see?" Molly asked hopefully.

"Yes, you can turn on the lights, but Ben, keep your eyes closed. I know it's hard but be patient." The wind started blowing harder and a loose branch hit the window. The mothers let out a gasp simultaneously, "Oh, no!"

Ben was worried. "What is it, Mother?"

Molly's fear could be heard in her trembling voice. "I'm afraid Mister Ash has stayed here longer than he should have."

The clock showed the time and Ash's mother nodded and said, "We must leave." She gave Molly a hug. Molly returned the hug and whispered, "Thank you so much." Ben smiled, still keeping his eyes closed, "I wish you luck on your journey." Ash and his mom ran to the ambulance.

Ash worriedly looked at his mother. "What was that fear I heard in your voice?"

His mother whispered, "I can't talk about it now, maybe later."

She was looking out the window as he drove through the

night. Ash's concerned voice broke the silence, "You are not getting off that easy."

She looked at him in exasperation. "Ash, not now!"

Ash knew to back off. "OK, OK!" He looked at his mother with concern. The sleeve of her shirt rose to wipe a tear out of one of her eyes. Ash just shut up and drove.

After about an hour, Ash pulled over. The night sky was cloudy, as if a storm was brewing. His mom looked at him.

"Well son, what is the plan?"

Ash put his hand through his hair. "Well, I guess it's not to get caught, for starters." A long pause of silence fell on both of them. She started to laugh uncontrollably, "Oh my, you don't have a plan, do you?"

Ash put his head back on the headrest. "Mom, it's been a long three days. One of the times I slept, an angel came to me in my sleep and freaked me out. He told me all this was going to happen."

His mother looked concerned. "Are you sure about that?"

Ash nodded, "Yes, mother, he was an angel." She took her arm and pushed on his shoulder. "No, I mean are you sure that you were asleep and it was a dream?"

Ash started wondering if he was insane. He whispered, "I don't know. It seemed so real to me. He seemed so real to me. Am I crazy, Mom? I'll believe you if you say I am."

She looked at him with confidence. "I know the angel you are talking about, and I don't think you were asleep. Angels appeared to men in the Bible. I know you're not crazy. Your problem is that you have the family gift."

Ash looked up at the sky. "I don't feel like it's a gift — more like a curse. Mom, sometimes I think I am going out of my mind."

Ash's mom shook her head. "No, son, it is your life's quest. We can make a difference in the lives of others, and you have seen this with your own eyes." Her lips trembled, and she broke down in tears.

Keys of Life

Ash tenderly put his arm around her shoulders and said, "OK, Mom, tell me what is going on." His mom just shook her head in refusal. "I'm just tired. Let me rest for a second." She closed her eyes and let out a big scream. She opened her eyes. "Oh no! Molly!"

Ash jumped out of his seat. "Mom, what happened? You're scaring the hell out of me."

"I had a vision that my friend Molly was murdered by two men who were looking for us," she said anxiously. "You know how I get visions from time to time. You get your gift from my family. We are all seers and healers. It might happen tomorrow or maybe tonight."

Visions were part of her family's history, and Ash learned as a child that his mother's intuition was always right.

Ash calmly answered, "Hold on for a minute, you never have said 'may happen' before. What do you mean by may happen? As long as I've known you, if you saw something, it came to be."

She looked at him in distress. "Well, you see, my son, I broke one the biggest rules. Molly may die from me breaking those rules."

Ash hugged his mom. "Tell me what you saw. Tell me everything."

She began describing her vision in a shaky voice, "I saw two men in Molly's kitchen. One of the men was getting ready to hurt her son, so Molly turned to the breadbox on the counter and flung it open. She grabbed a huge knife, and as she came back around, one of the men shot her twice in the head. I didn't mean for Molly to die so we could live." She let out a small sob.

Ash was so confused. "Mom, you left out something." She shook her head.

"No, no, I was afraid this was a mistake, and I was right." she said determinedly.

Ash spoke firmly, "Yes, yes, I knew something was going to bite us in the ass and when it comes to my ass, it is very sensitive. Over the last few days, it has been bare for all of Egypt to see, pinch, photograph and grab and I am not looking forward to having it bitten, too."

Yes, Ma'am

His mother snapped out of her state of fear to wonder, "Oh, son, tell me who was grabbing your bare ass? Is it someone I know? Is she a nice girl?"

Ash put his hands up, exasperated. "It was an old lady, but Mom, don't change the subject." His mother showed her disappointment that it had been an older woman. Ash coaxed her, "Mom, calm down, and tell me everything."

"Oh Ash, I didn't think it would be like this, but we are out of time," she answered sadly. "I don't know where to start."

Ash reassured her, "OK! Mom, will you just start anywhere?"

She closed her eyes, "OK, OK, I will start with Molly and the breadbox. You see for the first time, I interfered."

"Oh, I don't like the sound of that. What do you mean you interfered?"

Ash's mom explained, "You see, Ash, when you use your gift, it's meant to be spontaneous, not planned. When you see the future, those are things that have happened and should never be interfered with. If you do, you will make ripples in time. It's a huge responsibility."

Ash impatiently interrupted her, "Yea yea, Mom, I have heard you tell me that over and over again." She looked at him intensely. "OK, here it is, the can of worms, and it is a huge one.

"Well, let's start with Molly. You see, when I saw her with the knife and they had guns I thought she didn't have a chance. I decided to give her a chance, so I took the knife and replaced it with my gun." She put her head into her hands. It dawned on Ash what she had done.

"Holy shit, Mom. What are you doing with a gun?" he asked, astonished.

She answered furiously, "Oh let's see, I am sneaking out to meet my fugitive son, who is on the run from dangerous men." She rolled her eyes at him. "What he should be doing is getting married and giving me grandchildren."

Ash rolled his eyes back at her. "Mom, will you get serious and stop with the marriage crap?" She quickly reached over and

Keys of Life

smacked Ash upside his head. Ash yelled back, "Mom, ah, I am not a teenager anymore."

She yelled, "Then will you stop acting like one!"

Ash knew how to make her happy. "Yes, ma'am."

She took a deep breath and spoke, "Here comes the can of worms, you see it just wasn't any kind of gun I left for Molly. It was your father's gun."

"It's all right, they know my dad is dead, and you are my mother."

Ash's mom stared at Ash, looking worried. "I wish it was that simple, so here comes the bigger problem."

Her agitation increased. "I am just going to get to the point. You see, no officer in the German army would have been caught dead in the field without his gun. If they had any sense, they were going to figure out that when the tomb collapsed, your father was not inside."

Ash's head shot up. "You told me that's how Dad died." He thought about what his mother was hinting at, and Ash's surprised voice rang out, "Dad didn't die?"

Ash just sat there with his mouth open. He slowly turned to his mom with concern.

"If Dad isn't dead, then where is he?"

"I think that is where we should go," Ash's mom whispered softly. "You see, if there's anyone who can give you tips on running and hiding, it would be your father. He has been in hiding for years."

Ash was in disbelief. "Mom, that's not funny. Why didn't you tell me after all these years?"

She looked at him sadly. "Ash, if they had found him, they would have killed him. We both decided that you would not have to bear the pain if they did find him. In the end, it might be my stupid mistake, which will get him killed.

"I think it is time for you to meet your father. He is at the Monastery of Saint Catherine. Your father knows we are coming, and he can't wait to see you. You must remember he was a

Yes, Ma'am

younger man in the pictures I showed you. He just turned 69 but is doing great."

Ash sighed, "He may as well be on the other side of the earth with all the road blocks between us."

Ash's mom gave him her Cheshire grin. "Well, you forgot I saw this day coming, and your mom is a good planner. You remember your father's old plane? The one you learned to fly when you were young?" Ash nodded his head. "Yes, but you sold it when I went to college."

"No I didn't," Ash's mom said, smiling. "I had it moved to an airfield across town and had it refurbished. I let the owner of the airfield give rides to tourists in return for taking care of it."

"Mom, I can't fly anymore. It's been too long, and besides, I wasn't that good to begin with."

Ash's mom threw her hands up in the air. "OK, we will just turn down the street and head back home. I am sure they are looking for you. I don't think we will escape unless we go by plane. Ash, you can fly that plane."

Ash thought about it more, "I agree it is our only option. Which direction to the airfield?"

Ash started the ambulance and drove toward the airfield. As they went down the street, he saw a 4Runner just like his. It had stopped on the side of the road and the driver went into a building. He pulled in behind it and told his mother to wait for him. He walked up, seeing the truck was old and had no alarm system. He knocked out the window and unlocked the door. In less than a minute, he had it started, and he pulled it back alongside the ambulance and they transferred all their bags.

He slammed down on the gas pedal and they started off again. Ash's mom looked worried. "Are we stealing, Ash?"

Ash shook his head. "I know, Mom, it looks like we are, but we're just borrowing it. An old man told me if you stay with anything too long, they'll find you. The ambulance was due to be replaced. I want to see my father. I don't think that is a crime."

She put her arm on his shoulder and consoled him, "Oh Ash,

Keys of Life

I see things for you that you can't imagine. You know I can't tell you. If I do, you might try to change your future. You must trust your heart, that we will see your father."

It was a good thing Ash got rid of the ambulance because just after he turned to the next street two black Chevy Suburbans pulled up. Three men and one woman got out with machine guns and ran to the ambulance and flung open the door. The woman pushed on her headset and spoke into it with great frustration, "We just missed them, sir. The seats are still warm."

One of the men ran up to the woman. "They must have stolen a car. We found some fresh glass on the ground."

"Are you sure it was a car?"

The man with the beard nodded, "Yes, there wasn't enough glass for a truck."

The woman yelled out, "Damn it, there are too many homes and apartments to find out who the owned the car." The woman talked into her headset, "I'm afraid finding the next lead will take some time, sir."

The voice on the phone was commanding, "Then you better get to it. I want to be briefed every four hours, understood?"

"Yes sir!" She walked to the glass on the ground. An older Egyptian man with gray hair and wearing a white cotton shirt and khaki pants came out of a house across the street. He raised his arms in surprise and yelled at the group standing where his truck used to be.

"What have you done with my truck?"

The woman ran across the street and grabbed the man by the coat. "What kind of truck?" The angry man realized these people had guns and they pointed them at him. "It is a 4Runner." The woman put her gun in his face, and the terror on the man's face showed.

"What color is it? "

"Red."

"What year?"

The man's voice shook as he said, "It is a '96."

She pointed to one of the men. "You take care of the ambulance."

He nodded and ran down the road. He threw a grenade and the ambulance exploded into flames. She looked at the other man holding a gun and ordered, "Clean this up, and let's go." One of the three men reached in his pocket and pulled out a handgun with a silencer. He put it to the frightened man's head and pulled the trigger. The man fell to the ground instantly, while the shooter fired once more into the heart.

The woman got back on her headset as she headed back and opened the car door. "Sir, we are back on the scent."

The voice came back. "Well done, I want you to come in for a briefing. Let the others stay on scent."

"Yes, sir."

She ordered the men to continue the search. "I don't want anything to come back our way, understood? So get rid of the body."

They shook their heads and answered, "Affirmative." The three were moving fast and without talking, as if they had been doing this all of their lives. They were military contractors hired by the Children of Nephilim. They wanted to be untraceable with as they moved from country to country. They answered to no one.

She got into one of the Suburbans and drove off, wheels smoking and screeching with urgency. In ten minutes, she spotted a 4Runner in front of her. It has to be them, she thought, as she sped up to get a closer look.

Ash's mom let out another gasp, "Oh, no! We better get a move on."

Ash looked in the rearview mirror and said, "I think I see what you mean. It's a pair of headlights closing on us fast."

Ash turned at the next street and then at the next. He didn't see the lights but for a short time, and the Suburban was behind him.

He said reluctantly, "Mom, I think you're right, as usual. I think I can slow them down. They are bigger, wider, and heavier than us, so hang on."

Keys of Life

Ash turned off road and over the curb and they flew, not even slowing down. They were off-road and driving over desert sands until the 4Runner started to get stuck. Ash's experience in the desert paid off, and they made it through. As they turned the corner, Ash could see that the Suburban had gotten stuck in the sand.

The driver got out and started shooting at them. Bang! Bang! The bullets whizzed over their heads.

"Keep your head down!" Ash yelled. Ash kept driving and soon the distance grew. Ash pulled his mom up. "Mom, I think I bought us some time but not much. Which way to the air field?"

Ash's mom sat up and pointed. "You know the school where you won the triathlon in your last year of high school?"

Ash, nodding his head, said, "Yes!"

"It's right behind it."

Ash pulled the 4Runner back on the road. "I got it, and I know exactly where to go."

His mom smiled. "I thought you couldn't fly awhile back. You sure changed your mind quickly when you saw them chasing us."

"I can fly. I can do it," Ash said confidently. "I'm hoping it is like riding a bicycle." As he thought more on it and got closer to the airfield, he was determined. "I will make it work." He looked at his mom. "I don't think I have a choice, do I?"

"No, son, sometimes we just have to follow our heart."

All of the sudden, it hit him and Ash knew what true exhaustion was for the first time in his life. He knew that he couldn't fly without sleep and with his adrenaline so high, he wasn't sure he could sleep. Ash realized that whatever he decided to do, it had to be unexpected so that the ones hunting them would not find them.

Ash knew that every decision was life or death from here on out. Ash whispered, "No pressure, no pressure."

His mother looked at his pale face. "Ash, you aren't looking so well."

Ash stopped the truck. "I need to sleep, and I don't want to die."

Ash's mom patted his back, "Little kid, little problems, big kid, big problems. And what is a mother to do? I know where to go, and we'll be safe."

Ash looked up. "You do?"

Ash's mom smiled. "It's time you go to church."

Ash pulled up to the small Coptic church next to the airfield and started to think, this is pretty unexpected. He had gone to this church occasionally when he was small. Ash's mom climbed out of the car. "OK, son, get out and go in the church. The back door is always open. I used to help decorate on the holidays with flowers. If you're lucky, no one will be inside so you can go to the confessional and get some sleep."

Ash, exhausted and weak, opened the door. "Mom, what are you going to do?"

She went over to the driver side. "I'll get us ready to fly and then come back to pick you up." She pointed toward the church. "Now go and get some religion and some sleep."

He went in the open back door as fast as he could. Inside the simple but beautiful empty church, he ran to the confessional and jumped in, shutting the door. Through the screen, he could see a small glowing light in the room where the confessor kneels. A voice whispered in surprise, "Why Ash, you're still alive."

Ash jumped up to leave the confessional but then it dawned on him that he knew the voice. "Uriel, is that you?"

"Who were you expecting?"

"I was hoping for some peace and quiet so I could take a nap," Ash said in a tired voice. Uriel softly whispered, "I know what you need. Sit down and close your eyes, and I will keep watch."

Ash fell into a deep sleep. The next thing Ash knew, his mother was pulling at him, saying, "Come on, Ash, the sun will be coming up soon. It's time to go."

Ash smiled. "I had the best sleep. How long was I out?"

"About ten hours, I think?"

Ash looked at his mother. "Did you see him? He was sitting over here." He pulled open the door to the other side of the confessional, but no one was there.

"Who are you talking about?" His mom asked, puzzled.

"Uriel."

"It must have been a dream, dear. Ash, we need to go. We need to go now. They're getting close. I can feel it." Ash's mom led him to the back door. It was broken, as if someone had hit it.

"Did you do that, Mom?"

"Yes!" She looked all around her. "It has been a hectic ten hours, son." She pointed to a car. "Get in the car."

Ash climbed in. "Where is the 4Runner?"

"It was time to borrow another one."

Ash looked for his bag. "Mom, they didn't get my bag, did they?"

"No! I've got everything in the plane. I was on my way to pick you up when I saw a strange car come down the block so I jumped out at the turn and went up the back way to the church."

"So when you say 'they are close' do you mean like down-the-street close?" Ash asked, sounding concerned.

"No, I mean at-the-front-door close," his mom said curtly. "Now you just get in the black car over there."

Ash started becoming alarmed at what he missed. "Where did you get a black car?" Ash's mom climbed in. "It came with the church. The keys were next to the back door. I borrowed the parish car from time to time to pick things up for the church."

Ash smiled, "I told you, Mom, once you start breaking and entering, you go right to borrowing."

Ash drove forward slowly. When he pulled to the front of the church, there were roadblocks at either end of the road. He slowly pulled back behind the church.

Ash's mom sounded worried while her eyes were big with fear. "What are we going to do now, Ash?"

Ash could see that the corner of the church backed up to the high school drive. The school was private, and many archeologists, diplomats, and military members sent their children there. A fence blocked a small rocky path, which crossed an athletic field. Ash had used it when he was a kid late for practice. He

Yes, Ma'am

knew the airstrip was on the other side of the field. Ash put his seat belt on and motioned for his mom to do the same. "Hold on, Mom, we are going to make a road through the fence."

Ash pushed the accelerator to the floor, and they took off. They hit the fence, and it let out the biggest bang. The crash tore off the front bumper, while a second bang signaled the one-foot drop down the curb to the parking lot of the school. They headed to the back of the school, and Ash looked at the 12-foot fence around the airstrip.

Ash looked at his mom. She was smiling like she was having the time of her life. Ash didn't lose any momentum and hit the big fence. With a great crash, it came down. For the first time, Ash could hear gunfire in the distance. Bang! Bang! He knew that they were shooting at him.

The trouble for the shooters was the distance and the surprise. They had been drinking while standing guard at the roadblock. Ash pulled up to the makeshift hangar, which was made out of corrugated tin.

Inside the hangar was a plane in mint condition. They jumped in the plane. Ash was shaking. He hadn't flown in a long time. He started it up, and the engine purred. He started to pull out of the hangar, and his mother could hear him saying aloud, *stick, rudder, flap, speed, altitude.* He kept repeating it over and over. Ash taxied down to the far end and turned around.

Ash's mother thought about how she liked to think that her son was good at everything, but she was having second thoughts about his flying. He was all over the place. So finally she said, "Try to stay on the runway, son."

"OK, OK, I'm getting the hang of it." He could see the men who were chasing them were at the fence. He pulled the throttle wide open, and they started to go faster and faster. Ash yelled out, "Mom, get down, we're going to take some fire."

He could hear the gunshots now, and he was just about out of runway when he asked his mom, "What did you put in the plane?"

Keys of Life

"Everything!" she yelled over the plane engine. "You only had one bag, the one in the car, but I brought my suitcases, too. I had a feeling you were coming, and we were going to see your father."

"Were they heavy?"

"Why, yes, as a matter of fact, they were. I could hardly lift them onto the plane."

The two men at the fence figured they would shoot as Ash flew over but their position was all wrong. The plane was still on the ground, and its blades were coming at them so they ran for their lives. The plane chased them down a small hill onto the school field, which made a nice runway, and finally, the plane got enough speed. It started to take off, but Ash didn't know if they would miss the roof of the school. Did they have enough altitude?

They did it, but just then Ash remembered what was on the other side of the school. The church had a tall steeple, and it didn't look as if they would make it. Suddenly, a gust of air pushed the plane upward, and Ash tilted the nose to avoid the steeple. They could still hear gunfire, but they were out of range. Ash yelled at his mom, "Are you OK?"

She smiled. "Yes, Ash, you did it. That was some great flying, son."

"Thanks, Mom. Nice packing job! Women! What is in those suitcases, the kitchen sink?" They both started to laugh.

The laughter eased the tension.

"You are a great flier once you're in the air, Ash," his mom said. "How are you at landings?"

Ash shook his head. "Not as good as my takeoffs."

Ash's mom sighed. "I was afraid you were going to say that."

The airstrip by the Monastery of Saint Catherine was for emergency use only. It was short and treacherous. Ash knew that if he could land without killing them, it would be a miracle, because his landings were twice as bad as his takeoffs. Ash asked, "Mom, you said I had more surprises yet to come."

When there was no reply, Ash yelled at his mom. He yelled one more time before he realized that she was sleeping. His questions would have to wait for later — if there was going to be a later. It took about an hour, but Ash's heart started to beat normally. His mom had placed the coordinates and map for Saint Catherine's on the dashboard. He was flying well below the radar screen. It was too much excitement for one person to handle.

Ash was actually enjoying flying again. After all this time, he had forgotten what it was like to feel free of the earth and just soar like a bird. As they came closer and closer to the Monastery of Saint Catherine, the mountains got bigger and bigger. Ash could feel his palms getting sweaty, and he even started to shake. Ash let out a prayer, "Don't let us die!"

Ash's mom started to stir. "Son, did you say something?"

"Yes, I said I don't want us to die. I always say that on landings and on this one, it could very well happen."

Ash's mom calmly talked him through. "What happened to stick, rudder, altitude and speed?"

"Mom, it's too late for that, because you see, Mom, landing an airplane is nothing more than a controlled crash. Unfortunately, with me, it ends up more like an uncontrolled crash."

"I didn't see that coming or I wouldn't have had us fly," she said calmly.

"OK, Mom, you said there was more to tell me?"

His mom hesitated and then answered carefully, "Well, son, I am going to let your father tell you everything. It only makes sense."

"What do you mean makes sense?"

"Well, the way I look at it is, if we're going to die landing, there's no sense in me going over it now," she said calmly.

Ash insisted, "Mom, you should tell me now."

Ash's mom stubbornly answered, "Oh, Ash, we do not have enough time."

"I thought you had more to tell me."

Ash's mom sighed, "It is so complicated."

"You better get started."

Ash's mom stood firm. "We don't have the time." Ash leaned over the side as his mother pointed her finger and yelled, "There

Keys of Life

is the monastery. I have to start to pray for our landing." They both saw Mount Sinai looming in the background and the small monastery of red brick buildings surrounded by a wall at Sinai's foot. Ash broke into a cold sweat.

"Oh shit! It looks harder than I ever imagined."

"Is there anything I can do?" Ash's mom yelled.

"No, but that praying could come in handy." Ash could see a windsock, and it showed great news — no wind. That's good, he thought. The landing area was on the side of a small slope and there were several ruts on either side. Ash cried out, "Mom!"

"Yes, son?" she yelled. "I will pray louder. We're going to need it. You know, son, this is where Moses talked to God, so we have a better chance that he will hear us. I believe in you and love you, Ash. I always have. Just land this plane, and I promise I'll tell you everything."

Ash felt as if he was going to get sick, but then calm came over him. It felt as if there were a second set of hands on top of his. Ash yelled back at his mom, determined, "I can do this!"

He tilted the plane downward. He slowed down and got into position. Everything was looking great as — *bam* — he slammed into the runway. The plane bounced twelve feet in the air.

Ash let out, "Oh, shit!" and before he knew it — *bam* — down again, they hit the land and back up ten feet. The landing space was running out, and the mountain was getting closer. It was like a rodeo on a bucking bronco, down and up they went again, and back up each time with an *oh shit*! All of a sudden, Ash felt a smack on the back of his head. It was his mom. She yelled out, "Put it down now!"

The plane leveled out and set down. It rolled toward the end of the field, where a mountain awaited them. The plane came to a stop only a few feet before the mountainside. Ash started to smile. "Damn, that was fun!"

Ash's mom hurriedly climbed out of her seat and said, "I never want another landing like that in my future. I want to kiss the ground right now." They started to laugh.

Yes, Ma'am

They could see a small truck coming down to meet them. As it got closer, Ash's mom could see it was her husband, who she hadn't seen in 25 years. She started to run toward him. She threw her arms around him, and with tears in both their eyes, they kissed. The love was there, even after all these years. They hugged again and for the first time, Ash could see himself in the face of his father.

A healthy gray-haired man, Ash's father was tall, lean, and didn't look his age. But Ash knew it was his dad. A large lump came up in Ash's throat. He was starting to panic and get angry. How could this man leave his wife and child for all those years? Ash wanted to punch him.

Ash's smiling dad walked over to him, his arm around his mother, and he reached out his other arm to hug his son. Ash couldn't resist. His heart took over. He reached out, and they hugged for a long time. His father stepped back and said, "So, you must be my little Asho, all grown up."

Ash stepped back because he didn't like being called that name. He was Ash. He was angry now. "Why am I the asshole, old man, when you are the asshole for leaving us?"

Ash's father looked confused and turned to his wife. He shrugged his shoulders, and then he repeated, "No, you are Asho."

Now Ash was getting madder, and his mother jumped in, "Now, shut up, the two of you! You are both assholes." Ash and his father looked at each other, both mad, and this time, both shrugging their shoulders in unison.

She put her hands up. "Give me a second, and let me catch my breath, you two." Ash's mom calmly put her arm in Ash's and said, "He's not calling you an asshole. He is calling you by your name, Asho, A-S-H-O. In Egyptian, it means..."

Ash remembered the meaning and blurted, "It means Pure of Heart!"

Ash dad's looked puzzled, "Who is Ash?"

His wife put her hand on his. "You were not there when he was little. The children would tease him. He was in fights all the time so I shortened his name to Ash."

Keys of Life

His father looked sad. "You did this without asking me?"

Ash and his mom looked at the old man in the monk habit and nodded their heads in unison. "Yes!" Ash's dad knew he lost that battle. Smiling, he held out his hand. "I don't care what your name is my son. You are here at last. I have dreamed about this moment. Our family is together again. I have missed you so much."

Ash shook his father's hand, and the man had tears forming in his eyes. They both hugged each other. Ash could feel his father's fragile thin frame, but his strength was still there.

"Where have you been?" Ash's dad questioned them both. "I was expecting you two years ago." He hugged Ash's mother next. "Dearest one, you told me in your dream you saw him in his mid-twenties. The year puts him in his early thirties."

Aziza apologized, "Age is difficult to judge in the dream state. I'm sorry you had to wait so long."

Ash sighed, "If both of you knew this day would come, why didn't anyone bother to tell me?"

Ash's dad patted him on the back. "My son, let us get this plane hidden before someone sees it. I will show you where there is an old building down the road. My friend will take care of the plane."

He waved to his friend in khakis and a white shirt. He climbed in the plane and drove it to a building that looked like a storage shed. The monks opened the doors, and the plane fit perfectly inside. The monks closed the doors, and the bells from the church rang out.

CHAPTER 44

Bill and the Light Watchers

It was to the Watchers' benefit to be neutral. They were a huge intelligence operation spanning the globe. They were in governments, religions, and companies around the world. Both Watcher groups had obtained the video from the temple of Nefertari at Abu Simbel. Both sides were alarmed. They were unable to identify the robber, and they didn't feel the moths' interference was a coincidence. The Watchers believed in the One. The One created all things; therefore all things were connected to the One. It would put in play the theory that all things were connected in nature. Coincidences were little signs of these interconnections.

Bill McDermott had seen the crazy video from Abu Simbel. He laughed because he knew the Children of the Nephilim would be repeatedly mooned by the robber in their conference room. At the end of the day, they would come up empty-handed. The balance was shifting. One could feel it everywhere. The poles of the earth had shifted in the North, causing Tampa Airport to adjust the lines of their runway. The Arctic and Antarctica were changing, too. The opposite poles of the world were going through dramatic changes, and it could represent a change in the power of Children of Nephilim. Bill saw that their agenda created global domination and drained natural resources. The Children were at the height of their power. Sex trafficking, child stealing, war, and economic turmoil were making the world a dismal place. Many religious orders were calling it the end times.

He knew that things were getting ugly. In all his years as a Light Watcher, he had never seen the Children of the Nephilim grab so much power and money. The Dark Watchers had grown powerful playing with both sides. Bill was worried and now Cordy was on her way to Nova Scotia to see him. She was on the grid, something her father gave his life to prevent. Bill had tried to tell his son that eventually they would find him. The chief had emailed him saying he wanted to see his great-granddaughter. Bill had to obey his father-in-law. Annie, his late wife, would never forgive him if he hurt the chief.

He noticed she was tapping into her inheritance. Bob Schaefer was her portfolio manager, and Bill checked into his credentials. Frankly, he was impressed with Bob's talents and honesty. According to the Light Watchers, Bob was already stirring the pot by pulling all of Cordy's inheritance out of Stonehenge and moving it to new funds. Cordy impressed him with her intuition. Who would have guessed that she would pick a fast food waiter for her money manager?

Schaefer was brilliant, a genius in the financial world. The man was making Cordy more money than Stonehenge. Bob had connections all over the world from intelligence agencies to militaries. He had seen time in the Navy SEALs. Bill would have a talk with Bob. The question was how did a talented man slip through the cracks? How come no organization grabbed him? Or did someone have his allegiance? Bill was optimistic. Bob Schaefer could end up as a blessing in disguise. Bill raised his glass in salute to the heavens.

CHAPTER 45

Saint Catherine

Ash's father ushered them toward the church, "I need to see you later and discuss your escape. I believe you found something we don't want some very powerful people to possess. Is there anyway you were followed?"

Ash shook his head, "No, I flew below the radar, and no one should know we're here." His father patted his back. "Good, my son. You've bought us a few days, and you will come to understand that they have eyes everywhere, even here. We'll be leaving later tomorrow because there's something important I want you to see."

Ash gazed at the dusty road and scratched his head. "I thought it was a runway when I saw the air sock next to it?"

His father chuckled, "No, Asho, the area you saw was for the helicopters to land. The airstrip is farther down the road. It is a nice flat runway on the other side of the mountain that is well taken care of. I was impressed with your landing considering the small runway."

Keys of Life

Ash's mom explained. "Did you know, my love, that a landing is a controlled crash?"

"Is that what that was? I was thinking out of control and very lucky. My heart stopped for a few seconds."

Ash started bragging now that he was safely on the ground, "I had it under control all the time. I knew what I was doing."

Ash's father smiled at his son's confidence. "The plane engine worked great, but I did see some bullet holes on the bottom. I admit, I'm very impressed."

"I knew he could do it," Aziza said. "He is your son."

Ash's father eyes searched the sky. "We must get inside so they don't see you. We have much to catch up on and discuss. I will fill in the blanks, Asho."

Ash sighed, "Father, could you please call me Ash?"

Han was firm in his response. "No, I will call you by the name that I gave you at birth. It is a blessed name. You must trust me, Asho, and be patient. We will go to my office."

Ash's mom was so excited, and her eyes shined with happiness having them together again at last. She knew it was not going to be easy, but she knew her men. She knew that Ash's father would love him unconditionally. His father was very proud of him.

Ash had his bag from the plane in his hand. He never let it out of his sight. They headed to the monastery. A small man followed them and carried his mother's luggage. The weight of the luggage made him huff and puff. Ash's father didn't live in the monastery but in a small building just to the right side of the monastery. Ash's father's excitement showed.

"I can't wait to see what you have in the bag, Asho."

Ash stubbornly tried again, "I really wish, father, you would just call me Ash."

His father explained, "No, you will always be my little Asho. It is a wonderful name."

Ash just shook his head, and said, "It angers me. I was teased over and over again by my classmates. It isn't a great name."

His father shook his head. "Son, you will have to be patient with me because I am too old to change now."

Ash threw his hand in the air with frustration. "Whatever!"

Aziza squeezed between them and spoke, "OK you two, get over it and move on. Just call him son. I have something to tell you, my husband. You do need to know, my love. Your son has a special gift of healing others."

Han looked surprised and gasped, "Ahhh! I knew Asho was special. I would hold him when he was a baby after work. My back hurt due to excavating the temple and doing the stonework. The baby would smile at me and the next day, I felt great. I never felt as good ever again. The nagging back pain comes every day. I have to take medicine for it. He has the gift, doesn't he?" She nodded her head.

Ash's curiosity increased. "Father, I found something very special in the temple."

His father smiled. "Your mother's family comes from a long line of devoted healers and seers. I knew that you would be special, and that is why I named you lil' Pure of Heart."

Ash cringed and interrupted, "Dad, let's get back to what's in the bag. I found one of the 'Keys of Life' that was carried by one of the pharaohs. It has some hieroglyphics that I've never seen before." With a surprised look, his father turned and motioned for them to follow him.

The small house had just two rooms and a bedroom. One room was an office with a couch and the other a small kitchen. Ash saw bookshelves of ancient books. His mother went to the fridge and grabbed beers for everyone. Then she got to work and started cooking in the kitchen. Ash pulled out the stone box and opened it in front of his father. Ash's father whistled, "What do we have here? Stolen artifacts? Like father, like son?"

Ash's dad explained, "I was working in the temple in the star room and was shocked when I saw a drawing in great detail of myself on the back of one of the loose stones. I realized that it wasn't a younger version of me but was in fact, a picture of you with your star birthmark." It was like the person who drew the picture knew that you and I would find the treasure of the temple. I didn't steal anything from the temple, but I did prevent the discovery of the treasure until you could find it. I fixed the crumbling stone but knew it wouldn't last."

Inside the first box, Ash pulled out a small golden triangle.

"Interesting, what else is there, Ash?"

Ash pulled out the second stone box and opened it. Inside he pulled out a small rock crystal jar and a small Key of Life.

"The next item is the reason why I ran, because I knew it was too sacred to be placed in the hands of the collapsing government."

Ash reached in the bag and pulled out a full-sized Key of Life. It was a treasure no one in history had found but was seen in the paintings found on many temples.

"The angel warned me that I was going to have to run, and he was right."

Ash's father smiled. "Son, it looks like you've hit the mother lode. It is late, and I know you're exhausted. I need to analyze all this and talk to my friend Brother Michael. We will talk in the morning."

Ash's mother had made a feast for them both. His father wanted them to relax and enjoy their meal as a family. His mother was so happy, and his father was beaming with joy. Ash had to admit it was one of his happiest moments in his life. His father was alive, and he realized he would treasure tonight's memories. Later on after the meal, Ash helped clean the dishes with his mother.

Ash woke up to hearing romantic whispering voices coming from his father's bedroom. He got up from the couch and said, "Time to take a walk. I need some coffee." Ash looked at his tousled hair in the mirror. He needed to get some fresh air and let his parents have some time together. He grabbed his bag of treasures, and he walked out to see the grounds. An elderly monk waved to him.

Saint Catherine

Ash followed the monk to an office filled with books, and he motioned for Ash to have a seat. He closed the door and the ceiling fans circulated the cool air. Ash smelled the aroma of coffee, and delicious fresh-baked rolls were sitting on the table.

"Ash, would you like some coffee?"

He was dressed in the brown robes of a Franciscan. Ash knew the Franciscans had been given privileges and custody in the Holy Land. The monk pointed to the small table with coffee and rolls.

"Please, Ash, have a seat. Let me introduce myself. I'm Brother Michael and a friend of your father's. We have lots to talk about."

Ash shook Brother Michael's hand. "Glad to meet you, and thank you. The coffee smells wonderful."

Ash took a sip and it seemed to be the best coffee he had ever tasted. "Awesome!" Brother Michael grabbed an apple from a bowl of fruit on the table. "I want to show you something, Ash. He cut the apple through the middle and set the apple in front on Ash's coffee cup saucer. "Do you see the pattern of the apple seeds?"

Ash looked and saw a five-pointed star pattern. "It's a pentacle or a five-pointed star." Ash picked up a roll, honey drizzled on its top, and began eating. Brother Michael smiled. "You are right, and in the story of Eden, the apple plays an important part. It is the apple on the Tree of Knowledge that Eve gives to Adam after the serpent convinces her to eat the forbidden fruit. The apple has the pentacle within its structure."

Ash smiled and picked up the apple on his saucer. He took a bite. "I love apples. The Ancient Egyptians call it Seba for the five-pointed star. They thought the sky was a great ocean and star watching was a religious and spiritual part of their life."

Brother Michael continued. "It is a fruit which grows from a seed and is pollinated by the bees. The apple was a gift. The pentacle with its triangles leads to mathematics and geometry. Who would have thought picking an apple would lead to such great knowledge? I think the point in Genesis is that men and women

Keys of Life

have the capacity to understand that knowledge together. Genesis comes from the Greek word for origin. The word 'gene' is within the word Genesis, as is 'Isis,' the Egyptian goddess of fertility. It is where DNA, the building block of life, resides." Brother Michael took the other part of the apple and ate it.

"It is the Egyptian goddess Nut who has all the stars on her dress, and the temple's ceiling is decorated in blue with yellow stars. I have been told if you eat one apple a day, it keeps the doctor away," Ash said with a small chuckle.

Brother Michael smiled at Ash's joke but knew this was more serious and the joke was on Ash. Brother Michael asked Ash, "Can you hand me the Key of Life, please? I have something of great importance to the world to show you."

Ash looked puzzled as he pulled the large Key of Life out of his bag and handed it to the monk. Brother Michael took a breath when he saw its beauty and unscrewed the bottom seal on the Key of Life. He poured into his hand a bunch of tiny seeds.

Ash exclaimed, "It's seeds, of course I get it. Seeds are the Keys of Life."

Brother Michael smiled. "It really is the key because what I hold in my hand is from the heavens. The Israelites were given Manna from the heavens so that they could live in the desert and not starve. It is an insurance policy for mankind in case of great catastrophe. In Norway, there is a seed vault that contains more than 100,000 seeds from all over the world, but they won't have these seeds. In Noah's flood, the Bible talks about saving the animals, but nothing is mentioned about the seeds of plants. The seeds are part of an ark in case mankind is in a cataclysmic extinction crisis. Now, let us see the crystal jar please."

Ash handed him the small jar. Brother Michael opened it up and smelled it. "Oh my, it is honey and according to legend, from the Garden of Eden. We will need to get a small sample to send off to our laboratories for confirmation of its age. The Egyptians believed when we die, we become stars in the sky. We start the journey. The Duat was the symbol painted on the gate of the afterlife. It was a star surrounded by a circle."

Brother Michael picked up another apple. "It's a circle which surrounds the star. The apple has great symbolism like the star. It holds the seed of life for if you plant one of the seeds, then a tree will grow and bear fruit. It is the archangel with the flaming sword who guards the gate of Eden and the Tree of Life. What is the archangel's name?"

Ash looked at him with a new understanding. "His name is Uriel, which means God is my light. He is the fourth archangel."

Brother Michael nodded. "He is said to have warned Noah and taught him how to build the ark. Uriel aided Enoch and instructed him on the stars, the sun's movements, and the moon. In many civilizations, there is a story of a Great Deluge which destroys civilization. Plato's story of Atlantis and Gilgamesh's story of the flood are written similar to the Bible's story of Noah. The story is about the giants of old and the Nephilim, who came from heaven, teaching man sacred knowledge. We see the Great Pyramid and Sphinx and gaze in wonder at the knowledge that the Egyptians had in their grasp."

Ash understood. "They are discovering amazing stone carvings even older than the pyramids. I think somewhere the sacred knowledge got lost or hidden."

Brother Michael poured Ash another cup of coffee. "Why do you think it was lost or hidden?"

Ash sipped on the coffee. "Some men aren't wise enough to handle some technologies. Nuclear bombs are man's nightmare. It's a technology that man isn't ready for because of its destructive power."

Brother Michael sighed. "Some men want to be god and want the power of life and death over not just man, but all life. God didn't create the earth for a profit. The Tree of Life is not for sale, and it's not there to make money. We are in troubling times, Ash. An organization known as the Watchers tries to keep the balance between the Pure of Heart and the Children of the

Nephilim. Your father came to help us in this battle, and he has been a wonderful asset to the community. Saint Catherine of Alexandria was a brilliant woman who taught great men, and she was killed because of her wisdom. Educated women were considered a big threat to some powerful men. It is said the Holy Family traveled to Alexandria because of Herod's edict to kill the first-born. A legend said Uriel brought John the Baptist and his family to the city. The Pure of Heart seem to be hunted over and over again. You know how important the Pure of Heart are to the world. The all-seeing eye of Ra is used by the Watchers, and you must keep an eye out for it."

Ash sipped his coffee and grabbed another roll. "The eye of Wadjet, the goddess, has a cobra rising up. It means the risen one, and it protects one in the afterlife."

Brother Michael smiled. "The eye is part of the Egyptian measurement system. The eye of Ra contains the information about the Egyptian fraction system. You can read Egyptian hieroglyphs?"

Ash nodded, "Yes, I can."

Brother Michael handed him a paper with pictures on it. "What you are looking at is the 'Our Father' in Mi'kmaq writing. Do you see anything interesting?"

Ash immediately saw the star. "I see the star symbol for Wojak, meaning in heaven, and I see the ankh, but it's upside down. Even the star symbol is tilted sometimes. I find this circle with the cross interesting because in Egyptian, it means goodness, truth, and beauty. It looks like its Mi'kmaq translation means holy. I've read about the similarities in the writing, and its controversy in the academic sectors."

Brother Michael nodded. "It could be that the stars look different in North America versus Africa. The path of the planet Venus in the north is a pentacle and is tilted. In the Mi'kmaq oral tradition, a story is told of a great deluge caused by the sun god's tears when he sees the wickedness of man. A great flood destroyed all the people on the earth except for one older man and a woman. They produced all the people on Earth. The circle

Saint Catherine

with the cross, or Celtic cross, is similar to the ankh. It is the key of life, and it is holy and sacred. You were right to run because on the Key of Life, the hieroglyphs of the Egyptians and Mi'kmaq are combined. This wouldn't have seen the light of day. The Nephilim and Watchers have been looking for the Keys of Life for centuries.

"I want to show you something, Ash, so if you're finished with breakfast, could you please follow me?"

"Sure," Ash said as he took one last sip of coffee. Ash followed the monk. Brother Michael removed his shoes and pointed to Ash to remove his. The gesture is to remember that they walk on holy ground. Brother Michael took him into the church of St. Catherine.

Brother Michael whispered to Ash, "Saint Catherine is one of the holy sites protected by sacred documents written by Muhammad. The story of Saint Catherine is that she was a beautiful princess who was educated and brilliant. She converted many of the learned scholars of her day. She was to be killed on the wheel of torture, but the wheel broke. Her head was cut off, and her body left to rot. The angels were said to have transported her body to the place God had been. Her body was discovered at Mount Sinai, and now we have the monastery. The icon of her is very old."

He pointed above Ash's head to a painting of a regal woman with a crown being placed on her head by angels. She was sitting on a throne surrounded by books of all kinds. Ash looked very carefully and saw a crystal ball in the corner of her books. The ball held a picture of the structure of an atom or the elliptical movement of the planets. It was quite amazing.

"What is that?" pointed Ash. "I know I've seen many kings holding it as a sign of power."

"Some call it the globus cruciger," Brother Michael said. "We're not sure what power it holds but Brother Saunhac knows where the crystal ball is, and your ankh is to be inserted in a hole in it. Ash, you have the ankh, which is the key. We need to unite

Keys of Life

the crystal ball and the key. It will only work if a Pure of Heart inserts the key."

The monastery was home to the Codex Sinaiticus, one of the oldest versions of the Bible. The library held many sacred texts and was filled with illuminated manuscripts. Ash knew his father was in heaven here.

"Dad was in here every day, wasn't he?"

Brother Michael looked solemn. "He missed your mother and you every moment and every day. He did it to save your mother and you. He made the most of a bad situation. Your father has served the monastery well over the years."

Ash looked at him. "I guess some people get another chance after all."

Brother Michael smiled. "Don't underestimate heavenly power. I've seen many unexplained things in my lifetime. Your mother and father are going to take you to Mount Carmel today. Your father wants you to see something."

Ash looked surprised. "What is at Mount Carmel?"

"I'll let your father explain, Ash. It's important, and he wants to spend some time with you. He wants to explain what happened. All I ask, Ash, is that you give him a chance to explain. You know what it's like when the Children of the Nephilim are on your trail."

The monk added, "My connection in Nova Scotia, Chief Saunhac, could help you with figuring out the importance of the ankh. He's a shaman of great power and knowledge. He is the leader of the Pure of Heart. Saunhac can help you understand this mystery. His health is deteriorating and so time grows short for him. I told him about your birthmark of a five-pointed star."

Ash looked up. "How did you know about that?"

Brother Michael smiled. "Your father told me all about you, Ash. Saunhac calls you a star child. One of you popped up every generation or so. Saunhac sent me a letter asking about the oldest synagogue in Magdala and the stone that was found. Magdala has a connection to Mary from Magdala. I have a picture of it."

Brother Michael showed a large stone with two trees of knowledge and another of life, which had a vine wrapped in a serpentine design around the trunk. The picture of the carved stone showed the symbol for the Flower of Life, two hearts, two vases, a menorah, and two pillars.

Ash looked at him. "The Pure of Hearts and the Flower of Life. I have the Keys of Life, or Seeds of Life, from the Book of Enoch. I do have to meet Saunhac."

Brother Michael smiled. "Yes, I agree, and so does your father."

Ash walked out of the church with Brother Michael. His parents were waiting for him. His mother smiled. "Ash, we're going take you for a drive. Your father wants to show you something important. Our goal is to blend in with the tourists. It's time to move on. He has another passport for you, and we're going to test it out in friendly territory."

"My dad is a master of all trades and forger of passports. What other talents do you have?"

His father smiled. "I'm a great marksman with a rifle scope, too. Any other questions, Ash?"

CHAPTER 46

A Father's Wisdom

They rushed to get their bags into the car and drove for an hour. It was time to fill up the car, and Ash's mom went to purchase some drinks for them. Ash and his father were alone waiting for her under an olive tree. Ash's father knew if there was a time to say what needed to be said, now was the time, for nothing was certain in life. Ash had not gotten along with his father since they met. He was in a lot of pain and confusion. Why did they have to be separated? Why didn't his father fight?

Ash's demeanor was one of total disarray and confusion, like being on a roller coaster, up one minute and down the next. His father was hanging on to his traditional ways and could not understand Ash's outspokenness and rashness.

Ash's mom said she would have never come along if she knew she was going to have to be the referee to their childish games. She knew she needed to be patient with them, and she could see them gaining respect for each other after each skirmish. It was time to build bridges, not destroy them. Ash's father and mother

A Father's Wisdom

knew that they had stayed at St. Catherine's too long. They had decided to start a new beginning as an old couple whose love never died. Ash was on a journey, and they knew he wouldn't be coming with them later on. They intended to enjoy this short time together.

Ash's father couldn't imagine what it was like growing up without him. He could have taught Ash everything about the world. He regretted leaving them, but he wanted them safe. Ash thought about the greatness of his father's sacrifice to keep them safe and the loss of his father's companionship and learning. Ash's mom was the peacemaker. She knew that for this relationship to work, she had to convince them that they needed each other more than they knew. Ash idolized his father when a child, and now the idol was an old man set in his ways.

Ash's dad turned to his son and spoke, "Asho, you know one thing I'm sure of is that it all has something to do with the chosen ones, or the Pure of Heart. I've also heard them called the 'Clean Ones.' In their hearts, they can feel and see the light that illuminates the righteous path, and they always take it. Some say it has something to do with astrology — that at certain times throughout time, when everything is in alignment, the chosen ones return. The Pure of Heart are born throughout time. The masses just never connected the dots. Many religions and secret societies knew about their arrival, usually heralded by significant signs from the stars. The first-born sons were killed by King Herod when the Magi stopped and told him of the stars' prediction that a new king was to be born. He killed the infants in the search of the Pure of Hearts, Jesus, and John the Baptist. In that time, the Nephilim didn't have a system for finding specific children. It was word of mouth. But as the population grew, other ways were needed. Rome used a census, which was another way to try to find the Pure of Heart. The problem was that in the early years, they focused only on male children. It wasn't until the Mother Mary that they had realized their mistake. The dark ones knew that they had a lot of catching up to do and needed to become more efficient. The use of the Spanish Inquisition, witch hunts, and the general oppression of women even in the world today makes it much easier to find the Pure of Heart. The power of the Pure of Heart tended to be stronger as they grew older. The Nephilim would kill or set them up to fall early on so they would die or never recover. The earlier they identified them, the easier it was to get them, but some would not fall and so they were murdered. The dark ones were called many names through the years, but they've always been the Children of the Nephilim.

"They are the puppet masters working behind the curtain, and they've ruled until now. Legend has it that a second coming will happen at the beginning of the Age of Aquarius and at the end of Pisces, and we believe it is underway."

Ash's mom returned with refreshments for all of them and they continued their journey. The sun was shining, and the car followed the highway. The view of the Mount Carmel mountains was filled with oaks, olive, and pine trees. They pulled the car over to stretch their legs and look at the view. His mother went to gather some rocks for her collection. Ash and his father stood looking at the beautiful view together.

Ash asked, "What happens to the Pure of Hearts when they fall and lose the light?"

His father explained, "A Pure of Heart can be corrupted. Many have been recruited into the Watchers organization. The Watchers were long ago united, but they've divided into two camps, the Dark Watchers and Light Watchers. The Children of the Nephilim consider all Watchers the same, but they're not. The Nephilim hunt down the Pure of Heart, and their goal is to corrupt them or kill them. The only way to escape is to fake your own death. It's not easy to do. They have investigation teams that are impeccable and thorough, and if they find you didn't die, they'll make sure you do. The earth's population is spiraling out of control of the Nephilim's grasp, and more and more treasures that have been once forgotten are now starting to be found. The Nephilim try to discredit everything that challenges their order of things."

A Father's Wisdom

His father continued while Ash listened intently, "History has been written by many men controlled by the Nephilim. They have agents and have infiltrated the most powerful agencies all over the world — CIA, KGB, and Interpol. All ancient books, documents, artifacts — and anybody wanting access to those items — goes through them. They've systematically tried to control all information given to the public. They use huge databases to store all their information. You must only believe what you see and experience in your heart, not something someone else tells you. Trust no one, and you might live a free man. Always look to the light in your heart and hold tight to love. Your mother said someday we'd all be together again, and that belief in love is what kept me going. If I hadn't left, they would've found you. We loved you so much that the thought of losing you was unbearable. We decided that it would be better to sacrifice being together to protect you. I never told your mother where or when I would leave. It was better she didn't know."

At this point, tears were forming in the old man's eyes and his voice was getting shaky. Ash's father voice revealed his age and quivered softly, "Even if we died trying, we felt it was better to die with you than to have you die without us." Ash had tears streaming down his face as he pulled his father into his arms.

Just as they started to hug one another, Ash's mom witnessed the love of father and son. The tears trickled down her face as she watched them embrace. She put her hand to her mouth to not make a sound. She didn't want to interrupt the perfect moment in time. It only lasted for a second, but the memory would last a lifetime.

Suddenly, Ash's dad's cell phone rang. It was Brother Michael. He said a young Light Watcher saw a caravan of SUVs coming toward the monastery. Brother Michael and Han believed they belong to Nephilim who were on the lookout for Ash and his mother. The monks had hidden the plane, but chances were, the Nephilim would find out they were there. They got back into the car and stepped on the gas.

The road was dusty, but there was no traffic. Tour buses flew down the road toward Northern Israel. Ash grabbed a bottle of water out of the small cooler.

"I've been to Mount Carmel before as a student studying antiquities. What's so important?"

His father smiled and looked at his son in the rear view mirror. "It's a UNESCO Biosphere reserve. It's filled with trees of all kind and caves. They found the burial grounds of Neanderthals and Homo sapiens. It was home to Elijah and the Essenes, who were from a place in Galilee called Nazareth."

Ash answered, "I know the Egyptian king Thutmose III thought it was a holy mountain, and Pythagoras visited Mount Carmel and said, 'It was the most holy of all the holy mountains.'"

Han listened to his son with pride. "You have studied hard, Ash. Pythagoras was a mathematician. He is a very mysterious fellow who had long hair, was a vegetarian, and had a birthmark in the shape of a star on his thigh."

His parent's eyes met, knowing Ash bore the same birthmark. Ash looked up. "A star for a birthmark? What does that mean?"

Han continued, "It means Pythagoras and you have a connection with the stars. The studies coming out on the extinction of the Neanderthals are very interesting. It was thought that there was no interbreeding of Neanderthals and Cro-Magnons. The new research coming out is proving that interbreeding may have taken place. It's said that Neanderthal DNA makes up one to four percent of the DNA in humans who do not live in Africa. They were thought to be big and stupid. The latest discoveries are showing they were big, but they made tools. They didn't just eat meat but plants, too. It's even said that some of man's immunity from diseases came from them."

Ash's mom asked, "Why did they go extinct?"

"Climate change is one possible reason, and they lived in small groups," Han said. They were big but slow, and that isn't good when you're running from danger."

A Father's Wisdom

Ash chimed in, "The faster guys won. It's survival of the fittest. It's like the story of David and the Giant. The bigger they are, the harder they fall."

Han pulled the car over, and the family found a spot under a shade tree. The view of Mount Carmel was breathtaking. Ash's father wanted to take a few minutes to show Ash some important historical points on the way. Beside, it would make them look like typical tourists and less suspicious.

Han smiled. "The country here has amazing history. Elijah's story is a fascinating one. He lived here, and he was taken up in the fiery chariot to the heavens. He has an experience with an angel who tells him to go on a journey. Have you ever had an experience like that, Asho?"

Ash put his hands through his thick hair. "I had a dream about one crazy experience." His father looked at him. "You should be honored that you were chosen. Pythagoras walked here and declared Mount Carmel sacred, and the Essenes from Nazareth lived here. The Carmelite monastery has been here for centuries, and St. Louis from the Crusades visited here, bringing back to France some of the hermits. He also brought a special treasure from Mount Carmel. St. Louis's Bible shows an illumination of the Great Geometrician, which shows God holding a compass creating the world. St. Louis and his mother, Blanche Castile, placed the sacred knowledge of Pythagoras in the illuminated manuscripts and in their cathedrals."

Ash answered, "Pythagoras learned much of his mathematics from the Egyptians and believed humans were a divine race. Josephus wrote that the Essenes and the Pythagoreans had similar lifestyles."

His father nodded. "Mount Carmel is a holy place with a history of oracles and visions of prophets. I wanted you to experience this sacred place where many holy men walked. Our love will always be with you."

He grabbed his son's hand and his wife's hand. "I want us to remember this moment and remember the love and pride I have in my only son."

Ash's mother kissed her husband and hugged Ash. They hurried on with their journey.

Ash felt like he was in a dream, but he picked up from his father that his journey was pointing to Canada and Nova Scotia. Ash's mother looked at him. "I had a dream last night about a woman you are going to meet in the future. Her name is Samantha Lafitte, and you're going to have an interesting relationship with her. Her name has something to do with pirates long ago. I'm not going to say any more about it." She held up her hand, and Ash knew that sign meant she couldn't say anything else without violating her code.

His father held her hand gently. "Your mother and I are going to go into hiding and retire in peace. We're going to spend our last years together. I'll give you some codes so that you will know where we are if you need us. We are fighting a war, Ash. It's a war that has been fought for millennium. The Children of the Nephilim must not gain control of the sacred objects of power. We are talking World War III, and the magnificent Earth that we know won't exist. It will be a dark and toxic place for animals and humans. Your passport passed inspection through the rigorous Israeli border agents. Saunhac will tell you more when you see him. Ash, we can't afford to lose this war."

Ash looked at his father bravely. "Bring it on then, and let's kick their butts."

Ash laid on his back in the back seat and looked through the window at the clear blue sky. He listened to his mother and father chattering away, savoring the moment. He nibbled on a grape and thought, the prophet Elijah didn't have to deal with a crazy angel named Uriel. How did he get so lucky?

Aziza, Ash's mother, wanted to stop in Megiddo to show Ash a great discovery her colleagues had notified her about. Aziza published articles for Antiquities Group Magazine. Megiddo was home to the oldest Christian church in the world. Prisoners found a mosaic floor in a prison.

Ash watched his mother's eyes sparkle with excitement. He forgot how much antiquities research was a great passion of hers. The guide smiled and took them to see the floor. The tile floor was in great condition and a centered octagon showed two fish. One fish was bigger and blue, and the other, smaller fish, rose-colored. Ash knew it was a sign the Gnostics used dualism. The fish was a sign of Christianity.

His father answered, "And this is a sign for the Age of Pisces, which is when Christianity began."

His mother smiled. "It could be a reference to the miracle catch of the 153 fish. It's in the Bible, where the Beloved Disciple recognizes Jesus and tells the Apostles. Jesus tells them to place the net on the right side, and they catch 153 fish. A few theorists believe Magdalene was the Beloved Disciple."

Ash looked at the inscription in Greek, which said the woman Akeptous donated a table in remembrance of the Jesus Christ.

His mother clarified. "It is a woman. In fact, there are four women's names that are inscribed on the floor, as well as the Roman Centurion and designer of the floor. The checkerboard pattern indicated the forces of black and white and the net used to catch fish. I am happy to see evidence of women's participation in the early church. It was here the 'love feast' took place, and in the catacomb, pictures show women sat at the table of the feast and participated."

Ash took pictures of the floor and thanked the guide. They left to continue their journey.

Chapter 47

Jerusalem and Meeting an Old Friend

Ash's dad decided to take them to Jerusalem. Ash knew Jerusalem was home to many religions. Wars continued even today for possession of the city and its holy sites. It was getting late so they headed for the Church of the Holy Sepulchre. Ash's parents were always very spiritual people. They didn't believe any religion held all the answers, but in fact, they were all connected. The law of treating one another as you would want to be treated lived in their hearts. Ash's mother tried to teach her son this lesson all his life. The idea that angels were spiritual beings who spoke and guarded human beings was seen throughout many religions.

The Church of the Holy Sepulchre was where it was believed Christ was buried. At one time, it was a temple to the goddess Venus. Ash knew many church sites were built on temples of pagan gods and goddesses. Ash's father showed him the wall that the Crusaders marked with crosses. The crosses made a checkerboard pattern.

"Lots of great men lost their lives protecting this city. Godfrey of Bouillon was one," Han said, showing Ash Bouillon's sword

Jerusalem and Meeting an Old Friend

hanging in a box on the wall. "The Kingdom of Jerusalem cross is there," he said, pointing to a square made of crosses on the sword. It emphasized the four corners of the world. The mosaic floor showed a compass-like design indicating this was the center of the world. Hans told Ash about the legend of the Templars and Crusaders who brought back something hidden in the tunnels under the Dome of the Rock.

They departed and headed for a restaurant that had an incredible view of the Dome of the Rock. The waiter motioned them to a table on the veranda, where Brother Michael waited for them. Hans wanted them to sit outside and enjoy the magnificent view of the golden dome shining in the lights.

The night was enchanting, and the food was delicious. Brother Michael sadly looked at his dear friend. "I fear this will be the last time we will break bread together, my friend. My sources have told me that we've overstayed our welcome, and we must all depart and separate."

Ash looked at his father sadly because it meant they were going to be apart again. Brother Michael showed Ash the video titled *Looking for Magdalene* by Cordy McDermott on his cell phone. The picture showed the symbolic hand positions on the Magdalene statue. The hands were crossed and made a square, which was connected by crosses. He pointed to Cordy's necklace, which had Mi'kmaq hieroglyphs and the Mi'kmaq star.

Brother Michael said, "The hands of Magdalene are like the Jerusalem Cross of the Crusaders and Godfrey of Bouillon. It meant a great secret resided here. Ash, here is her email. Our intelligence told us her name is Cordelia McDermott, and she's on her way to Montreal. You need to meet her. It's very important while you are in Canada for you to visit Chief Saunhac."

Brother Michael handed Ash his phone, and Ash emailed Cordy about the interesting statue. A beep returned on the cellphone. Cordy emailed back her thanks. Brother Michael urged Ash to try and meet her.

Ash's mom looked at the picture. "Oh, Ash, she is very pretty."

Ash rolled his eyes. "Mom, this is important work. I don't have time for women."

Ash's dad winked at his mother. Ash wrote in his email that he was an archeologist in Egypt and would be coming to Canada for business. Ash forwarded his website at the university and asked where could they meet in Canada.

Brother Michael smiled. "Good work, Ash, and send her your picture so she will recognize you. The Notre-Dame Basilica at Montreal would be a great place."

The cellphone rang and Cordy replied, "I'm going to Montreal. Perhaps we can meet there."

Ash wrote back, "Great. Look for me at the Basilica in Montreal." He sent her his picture. "You can also contact me through the university website. The statue has some interesting connections with Rennes Chateau in France. I hope we can meet. Ash."

Cordy responded, "Hope so, Professor Ash."

Everybody raised their wine glasses to celebrate their last supper together. The meal was delicious lamb and rice spiced with ginger and curry. Night fell on Jerusalem, and the stars shined in the sky. The golden Dome of the Rock was lit and all of a sudden, a strange light hovered over the dome.

Everyone turned and a hush of absolute awe fell on the patrons. Then chattering and screaming filled the air as people watched, amazed, a circular light object hovering over the dome. Cellphones popped out and cameras were flashing because it was an amazing sight. Suddenly, there was a flash of bright light and a rush of air as the object shot like a missile straight up in the air. People screamed in shock and fear as they watched the object instantly disappear.

Brother Michael looked at Ash's father. "Any relation to the star room and the objects that Ash found?"

Han rubbed his forehead. "I don't know, but maybe? We're not the only ones aware of their discovery."

Ash was stunned. "What are you guys talking about? That was

Jerusalem and Meeting an Old Friend

amazing. What was that? It was right over the Dome of the Rock and the Well of Souls."

Aziza looked at Ash. "Son, some things are unknown, even to us, but the heavens know. It wasn't an airplane because air space over the dome is forbidden."

Multiple sirens rang throughout the city, and they all agreed it was time to leave. Ash hugged his crying mother and hugged his father. He shook Brother Michael's hand and his parting words to his parents were just, "I love you."

Ash's tearful dad broke the bad news, "You have to leave for Canada, but we have no money to help you with, Ash."

Ash shrugged his shoulders. "What else is new? I've made it on my own this far, so here I go again. I can always go back to grave robbing like my fugitive father."

Han laughed. "That's my boy. Make me proud."

Brother Michael apologized for his lack of funds, but the Franciscans kept him on a strict budget. His parents and Brother Michael waved goodbye, and they separated, letting fate guide them.

Ash walked out of the restaurant with no money and no promise he would see the sun the next day when he heard a familiar laugh from a crowd down the street. It was Dirty Dottie. "Well, I'll be damned," he said, looking up at the stars. "This isn't funny, Uriel!"

CHAPTER 48

Children of the Nephilim and Ellen's Initiative

After watching hours and hours of close-up shots of the mysterious tomb robber's ass, Ellen spotted it.

Her head leaned forward for a closer look. "Well, I'll be damned. There it is."

She was alone because everyone had given up in the monitoring room. Ellen's gift was being persistent and stubborn. It paid off, for on the screen, enlarged, was a small red star birthmark on the front of the tomb raider's thigh. She would remember this, and she printed a copy of the screenshot.

Ellen's cell phone rang. She recognized the number of the informant within the Watchers. Ellen never said who it was. She was the only one who knew him. She had told the chairman that she had an insider. He was the only one who knew. She placed the phone to her ear.

"Hello my dear, I have some news for you. I believe the artifact you seek has been found."

Ellen smiled. This was the big break she was looking for. Ken would be so ticked off if she beat him out of the biggest find of the Nephilim.

"Where do I go to acquire it?"

He whispered, "I believe you need to pack your bags and take a holiday to Canada. I will give you instructions when you get here."

"I'll slip into some of my sexy lingerie, and we can mix business with pleasure," Ellen seductively suggested.

He chuckled. "I'll be waiting for your arrival and will text you with more information. It will be the greatest moment in your career, my dear, and mine. See you later, darling."

She heard the click and smiled — two big discoveries in one day. She held the photo of the well-endowed naked man with the red star on his thigh. It was a sign of a "star child," as the old ones called them. She hadn't heard of one for more than a century. He could be the only one, but they usually came in pairs. They usually were "Pure of Hearts."

She enjoyed the sport of hunting them down. "I'll find you. I always do."

CHAPTER 49

Cordy Goes to Montreal

Cordy ate breakfast after she worked out. Her cell phone rang. The woman on the other line identified herself as Bill McDermott's secretary, Molly. She had a sweet voice and was very cheerful. Molly told her, "He is excited to see you. You are to fly to Montreal by his private jet. The limousine will be there to pick you up at eight in the morning. You'll be a guest at the Hotel Champlain in Bill's penthouse suite. Do you have any questions or any places of interest you wished to see?"

Cordy quietly replied, "It sounds fine, Molly."

"I guess we will see you soon, and if I can do anything to make your trip more enjoyable, just let me know. My number will be in your email."

Cordy laughed. "Can you include a cute pilot or two for the plane trip?"

Molly giggled. "I'll see what I can do. Your grandfather is very happy you're coming. We'll be seeing you soon."

"Molly, could you inform my grandfather that I want to visit

Chief Saunhac as soon as possible?" Cordy asked in a tentative voice. "If he doesn't want to come, that's OK, but I want to see my great-grandfather."

Molly assured her, "I will let Bill know."

Cordy quietly whispered. "Thanks, Molly."

Molly hung up and Cordy held onto the phone. It would have been a nicer touch if her grandfather would have called her himself. She told herself not to get her expectations up or chances were that he'd be disappointing.

She opened up the paper to see an article in the Times Register about an anonymous donor giving $2 million to the Making the World Green Fund. The fund donated to local women who were planting trees all over Africa.

Bob had started work immediately. Bob emailed her that the office was in full swing, and if Cordy needed anything in Montreal, just to let him know. She emailed him telling her plans and her grandfather's address. Bob sent her a dossier on her grandfather. He was a self-made billionaire and well-respected Canadian businessman. He gave money to many charities and was a thirty-third-degree freemason of the Grand Lodge of Nova Scotia. His wife was Annie Saunhac, who died at age forty. She was a daughter of the retired Chief of the Mi'kmaq Indians. Her great-grandfather was over ninety years old and still alive.

Cordy got tears in her eyes. No one had told her that her great-grandfather was still alive until now. He was a great leader of the Mi'kmaq Indian Nation and a much-respected leader. Bob did a fantastic job of getting her information even her family didn't give her. She decided she wanted to see him as soon as possible.

Cordy was packed and waiting for the limousine to pick her up. Cindy was helping her get ready, and she heard Cordy's email come through on her cellphone with a picture of Ash.

"What a hunk, Cordy. Who is this absolutely gorgeous man, and where have you been hiding him?"

Cordy picked up the email and saw Professor Ash Von Lettow's picture on his university website. "Oh, that's Professor

Ash. He wanted information on the statue of Magdalene at the school. He saw it on Maggie's video. He said he would be in Canada at the same time, and we might meet."

Cindy gave a deep sigh. "Oh, Cordy, he is definitely sperm daddy material."

Cordy grabbed her phone. "Goodbye, Cindy. You're slowing me down," she said as she pushed Cindy out the door.

Cordy had gone shopping and updated her wardrobe. Her long chestnut hair fell over her shoulders. The white cashmere sweater dress with a low V-neck was covered with a tan wool shawl. Her tan leather high-heeled boots showed off her spectacular legs. Her light tan long-sleeved leather gloves touched the ensemble off.

Cordy would show her grandfather that her tastes were simple but elegant. She knew deep down that she wanted to make a good impression on him. The limo arrived, and the driver picked up her bags. She was off to Montreal and Nova Scotia. The corporate jet was waiting for her. She climbed the stairs and entered through the door. The stewardess smiled and pointed in the direction of an older, distinguished-looking man sitting in the back.

Cordy walked toward him, and he got up, smiling the whole time at her. He extended his hand to her. "May I introduce myself, I'm your Grandfather Bill."

He pointed to a seat, and she sat next to him. Cordy gave him a shy smile. He was not what she had expected. He was a handsome gentleman whose looks got better with age, and he was in great shape. She could tell he had a personal trainer. Bill wore a grey sweater over his white shirt and black wool pants.

"Please, Cordy, have a seat. I hope you are all right with me calling you Cordy."

Cordy kept smiling at him. What was the matter with her? Why was she so quiet and shy all of a sudden? Snap out of it, Cordy thought to herself. She sat next to Bill and buckled up.

So many emotions ran through her head when she looked into his blue eyes. Her father's eyes stared back at her. "Why don't I call you Grandpa Bill? I've always wanted to say that, for so many years. My dad called you that when I was tiny. My dad loved you, Grandpa Bill, and he told many fish tales with you in most of them. He loved fishing and sailing with you."

Tears welled up in Bill's eyes. "Your father and I had some wonderful times together. Unfortunately, we sometimes didn't see things the same, but I loved him always."

Cordy grabbed her grandfather's hand. "Grandpa Bill, Dad wrote a letter to you before he died. He left it on the table before mom and he left on the plane. I've kept it all these years for some reason. I never opened it."

She pulled out of her purse a white envelope addressed to him. She handed it to him, and Bill reached for it tenderly. The plane had taken off but both of them were oblivious. The stewardess asked them if they would like a drink.

Bill answered, "Sallie, I'd like a cup of coffee, please."

Cordy asked. "Do you have any hot tea?"

"We have everything, including champagne."

Cordy shook her head, "Tea is just fine."

Bill looked at Sallie. "We'll have some cheese, bread, and salad for lunch. And if you have some croissants back there, bring them, too. Thank you, Sallie."

Sallie hurried off and the pilot came on the intercom, "Ladies and gentlemen, we'll be arriving into Montreal in three hours, so relax." Bill's hand shook slightly as he opened the letter from his son.

Dear Dad,

I am taking my wife on our first trip since Cordy was born. I know you and I haven't seen eye-to-eye on many things. Mom said we were too much alike and both stubborn. I'm a father and older now, so things look different. I wanted you to know that lately I have had the feeling that my family was being watched. You warned me about the

Keys of Life

danger we were in. I'm worried, Dad. If anything happens to me, please watch over Cordy. I miss seeing the chief. I want him to see his great-grandchild. He would be proud of her. You would be proud of her. She has the Saunhac gift. I plan to take Cordy home to Nova Scotia and visit the family. That includes you, Dad. The chief told me it was time to bury the hatchet. It was a dream visit. I knew when I woke up that it was true. I want to say I'm sorry for getting angry with you, and I love you, Dad. Mom and you were wonderful parents, and I hope I can be, too.

Your loving son

Inside the letter, Bill pulled out a picture of his son's family. Cordy was seven then, dressed in her First Communion dress. She was holding her father's hand and her mother's hand. Bill could not stop the tears from running down his cheeks. He knew that the Nephilim had assassinated his son because he was a Pure of Heart. Cordy had tears in her eyes and looked at him with sorrow.

"Can I ask what he said, Grandpa Bill?"

Bill showed her the picture. "He was going to bring you to see me, and he told me he was sorry for getting angry. He told me he missed the chief and me. Life plays cruel jokes on some of us, Cordy. I missed out on being with you all those years, and we are going to make that up now. I want you to wear this pin for me. It's a family heirloom."

He handed her a tiny gold pin, which had the McDermott heraldry on it. "The crosses stand for the Crusades. The family participated in three of them." He pinned it on her sweater. "The McDermotts were fighters, and one of them fought for Ireland's freedom. It is yours now. I would like you to wear it as often as you can. I have found it to be a good luck charm." Cordy smiled as he pinned it on. "I'll wear it proudly, Grandpa Bill."

Sallie handed Cordy the teacup with assorted teas and Bill, the cup of coffee. She placed an assortment of cheeses and breads before them. The salads came later and champagne was poured into their glasses. Bill raised his glass in a toast. "Here is to family and good times to come." Cordy raised her glass, too.

Cordy started eating the delicious cheese and bread. "Grandpa Bill, why didn't anybody tell me about great-grandpa? I want to see him."

Bill looked at her determined face. "Don't worry, Cordy. I'll take you to see the chief. He is retired Chief Saunhac now, but he is still getting around at the old age of ninety. I believe Mother Agnes was the one who didn't think it was best for you to know he was still alive. I don't know why, but she could've been worried that you would leave school. The chief and Mother Agnes didn't always see eye-to-eye on things. They both are very religious, but he has the Mi'kmaq spirit and abides by the old laws. I think she was afraid you would fall under his spell. He is quite a character and a real snake charmer. I mean that literally, a snake charmer. Your grandmother Annie and he would always argue about the old ways changing or being lost. She did everything she could to hang onto her heritage. I think she would be so happy that you're meeting him. I have some business in Montreal, but the next day we'll drive into Halifax. We'll see the chief and take a family boat trip. I hope you don't get sea sick."

Cordy gave him a sheepish look. "I guess we will find out."

Chapter 50

Dottie Takes Ash for a Ride

Ash walked toward Dottie's voice. As he got closer to the sound, he passed many outdoor restaurants lit by strings of lights dangling on their roofs. He could now see her with four other elderly women. Ash yelled out to be sure, though Dottie was hard to forget, "Dottie, is that you?"

Dottie laughed, surprised to see him. "Is that my Ash man?"

The elderly women were hard of hearing, and they mumbled, "Ass man?"

Dottie sighed, "No girls, that's his name — ASH. You need to turn up your hearing aids."

Dottie winked at him. "I see you made it out of Egypt in one piece, but I'm a little disappointed because you have more clothes on."

The girls' hearing perked up. "What are you doing in a holy place like Jerusalem, Dottie?"

Dottie laughed. "I'm on a Mediterranean bachelorette party, and the girls wanted to see Jerusalem. At our age, you can never

Dottie Takes Ash for a Ride

pray too much, and we heard that during the Crusades they forgave you your sins here. Let's face it, I have a million and can use the indulgences. Why the long face, Ash?"

Ash said glumly, "I'm desperate to get out of Israel, Dottie. I have to get to Canada, and it's an emergency."

Dottie smiled. "Maybe we can work out a deal. How about you pretend to be my last fling before my wedding? I can get you to Greece, and it's in such an uproar and mess, you can slip through the authorities easier. I'm willing to pay you for your time. You can pick up a cruise ship that goes right to Montreal."

Knowing Dottie, Ash said, "I'm making it perfectly clear, Dottie, that there's no hanky-panky. Just a good show. How much is it worth to you?"

Dottie looked him over. "How about one ticket to Canada?"

Ash smiled. "Sold!" He turned his head up to the sky and whispered, "Curse you, Uriel." Dottie laughed and introduced him as her escort to her stunned friends. They headed to the cruise ship waiting at the docks to take them to Greece.

When they got to the cruise ship, Ash was already regretting his decision to go with Dirty Dottie. He had no money, and Dottie was already saying Ash was going to owe her big time. The girls just roared with laughter. As they turned the corner, the ship was docked at the pier. Joyce, Dottie's best friend, pushed everyone back. "DD, they are watching the ship." Dirty Dottie's close friends called her DD for short. The ship gate had about five Israeli soldiers and three undercover officers patrolling it.

Ash said, "They could be part of the Duvdevan, an undercover unit of the Israel Defense Forces." It was the first time Ash worried about his parents. How could the Nephilim get governments to mobilize on such short notice? Ash was thinking to himself that it would be a miracle if they lived much longer.

"I've got an idea," Dirty Dottie said. She started to take off her clothes. The older women, Dottie's friends Brigitte, Joyce, Margie and Shari, were used to her naughty escapades. Her friends let out a small yell in unison, "DD, what the hell are you doing?"

Keys of Life

She answered, "I am going to act drunk, so Ash, you put on my dress. Brigitte, you give him your hat. Joyce, you give him your shawl, and Margie, you take off your high-cut boots. Shari, lend him your scarf.

"This is crazy," Ash said. "I'll get caught."

The light illuminated Dirty Dottie's silhouette. She was the best-preserved woman in the world. Ash thought, with a body like that, they wouldn't be looking at anything else.

"Well, Ash man, what do you think? I do give some of the credit to my push-up bra and Victoria's Secret panties," Dottie said with a wicked laugh that she must have practiced her whole life.

"DD, I am in, and this may just work."

Dottie winked at him. "I wish you were in, Ash."

Joyce said, "Damn it, DD, you have company, you wicked woman."

Ash reached in his pocket and pulled out Dottie's knife. Dottie smiled, "I see you still have something to remember me by, Ash."

He smiled back, and he cut the back of the heels from the boots. His feet were too big for them, but everything else fit well. With his blond hair, his beard was barley noticeable as they started to turn the corner. Dottie said, "I wish my ass looked that good in that dress."

Joyce got on one side of Dotty and Bridget got on the other, while Ash, Margie, and Shari walked behind. As they got closer to the boarding area, the men started to laugh at Dirty Dottie. Ash noticed everyone's eyes were on Dottie. She stopped when she got right up to the soldiers, and Ash, Margie and Shari went right up the gangplank. They got to the top. Ash didn't have his identification to get on the ship and was stopped.

Margie whispered to the ship's Officer Antonio, "For God's sake, this guy is a surprise stripper for Dottie's birthday party. We will make sure he's off before the ship sails. Come on, Antonio, here's a hundred."

274

Dottie Takes Ash for a Ride

Antonio winked and pocketed $100 bill. That was all it took.

Money on a ship makes the rules, and the girls were loaded with cash. They took Ash to their cabin as fast as they could. It was about ten minutes before Dirty Dottie, Joyce and Bridget showed up and then the party began. They couldn't believe that they had just smuggled a fugitive aboard. Ash had been to some wild parties in college, but these old girls were out of control.

Around three in the morning, it started to wind down, and Dotty said, "Ash, it's time to go to bed. Let's go." She grabbed his hand and they went down the hall. Ash started to worry as he pictured a stateroom with only one small bunk. She might be expecting him to share it with her. She walked up to a door that said Presidential Suite.

Ash said, "DD, you are going to get us in trouble?" She put in the key and unlocked the door. In she fell, Ash grabbing her before she hit the floor. "Come on, girl, let's get you to bed."

"Ash," Dottie said, drunkenly slurring her words. "I know you're a virgin, and I can't believe it. You are just so damn good-looking. I have a king-size bed, and I promise you will be a king when we get to Greece in two days. Will you give a girl a chance to have some fun? Just talking as if we, well you know..." Dottie winked.

"Dottie, I appreciate the offer to share the bed, but I don't think you got that nickname for nothing," Ash said, winking.

Dottie laughed, "You are too smart, Mr. Ash from Egypt."

Ash assured her, "I will be just fine out on the couch, but you did save my life, so anything you tell the girls, I will just go along with."

"Oh, Ash man, you're the best. This will be the most fun I've had in years." Dottie thought to herself and then said, "I will get you some clothes early in the morning, but you can use my robe until then."

Dottie went into the bedroom and brought out a thin, white silk robe. It was sheer. Ash smiled. "Thanks, Dottie. The robe will work. It was that or your black dress."

At least Shari was able to hide Ash's backpack in her shopping bag, but she had no room for his clothes. Dottie threw Ash a pillow and blanket and then, as she was closing the door to the bedroom, she let him know with a wink, "If you change your mind, the door won't be locked." Ash rolled his eyes after that comment. Dottie collapsed on her bed and soon was snoring.

Ash hit the couch hard and was out instantly. As he drifted off, he had no idea how his mom and dad were going to get out. Ash woke up, and he was lying on his stomach hugging his pillow with both arms and having a morning erection that just wouldn't quit, before he realized that Dottie was sitting next to him, rubbing her hand over the silk that covered his firm ass.

Ash didn't even look around. He whispered, "Dottie, I know it's you."

She just giggled and said, "Oh, to be young again!!"

Ash asked, "Dottie, what time is it?"

She got up and opened the drapes revealing a beautiful view of the ocean. "It's two in the afternoon, and I already have your clothes and a swim suit for you. I took one of the boots with me and got you a pair of saddles that were about two inches bigger and some tennis shoes. I hope you love everything and it fits."

"OK, DD, you can stop rubbing my ass now," Ash said as he lay there. " I can't move right now because I might poke your eye out, if you know what I mean."

Dottie smiled wickedly. "You know, as a matter of fact, I do, Ash. You see, when I went to get your clothes early this morning, you didn't have your blanket on, and the robe was pulled apart, and let's just says you were standing at attention."

"Oh, Dottie, I'm sorry," Ash said, red-faced.

Dottie smiled. "I'm not. It was quite spectacular, and I've seen a lot of soldiers salute, if you know what I mean."

Ash laughed. "I bet you've lost count by now. Did you have the decency to cover me back up?"

"What do you think, big boy?"

Ash shook his head. "I was afraid of that."

"I just decided to sit back and enjoy my first cup of coffee for twenty minutes because I was timing just how long it would stay

Dottie Takes Ash for a Ride

at attention. I could have taken a picture, but it's burned into my memory forever," Dottie said, rolling with wicked laughter.

Ash smiled sheepishly. "Well, get ready to be saluted one more time. I'm getting up." Ash jumped up, and mister happy was peeking out of the curtains of the robe. Ash asked Dottie, "Where's the shower?"

Dottie pointed to the bedroom. "Go in the bedroom, and it's on the left."

Ash stayed under the shower for what seemed to be an hour. When he got out, Dotty was sitting by the bedroom door sipping her coffee.

Dottie whispered, "Ash, do you remember what you promised last night?"

Ash nodded. "Yes, I would go along with whatever story you would tell the girls." Dottie laughed, "Well it's show time. The girls are out in the living room, and I put up the pillow and blanket, so let the games begin."

Ash had a towel wrapped around him, and he decided to give the lady's a show. He walked out as if he didn't know they were there and said, "Dottie, honey, where are my clothes?"

He acted surprised to see the ladies and turned around and went back in the bedroom. He could hear them laughing. Dottie yelled out, "I put them in the closet next to the bed on the right."

Ash decided to play the part. After all, Dottie probably did save his life. Ash yelled, "Thanks, darling. I see them."

Ash started to look through the many packages. Dottie had purchased a small wardrobe for him, and everything was expensive. There wasn't a price tag that was under $500. Ash put on a pullover shirt and some white jeans. It was the first time in a long time he put on white bikini-brief underwear. She even got him two duffle bags and a book bag. Ash knew it was because he was on the run. Dottie, somehow, deep down, understood what he was going through.

Ash was still playing the part. "Dottie, get your boney little ass in here so I can thank you proper."

Ash could hear more giggling and laughter coming from the front room and thought, do women giggle until the day they die? Dottie let out a "Coming, dear" and came into the walk-in closet only to see Ash standing in front of her dressed to the nines. Dottie couldn't believe her eyes. To say he was the most handsome man on the ship was an understatement.

Ash walked up to Dottie and said, "From the day I met you in Egypt coming out of the water, I have been in need of clothes, but Dottie, this is too much."

Ash reached over to hug Dottie and as soon as he did, he realized it was a mistake. Dottie's hand went right to Ash's butt cheeks. Ash pulled her arm off his ass. "Dottie, Dottie, I don't think you stop for a minute, do you?"

Dotty giggled. "The day I stop grabbing is the day I start crabbin', and no one likes a crabby old woman. Beside, it keeps me young at heart. To be honest, men put up with me, and sometimes, I even get lucky."

Ash laughed. "Dottie, you will always be young at heart."

Dottie pushed the door open. "Come, Ash. You need to get packed because we're docking tomorrow. I hope you have a passport. I'm not getting off the boat in my underwear. You'll have to swim for it."

Ash nodded. "Yes, Dottie, I have two passports, one under Ash and one my dad had made for me under my real name."

"Your real name. What's your real name?"

Ash knew what was coming. "Why don't you laugh first and then I will tell you."

"Come on, Ash, it can't be that bad."

"It's Asho," he mumbled.

Dottie looked puzzled. "Oh, that can't be. I don't hang out with assholes." She started to laugh. "If I were you, I would keep that one to myself. What were your parents thinking?" Ash shook his head. "They weren't thinking, but it means 'pure of heart.'"

Dottie patted him on the shoulder. "Well, they did get that right."

Dottie Takes Ash for a Ride

"Thanks."

"You should stay in the cabin until the ship docks because you are too good-looking for people not notice you. I'll bring you some dinner back later."

Ash started packing and realized he needed to somehow disguise his artifacts. He placed the "Made in China" stickers from his clothes onto the boxes and the Ankh.

"The girls and I better get back out there. I'm sure everyone is missing us. Get your rest. I want you rested if you change your mind tonight." Dottie open the door as she laughed.

Ash walked into the front room and thanked the ladies one more time for getting him on the boat. As they marched out the door, Ash yelled out to Dottie, "Bring back some chap stick, DD. My lips are chapped from all that kissing last night."

He could hear giggling and laughter down the passageway even with the door closed. A surprise awaited DD when she arrived later that evening. Ash was asleep on the couch in his white bikini underwear. Dottie knew he did it just for her, and in return, she just let him sleep. She poured a stiff drink and headed for bed. As she walked through the bedroom door, she thought, "Maybe I am slowing down or maybe for the first time, I finally met a nice guy. It took a few years."

The sun shone through the cabin window as she woke up. Ash was already out of the shower and dressed. Dottie yelled out, "Ash, I got you a travel gift card for cruise liners and airlines. It has ten thousand on it. That should take care of where you need to go. I have the money. You were worth it."

Ash came into the bedroom only to see Dottie lying tastefully naked with a white sheet covering strategic areas. Ash shook his head and covered his eyes. "Dottie, you never give up, do you?"

Dottie seductively said, "Would you have me any other way, my Ash from Egypt?"

She dangled the gift card. Ash knew he had to come over and get it, and she pulled him in for a hug. Ash knew what was coming but leaned in for the hug as he felt Dottie's hand grabbed his

Keys of Life

ass. This time she squeezed and shook it as if she was shaking a hand. She laughed, "You're so nice-looking, Asho. I'll never forget you." Dottie gave him a sweet smile. Ash took the card and said, "Dottie, how will I ever be able to repay you, besides sex?" "If you get out of this alive and you settle down, get married and you have a baby girl, promise me you will name her Dottie. I'll know when I'm long gone, you will smile and remember me. This would make me a happy woman."

Ash played along. "I will, my love." And then he turned and was gone. As he reached the door, he could hear a vibrating sound coming from the bedroom and smiled.

CHAPTER 51

Montreal, Canada

Matthew 5:8 Blessed are the pure in heart: for they shall see God.

Cordy and her grandfather stopped in Montreal first. He had some business to attend, and he wanted to show her the city. Cordy's Canadian passport worked without a hitch. Her dual citizenship was approved, and she had no difficulties getting through customs. Bill gave her a bit of Montreal history.

"Montreal is the second largest city in Canada. Its original name was Ville Marie, which means City of Mary. Mount Royal is the triple-peaked hill in the center of town."

Cordy looked out the window to see the beautiful city. French was its official language. Bill could speak fluent French. Cordy learned to speak French from her father when she was little.

Bill continued, "The Iroquois had been the first residents of Montreal when Jacques Cartier arrived. But by the time Samuel Champlain arrived, the Indians had abandoned the city. Their population was decimated by disease brought over from Europe. You talk about bioterrorism: bring smallpox and measles into a population which has no immunity. It was devastating."

Bill took her to his penthouse and introduced her to his staff. Rose was the chef, and Maria was the maid. They were two middle-aged ladies who had worked for her grandfather for years. An older man named Jacques had been his butler for years. Jacques helped coordinate dinner parties and made sure Bill looked his best. He made sure the household ran smoothly. Cordy could see that Bill was committed to his business. Her grandfather was a workaholic whose life had been running his companies. Her father realized this and so did she in the little time she was with him. It would be a couple of days before she saw the chief, and she wondered what he would be like.

Her room had a breathtaking view of the city. Everything was done in a contemporary European style. It fit Bill's sleek, fast-track lifestyle but missed a woman's touch.

She did spot a picture of her grandmother. A petite strawberry blond with green eyes stared back at her. It wasn't what she expected. Bill had told her the Mi'kmaq's history went back to when the Europeans came to the New World. They intermarried with the settlers.

Rose knocked. "Miss Cordy, do you need anything?"

Cordy opened the door. "No, everything is just wonderful, Rose. I'm unpacked, and I love the wonderful view of the city. You have to understand this is all new to me. I'm not used to being waited on."

Rose smiled. "You let me know if there's anything I can get you."

Cordy walked into the front room and looked at Bill as he sat on a white leather couch reading some mail. He looked up at his amazing granddaughter in front of him. His heart tightened and he realized how lucky he was that she came to see him. He had not realized until that moment how lonely he was, and Cordy resembled his beautiful Annie, especially when she smiled.

Bill asked, "How is everything, Cordy? If you need anything, just let Rose know and she'll get it for you."

Cordy sat next to him. "Oh, the room is wonderful, and the view is magnificent. I saw a picture of Grandma, and she had such a sweet smile."

Montreal, Canada

Bill smiled. "Don't let that smile fool you, because she was quite a wild one. A mountain climber, pilot, expert marksman, and the best cook in Canada, she was the most incredible woman. I never could find anybody to compare to her. You look like her, and you're fearless like her, too."

Cordy smiled at him. "It sounds like she was a pioneer for women's rights."

Bill had a twinkle in his eye. "She was one helluva wonderful woman, and I loved her madly." He changed his voice to a more serious tone. "I hate to do this, but I have to go to the office for a meeting. I want you to walk around the city and see Montreal while I'm gone. I'll be back for dinner, and I have a reservation at Andre's."

Cordy smiled. "I'll take a walk in the park across the street." She didn't tell him that she too had a meeting. Bob was in town, and he was going to have lunch with her and give her an update on their business endeavors. She got up and picked up her sweater. "I'll be just fine," she assured him.

Bill got up and hugged her. "OK, then I'll meet you here at about six for dinner. I'll pick you up and call you on your cell phone." He walked to the door and looked back at her. "I'll see you soon. I love having you here."

Cordy smiled and waved to him to go. "I love being here. I'll be fine."

Cordy walked through the streets of Montreal. She had bought a guidebook with a map at a local shop. One of the oldest buildings in the city was the Saint Sulpice Seminary, founded in 1641. Father Jean Jacques Olier founded the Society of Saint Sulpice. The Seminary was headquartered in Paris, France. It was known for its great academics at a time when schools were very few in number.

A Vincentian seminary was created by Bishop Dubourg in Perryville where her family had lived. Olier was good friends with Saint Vincent de Paul, and they created the secret society Compagnie du Saint –Sacrement. It was a charitable society but also a militant association for the defense of the Church.

Cordy's aunt was a Daughter of Charity, which was founded by Saint Vincent de Paul and Saint Louise de Marillac. Saint Louise de Marillac was born out of wedlock, and her father was Michel de Marillac. He was an advisor to Queen Regent Catherine de Medici. Her uncle married his daughter to Antoine le Gras, who was a possible relative of Cordy's mother's de Grasse family. The sisters' main focus was helping the poor and the sick. The Daughters of Charity created a hospital system throughout the world.

Cordy looked up at the heraldry above her, which showed the symbol of the Saint Sulpicians. The elaborate symbol was made of triangles connected to each other. Cordy's hand went to the golden triangle in her pocket that she had gotten in the statue repair shop in St. Louis.

The Sulpicians were the feudal lords of Montreal. They encouraged settlers to come from France, Ireland, and Scotland and gave them land. The Sulpicians convinced the Mohawk to move, and King Louis XIV granted them Kanesastake. The Mohawk later found out that the Sulpicians had changed the grant, replacing the Mohawk name with theirs.

Notre Dame de Bon Secours chapel was the inspiration of Sister Margeurite Bourgeoys. Cordy had read about this incredible female pioneer. The men realized that the colonies would not exist without women. She braved the voyage to the New World. The Ursulines offered to let her to stay with them, but she refused. She didn't want the cloister life but instead preferred to be more active and helpful to the poor.

Cordy liked her because she compared her sisters to the Apostles. Magdalene was called the Apostle to the Apostles, so Margeurite saw her sisters doing the same work. The priests felt threatened, and the bishop kept fighting her for being too active. The fear was that the sisters would preach and teach the word. It was a job left to the priests. She persevered and won. She was friends with Olier and Saint Vincent de Paul.

Cordy toured the inside of the beautiful chapel of Notre Dame de Bon Secours. Our Lady of the Harbor stood at the top

Montreal, Canada

of the chapel. Stars circling her head and she rested atop a globe. Inside the chapel, there was a beautiful picture Mary the Mother with her feet on the crescent moon. The imagery was very similar to Cordy's miraculous medal.

A statue of an archangel stood next to Mary with a scale in one hand and a sword in the other. Cordy looked at her guidebook. "I wonder what the archangel's name is?"

A tall, sandy-blonde-haired man in his thirties was looking at the angel, too. He heard her question. "He's Archangel Uriel, if you want to know. He is one of the seven archangels who have an especially weird sense of humor."

Ash thought of his dream and continued, "He stands at the gate of Eden with a fiery sword. Uriel is the angel of repentance."

Cordy looked at him confused. "Uriel! I was thinking of Michael."

Ash smiled. "Uriel and Michael get mixed up and interchanged sometimes. They have the same job delivering justice." Ash took in the gorgeous woman standing beside him. There was something familiar about her. She was mighty fine. Long thick hair, curves that would drive men wild, and a sweet smile. Her voice was musical and her laugh infectious. It suddenly came to Ash where he knew her from and Ash couldn't help himself.

"You know in Egypt there is a god who weighs the heart on a scale to see if one goes to heaven. Thoth records the man's life, and Maat's feather was placed on the scale to see if the heart was true. If it was too heavy, then another god called the gobbler ate it. The soul would cease to exist. Maat was the goddess of truth and justice. They were looking for only the Pure of Heart to go to heaven."

Ash stuck out his hand. "Let me introduce myself before I get too boring. My name is Professor Ash Von Lettow, and I recognized you from your video, 'Looking for Maggie.' I'm an archeologist here on vacation, and I believe we've corresponded via email. I was hoping to get to meet you while you were in Canada."

Cordy couldn't believe it, and she recognized him as soon as he said his name. She smiled and shook his hand. "I've seen your

Keys of Life

picture on your website. What a small world. Yes, my name is Cordy McDermott, and I'm so glad I'm meeting you, Ash. I was just thinking I needed to email you. The Pure of Heart are special and supporters of truth and justice. It seems that Archangel Uriel is part of that legend, standing up there with his scale. I've heard stories about the Pure of Heart. It could be compared to the Sacre Couer or the Sacred Heart."

She pointed to the symbol on Christ's chest of the flaming heart on the statue next to the door. Cordy's surprise showed. "It's amazing that we should meet like this."

Ash laughed. "Yes, what a coincidence. I was hoping we would bump into each other someday." The surprise and delight showed in his voice. "I want to know more about the statue. I'm heading over to the Notre Dame Basilica. Do you want to come with me?"

Cordy looked at her watch and answered, "I have time, and I'd love to."

Trees lined the street. Ash was nervous and when he was nervous, he babbled away. "You know, that picture of Magdalene was unusual because of her hands. They were folded in a mysterious symbolic way. Some say it indicates a secret. At Rennes Chateau in France, another Magdalene kneels with her hands in that same position. Rennes Chateau is full of mystery because of an Abbe Sauniere who was said to have found a secret. I did some research, and it's been seen in other places. Others believe it holds the key to a mystery." Cordy listened to Ash as they walked closer to the towering Notre Dame Basilica. She added, "I went to where the children bought the statue. Mr. de Villiers said he didn't know what it meant, but I'm not sure I believed him. He did know about Rennes Chateau and the mystery there. He acted very strange, and he gave me a mysterious looking antique box for curing his cat. My friend emailed me that the shop was destroyed after I saw him. I'd like to show you what was in the box since you're an archeologist."

Ash picked up her worry. "I would love to see it, but I can't promise anything."

Ash and Cordy looked at a statue atop the fountain of an early French settler, Paul de Chomeday, holding a flag. He had erected the cross on Mont Royal and was the first governor of Montreal. Water spewed out of the mouth of what looked like a pagan water god. On the corner was a man named Charles le Moyne holding a sickle and wheat. A man with his gun and faithful dog stared at them.

Ash read the plaque, "It is a tribute to the men who defended Montreal against the Iroquois."

Cordy looked at the woman holding the little girl. "She is Jeanne Mance and one of the founders of Montreal. She was supported by Anne of Austria, King Louis XIII, and the Jesuits. She helped convert the natives. She built the first hospital and was the first lay nurse in Montreal."

Cordy pointed to the Montreal flag symbols of the fleur de lis for the French, the thistle for the Scots, the shamrock for the Irish, and the rose for the English with the red cross of the Crusaders on the white background. They arrived at the Basilica, and Cordy read from her guidebook.

"The Jesuits were the first owners of a small chapel but in 1657, the Sulpicians decided to build a bigger one. In the 1800s a bigger church was built and later called Chapel of Notre dame du Sacre Couer. It was consecrated in 1891."

Ash smiled and said, "The 'Sacred Heart,' as I said, has similar symbolism in Egyptian stories."

Cordy continued, "Sainte Chapelle was used as an inspiration. Sainte Chapelle in Paris was built by Saint Louis and was where he housed the crown of thorns. It has twin towers. The eastern tower holds 10 bells, and the opposite tower holds 12 and is called "Le Gros Bourdon."

Ash laughed, looking up at it. "The large bumblebee."

Cordy gazed at the church. "The Virgin Mary represents Montreal, John the Baptist represents Quebec, and Joseph represents

Canada." She pointed to the statues on the outside of the church. Cordy impulsively said, "Are you bored? Because I'm not. I like you, Ash."

Ash smiled back. "The feeling is mutual. I'm not bored. I love this stuff. I find it fascinating to see Egyptian imagery interconnected with Christian symbolism."

They both walked in to see a sapphire blue interior and a ceiling filled with gold stars above their heads. It was like looking up into the starry skies. The stained glass windows had come from Limoges, France.

The altar front showed a woodcarving with a copy of da Vinci's *Last Supper*. The feminine-looking John sat next to Jesus, who had in front of him a gold cup. Cordy pointed to the cup. "The Holy Grail, if you remember the stories of Arthur and his knights. It is quite beautiful."

Ash pointed to the center of the altar, which depicted the Crucifixion. Mary Magdalene was kneeling at the foot of the cross. Her hand was touching his feet and her head bowed directly below his feet. It almost looked like she was being baptized in his blood. It was extremely intimate, and it showed the deep connection Jesus had with her. A vase stood next to her.

Ash recognized the Ark of the Covenant to the right. "Moses is standing by the ark with the rays coming from his head. Aaron sacrificed his lamb. Melchisidech offered bread and wine over a stone altar, and Abraham offered Isaac. The theme was about sacrifice, human sacrifice and animal sacrifices."

Cordy caught a glimpse of it. "The golden triangle is above the pulpit." The pulpit was a spiral staircase. The prophets Ezekiel and Jeremiah were sitting below, but a golden triangle with golden rays coming from it was at the top. Ash whispered to her, "Archeologists know of the story of the Ark and its construction. The Egyptian mystery schools may have been a source for the prince of Egypt named Moses. The golden triangle was called the Tetractys and was composed of ten points. It was a sacred symbol to Pythagoras. The Egyptians knew their geometry. I can verify that for you. You sometimes see written in the middle of it the Tetragrammaton."

Cordy looked puzzled. "OK, you're starting to use big words on me."

Ash chuckled. "I'm sorry about that — occupational hazard being with a history buff. It's the hidden name of God. It's believed that the golden triangle resided in the Ark of the Covenant."

Cordy pulled out of her pocket the gold triangle. Cordy's serious tone took over. "Ash, could you please take a look at this?" She placed the golden triangle in his hand, and sure enough, it had the Hebrew letters YHWH or the Tetragrammaton. Ash's hand felt warm when the gold triangle sat in his palm. He felt a tingling in his hand as the triangle glistened. "It's solid gold. Have you heard of the Golden Triangle of Enoch?"

Cordy shook her head. "No, what is it?"

Ash sat down in a pew and Cordy with him. Enoch was a prophet who had a vision of a mountain and a golden triangle showing the rays of the sun. Cordy and Ash looked at the golden triangle above the pulpit. It had rays coming from it.

Ash whispered, "The Egyptians believed in sacred words, and there's a story about Isis tricking the great god Ra to reveal his secret magic word. The Hebrews believed there was great power in God's name. I find it sometimes ironic that the Christian prayer Our Father or Pater Noster finishes with the word Amen. Amen means 'hidden one.' It used to be the name of Ra who was called Amen Ra or Amen Osiris. The Our Father has aspects similar to what is written in the Egyptian Book of the Dead and Maxim of Ani. The Freemasons use the golden triangle, as do Christian churches. It is an expensive and rare gift."

He pulled out his cell phone and pulled up a picture of an illuminated manuscript from St. Louis's Bible. "It shows the Great Architect with his compass. It was a picture of God bending over using a compass. Geometry and mathematics were considered sacred knowledge from the heavens. St. Louis knew this was divine knowledge and placed it in his Bible. Royalty passed the knowledge down to their families."

Cordy was fascinated. She knew all about Saint Louis and his history. "Ash, do you think secret sacred knowledge was brought back from the Crusades like myths talk about?" Ash nodded. "It seems St. Louis's Bible hints to that fact. Egypt is in turmoil with politics but rumors abound that something strange has been found at the Great Pyramid. Other Bibles show the Great Geometrician such as St. Louis's mother, Blanche of Castile. She was around during the building of the Notre Dame Cathedral at Chartres. The beautiful Gothic cathedrals were built during this time. It's a mystery, Cordy."

The phone buzzed in Ash's pocket. He got a text message from his mother. "It's my mom. She wants to know what I'm doing." Ash quickly texted her back, "I am sitting with a wonderful woman talking history."

He got another text. "Is she married?" Ash laughed and showed Cordy what she wrote. Cordy looked pleased. "You can answer her back no."

Ash blushed slightly. "I'm sorry about that, Cordy. My mother always wants me to settle down. I just never met the right woman at the right time. You made an old woman very happy." They both laughed.

Cordy looked at her watch. "Oh, Ash, I have to go. Can I get your cell phone number?" Ash looked delighted. "It's usually the guy who asks for the girl's number. Of course you can have it. I hope we can see each other again. I had a wonderful time."

He wrote his number on a piece of paper and gave it to her. Cordy asked, "I want to invite you for a fishing trip with my family. I have some other things to show you. I could use an expert's opinion. It will be in a couple of days."

Ash answered without hesitation, "I would love to. Do I bring my fishing pole?"

Cordy started walking out of the cathedral. "No, just bring you. The directions will be in your email. I'll hope to see you soon."

Montreal, Canada

Ash watched the gorgeous woman run down the street. He couldn't take his eyes off of her. Cordy turned around and waved back at him.

CHAPTER 52

Lunch with Bob

Cordy went for a run, thinking it felt good to get the exercise. She was excited and glad Ash was really a nice guy. Cordy couldn't believe she asked him out. He was a stranger for goodness sake. She saw the café, and Bob, dressed in a gray suit, sat outside having coffee and reading the newspaper. He looked so different in a suit instead of his Bingo's uniform. She yelled, "Bob!"

His head shot up when he heard his name called.

"Bob, I'm so sorry for being late. I forgot the time while looking at the beautiful sights. I love Montreal, and the people are so friendly. Will you forgive me?" Cordy gave him her puppy-dog-eyes look.

Bob tried to look mad but melted when he saw her face. He took great pride in being tough but with Cordy, he was a marshmallow. Bob said, "I bet you haven't eaten anything or drank anything all day. You're going to eat something while you are on my watch."

Lunch with Bob

The waiter delivered an omelet with spinach and mushrooms and a lovely strawberry spinach salad. He poured Cordy a cup of tea. She answered playfully. "You read my mind. I miss your Bingo's hat."

Bob smiled. "I still have it as a matter of fact."

Cordy was enjoying the food and grabbed a croissant roll from the breadbasket. She could tell he was happy to be back at his old job. Bob went to business straight away.

"How are you and the long-lost grandpa getting along?"

Cordy looked at him. "It's good. He really has been very nice to me."

Bob leaned over. "But..."

A serious and troubled look came over Cordy's face. "I don't know what it is, Bob. I feel like there's something he's hiding from me. He definitely is dedicated to running the company. It seems all consuming but then I would guess running a multibillion-dollar corporation would be."

Cordy finished her lunch in a flash. Bob knew she was starving. He snapped his fingers and like a magician, the waiter placed before her a red velvet cupcake. A glass of red wine was delivered, too. Cordy beamed. "What would I do without you, Bob?"

Bob, with a knowing look, simply said, "Starve!"

"You're telling me you don't trust gramps."

Cordy looked at him intently. "Nope!"

Bob shot back at her. "He wants to meet me along with his lawyers to make sure your estate and trust are legally safe. You are his only heir, and he doesn't trust me. I'm going to get checked out, and if he has his way, probably shipped out."

Cordy munched on her cupcake. "He told me you checked out, and I was lucky to have found you. I'll admit that I would like to have a family. He's tired of being alone, and so am I. I love him, and my father loved him. He's pretty incredible when you get to know him."

Bob leaned back. "He's family when it gets down to it."

Cordy nodded. "Yep! I just wish I knew what he was hiding from me."

Bob pulled out a small red friendship bracelet from his pocket. He took her arm and attached it to her wrist. He smiled. "We are friends, and so I got you a friendship bracelet. I just want to make it clear that this doesn't mean we are going steady. I have found it isn't good policy to date the boss, and beside, I have only been in love one time in my life and that was five minutes in an elevator. I don't think you're my type. The woman I loved never knew I loved her, and I've been empty ever since she walked out of that elevator."

Cordy got a suspicious look on her face. "Five minutes, Bob, is that what I should call you?"

Bob grinned. "It was glorious. I'm a fast worker. What can I say?"

Cordy pointed to the bracelet. "Yeah, so what's with the bracelet?"

"Oh, don't think we're getting married, cupcake. This bracelet has a device that will keep track of you while you're with gramps. I know you're not going to want it, but just trust me. I want you to text me every day and update me. You have your own business now, and I may need to ask you a question every now and then."

Cordy saw through that one. "I trust you, Bob, to make those decisions. What is worrying you?"

Bob waved for the check. "Gramps plays with some very powerful organizations, and now they know you are his sole heir. You have made him vulnerable. I know you can take care of yourself, but, Cordy, just be careful and follow your instincts."

Cordy realized he was serious. "OK, just because you're my friend. The bracelet does fit perfectly."

Bob paid the bill and started to get up. "I never told you, Cordy, why I left the Navy SEALs. I got insubordinate with a commanding officer. He was a real jerk. I lost my temper when I lost some of my brothers in an operation. He told me I was too protective. The bracelet is an insurance policy. You keep that bracelet on and update me every day, and I'll be a happy man." Cordy looked at the bracelet and then at Bob. "I promise, Bob."

Bob smiled and told her, "Cupcake, let me make something clear. First, you are not my type because you are way too tall, second, you are too nice, and third, you make more than me." Cordy smiled back at Bob with a twinkle in her eye. "Hey, Bob, I want to make something clear between you and me. Don't ever call me cupcake again, or I'll knock that smile off your face."

Bob laughed. "Oh, now that's my girl. Aye aye, boss lady." Bob looked at his watch "Gotta go meet Grandpa and his gang. It's good to know I passed the test." He paid the bill and took off. Cordy waved good-bye.

She looked around her as she sipped the last bit of her wine. An older man was sitting on a bench feeding pigeons. He looked familiar. Something about him reminded her of someone she had met. Cordy watched him get up and leave and thought maybe her eyes were playing tricks on her. My goodness, Bob had gotten her paranoid now. It was time to head back to the penthouse. Her grandfather would be taking her out tonight. She admitted it felt good to have family. Her grandfather turned out better than expected.

CHAPTER 53

Dinner with Bill

Cordy greeted the doorman, and he opened the door for her. Cordy smiled to herself. "So this is how the rich live." Rose opened the door to the penthouse and greeted her.

"Hello, Mademoiselle Cordelia, and how was your walk?"

"It was wonderful, Rose, and thank you for asking. Is my grandfather home yet?"

Rose answered, "No, Mademoiselle, he told me to tell you business has delayed him. He apologized and will be here shortly."

Cordy smiled to herself. She knew what business was going on — Bob's interrogation. Cordy said, "Then I'll have time to freshen up."

She headed for her room with a view of the city of Montreal. The skyline of buildings lit from inside was beautiful. Cordy picked out a strapless, silk black dress with small white and red flowers embroidered on the skirt. Her mother's pearls were simple but elegant, while her black high heels accentuated her long legs. She put her hair up in a bun, letting tendrils curl around

Dinner with Bill

her face. Cordy looked in the mirror and almost didn't recognize herself. She decided to wait for Bill in the living room.

Cordy walked around the contemporary furniture, which had an interior decorator's touch. It seemed sterile with its white couch and silver cocktail table. Family pictures stood in the corner on a tiny table by the window. A vase with one red rose stood next to her grandmother's picture. She was very beautiful and wore a loving smile as she held her prized possession, her father as a baby. Her beaming, handsome young grandfather had a protective arm around her. Cordy saw a picture of a tall man wearing his Mi'kmaq coat. His arm rested on a tiny woman wearing a pointed tribal hat and Mi'kmaq dress. They both had regal bearing and pride on their faces.

The picture of her parents holding Cordy as a baby caught her eye, and she picked the frame up tenderly. His soft voice came from over her shoulder. "I miss them every day, too." Cordy's voice trembled, "I was at school when I got the phone call that they were killed. It took a good year before I realized they were never coming back." She patted his hand and turned, giving him a hug. "OK, Bill, I'm hungry so where is this dinner you promised me?" Bill smiled, "Mademoiselle, you are in for a treat. We are dining at Antoine's."

Cordy grabbed her black sweater and purse. They headed downstairs to the limousine waiting for them. "We will be visiting the chief at Cape Breton. Cape Breton is an island in Nova Scotia. The Bras d'Or is one of the world's largest salt-water lakes in the world. It is a sacred place for the Mi'kmaq nation. The Grand Council met on an island called Mniku in the old days. Now it's called Chapel Island. The Mi'kmaq are mostly Christians due to an alliance with the French Jesuits when they arrived to Nova Scotia. The French wouldn't have survived without the help of the Mi'kmaq. They intermarried and became allies to the French during the war. France lost, and then the Great Expulsion happened when the British took the land from the Acadians. The Mi'kmaq had their land seized by the British. In 2010, Canada

Keys of Life

and Nova Scotia consulted the Mi'kmaq Nation on any activities that would affect them. The chief is retired, but he's been fighting for recognition for a long time. We will visit the chief tomorrow, and then we'll go on a fishing trip the next day. I know, I asked this before but do you get sea sick, Cordy?"

Cordy answered. "I went on a cruise and had no problem."

Bill laughed. "The fishing boat is a bit smaller than that, so I'd bring some medicine for sea sickness just in case. If you have the sea men's blood that runs in the family then you should be fine."

Cordy agreed, "I'll take your advice."

"The family business started with fishing, and we've now branched out into different businesses. I have a fishing fleet that does cod, lobster, and shrimp."

Cordy thought about Ash. "Grandpa Bill, can I ask a friend to come with us fishing? His name is Ash Von Lettow. I invited him to come along with us fishing. Is it OK?"

Bill answered, "Why sure it's OK, Cordy, but make sure he doesn't get sea sick or this fishing trip will be miserable for both of you. Are you and he seriously dating?"

Cordy laughed. "Oh no, Bill, it isn't like that. He's just a friend."

"What does he do?"

"He's an archeologist specializing in Egyptian antiquities."

Bill looked surprised. "Where did you find him?"

Cordy shook her head. "On the Internet, and, I know, not a good place to meet people. You can check him out."

Bill's face turned serious, and he looked at the window, softly whispering, "Oh, don't worry, I will."

The limo dropped them at Antoine's, where all the rich and famous in Montreal could be seen. The waiter knew Bill well and had his favorite table ready. Bill was enjoying all the men in the restaurant looking at his gorgeous granddaughter. He chuckled to himself as the thought of them thinking he had a new girlfriend. Bill didn't have time for women. Most of them were untrustworthy, time-consuming, and high maintenance. He enjoyed the

Dinner with Bill

occasional one-night fling only to wake up and find the woman was a fortune hunter. His granddaughter was naïve and innocent in this world of sharks. The lessons were going to begin tonight.

The table overlooked Montreal in all of its glorious lights. The waiter poured the wine, and Bill asked, "Well, Cordy, what would you like to eat?"

Cordy was a bit overwhelmed. "How about you order for me since you've been here before?"

Bill smiled. "The mademoiselle will have the lobster, and I will have the steak."

The waiter went to tell the chef. Cordy apologized, "I'm afraid I know nothing about the fishing business. Dad and I fly-fished for trout at Montauk, but otherwise, I'm clueless. The biggest water source was the Mississippi."

Bill laughed. "It isn't hard, and I'll teach you everything I know. The chief is coming along with us. He is so excited to see you. He has called my secretary seven times."

Cordy smiled back. "I am, too."

Bill asked, "What did you see on your sightseeing trip?"

Cordy relaxed. "I walked to the Basilica Notre Dame and the Saint Sulpician Seminary. The gardens at the seminary were lovely. I met Ash at Our Lady of the Harbor by accident. He was sightseeing, too. I didn't know who the archangel was with the scales in his hands. Ash told me he was Uriel. The Egyptians believed that the heart was weighed after death and it had to be lighter than a feather."

Bill looked down at his wine. "Did he talk about the Pure of Heart?"

Cordy nodded. "He talked a little bit about it."

Bill's voice took a serious tone. "Did anybody else talk to you about it?"

Cordy looked at him. "Sister Agnes told me about them. I didn't quite believe it."

Bill poured her some more wine. "You can believe it. Jesus said, 'Blessed are the Pure of Heart for they shall see God.'" Bill

Keys of Life

sat back and sipped on his wine. "History repeats itself. Why? Because men make the same mistakes over and over again. The Pure of Heart arise when times are dire and dark. They have the power to change the world, but alas, that is why they are hunted down. I don't want to scare you, Cordy, but I do want you to understand that you are a Pure of Heart. That's why you were hidden by our family."

Cordy had an incredulous look. "How do they change the world?"

Bill gently answered, "They take their skills and plant trees over desolate farmland in the third world. Do you know someone who did that?"

Cordy's face blushed for a second. "Bob did it."

Bill continued, "Who gave him the order to do so?"

Cordy looked him in the eyes. "I did, but I don't regret it. We really are helping the environment and the people."

Bill threw up his hands. "You are changing the world, and some people don't like it. In fact, they will kill people to keep the status quo. I just want you to promise me that you will be careful. The legend goes that Joan of Arc was a Pure of Heart. That's why she was burned at the stake. Gandhi was another Pure of Heart who freed India and then was shot. How did you meet Bob? This was a lucky find, by the way."

Cordy noticed he changed the subject. "Bob was a miracle and a coincidence. I just happened to be eating at the restaurant, and he saw the portfolio. We sat down and hit it off. Bob's an honest man and because of that, he got into trouble with his boss."

Bill nodded. "I checked him out with my associates. He seems like the real deal and quite an incredible find, Cordy. Bob has made more money than my money managers this year and in a very short time. I'm a little jealous that he works for you and not me."

Cordy drank her wine and giggled. "You can't have him, Grandpa Bill."

Bill laughed. "I have to admit I thought about it. I like Bob, and he's quite under your spell. Do you love him?"

Dinner with Bill

Cordy laughed, choking a little on her water. "You don't mess around do you? It was a miracle I found Bob, but I don't love him, if that's what you're fishing for, fisherman Bill. No. Definitely N-O."

Bill smiled. "Good girl. Loving your financial planner is a no-no. I was just checking. I think we should order dessert." The waiter came, and Bill ordered a maple crème brulee and Irish coffee for both of them.

Cordy shook her head. "Everything was so delicious, and I'm so full. I'm not used to this rich food."

"The coffee is very good and has no calories. I have a bedtime story to tell you, my granddaughter."

Cordy laughed. "I haven't heard one in years. Does it have mean ogres?"

Bill sipped on his coffee. "No, this one has giants in it. I want you to read Genesis in the Bible. It has some interesting parts. I want you to pay attention to the parts that deal with the Nephilim."

Cordy looked puzzled. "Nephilim? You mean the bad guys?" She had a small taste of her rich brulee. She thought to herself, a woman could get use to this pampering. Bill smiled at her enjoyment.

He continued, "In Genesis, the sons of God came from the heavens and took wives from Eve's daughters. They produced a race of giants known as the Nephilim. The flood destroyed most of the Nephilim but not all of them. The Children of the Nephilim is the name of a secret group that believes mankind is just sheep. They want to rule over them and make them slaves. The group is secretive, and the members are some of the richest and most powerful men in the world. One of their main objectives is hunting Pure of Hearts and destroying them. I know you are a black belt karate expert with other talents. You inherited one of your talents from your grandmother and mother. That's the gift of healing and the ability to communicate with animals. I want you to be extra careful because when you saved Minah in St. Louis, that may have put you on the Nephilim radar screen."

Cordy grabbed his hand. "Grandpa Bill, don't you worry about me. I can take care of myself. Master Wong took me with him to train in Tibet. I took a vacation right after vet school. I love the focus and internal calm of the Tibetan teachings. Wong taught me on various weapons. I had some anger issues, but he helped me work through them. He is 60 years old and can still knock me down when he wants to."

Bill looked at her. "I know you can take care of yourself, and I'm very proud of you. I just want you be careful, Cordy." He looked at his watch. "It's getting late. Let's go. We've got a big day with the chief."

CHAPTER 54

Ash and the Sweat Lodge

Ash had the physical and email addresses that his father had given him. The Pure of Heart had certain commanders throughout the world. His father was in charge of the Middle East while the chief was in charge of North America. He emailed Chief Saunhac when he arrived in Canada, thanks to Dottie's gift card. He had made it to Montreal and was waiting for further instructions. He checked the computer Dottie gave him, and Saunhac emailed him right back. Ash had written in the subject line: Looking for Mary Magdalene. The chief wrote that Ash was to bring what he found with him. A Mi'kmaq would pick him up by the Saint Sulpice Seminary.

Ash wrote him back that he would be waiting and knew where it was located. Ash left, and he stood under the Sacred Heart of Saint Sulpice's door. He saw coming down the sidewalk a tall heavyset man with long, thick dark hair pulled together in a ponytail and wearing a bracelet with intricate Indian geometric designs. He was dressed in plain jeans and a T-shirt. If it weren't for the bands on his wrists, Ash wouldn't have been able to tell he was a Mi'kmaq, but the band designs were like the hieroglyphs Brother Michael showed him. His name was McDonagh, and he looked like a football player.

The Mi'kmaq walked right up to Ash with a stern look. He didn't look very happy to see Ash. Ash held out his hand. "Hi! I'm Ash. What's your name?"

The Mi'kmaq just stood in front of Ash in a very intimidating stance. "They call me Little Louie. Follow me if you want to meet the Chief."

Ash smiled. "I wouldn't have guessed that one. Little Louie, lead on."

Little Louie pointed to his pickup truck parked across the street. Little Louie started running to his car and Ash ran, too. "We have to beat the traffic, so we don't have much time." It was a long drive to Nova Scotia.

Ash couldn't help himself, and he had to ask, "Why do they call you Little Louie?"

Little Louie cracked a smile. "I was the smallest one of my brothers, and then one day, I wasn't. The nickname stayed, and I've lived with it all my life. We will have to relieve each other driving so you better get some sleep."

Ash took his advice and put his head up against the window and fell fast asleep. He was awakened by his cell phone, which showed an email from Linda containing a picture of Leo with Mahd. Rosh gave Leo to Mahd since he tore up his garden the next day. Mahd had told Linda that the news was a naked man had been spotted on the Abu Simbel camera security system. It was quite a mystery — a naked man who didn't take anything from the temple. No one had been caught for the crime. The government announced that it was a prankster.

The bad news was that Rosh was killed in a car accident shortly after he gave Mahd the dog. Ash emailed her, typing, "Thanks for the news and the picture of Leo." He told her to study hard and behave herself.

Ash and the Sweat Lodge!

Little Louie changed seats with Ash. Louie snored away as Ash drove into Nova Scotia following the GPS. Ash couldn't believe Rosh was gone, and he had a feeling it wasn't an accident. Mahd's family would protect Mahd. They were part of a great tribal system and they watched their own. Ash thought the Mi'kmaqs weren't that much different from the Egyptians. They protected their family. It was about the tribe.

Little Louie switched seats with Ash again. "We are almost there, Ash." Ash got a text from Cordy giving him the directions where to meet for the fishing trip. He had to admit that he was looking forward to seeing her again. The truck pulled up in the driveway. A tall older man in a Mi'kmaq war bonnet made of lovely white, red, grey, and brown eagle feathers walked toward them. He was in his tribe's formal dress. The smiling elderly man with weathered skin wore a leather coat, pants, and moccasins with beaded Indian symbols. He was ancient and yet timeless.

"You are just in time for the sweat lodge ceremony, my friend." He pointed to Little Louie. "Little Louie, escort Ash to the medicine tent for the purification."

In his backyard, the Chief had an arched structure made of branches covered by a leather top and more branches from the trees. Ash walked into a room filled with men sitting cross-legged around a fire surrounded by a circle of stones. Ash was given an Indian headband and a beaded vest with Indian geometric designs.

The chief came in and all the men bowed their heads in respect, even Ash. He sat next to the chief. The elderly man looked at Ash. "I am a healer, or what my people call the medicine man of the tribe, like you and your family. I am going to take you on a spiritual journey. You will walk with the ancestors alongside me."

The door faced the fire in the middle. Five men sat around the fire with bowed heads. Little Louie started to chant in a deep vibrating voice.

Two other men started beating on their drums in rhythm with Little Louie's chanting. Little Louie fed the fire, and it got hotter

Keys of Life

and hotter. "He is the fire-keeper," the chief whispered to Ash. He pointed to the door of the tent and a younger man. "He is the protector." Ash felt a stirring in his whole body as he listened to the mesmerizing drumming and chanting. He started to perspire from the heat in the tent. The chief smiled. "It's the purification process. The toxins are released."

He handed Ash a long pipe with feathers after he took two puffs. The aroma from the pipe was intoxicating. Ash said, "I don't smoke," but decided he better take a couple of puffs after looking at all the men giving him an intimidating stare. "OK, maybe just this one time." He took a couple of puffs and inhaled the exotic smoke. He coughed a couple times, as he wasn't used to it. Ash passed the pipe to Little Louie, and it continued around the tent. Saunhac picked up a long gold spoon with an open hand. Mi'kmaq hieroglyphs were carved into the gold. Ash saw it and recognized the similarity to the incense burners in the Egyptian temples. He asked, "Where did this come from? It looks Egyptian."

Saunhac smiled. "My family has passed it down for centuries. It holds the great incense that purifies the air of dark spirits."

The chief told Ash, "You must close your eyes and tell us what you see."

Ash closed his eyes as everything swirled around him and *whoosh*, he flew down what looked like a tunnel or black hole and landed in a strange land. In front of him, the Easter bunny with his basket said, "You don't want to be late for the main event."

The chief stood next to Ash in his dream. "Ash, ask him what main event?"

The bunny's nose and whiskers moved as he talked. "The time has come to bring the Pure of Heart out of the shadows. One who was lost will be found. The ancient ones' gifts will be found by the Pure of Heart and united so they may save the world."

A Crusader knight dressed in a white tunic with the red cross appeared. He stood protecting the little bunny and Ash. Antar

Ash and the Sweat Lodge!

came into the dream and faced the Crusader. "You think you can protect your lil' bunny from the Nephilim? I don't think so."

The Crusader pulled out his gleaming sword. "I am Guillaume de Saunhac, Templar Grandmaster and protector." The knight Saunhac turned his sword downward to make it look like a cross and pulled from his pocket a crystal ball that lit the room.

Ash looked in the lil' bunny's basket. In it shined a golden triangle. The bunny whispered, "It's yours. Command him to go."

Ash pulled the golden triangle out of the basket, and it glowed with a fiery intensity. He saw Uriel standing next to him and another archangel with a spear. The Crusader yelled to Ash, "Repeat these words with me, O Pure of Heart, 'NinAlasotmoinoi gil Mento Tooe.'"

Ash chanted the words and Antar left, and Ash woke up from his dream. Ash looked in great puzzlement at the chief. "What did I say?"

The chief rose up. "Ash's name in the tribe will be known as Little Rabbit, and what you chanted in your dream was an old Mi'kmaq saying. It means 'I am Catholic, you are the devil, get out.'"

Ash felt woozy after the spiritual experience. The chief instructed Little Louie to take Ash home and let him sleep. The chief told Ash before he left, "It is the golden triangle they seek and the ring. It contains the power to rule over all the angels."

CHAPTER 55

Cordy Meets the Chief

It was a sunny cloudless day when Bill and Cordy set off to see the chief. They took the corporate jet to Halifax. Bill's SUV was at the airport. They loaded their luggage in the back and off they went. Bill began to act like a tour guide as he drove, giving the history of Halifax, Nova Scotia.

"Halifax is the capital of Nova Scotia. The British took it over from the French and Mi'kmaq after the Great Expulsion. It has been a naval stronghold for Britain. Fishing was the major industry and then banking." He showed her the small house where her father was born. It was a tiny, bright blue two-story house. Many of the houses were brightly colored, giving the city a cheery look.

Her father had told her tales about the sea. She wondered at the ocean's magnificence. Cordy wondered if her father regretted leaving his ocean home. He loved his farm and his family. If he regretted anything, it was leaving his father and his friends. Cordy breathed the ocean air and saw the seagulls flying over the ocean. The harbor was filled with boats of all kinds. It amazed her how

Cordy Meets the Chief

her father came from Halifax to a small farm off the Mississippi river. Cordy asked Bill, "What was the Great Expulsion?"

Bill sighed. "It was the expulsion of the French Acadians. They refused to swear an oath of loyalty to Britain so their land was confiscated and they were taken as prisoners to other settlements. Longfellow told the tale of Evangeline, which is all about their hardships. The Mi'kmaq had made allies with the French and suffered for it."

Bill took Cordy by the highway that went along the seashore of Cape Breton. It was breathtakingly beautiful. Trees dotted the land and the cliffs were jagged and worn by the cold winds. The view of the ocean was magnificent. The chief lived on an awesome island.

Bill told her, "The Mi'kmaq Indians were here before the settlers like Cartier came. They converted to Catholicism easily. Their religion had similarities to Christianity. The chief is retired but still is a respected shaman and medicine man." He pointed to Bras d'Or Lake. "It is a salt water lake. It means arm of gold, because when the sun shines on it, the gold shimmers from the rays on the water. It is highly respected and protected by the Mi'kmaq."

A white flag with a red cross waved in the breeze. On it was a crescent moon and a five-pointed star. Bill pointed to it. "That's the flag of the Mi'kmaq Nation. The white background means purity and the red cross represents mankind and infinity. It reflects the four directions and their Christianity. The star for the sun and the moon represent the forces of day and night. The Mi'kmaq have an old saying, 'I am Catholic, you are a devil, get out.'"

Cordy smiled. "The flag looks like the flag the Crusaders waved in the Crusades."

Bill thought Cordy's intuition was pretty perceptive. Bill looked at her. "The chief is from the Saunhac family. The family had a Grand Master of the Knights Templar in their history. His name was Guillaume de Saunhac. He fought in the Seventh Crusade with Saint Louis. He died at the battle of Fariskur. He had lost an eye in the previous battle, but that did not stop him and he continued to fight with one eye. His bravery in battle was his legacy. In fact, other Acadian families had a history of families participating in the Crusades. The McDermott's participated in the Crusades. On their crest, the cross of Jerusalem is on their heraldry."

Cordy said proudly. "We come from a long line of fighters."

Bill continued, "The name Mi'kmaq means 'People of the Red Earth' or the 'Red Earth people.' The Mi'kmaq after many centuries now get a voice in what happens on their lands. The chief worked very hard for it."

Cordy shook her head. "It's amazing he did it with the way governments are now."

Bill pointed at a statue of a woman off to the side of the road near a small church. "Saint Anne is their favorite saint. She was mother to Mary and grandmother to Jesus. The grandmother holds a very high place of respect in the family."

Cordy asked him, "The Algonquin, are they related to the Mi'kmaq?"

Bill thought for a second. "The languages are the same. They are called the 'Wabanaki' People of the Dawn."

Cordy answered him, "I read that the Algonquin language was very similar to ancient Gaulish or Basque language."

Bill shook his head. "You're right. Some Gaelic words are very similar to the Algonquin word. In fact, the French brought a Basque translator who helped communicate with the Indians. The Basque fisherman had been trading with the Indians before the French established settlements. The Iroquois and the Mi'kmaq battled for territory. The Iroquois adopted the children of the tribes they defeated. Women in the tribe were highly respected and were allowed property."

Cordy smiled. "People thought the Indians were primitive, but they were ahead in women's rights compared with the Europeans."

The road wound around the coastline like a snake. Cordy's cell phone vibrated. Bob had texted her. "It's Bob, just checking in. I didn't know a man could act like a mother hen."

Cordy Meets the Chief

Bill smiled at how Bob kept tabs on Cordy. "The chief is a high-level medicine man. They are called 'Midewiwin.' It's a secretive religious group of healers. My mother told me that they were created to give secret medicine to the people."

Cordy gave him a skeptical look. "I don't believe in magic."

Bill nodded. "People here consider him a magician or great medicine man. I want to prepare you that he may talk a bit strangely or do some strange things. He did a birth rite ceremony when you arrived at Nova Scotia as a baby. Hundreds attended the ceremony and your Mi'kmaq name was "Star Child." The surprise on Cordy's face was comical. "Dad never told me my Indian name. Why did he name me 'Star Child'?"

Bill laughed. "You will have to ask him about it."

They pulled onto a narrow road and saw a small white house with a white picket fence around it. Oak, maple, and evergreen trees surrounded it. It would have looked like a typical Nova Scotia home except for the wigwam in the back yard, which had smoke coming out of it. Cordy laughed. "Was he sending smoke signals?"

Bill chuckled. "I wouldn't put anything past him."

An older chubby woman wearing an apron and a big smile came out of the door. "Hello, Bill, long time since I've seen you." She hugged Bill.

"Mary, you look as young as ever. I want you to meet my granddaughter Cordelia from St. Louis in the States."

Mary held out her hand and Cordy shook it. "It's nice to meet the chief's great-granddaughter."

Bill explained, "Mary watches after the chief for me. She makes sure he behaves."

Mary laughed. "If he doesn't, he gets no homemade apple pie. I'm supposed to bring you to the Great Lodge." She pointed to the smoking wigwam. "He is doing some sweat lodge ceremony with a young man. He should be almost done."

The door of the wigwam opened and out stepped a tall man with an ageless face dressed in leather breeches, a white-colored

Keys of Life

shirt, and a dark blue jacket with gold embroidered sleeves. He was concentrating on the young man who was naked from the waist up. His chest had paint and designs on it, but it was the sculptured body that got Cordy's attention. She recognized him immediately. "Ash, is that you?"

Ash had a drunken smile on his face. "Hellloo," he said leisurely, the words coming out in a slur. The chief called for Running Bear, a tall Mi'kmaq coming out of the wigwam. "Running Bear, take Brother Lil' Rabbit to your house to sleep so he can continue his spiritual journey."

Ash waved goodbye to Bill and Cordy and almost stumbled, but Running Bear caught him. Running Bear grabbed his arm, putting it over his shoulder, and guided the staggering Ash to his car. Cordy's face showed her surprise and her worry for Ash. "Is he going to be OK?" The old man smiled. "Do not worry, Star Child, over Brother Lil' Rabbit. A good night's sleep and he will be a new man. Star Child, please give this poor old man a hug."

Cordy couldn't help herself and hugged the chief. Bill whispered to the chief, "Did Ash do well through the ceremony of initiation?"

Chief nodded and whispered back, "He did the best I have ever seen, Bill. He traveled far."

Bill's face had a serious look. "He is a Pure of Heart?"

The Chief smiled, "Indeed he is, and he has great power."

Cordy followed Mary, who took her to see pictures of her great-grandmother Catherine and her grandmother when she was little. Mary brought Cordy and Bill to the table, which had a hot pot of tea and small cakes. They sat down together and the chief told her stories of her grandmother Annie, who was his only child.

The chief showed her all his sacred Indian mementos. He told her of the Great Spirit creation story. Chief's voice enchanted her.

"The Great Spirit created the universe. He created the stars and galaxies. He had a day of rest and decided to create

Cordy Meets the Chief

Glooskap. Glooskap had special powers." The chief pointed to a beautiful decorated pipe. "The Great Spirit and Glooskap shared the sacred pipe. The Great Spirit looked at some red clay and said, I will create a people in my own image and call them the Mi'kmaq. After he created them, he had some leftover clay made into a Minnego, an enchanted island. He placed the magical island in the singing waters of the Gulf of St. Lawrence."

Cordy held the pipe. "It is so beautiful, the island, and amazing."

The chief told her, "Our history has many mysteries and legends. We have a story similar to Noah. Evil ruled the day in the hearts of men, which caused great sorrow in the eyes of the Creator sun god. He cried great tears, which caused a great flood. Only one old man and woman survived to populate the Earth. We have a tradition of telling our stories to our children. I want you to tell your children these stories on the cold nights. It is why I am so glad you came to see me."

Cordy nodded. "I promise I will tell them, Chief. My mother told me many Irish tales of fairies, giants, and Tuatha Danaan. Her family had the same oral tradition."

The chief pointed to a statue behind her. "Glooskap is the Mi'kmaq's big giant hero." She saw a statue of a tall, red Indian man with long black hair wearing an Indian tunic and pants. Chief went over and picked him up. "Glooskap was a twin. He was all that was good, while his brother was all that was evil. Glooskap helped create the good world and knew that hunters should not kill all the animals or destroy the Earth. Mother Earth must be treated with respect. Glooskap is not happy with the imbalance and how mankind treats his creation. That's why the Mi'kmaq chiefs were taught the Great Earth Magic. I admit my family comes from a long line of great wizards."

He handed her a rock with a petroglyph carved on it. It had an eight-pointed star surrounded by pentacles carved on it. The chief placed it in her hand. "Your Indian name is Star Child, and you wonder why. Because you come from the stars. We are made of star dust, and our ancestors resided in the stars. This star was carved on the rocks around Nova Scotia long ago. The story goes that the eight arms of the star point in four cardinal directions and reveal a great mystery."

Cordy whispered, "What great mystery?"

The chief smiled mischievously. "It tells us that there is something more than just what we perceive with our eyes. Once on Earth long ago, four people lived on the planet. The red, white, yellow, and black people sailed in four different directions and settled the lands there, where one day they would unite to settle in the center of the world and live in peace. The star represents the clans of the world and a compass. Its power is great."

He handed her two crystal stones. Cordy recognized it. "Feldspar and Iceland spar crystal stones. One is used for navigation for its properties with the sun, and the other, moonstone."

The chief smiled and nodded. "We know the Great Spirits or as some would call them, angels or saints, are the protectors while some are the destroyers. We must know when to call upon them, and only a Pure of Heart has the strength to handle such power."

Cordy nodded. "I agree, Chief. Our brothers and sisters, the animals are going extinct because of the imbalance. The bees are dying in incredible numbers. Something has to be done."

Chief sighed. "Imbalance brings chaos and a reckoning. That's why the Pure of Heart will return to restore balance to the world. Glooskap taught the Mi'kmaq knowledge of good and evil, magic, fire, and how to make canoes. You can see why the Mi'kmaq had no trouble converting to Christianity. Jesus's love for mankind, his gifts of healing, his kind treatment of women, children and animals and his pure heart made it easy for the Mi'kmaq to embrace. The legends were similar. The Great Father and Mother protect their children and love them. We await Jesus's coming as we await Glooskap's return."

Cordy listened to the stories intently. "It must've been hard walking between two cultures. Indian and European cultures are so different."

Cordy Meets the Chief

The chief nodded. "Many of the Mi'kmaq died fighting in the wars defending their land. One tribe became extinct. A story is told of a great tall warrior, seven foot in height, who went to greet the new explorers. He approached them in greeting but his size terrified them. He was shot when he tried to greet them. They took his wife, and that was the last of his tribe. Many died due to disease. You come from a line of great warriors. We have fought many wars. I fought in World War II."

A wooden carved whale stood on a shelf, and Cordy picked it up.

"You want a good fishing story?" laughed Chief.

Cordy nodded. "Yes, I bet it is a big one."

Chief went on. "Glooskap and a great giant went fishing for a whale. The giant made a canoe of rocks and a spear of rock to hunt the whale. The giant used the great spear to kill the whale and lifted the great fish to the clouds. He was so strong that he lifted the great whale and placed him in his rock canoe with Glooskap. They had him for dinner that night. It is similar to Norse stories that feature the great Thor. The Vikings have now been found to have discovered America before Columbus, who lost his shoe in 1492."

Cordy agreed. "History changes over time. I have read about the discoveries. I'm surprised at how tall the Indians are in the family. You're over six foot, Chief."

Chief smiled. "I was six foot, seven inches but old age has shrunk me. The land of giants is Nova Scotia. Glooskap was friends with them."

Cordy remembered her mother's tales of the Irish Tuatha Danaan and the great giant warrior Cu Chulainn.

Bill helped Mary in the kitchen while the chief showed Cordy around. Bill got the dishes and silverware to set the table. He casually asked, "How is the old chief doing?"

Mary sighed. "He is stubborn, Bill, and he never listens to me. I see him get short of breath and in pain. Cordy visiting him energizes him. He takes more naps now." Mary's eyes teared up. "He tells me the Great Spirit's voice is calling him, and it gets louder and louder. I will miss him, Bill, even though he is the most stubborn old man in the world."

Bill gave her a hug. "I appreciate everything you have done, Mary, and you know I love that old man."

He went to set the table and watched the chief show Cordy his tent in the backyard. "Woof woof," barked a grey wolf-looking dog running toward the chief and Cordy. It was Grey Smoke. Cordy couldn't believe her eyes at the magnificent wolf-dog. He was a hybrid, probably from a grey Arctic wolf and an Alaskan malamute. Chief smiled. "You like Grey Smoke?"

Grey Smoke came up shyly, and the chief laughed, petting his head. "Grey Smoke, meet my great-granddaughter." The wolf-dog wagged his tale and went over toward Cordy. She put her hand on his thick, luxurious fur and petted him. "Where did you get him, Chief?"

The chief smiled. "It was cold, and I found him next to his mother who was shot by a hunter. I raised him from a pup. He is very shy around strangers, but he likes you."

Cordy got on her knees to look him over and pet his silver-grey coat. "His hair is wonderful."

"He looks as white as snow when winter comes."

Mary hollered out the door, "Dinner's ready!"

Cordy felt like she was in a dream. Grey Smoke lay on the floor watching the laughing and smiling family. It was a family dinner in every way. Jokes made by the chief and Bill kept her and Mary laughing. Cordy told them about her adventures and her veterinarian clinic. Mary got up to get dessert, which was a blueberry cream cake.

Cordy thought it was time to show the chief her strange box with the Egyptian-looking cup. Cordy smiled at Bill and the Chief. "Sister Agnes told me to ask the chief if I had any questions. I have a huge one for you, Chief."

Chief had a knowing look on his face. "I am ready, so go ahead and ask, Cordy."

Bill's attention focused on the box she was holding. His voice got very tense. "Where in the hell did you get that, Cordy?"

Cordy Meets the Chief

Cordy was stunned at his tone. The chief placed his calming hand on Bill. "I knew she would bring it. Let her show us."

Cordy pulled out the white cup with the Egyptian hieroglyphs. Bill was shocked. "It's the wishing cup."

Cordy began worry. "Did I do something wrong? I was just wondering if it was real."

The chief gently took the cup from Cordy. Bill warned him, "Be careful, Chief." The chief reassured him. "Only the Pure of Heart have the ability to harness the power of the wishing cup and you, Cordy, have passed the test."

Cordy looked at both of them, and she knew that she was a Pure of Heart. The chief placed the wishing cup back in the box. "This will be very useful when the time comes. It allows one wish to the person who drinks from the cup. How did you find the cup, Star Child?" Cordy said, "It was a gift from de Villiers for curing his cat."

Bill shook his head, worried. "You are on the grid now, Cordy. De Villiers is a Dark Watcher Master. His life-long ambition is getting complete power over the world."

The Chief smiled. "Everything is all right, and you did the best thing by bringing the wishing cup back into the hands of the Pure of Heart. Let's talk about our fishing trip. We are going fishing near the Magdalen Islands, which are very beautiful."

Bill answered, "We have had reports of pirates and interference with some of our boats. Chief, have you heard anything?"

The chief nodded. "It would be coming from Sainte Pierre and Miquelon. They have a history of pirating that goes way back. The law means nothing to them. The Lafitte family owns a bank on the island and a business. Their wealth comes from avoiding the laws and taxes."

Cordy smiled. "Lafitte? Isn't that a famous Louisiana pirate?"

Bill's concern showed. "The Lafitte family is still in the pirate business. They made millions during the Prohibition days selling alcohol. They have moved into the gambling business last I heard. The head of the family, Jon Lafitte, is bringing the family into legitimate businesses. They are very territorial so anybody that crosses into their fishing or business will encounter serious trouble. No one knows what happened to the Louisiana pirate Lafitte. One legend said he moved and lived in St. Louis under another name. It would be his children and cousins who run the multimillion-dollar business. Many settled here because they had family here once. Nova Scotia had a connection with Louisiana. In fact, the Acadians settled there after the Great Expulsion."

The Chief looked at Cordy with a serious face. "Many have come from Europe to escape death. They fled persecution and brought the sacred knowledge with them. The New World was a free world. The Mi'kmaq became their friends and allies. The belief in One Creator who was Our Father was not hard to believe for us. Christianity was not a hard sell. The Great Mother has our great respect, but Grandmother Saint Anne is our patron saint. The role of grandmother in the Mi'kmaq is one of the most highly respected places in the Indian family. Women have held property and seats on the Council."

The chief's eyes twinkled with mischief. "How do you know Little Rabbit?"

Cordy laughed. "Who is 'Little Rabbit?' Oh, you mean Ash."

Chief chuckled. "I call Ash Little Rabbit for it is his spirit name. He came to meet me, and he wanted to know about the Mi'kmaq hieroglyphic writing. I helped interpret some artifacts he found. He showed me that the Mi'kmaq and Egyptian hieroglyphs were similar." Bill's ears perked up as he sat quietly listening. Cordy smiled. "I was wondering why an Egyptologist would be in Nova Scotia. He is doing research."

The chief asked, "He told me that you and he met because of a video you made of Mary Magdalene."

"I helped make a video on Magdalene for a little girl I babysat for a friend. I didn't know it would get so much attention. I had Ash write me about it and another scholar from Oxford wrote me about the Magdalene statue in the video. The statue hands are similar to the hands of Mary Magdalene at a place in France called Rennes Chateau. The hands on the statue are very mysterious, and then I found a painting with the same hands on Mary at the Miraculous Medal Shrine. What does it mean? Why would the Mi'kmaq have hieroglyphic writing?"

The chief smiled. "The hands in the paintings and statues are a great mystery. I feel the Pure of Heart placed them there. Templar families and other groups watch over great mystical treasures. The crossing of the fingers form crosses interlinked with each other like an endless knot or the Jerusalem Cross. The Crusaders placed crosses on the wall of the Holy Sepulchre, which are endlessly linked. They are all connected like the hands crossed. Many have wondered why the Mi'kmaq have the hieroglyphic-like writing. We wrote on bark, and the French missionaries had the children write it on paper. It has been the Mi'kmaq writing for as long as the Elders can remember."

"The Mi'kmaq flood story is a like another flood story." Bill looked at Cordy. "It's another version of Genesis and Noah's Ark. It is about wicked mankind, and only one family being worthy."

The Old Chief went on. "The Arikara believe the floods wiped out the giants and made the world safer. The Sumerians have their flood and Gilgamesh. The Egyptians say Ra got very angry with mankind and ordered Hathor to punish them with a great flood. He ends up saving a few so they can start fresh. Little Rabbit is looking for answers to the question of why some Mi'kmaq hieroglyphs are similar to Egyptian ones. He wondered about the connection. Everything is connected, and evidence shows more and more that the Earth had a mass extinction event."

Bill joined in, "In the Book of Enoch, the story goes that the Nephilim were children of the sons of God. They were called the giants of old, such as Hercules or Orion. Some were good and some were wicked, so the result was killing their brothers. It seems the Great Flood was viewed as a punishment and attempt to exterminate the giants. It is why the Children of the Nephilim began as an organization bent on revenge and extermination of the Pure of Hearts. Noah was considered a pure one or a Pure of Heart. The Watchers have their place in this battle. They are divided in two camps. Light Watchers are the dedicated and loyal defenders of the balance and the survival of the Pure of Heart. The Dark Watchers use the ancient knowledge and objects of power to cause chaos. They become more powerful using chaos as a tool to rule the Earth. It is a battle our family has struggled with over the centuries. The Nephilim killed my son and his wife because they were Pure of Heart. That's why, Cordy, you were hidden and protected by us for so long."

The chief sighed. "We don't know if the Nephilim killed them, or it may have been the Dark Watchers. Star Child, you come from a long line of warriors, healers, and shaman. I was not surprised that you became a vet."

Cordy felt anger that her parents may have been assassinated. *Grrr,* a rumbling growl came from Grey Smoke. He looked at the chief. The chief rose up from the table. "Grey Smoke wants to go out. He heard something or somebody."

Bill looked knowingly at the chief. The wolf-dog rushed out the door. Cordy's emotions were all over the place. Bill and the chief were telling her that her parents were killed by a crazy organization. She didn't know if it was true or if they were just paranoid. Her experience with Minah made her believe it was possible. "Is Minah a Pure of Heart?" she asked, looking at Bill intensely.

Bill nodded. "Yes, and the name Cordelia means heart. Your mother picked it out, and it suits you. You do have a tender heart for people, animals, and the sick."

The chief spoke with pride, "She was a warrior, too. Don't let her fool you. Acadians are a mixture of many bloodlines. The Saunhac name goes back to France and some of the Acadian families, who came from France, can trace their families back to the Crusades. They met the Mi'kmaq and married while here in Nova Scotia. The red cross of the Crusaders is very similar to the Mi'kmaq flag with its star and crescent moon. We believe in the Queen of Heaven."

Bill explained. "The symbols date to the Sumerian times, and the star symbol was a sign of Ishtar and Isis. The Fertile Crescent was a crescent land between Mesopotamia and ancient Egypt."

The chief continued. "Lil' Rabbit seems to think some of the hieroglyphs of the Mi'kmaq are similar to the Egyptian. A few symbols are similar, such as the five-pointed star, which represents heaven. The DNA of some of the tribes on North America's east coast has Haplogroup X, which is seen in Europe. It supports a theory that America was colonized from Europe sooner than we thought. The Druze had the Haplogroup X. They lived in Galilee, Lebanon, and Israel. The Soultrean hypothesis is a controversial theory that believes America was settled by a people in France and Spain dating back to 20,000 B.C. It seems that the native Indians' origin is of interest in the archeology world."

A man in black had his rifle pointed at the window of Chief's house. The crosshairs on the infrared scope were pointed at the chief. It moved toward Bill and passed by Mary but finally fixed on Cordy. He got ready to pull the trigger when near his ear, he heard a menacing growl.

He didn't hear Grey Smoke come up behind him. The wolf dog buried his jaws in the man's neck. The man wrestled with the huge animal while trying to reach for the gun. The white, female wolf-dog bit his hand, but Grey Smoke's tightening jaws muffled his screams. A black wolf-dog grabbed his leg. The whole pack emerged and took part in the kill. The night went quiet again.

Grey Smoke scratched on the door. Mary opened it and bowed her head knowingly to Grey Smoke. He settled by the fireplace. The wolf pack would eat well tonight and only a few bones would be left scattered across the wilderness along with a torn black patch with the symbol of an eye.

The chief rose and grabbed the decorated pipe. He placed an herb from a jar in the pipe. "It's time to smoke the peace pipe." He took two puffs and handed it to Bill. Bill took two puffs. An intoxicating smell filled the air. He handed it to Mary, who took two puffs. Cordy felt the reverence of the moment. She was being initiated into the Mi'kmaq ways. The smoke filled the air with a rich smell of herbs. Cordy could smell a touch of sage, which clears the air of evil spirits.

The chief handed her the pipe. "We welcome Star Child back home with her Mi'kmaq family."

Cordy took the long pipe and inhaled the smoke. She got a dizzy feeling and in her mind, she heard the voices of Indian women singing a song. She handed the pipe back to him. "I will teach you our ways, Star Child. Here is a book which I wrote about your family."

He handed her a small red book with the name Saunhac on the front. Mary and Bill clapped and sang a Mi'kmaq welcome song and the chief picked up his drum. The chief had the most enchanting voice, which vibrated throughout the house. Grey Smoke lifted his head and howled along to the music. Cordy felt something stir deep inside her, and she felt a pride in her family. It was a night to remember.

Chapter 56

Ellen Undercover

It was late at night and she was waiting for the Dark Watcher. He had been feeding her information for more than a year. The chairman was aware of it and wanted her to get more information. Ellen knew most men's weakness was sex. He would be putty in her hands by the end of the night. She was dressed in a black corset with black laced-trimmed thigh-highs and high heels. He liked her in black because it showed off her silky skin.

She tied the black silk robe around her. A bottle of champagne stood chilled, ready to be poured. He told her to get ready to celebrate. The news he brought would be the best. He was an distinguished, well-educated man like the chairman. It seemed powerful men tended to find her sharp wit a big turn-on. Ellen heard a turn of the key, and he walked in. The Dark Watcher walked in to see a delicious Ellen sitting on the bed in a silk robe with her long legs crossed. He had to admit she was delicious-looking and lethal.

The Watcher came over and kissed her hard. "My dear, you look absolutely ravishing tonight."

She gave him a seductive smile. "Well? Did you get the information?"

He handed her a file. "I did, and what is in it will ingratiate you with the chairmen. Ken will be working in the mail room after you show him that folder."

Ellen beamed. "What's in the file, darling?"

The Dark Watcher grabbed the bottle of champagne. "It has the names of two very important Pure of Hearts and their whereabouts. They have been hidden from all of us for a long time. The file shows that the retired chief of the Mi'kmaq has in his possession the wishing cup. The cup gives the imbiber secret knowledge from the Tree of Knowledge in the Garden of Eden. One who drinks from it will get his wish. Saunhac plans on giving it to a Pure of Heart. The other goodie is that the other Pure of Heart carries the honey from the Tree of Life. The honey has special qualities.

"Chief Saunhac is going to take them to get the Pure of Heart's priceless stash because he is too old to protect them anymore. They have hidden their treasures close to these coordinates, but we don't know exactly where. The Pure of Heart died during torture before we found out the exact location. You're going to need to follow them and radio my men as soon as possible when you find out. I have given you the number to the Lafitte family, who are Dark Watchers and will aid you. They know the territory well. We will split the treasures between us and after this, the chairman will be pleased and give you whatever you want."

The glasses were filled with champagne, and they both raised their glasses in salute. Ellen untied her silk gown, revealing an enticing view of large breasts and a voluptuous body. "I think you deserve a big reward."

The Watcher smiled. "I can't wait to see what surprises you have in store for me. I might have a surprise or two for you also. Let the games begin."

Ellen giggled, and he clicked the bedroom light off.

CHAPTER 57

Jon Lafitte's Promise to Pappa

The distinguished elderly man sitting at the café on Saint Pierre Isle motioned for Jon to have a seat. His face was worn from the sea, which made him look even more handsome in his old age. Jon's father had a certain charm or charisma about him. Women found him irresistible when he was younger, but the love of his life was Evangeline.

Jon's mother was named after the Acadian woman in Longfellow's poem. It fitted his mother because she was a Cajun from Louisiana. She was from a wealthy Southern family and was singing in a Broadway play when his father became smitten. Jon's mother had passed away from cancer a year ago. His father missed her every day. The older man smiled at his handsome son. He was the spitting image of his father with thick curly dark hair with a sprinkle of light grey and dark eyes.

"I am glad, Jon, that you have come. Are you still having your dreams?"

Jon nodded. "Yes, they seem to have increased."

Keys of Life

His father pulled out a crest with three blue boars and three Crusader crosses on it.

"You know what these symbols mean, Jon?"

Jon shook his head. "No, but it's a family name and their crest, Pappa."

On the crest were the words "Honor and Virtue." Jon thought, that is not the Lafitte motto. The Lafitte motto was "Don't ever get caught." Pappa looked at him seriously while he sipped his wine. "I want you to promise me that you will help whoever wears this crest."

Jon smiled at his father. "I promise, Pappa, but why do you want me to help them? Do we owe them a favor?"

His Pappa nodded. "The family saved our family a long time ago. Our family made a promise to always aid them."

The family had a history of privateering — gun running, alcohol, gambling, and fishing businesses were all part of their past. Jon was bringing the family into the legitimate business world by running gambling casinos around the world. The Lafitte family business had grown into a large corporation.

His father started to get up to take his afternoon walk. "If you keep your promises, the angels smile at you."

Jon patted his father's shoulder. "Have a good day, Pappa, and I will remember my promise." His father grabbed his arm. "You will tell your grandchildren about this promise. It was made to help them forever. It goes back further than my grandfather."

The Lafitte family was close, and they would do anything to protect each other. Jon was in line to head the family business.

"I must feed my birds. They grow hungry."

Jon waved goodbye to his father. As Jon walked to his office, his cell phone rang. A woman's voice asked, "Jon Lafitte? I heard you have a company in the import and export business. I need to hire you for a very special job. I'd like to start with a million dollars for your services, and I want complete secrecy. Are you my man?"

Jon smiled. "Are you as enchanting as you sound, mademoiselle? Yes, I am your man."

Chapter 58

Pure of Heart Arise

The sun's rays peeked through the window, waking Cordy. She went to get up but found the wolf-dog lying by her bed on the floor. She reached to pet his head and he leaned toward her. Cordy whispered. "You are magnificent, Grey Smoke." She smelled breakfast cooking in the kitchen. She looked out through the window and saw the chief with his arms raised in the air, welcoming at the sunrise.

Cordy grabbed a cup of coffee and walked out to listen to Chief sing to the sun. His low voice vibrated with the Mi'kmaq prayer, and Cordy felt something stir in her heart. The chief smiled at her when he was finished.

"Many spirits live in this world, and they awaken for the great battle."

"Great battle, what great battle?" asked Cordy.

Chief's voice had a serious tone. "The great battle from the beginning of time where brother fought brother. You must bring the box you received from de Villiers with you, Star Child, on our

Keys of Life

fishing trip. I can see in the great astral sea. Time has no meaning there, and I can travel time and distance. The box contains many holy things."

Cordy took a sip of her coffee, "I don't know what they mean. A Book of Enoch, the Magdalene statue with the strange hands, and a beautiful wishing cup."

The chief smiled. "You are a Pure of Heart. You can touch it, but for others it means death. The wishing cup is Egyptian, and it dates to the time of Moses and the Ark. The cup was sacred to the Egyptians. The Mi'kmaq have had contact with the Vikings and some say with Crusaders who were trying to escape the Inquisition. Nova Scotia was a land where the Inquisition could not reach. In the later years, when the French came over after the Revolution, other sacred items made their way here for protection.

"The Children of Vincent were the great protectors, especially the nuns. Your aunt is a great and wise one. She is a warrior with great bravery, and she was right to hide you from them. Are you ready, Star Child, for the great battle?"

Cordy looked in the older man's eyes. "I am, but I'm not sure what the battle is about." The old chief spread his arms out to the land. "Have you not noticed the earth changes? The increased extinction of the animals, the warming of the seas, and the increased frequency of wars all over the world. The signs are there. The Children of the Nephilim and the Dark Watchers have united. They believe they can be gods, and they want to be creators. The Tree of Life is not to be tampered with, but they have changed the DNA of animals and seeds that have been on Earth for thousands of years. The Pure of Heart must rise up to defend the Great Mother of us all, and the flaming sword that protects the Tree of Life looks for justice. Your great ancestors look on you, Star Child, with great love. I am very glad to have seen you, Star Child, before I die."

Cordy blinked away tears. "I love you, too, Chief." Chief hugged her, and Cordy felt how frail he was through his sweater.

Pure of Heart Arise

"I will soon leave this world and take the journey to the ancestral home of my family. They wait for me. I will always be with you, Star Child."

Bill yelled from the door of the house, "Hey you guys! We have a boat to catch."

They placed their backpacks in the back of the car and as they did, Grey Smoke wagging his tail, jumped in. Cordy asked, "Is Grey Smoke a sailor?"

The chief laughed. "Grey Smoke loves fishing."

Bill laughed along, too. "I hope he likes Ash."

Cordy sat in the back petting Grey Smoke. The chief and Bill sat in the front talking about sports. It seems the chief had another special power. He loved football and could predict the winner of any game. Bill explained that the chief had the power of sight. He used to get up every morning and without reading the sports section, know the winners. It took years of developing his seer ability, but he practiced it on the games.

Cordy realized something. "You could make millions if you knew the winners."

The chief shook his head. "If I use the sight for the wrong reasons, it would be lost forever. Bill and you are the only ones who know."

Cordy promised to keep the family secret. The ocean sparkled when the sun shined on the waters. The blue sea and thunderous waves hit the jagged coastline. Bill took the scenic route. The road hugged the coastline.

Ash was waiting for them at the dock. The boat was named the Lady of the Sea. She was a small fishing vessel. Bill shook Ash's hand. "Good morning, Ash."

The chief smiled. "Hello, Little Rabbit, and how are you feeling this morning? I brought you some medicine for your stomach."

Ash chuckled. "I might take you up on that, Chief."

Grey Smoke crept on the boat past Ash. He saw the huge grey wolf-dog. "Whoa, that is one big doggie!" Grey Smoke growled.

"He doesn't like being called a doggie, Ash," laughed Cordy as she petted Grey Smoke. Bill waved to the crew and skipper of the Lady of the Sea. "Let me introduce the crew, Captain Joe, Big Ed, and Tim."

Ash asked, "Where we heading?"

"Magdalen Island, which has some of the best fishing," Bill replied. "It had huge salt deposits which were used for centuries to preserve cod."

Ash looked at Cordy, her long brunette hair streaked with blonde and red highlights that glistened in the sun. Ash was not a saint, and he enjoyed the vision of her in a black skintight skiff suit. Cordy had gorgeous long legs, and the suit showed her athletic figure.

The chief smiled. "Did you bring the box, Little Rabbit?"

"Yes, Chief, I brought it like you told me to."

"Good, Lil' Rabbit. I will show you something special when we get to Magdalen Island. Did you find your spiritual journey enlightening?"

Ash gave him a knowing look. "I was lost but now I found the truth. You were a great guide, Chief. I want to thank you for everything." Chief patted him on the shoulder. "The Great Spirits are with you."

Cordy's eye wandered to where Chief and Ash were talking, and she had to admit Ash was one good-looking guy. Grey Smoke relaxed around him, even letting Ash pet him. Cordy got her camera out and took pictures. She took a picture of Ash because her friends would be drooling at the eye candy. Bill looked suspiciously at Ash. The chief assured him that he was a Pure of Heart but Bill wasn't so sure. He didn't trust him. Bill's men on the boat were Light Watchers and if Ash blinked wrong, it would be the last thing he did. Guns and ammunition were down below, and Bill carried his revolver on him at all times.

The Lady of the Sea made it out of the harbor, followed by sea gulls looking for a treat. They knew fish was on the menu. Cordy screamed with pure joy watching the dolphins follow the ship.

One of them jumped in the air while following the boat. Bill sat there, amazed at how animals were so attracted to her.

Ash explained, "The dolphins use the wake made by the boat. In old legends, dolphins used to save sailors at sea."

Cordy smiled while listening. "I love dolphins. They are so graceful."

Big Ed and Tim came up to Chief and bowed. They were Mi'kmaq and knew the chief. "Please, oh great Chief, could you call the fish spirits?"

The chief answered. "You want me to sing the fish song. I will call to our brothers."

Bill pointed to the chief, explaining to Ash and Cordy, "The Mi'kmaq believe that all animals have souls or spirits. Man must live in harmony with the spirits of his brothers. They never over fish, and they ask permission of the fish to hunt them."

Ash asked, "How do you call the fish, Chief? You text them?"

Chief spread his hands over the sea. "I have no need for cell phones, Lil' Rabbit." His words vibrated and the song he started to sing was mesmerizing. "Come, my brothers and sisters, we ask for your blessing. Aahhh tahhh oooo, we give you thanks."

Big Ed and Tim lowered the nets and then pulled them up. The nets were filled with fish. Big Ed and Tim laughed and bowed to the chief. The chief bowed back. "Now it is time for Star Child to call the fish. Come, Star Child."

Cordy shyly went over to the chief and spread her arms over the ocean like him. She followed his words, and she felt a vibration all through her body. A force deep inside her emerged and came out in her voice. "There she blows," yelled an excited Big Ed, pointing to the right of the boat.

Bill scratched his head in awe. "Well, I'll be damned!"

Ash looked in amazement. Cordy had called a family of whales. They were heading toward the boat. The chief looked at Star Child with pride. She had the gift. The whales blew fountains of water from their air holes and sprayed the whole crew as Grey Smoke barked a friendly hello. Ash realized at that moment

Keys of Life

that Cordy had a special gift with animals.

The nets were filled with fish, and the boat traveled along the jagged coastline of Magdalen Isle. The cliffs had caves cut from the erosion of wind and the waves of the sea.

Bill was first to see the three boats coming at them. Two of the boats were from Saint Pierre, the notorious pirate island. He recognized the Lafitte family markings on the fishing boats. They didn't take kindly to competition. They were Dark Watchers who sided with whoever they wanted and held no loyalty. They had pirate blood running through their veins. Their reputation was for using intimidation to get the fisherman to leave the fishing area or to sign with their company.

Bill ordered Big Ed and Tim to bring out the guns. "We've got trouble, Joe. Run her at full throttle."

Joe saw them coming and turned the boat around. They started running away as fast as they could. Bill ordered Cordy, Ash, and the chief below and Grey Smoke followed, hiding under the bunk.

Ellen was in the lead, followed by Lafitte's men. Ellen laughed. "We got them. Fire at will, boys" Her men opened fired on the Lady of the Sea. Bill fired with his machine gun. Ellen ducked down hearing the bullets whistle over her head. One of her men was hit and fell off the boat.

Lafitte's boats caught up with Ellen and waved his support. Lafitte's deal with Ellen was to just give support and chase down the boat and make sure they would not escape. Ellen was going to be the one leading the attack. Tim was up top firing on Ellen's boat as he gave out the Mi'kmaq war call. He was drawing their fire. Ellen's boat was the fastest, and it drew closer. Tim was hit by the Nephilim. Knowing he was fatally wounded, he stood up and continued firing his machine gun at Ellen's men. They riddled his body with bullets, and he fell into the arms of the sea. Big Ed screamed, "Tim is gone!"

Chief, Cordy and Ash were below, listening to the gunfire, when bullets tore into the compartment. The chief stood up. "I'm tired of this shit."

Pure of Heart Arise

The old man pulled out a gun from the locker and loaded it like he had used it often. He shouted a Mi'kmaq war whoop and opened the door. Cordy pulled out a sniper gun. "This will do very nicely. My father taught me how to shoot when I was little. I'm pretty good, too." Ash pulled out a machine gun, "I've always wanted to use one of these."

Cordy pushed off the safety on his gun. "You need to take the safety off first. Ready, let's go!"

They both ran for the door. Chief was shooting from behind the bell on the boat. He yelled, "Lil Rabbit, point and squeeze the trigger."

Ash looked at Cordy. "I usually let ladies go first, but not this time."

Cordy opened the door. Ash ran to the front of the boat, blasting away with the machine gun. He positioned himself on the other side of Bill. He didn't hit any of the shooters, but he hit the mast on the boat, which knocked two of Ellen's men off the boat. The chief ran to where Joe was at the wheel driving the boat. Chief fired to protect him and give him cover. Joe smiled at the chief. "We fight for what is right, old wise one." It was then a bullet hit him in the head, and he slumped over the wheel.

Antar knew that time was running out for the leader of the Pure of Heart. Chief Saunhac and Antar had their encounters over the years. He was a "Spirit Walker" who was one of the greatest warriors that Antar had encountered over the centuries. They had many skirmishes, sometimes ending in a draw. The chief had many powers and was fearless in battle. The old man's time was running out, and Antar wasn't going to miss this. No one could see Antar but the chief.

The chief saw Antar watching them being annihilated with a smile on his face. The chief dropped the gun and grabbed the wheel of the boat. He looked at Antar. "Why do you smile, brother?"

Antar snapped back at him, "I'm not your brother!"

The window in the cabin shattered from the gunfire and the chief ducked. "We are all brothers for we come from the Great

Keys of Life

One of all things. He is all forgiving, all compassionate, and loving. Forgiveness is beyond you. Do you not love your own children?"

Antar snapped, "It is for the love of my children that I want revenge for their annihilation."

The chief looked at him with intensity. "You will regret your aid to the Dark Watchers and the Children of Nephilim. A father who cannot recognize his children is no father. Remember this Father of the Nephilim. I forgive your ignorance. You will learn a hard lesson."

Antar arrogantly replied, "You forgive me. The insignificant puny human thinks to forgive me. You waste your breath, old man, and the long journey awaits you. It comes soon." The boat ran fast and the chief swerved to avoid the gunshots. Antar was amused at how the Pure of Heart always had hope when there was none. "I have known, I would someday go to sleep when I woke up from my mother's womb. Death has no meaning for me. Your ignorance shows, Father."

"Quit calling me that. And if death has no meaning for you, then what of your charming great-granddaughter? Your trinkets will not save you. I'm going to enjoy watching your death. Goodbye, Chief." Antar disappeared. Chief smiled. "I hope it will be the last time I have to listen to you."

Ellen was down to only two men now. Ellen's men shot Big Ed, who fell off the boat riddled with bullets. Cordy screamed, "Big Ed's down!" She placed her scope on the top of the roof of the ship. In her scope, she saw a man with binoculars looking straight at her. He was smiling.

Lafitte was admiring the lovely woman in a skintight wet suit that revealed a wonderful figure. She was one the most ravishing woman Lafitte had ever seen. He then saw it, pinned on her shoulder, and he froze. It was the pin with the three blue boars and the three crusader crosses. "I can't believe it!"

His father's words echoed in his mind. "You must promise me to help the one who wears this symbol. We owe the family a great debt." Right then, a bullet whizzed and hit his hat, which flew off his head. He looked in his binoculars and saw Cordy giving him the finger. "Ma cherie is a naughty girl," smiled Lafitte.

The chief knew all would be lost if he didn't call up the dragon. It was old medicine, and it was time. He started chanting the old words from his ancestors. The breath of the dragon was the greatest of earth magic. Only the great ones used the magic of the dragon. The earth medicine called on the dragons of earth, air, water, and fire. He repeated the words over and over again as his father had taught him. Cordy could hear the words and the power that emanated from them.

It came suddenly on them. The sun went dim under the clouds, and darkness started to come with a thick mist turning to fog. Lafitte ordered his boats to stop because the coastline of Magdalen was dangerous and unforgiving. More than 400 boats had sunk over the years in these treacherous waters, which only the best seamen knew how to sail. It gave him an excuse. He would tell Ellen that they got lost in the fog. He told his men to stop.

Cordy saw the handsome dark haired man wave goodbye and salute her through her scope. He disappeared in a cloud of foggy mist.

The chief had been to the cove many times when he was a child. It was sacred. The rock's arch was cut by wind and sea, producing a splendid cut-out cliff with a cave. The boat was shot up and the engine gone. The waves coasted them into the beach where they ran aground.

"Cordy and Ash, bring the boxes. We don't have much time," ordered the chief. Grey Smoke scrambled out from under the bunk and jumped into the water, swimming onto the sand. The grey wolf-dog climbed the cliff and rushed toward the woods. The fog was too thick to see where he ran.

Chief assured Cordy, "Grey Smoke can take care of himself and has friends here. He was born here."

Cordy looked at the cave in the fog. It looked spooky. The cave had been used by many of the Ancient Ones and was a Mi'kmaq

Keys of Life

hiding place. It was used to hide very precious treasure. Bill grabbed guns and water. Ash brought his bag, which had some granola bars in them. It was just them now.

Ash, Cordy, Bill, and the chief headed in the water toward the sandy beach. Cordy held onto her grandfather who struggled with the strong waves. They climbed up into the cave. The chief took out a container of spices from the medicine bag around his neck and placed it in the rose quartz cup. He handed it to each one and told them to drink the mixed Mi'kmaq concoction. They all drank from the cup because Bill said they had to conserve water.

He checked the radio but it was shot. No radio transmission was coming from there. Ash asked the chief what was in the drink. The chief smiled. "It is an old Mi'kmaq potion to ward off evil spirits and provide nourishment."

"Does that mean ward off diarrhea? I must say this is the most exciting fishing trip I've been on," laughed Ash.

The chief took the boxes out of the bags and disappeared into the cave. He placed the boxes in the holes of the cave and placed a rock over them. The Mi'kmaq had hid secret treasures in this cave for centuries. The knowledge was passed down from family to family.

It had turned night, and the dark engulfed them. Bill was down at the boat getting emergency supplies. He was grabbing a red emergency bag when he turned around to see Ellen's man Pea Brain had snuck up behind him.

Bill felt his presence and took the bag and swung it at his arm. Pea Brain dropped his gun so he swung at Bill, missing him. A more-experienced Bill hit Pea Brain in the jaw. "I think you knocked my tooth out, you son of a bitch," Pea Brain yelled, wiping the blood from his mouth.

"Pea Brain, don't kill him yet. That's an order!"

Ellen had a gun aimed at Bill. "Bill, nice to see you again. I believe you have something we need. Why don't you be a good little Watcher and come and watch. We are going to have some fun with the Pure of Hearts."

Pure of Heart Arise

Doug stood beside Ellen with his gun on Bill, too. Ash jumped out from behind the rock, knocking Doug down. His gun fired randomly. Bill hit Pea Brain again in the face. Cordy kicked the gun out of Ellen's hands.

Ellen assumed her fighting stance. "You want to fight? I'll give you a fight." Ellen kicked at Cordy but was easily blocked. Cordy punched Ellen in the face and drew blood as she made Ellen bite her tongue.

Doug had his hands around Ash, but Ash head-butted him, making him scream in pain. Doug released Ash after Ash punched him in the face, loosening a couple of lower teeth. Doug spotted his gun in the dirt and grabbed it. He pointed the gun at Cordy. "Unless you want her dead, everybody, hands in the air."

He grabbed Cordy and pointed the gun at her head. "Nice job, Doug," smiled Ellen. "Where is the old man?" Pea Brain yelled out. "Old man, if you want them alive, you better surrender." The chief raised his hands up in the air as he stood in front of the cave entrance. They climbed up the cliff and met the chief. Ellen had them all enter the cave.

Ellen looked at him. "Hello, Chief, head of the Pure of Hearts. It is time for you to retire."

Chief looked at her. "If you're here to kill me, then cancer got me first. I've been waiting to meet you, Julia. We met once when you were a child. I knew your parents."

Ellen screamed, "My name isn't Julia. It's Ellen. You have the wrong girl, old man." The chief looked at her tenderly. "Your real name is Julia Villiers. You were taken as a small child by the Children of the Nephilim after your parents were brutally killed by the chairman. You were born in South Africa. I have waited many years to save you from him." Ellen had in her mind at that instant a flash back of a little girl in a party dress with her parents. They cried out her name, "Julia." Ellen got very angry. "Shut up, old man. We are not here on a witch hunt. Where is the wishing cup? I knew where your sacred cave was thanks to information reported by the Dark Watchers, and you helped lead us to it. It's not a secret anymore."

Keys of Life

Ellen smiled at the blonde-haired Ash, and pointed her gun at him. "You pull down your pants!"

Everyone looked surprised at the command. "You heard me, pull down your pants! If you don't pull down your pants, I'll shoot the old man. Don't be shy!"

Ash answered, "OK." He started to pull down his pants in front of everybody. He had learned his lesson and wore underwear this time. He stood in front of them in his red boxers. Cordy looked at the boxers and was surprised. She pictured Ash as a brief type of guy.

Ellen insisted, "Pull down the undies, too. Don't be shy. I've seen many naked men in my life, and I believe you have a unique marking on your thigh. A birthmark of a star is on your right thigh. I want to see it before I show the chairman."

Ash stood there in front of everyone in all his glory. Cordy tried not to look but couldn't help herself. She whispered to Chief, "I don't think Lil' Rabbit is the right name, Chief."

Ash looked up at the ceiling of the cave. He tried to remain calm, and thank goodness it was cold. Doug looked on his thigh. "He has the birthmark just like you said Ellen."

Ellen smiled with smug satisfaction. "I knew it had to be you. You are the naked robber of the Temple of Abu Simbel. I spent hours and hours watching videotape with extreme magnification, and I alone found the birthmark. OK, show's over, put your clothes back on."

Ellen looked at the chief. "You know what I want. Get it or they die. Old man, you will bring me the wishing cup."

The chief went to a hole in the cave wall and pulled out the cup.

Ash interrupted, "What in the world is the wishing cup of King Tut doing here?"

The chief brought it out gently and with reverence. "My family has been guardian over the wishing cup but it was lost to us. Cordy was given it by the Dark Watchers and brought it back. They used it to test if she was a Pure of Heart. The Templar Grandmaster Guillaume de Saunhac was in charge of keeping it safe."

Ash saw the Egyptian hieroglyphs. "It should have an inscription on it, 'Beloved of Amun Re, lord of thrones and lord of heaven.' It's a spell and gives the drinker a wish."

Ellen pointed the gun at Cordy. "Let's see the rest, Chief." The chief went in the cave and brought over the small quartz jar carved with the Egyptian hieroglyph symbols of the bee and the ankh. The other ancient Egyptian symbols carved in the alabaster were of Thoth carrying the Ankh in his hand, Seshat the goddess of Wisdom, Wedjet a goddess holding a staff with a serpent around it, the goddess Isis, and the eye of Ra.

The chief continued, "Ash found this in Egypt. At Abu Simbel temple, he pulled it out from the wall. It is the legendary honey from the Tree of Knowledge from the Garden of Eden. He who drinks will obtain the great secret knowledge. The Children of the Nephilim have been waiting for the Pure of Heart to obtain these."

Ellen looked at the jar. "What's in it?"

Ash answered, "I got an analysis report that it's honey but it has an unknown substance in it. It looks like it's ancient Egyptian honey. The Egyptians believed the bees were sacred and honey was a gift from the gods. According to Egyptian legend, the bees were created from the tears of Ra. I have never seen it connected to the Tree of Knowledge."

The chief explained. "On the Tree of Knowledge grew apples of which the serpent gave Eve to eat. It was said a beehive was in the tree's upper branches. The honey here would be very ancient and from that tree."

Cordy whispered to Bill, "The bees are dying everywhere in the world and are a major player in the process of pollination. They give us all the flowers, fruits, and most of our foods. I can see why the ancient people thought they were sacred. The bees have been around the earth longer than mankind."

Ellen thought for a second. "We have to test it before I call the troops in. It's crystallized but we can take the lighters to it."

Doug grabbed his lighter. The lighter burned the quartz bottle at the bottom and the honey dissolved to a liquid. She

Keys of Life

pointed to the Chief. "You drink it, and be very careful because I'll kill all of them if you do anything stupid."

She poured the honey in the cup and handed it to the chief. "Drink it."

The cup had a bluish-tinged liquid in it. Bill yelled out, "The honey has to be rotten. It has been in a tomb for thousands of years."

Ash answered, "He'll be all right. They've found honey in the tombs that is more than three thousand years old and it's still good. It may have a tinge of the blue lotus in it. That stays good for years, too."

The chief took a sip from the wishing cup, grabbing both handles. "It is very sweet." Ellen grabbed the cup from him. After fifteen minutes, the chief was still alive, showing no symptoms.

Ellen looked at him. "The honey is supposed to give him great knowledge, especially of the future. We need to test him."

Pea Brain asked, "How do we do that?" Doug answered, "Let's ask him about the football game winners for today. The scores are just coming in. It's random, and it'll tell us if he can see into the future. He couldn't know today's results, and I have the winners on my cell phone."

Chief smiled. "Fire away!"

Doug asked, "New York or New England?"

The chief answered without hesitation, "New England, of course!"

Doug smiled. "He's right! Saints verses Cowboys?"

The chief calmly answered, "Cowboys, and the score is 14 to 10."

Everybody looked in surprise at the chief. After half an hour, the chief got every winner of the games right. Doug looked at Pea Brain. "This knowledge could make you millions in Vegas. It could fund the Nephilim for years." Ellen smiled. "Exactly! I'm going outside to try to call the Nephilim. The reception in here sucks. How's your cell phone, Doug?"

Doug checked it. "The rocks must have some magnetic properties because my phone just comes and goes. I'm lucky I got the scores."

Pure of Heart Arise

Ellen looked out at the boat. "I'll try by the boats. Doug, you watch them. Pea Brain, go search their boat for any other precious items. Doug, search their back packs, and don't let that cup out of your sight."

Doug walked over to Bill. "I'll take great pleasure in shooting you, Watcher." Doug wiped the blood from his mouth. He put the gun to Bill's head. "Maybe I should get it over with!"

The chief spoke to Doug and glanced toward the cup. "It's too bad that the knowledge and cup will go to your boss and not to you who found it. It's a shame. You said it yourself. A man could make millions."

Doug moved over to the cup and looked mesmerized. "I'm tired of being the slave around here. You have a point old man. I don't trust you, so let's have him and her drink, too."

Doug picked up the wishing cup and could feel something stir in his heart. "It does have a power. I can feel it," he whispered.

He pointed to Ash and Cordy. "Each of you take a sip."

Cordy grabbed one handle and Ash grabbed the other. The chief looked at them with confidence. "It is a wishing cup, so be sure to make a wish."

Doug laughed, "I'd be wishing I live if I were you two."

Ash looked at Cordy. "Guess I'll go first." Ash whispered the ancient prayer. He took a sip, and then Doug put the gun to Cordy's head. "Drink up, sweetheart."

Ash whispered the prayer and Cordy recited it after him. She took a sip. Cordy and Ash stood there feeling a certain rush go through them. They had no side effects. Doug grabbed the cup. "My turn. What the hell!" He grabbed the cup and took a tiny sip and swallowed.

"It is sweet and gives you a bit of a rush! If anybody tells Ellen about this, then they're dead."

Five minutes later, Pea Brain walked in. "Ellen needs you to help with connecting to base. The instruments are acting screwy. I'll guard them."

Keys of Life

Doug walked from the cave. "I always have to do everything around here." Pea Brain sat on the rock, smiling at them with his tooth missing.

Ash whispered to Cordy, "I think he looks better without his teeth."

Pea Brain yelled, "Shut up over there."

He went over and grabbed Cordy's hair and smelled it. "My, you smell good, sweetheart. Maybe after this we can have a little fun together."

Cordy pulled away from him and he laughed. The chief calmly asked, "You really think the Nephilim are going to reward you for this? You will do all the work, and they will make the millions. It's all because you are afraid to drink from the cup. Doug just drank from the cup while you were gone. He told us not to tell Ellen."

Pea Brain yelled, "I'm not afraid of anything, old man. Doug drank from the cup, you say? Well, two can play that game."

He grabbed the cup and took a big gulp. "Pretty soon nobody is ever going to call me Pea Brain ever again. Las Vegas, here I come. Don't tell anybody or I will shoot you."

Ellen entered the cave. "Finally, we got reception, and Doug is typing the coordinates to headquarters. I emailed my friends the location. They'll be here soon. Pea Brain, go search their boat for some maps and give what you find to Doug. We don't want them to miss us. I'll watch them."

Ellen's tongue hurt where she bit it when Cordy hit her. The wishing cup glistened, and Ellen couldn't take her eyes off the beautiful cup. It attracted her. The chief whispered, "It is fascinating and bewitching, isn't it? Knowledge is power. The Nephilim has never had a woman as their leader. It is a wishing cup and think of the secret knowledge withheld from you. You could be the first. You would be free."

Ellen picked up the cup, mesmerized. "One sip can't hurt, can it? I would possess all the secret knowledge of the Nephilim. I will be free."

Pure of Heart Arise

Ellen took a sip of the sweet honey. She felt a tingling coursing through her veins. "A female head of the Nephilim. Could it be me?"

The chief looked at her with sadness. "Only the Pure of Heart can drink from the wishing cup. Ellen is not a Pure of Heart, but Julia Villiers is a Pure of Heart. I have come to free you from bondage, Julia Villiers. You are she, Ellen. The chairman killed your parents and became your guardian. He wanted a Pure of Heart who would obey him. You were trained at a young age to fear and obey him. You will remember everything, Julia, and you will see the Great Spirit who will tell you the truth. You will get your wish."

Ellen felt sick to her stomach. "Shut up, old man! I am not Julia." Ellen fell to her knees. "My stomach hurts. It's on fire." A trickle of blood came from her mouth.

The chief grabbed the half bottle of water sitting on the side of the cave wall that he put the herbs in and brought it to Ellen. "You must drink this, Julia, for it will help save your life. Drink it, Julia."

Ellen drank from the bottle and then screamed in agony. She fell on the ground, shivering. Chief pulled out of his bag an ampule and syringe. He ordered, "Cordy, this must be given immediately intravenously for it is antivenom serum."

"We drank snake venom?" Cordy took the syringe and filled it with the serum, wrapping a shoelace from her shoe around Ellen's arm as a tourniquet. She injected the serum.

Bill grabbed Ellen's gun and ran down to the boat. He found Doug seizing and frothy sputum coming from his mouth. His eyes rolled upwards and his whole body seized. He stopped breathing.

Bill spotted Pea Brain lying in his own urine, catatonic. He had a grand mal seizure and became non-responsive. Bill checked for a pulse, but there was nothing. Bill ran back to check on Ellen.

The chief held her in his arms, and Ash had wrapped her in his jacket for warmth. Ellen looked up at the chief. "Am I going to die?"

Keys of Life

He said gently, "You will live, Julia. You are a Pure of Heart."

Ellen asked, "Are the others dead?"

Bill answered her, "Yes, both of them."

Ellen looked at the chief. "You drank from the cup. Why aren't you dead?"

The chief gave her more medicine from his bag. "Take this, Julia, and drink. It will ease the pain. My family has immunity to certain snake venom. Your family has a tolerance to snake venom. The legend says that the honey came from the Tree of Knowledge. The serpent tried to take the honey from the great bees. The bees stung him on his nose and a drop of serpent venom landed on the honey in the beehive."

Cordy looked at him. "All three of them drank snake venom and we did, too. They wouldn't have gotten sick if it wasn't for the cuts in their mouths. You didn't have a cut in your mouth, Chief and Bill, and neither did Ash and I. I hit Julia in the mouth, making her bite her tongue. Pea Brain and Doug lost their teeth."

The chief smiled at how smart his Star Child was. "You are right, Star Child. The venom can be drunk but no entry from a cut can allow it to enter the blood stream. We must bring Julia back home and to the hospital. The antivenom should help save her."

The chief whispered into Ellen's ear, "Julia, do you hear me? You must investigate Julia Villiers when you are better."

Julia grabbed the chief's rough old hand and whispered, "Thank you! I will be free at last."

Cordy looked at Julia. "She is losing consciousness."

The chief put his hand on her forehead. "The object of power can be a two-edged sword. One edge gives great beauty and power, and the other edge gives death. Julia will receive her freedom, and Ellen will die. I have fulfilled my promise to her father."

The Chief went into the cave and grabbed the boxes. He placed the wishing cup and the jar of honey back in them. He put them in a backpack and handed it to Cordy. "You must keep them safe and protect them. All your treasures are in the backpack. I almost forgot, there is one more thing."

He ran back into the cave. Bill heard the sounds of a Blackhawk helicopter coming their way. "Everybody grab a gun. The Nephilim are coming."

Cordy grabbed the sniper rifle. She looked through the scope and saw a man dressed in black with a bulletproof vest. Her finger was on the trigger, ready to fire. His back was turned to her, and then he turned around and waved.

"It's Bob!" Cordy screamed in relief.

Bill smiled and hugged Cordy. "Well, I'll be damned!"

Bob dropped a harness down to them. "I've got her!" Ash picked up the backpack and then the unconscious Julia. He put the harness on, and he held onto her with all his strength. Bob cranked the wire and brought them up. Bob grabbed Ellen. Ash yelled to Bob, "She needs a medic!"

Bob yelled, "Jerry, take a look at her." Bob carried her gently over to the stretcher and placed a blanket on her.

Ash yelled at him, "She drank snake venom, and we gave her one dose of antivenom." The medic pulled out a syringe and injected Ellen and then started an intravenous line.

Ash placed the backpack in the cargo bin. Bob handed Ash a bulletproof vest. "Here, put this vest on. You may need it."

Ash smiled. "Let me introduce myself, I'm Ash and a friend of the family. I'm sure glad to see you."

Bob was dressed in black military fatigues with a bulletproof vest and yelled at the pilot, "Ted, keep her steady. The next one is coming up."

Bob pushed in the magazine in his assault machine gun. Ash looked down and asked, "How do you know Cordy?"

Bob smiled. "I'm her accountant."

Ash looked at him in disbelief. "You don't look like an accountant."

Bob had a wicked grin on his face. "You don't look like a stuffy

Keys of Life

archeologist, and don't ask me how I know that or I might have to kill you."

Ash did a double take of Bob's grin. The harness came down again and Cordy came up. She hugged Bob. "I'm so damn glad to see you. How in the world did you find us?"

Bob pointed to her friendship bracelet. "You didn't check in, cupcake! It has a tracking device in it."

Ash grabbed the harness. "I'll go down and get the chief."

Bob nodded and let Ash down. He gave the harness to Bill. "You go, and I'll bring the chief. Where is he?"

Bill put the harness on. "The chief is in the cave. He is bringing the other backpacks. Hurry, Ash, the Nephilim are on their way. I can feel it."

Ash ran to the cave. "Chief, come on!" The chief smiled while running. "I had to get everything out of the cave because it was compromised by the Dark Watchers and the Nephilim. I am ready for a ride, Lil' Rabbit."

Ash placed the harness on, strapping the backpack on the harness and a rope around the chief. Ash gave Bob the signal. The harness pulled them up as the wind rushed around them. Bullets flew over Ash's head. Bill and Bob went behind the cargo door for cover when they heard the gunshots.

Cordy pointed at the cliff where two snipers were firing at the helicopter as Ash and the chief were dangling from the cable. Bill screamed, "Dark Watchers!"

Bob's machine gun sprayed bullets by the rocks to give cover, and the dirt sprayed in the sniper's faces. Ash screamed up at Bob, "Not bad for an accountant."

Bob screamed, "Incoming, everybody get some cover."

The helicopter took fire, and the bullets cut through the steel door. Bill, Bob, and his men aimed their machine guns at the cliffs. The crane kept pulling up Ash and the chief. The sniper focused his scope's crosshairs on the chief and squeezed the trigger.

Cordy saw the chief's body jerk with the force of the bullet that hit him. Cordy cried out in anguish, "Chief is hit." The bullet had ripped through the old man's chest and lung. The chief suddenly felt very weak. He was surprised the pain wasn't very bad.

Bill lowered his gun and looked over to the edge of the helicopter, where the chief looked up smiling at Cordy and Bill. He spoke the words while tenderly looking up at them, "I love you."

Ash sadly looked at the chief, and the chief smiled serenely as the blood flowed from his chest. His gentle voice whispered with resignation while he looked at Ash, "A sacrifice must be made, and I am a warrior of the Mi'kmaq. Goodbye, Lil' Rabbit!"

He pulled a switchblade knife out of his pocket and cut the rope around his waist, falling into the icy water. Ash screamed, "No, Chief! No!"

Cordy cried out, "Chief!"

Ash unbuckled the harness and dropped straight in to the ocean. Cordy instinctively jumped out of the helicopter, which hovered over the water at 50 feet. She fell straight down, feet first into the cold water, holding her chin and clenching her muscles. Her body dropped down in a free fall as she heard the gunshots whizzing at her head. The cold water took her breath away as she crashed into the ocean. Cordy thought to herself, swim damnit, swim, and she kicked her feet furiously. She rose to the top taking a gulp of air.

Bob was incredulous as she splashed into the freezing water. "Well, I'll be damned!" Bill screamed hysterically, "Cordy!"

Bob grabbed Bill by the shirt and started yelling at him, "Bill, they need cover. Don't get any ideas." Bill and Bob looked at each other and sprayed the snipers with bullets, making them duck for cover. The harness came up and Bob cut the tied backpacks off with his knife and lowered the harness back down again. Bob prayed silently to himself and then he saw Cordy wave to him that she was all right.

Cordy took another deep breath and dove down to find Ash and the chief. Ash saw her as the chief's body fell into the deep dark waters. He swam toward the chief, deeper and deeper. The smiling chief pulled out of his shirt a white crystal ball. It lit up with a luminous bright light, and he handed it to Ash.

Keys of Life

Cordy swam toward the light and grabbed the smiling chief's cold hand. He pulled off his necklace in one jerk and handed it to her. Time slowed down in that moment as Cordy kissed his hand. She could hear in her mind the chief's voice. "Let me go."

His eyes grew fixed and his breathing stopped. Ash realized he was taking the journey home to his ancestors. Ash shook his head at Cordy not to follow him. He pointed upward. Cordy and Ash watched the chief's body drift to the depths of the ocean. His arms floated, making it look like he was a waving goodbye.

Cordy placed the necklace in the pocket of her shirt. She grabbed Ash's hand, which held the crystal ball. The ball lit upwith sparkling brilliant light, and a shock wave propelled them up to the top. Their lungs were screaming for air and the force of the energy that hit them was incredibly powerful. Ash placed the crystal ball in his T-shirt and swam to the top, gasping for air. A hand grabbed his arm and pulled him into a boat. He was coughing and spitting water onto the deck. Cordy gasped as she got to the top and aspirated water into her lungs. The ice-cold water made her arms feel like dead weights. She realized she was drowning and felt she was loosing consciousness.

Suddenly, he grabbed her hand and pulled her up into his warm arms. Cordy was limp and nonresponsive. She was not breathing. Lafitte placed the pale cold woman on the deck of his ship. Machine guns were firing all around them, and bullets sprayed the boat. Cordy felt his lips over hers and the warmth of his body covered her. An electrical shock filled her body with a tingling and aching. He breathed air into her mouth and pressed his hands over her heart. "C'mon, ma cherie, breathe!"

His strong, passionate voice resonated through her mind, bringing her back to the world. Cordy breathed in air and rolled over and coughed out the water in her lungs. Ash tried to stand but weakness overwhelmed him, and he grabbed for the nearest thing he could get his hands on. A woman with thick blonde hair proceeded to slap his face. "He is not dead, Jon, but if he grabs my boob one more time, I may kill him."

Pure of Heart Arise

Ash made the mistake of grabbing onto her nice firm butt. The woman slapped him again. "You are a slow learner, aren't you? I have killed men for much less."

The blonde woman walked away from him. The snipers on the cliffs fired on the boat, and Ash saw the rifle pointing at the blonde woman. He pushed her down on the deck, and the bullets hit him in the back.

Ash grimaced, "I've been hit. I'm dying. Do you forgive me for grabbing your ass?" The blonde woman smiled and kissed him. Ash felt in his heart a strange aching. She slapped him again and pushed him off of her to see his wound. Ash rolled over, smiling, and she saw his bulletproof vest had two holes in it. "Get up, handsome," she yelled as she pulled him up.

The boat was sinking because of all the holes and damage. "Andre, hurry! We are sinking!" She shouted into the darkness. A small boat positioned itself next to the sinking one. The blonde haired woman jumped aboard. "Jon, hurry up so we can get the hell out of here." She picked up a machine gun and fired at the cliffs.

Jon wrapped Cordy gently into a warm blanket and placed the harness over her shivering body and wrapped a rope around Ash. Ash's arms surrounded Cordy and the crystal ball illuminated, causing a bright light to flash. A blinding bright light surrounded both of them, making it impossible for the snipers to shoot at the targets. The night scopes burned their eyes with searing pain. Bob lifted them up to the helicopter. The light disappeared when they reached the helicopter.

Ash handed Cordy over to Bill. Bill tenaciously held the cold, wet, and weak Cordy in his arms and cried, "Cordy, thank God you are all right."

Ash was grabbed by Bob and pulled up into the helicopter. Bob patted Ash on the shoulder and whispered, "You did everything you could, Ash."

He placed another blanket over him and handed him a machine gun. "I don't know who they are down there, but they just saved your life. They need some cover." Ash and Bob fired at the cliffs to help protect the bullet-ridden sinking boat. Lafitte's other boat was getting away. Bob smiled at Ash. "Not bad shootin' for a professor. I think you're getting the hang of it."

Cordy and Bill looked down and heard the handsome, grinning captain yell out and wave, "Ma cherie, 'til we meet again."

He pulled off the hat, which had the bullet hole she had shot earlier in the day. The devilish grin on Lafitte's handsome face showed his perfect white teeth as he waved and bowed to Bill McDermott and Cordy. Bill nodded back and saluted, acknowledging that Lafitte's family had remained true to their word. It was a time when Dark Watcher families and Light Watcher families united because of a debt owed in their families long ago. Jon Laffite's other boat flew out of the snipers' range and into the dark night with the mysterious blond-haired woman. The other damaged boat exploded into pieces and sank into the cold sea.

Bob's men fired back at the snipers on the cliffs. The helicopter took bullet hits all over, and it was very vulnerable. One stray bullet hitting their fuel tank could cause an explosion. The light was gone and their dark night scopes were working again. The two snipers had Ash in the helicopter sitting by the door in their crosshairs. The fingers of the snipers were on their triggers of the rifles ready to fire when they heard low growls behind them.

Grey Smoke had picked up a group of hungry wolf-dogs that viciously attacked the two snipers. The men were no match for wolf-dogs. Everyone on the helicopter could hear their screams. The group of wolf dogs ripped the two men to shreds.

In the moonlight, Cordy watched Grey Smoke leading the group back into the forest. Ash was shaking from the cold. Cordy hugged him with all her strength. Bob placed another blanket over him. Ash had tears in his eyes. Everything hit him at once.

"He's gone, Cordy! I'm so sorry! I tried to save him, but he wasn't breathing. He wanted me to let him go. I think he wanted it this way, and somehow he knew that this was his last trip."

Cordy was crying and put her arms around Ash. "You did everything you could, Ash, to save him."

Bill grabbed more blankets, placing one on Ash and another on Cordy. He thought the sacrifice was going to be him, and all along Uriel knew it would be the chief. Uriel had tried to prepare him. Bob went over to see how Ellen was doing. He put his hand in hers and their eyes met. "You are going to make it. Hang in there. I don't know if you remember me, but you and I have met before."

Ellen weakly whispered, "Your retirement day on the elevator, I remember."

She squeezed his hand and smiled, falling into a deep sleep. The medic said, "She's stable, and the hospital is waiting for us." The helicopter headed back to Halifax and Bob promised Cordy that he would find Grey Smoke and bring him back home.

Chapter 59

Julia's Dream

She was in a dream. It was her birthday party, and there were six candles on the cake. She could hear, "Happy birthday, dear Julia, happy birthday to you."

The child watched the men in black shoot her parents in front of her. A younger chairman saw her hiding in the corner. The other men were ready to kill her. The chairman picked her up. He used a coaxing voice, "You don't remember anything, Ellen. Your name is Ellen now. You're my good little girl. Aren't you? If you ever do remember, then you will die just like your parents. Do you understand, my dear?"

The little girl was in total shock and nodded her head. Ellen was placed under the chairman's guardianship after her parents died. The Villiers estate and trust were under his control. He molested and raped her when she was ten. It was then the cold-hearted Ellen took over completely. Ellen's personality replaced Julia Villiers's. Ellen was a survivor, and Julia Villiers's memories were pushed back, too painful to remember.

Julia's Dream

The poison in her system put her whole body into shock. Julia Villiers had returned, and Ellen was dead. All her childhood memories came back, including her parent's faces. She looked up in the fog and saw Bob's face looking at her and holding her hand. "You are going to make it. Hang in there."

Darkness came back, and Julia slept. The helicopter landed on the hospital tarmac. Bob picked Julia up and set her on the stretcher. Bob, the medic team, and Cordy ran into the emergency room and rolled Julia into the trauma room.

Cordy looked at Bob. "She is going to need guarding, and it has to be a secret. The chief saved her life for a reason. I think it was all about her. She is a Pure of Heart."

Bob winked at her. "I'm on it!"

Bill looked at Cordy. "She is a high-ranked Child of the Nephilim. The chairman trained her himself. She is dangerous."

Cordy smiled. "She is a Pure of Heart now. The insider knowledge she possesses will bring the Nephilim to its knees. It was all about saving her. The chief sacrificed his life to save her for a reason. I know it."

Bill looked through the intensive care glass window at the lovely, innocent-looking woman sleeping. "I hope she was worth it."

Cordy confidently answered, "She could have killed all of us, but she didn't. Julia is a Pure of Heart. Is it a coincidence that my journey started with Mary Magdalene and it ended on Magdalen Island with the wishing cup? Magdalene was a Pure of Heart, too, and the Bible stated she suffered with seven demons. If Magdalene was saved, then doesn't Ellen deserve a chance? Is it all a coincidence? I don't think so."

Bill put his arm around Cordy's shoulders and they walked out of the hospital.

Chapter 60

Ellen and Bob

Ellen was dressed in a black business suit, her short skirt split on the side, allowing all the men to admire her long legs. She crossed them in front of the long-haired Bob, who was giving the board a hard time about their unscrupulous corrupt dealings. She caught his eyes on her legs while he was blasting away at the numbers on the accounts. He was no dummy, and he wasn't going to play their games.

Ellen thought, "He is kinda cute when he gets his temper going. If he doesn't shut the hell up, the Nephilim are going to exterminate him."

The board asked him for his resignation, and Bob willingly gave it to them. The meeting was adjourned, and Bob glanced at her legs again before he stormed out of the room.

Bob collected his things and headed for the elevator where Ellen was waiting for him. Ellen smiled at him. "You sure gave it to those idiots, and I thought I would give you my condolences before you left."

Ellen and Bob

Bob smiled. "They're just a bunch of corrupt jerks. Thanks, and may I say those legs are the best thing I've seen today."

The elevator door opened on the 54th floor, and Bob walked on the elevator with Ellen. Ellen's white blouse was open, revealing her plump breasts. Ellen turned to watch the elevator door close and then pushed the elevator stop button.

"I thought you deserved a proper send-off after all the hard work you did." She pulled off her black lace panties and placed them over the elevator camera in the corner up above. Bob contemplated it for about five seconds. "Oh, what the hell, why not!"

He grabbed her and pushed her against the elevator.

His hands went up her shirt, and he kissed her hard, leaving Ellen breathless. She had never felt like this with a man before. A pressure and flutter in her chest made her tingle all over. It was a different sensation never felt by her before. Ellen kissed him with a passion she never knew. Bob's strong arms cradled her and he kissed her tenderly, looking into her eyes.

The people waiting for the elevator heard strange noises and wondered what the hell was going on up there. Ellen buttoned her shirt and smoothed the wrinkles on her skirt while Bob smiled. He grabbed Ellen's black panties off the camera and smiled. She released the emergency stop button and the elevator moved downward.

"I have to say, this was the best resignation perk I've ever gotten in my life. You are going to need these."

Ellen smiled and pushed the elevator button to start the downward descent. "You keep them as a souvenir to remember me by."

Bob took the lace panties and placed them in his coat pocket. "My name is Bob, what's yours?"

Ellen introduced herself, "I'm Ellen, and, Bob, my advice to you is if you want to live, then you better get the hell out of New York. I would hate to see you meet with an untimely accident. Have a nice day!" Ding!

The door opened and everybody watched Bob and Ellen walk

off. In the crowd of people waiting near the elevator door, Ellen saw Chief Saunhac, but he was wearing Crusader armor with a white tunic adorned with a red cross, pentacle, and crescent moon. "You need to find Solomon's ring, Julia."

Julia woke up with Bob holding her hand. Bob smiled at her. "You're awake, sleepy head, and I have a nice hospital breakfast for you."

Julia looked around. She was in a hospital bed with intravenous fluids running and a cardiac monitor hooked onto her. She recognized Bob as the guy in the elevator. Her memories started coming back like a flood, and she remembered who Julia Villiers was and how her family was killed.

Bob buttered her toast. "You gotta eat something. Doc's orders."

Julia grabbed the toast and took a bite. "I remember you."

Bob smiled. "I never forgot you or those five minutes in the elevator."

Julia eyes locked with his. Bob gazed back at her intensely. "What are you going to do?"

Julia took on a steely cold venomous look. "I'm going to find out what the truth is and when I do, then I'll make my decision."

Bob held her hand gently. "You don't have to. You could run and hide. We have hidden you from them."

"Running isn't my style, but I assure you I'm going to find out the truth."

Bob looked hard at her. "Beware of a ticked-off woman."

Julia drank her orange juice. "You may have all been better off leaving me for dead." Bob kissed her on the lips gently. "I'll wait for you while you figure it all out." He handed her a red rose. "Here's something to remember me," he said as he waved goodbye and walked out the door. Who was she? Ellen or Julia, it was time to find out.

CHAPTER 61

The Chief's Funeral

Genesis 3:22-24
22 And the Lord God said, Behold, the man is become as one of us, to know good and evil: and now, lest he put forth his hand, and take also of the tree of life, and eat, and live for ever:23 Therefore the Lord God sent him forth from the Garden of Eden, to till the ground from whence he was taken.24 So he drove out the man; and he placed at the east of the garden of Eden Cherubims, and a flaming sword which turned every way, to keep the way of the tree of life.

The Mi'kmaq tribe was all there to celebrate the chief's journey home. Bill and Cordy set up a foundation under Chief Saunhac's name to give scholarships to Mi'kmaq children. His name was added to his wife's grave. Flowers filled the top of the grave. Bill spoke at the funeral mass, telling the great stories and accomplishments of the Chief. The words engraved in stone on the chief's grave read, "Here lies Chief Saunhac, son, husband, father, grandfather, great-grandfather and warrior of the Mi'kmaq. Blessed are the Pure of Heart for they shall see God."

Cordy, Ash, and Bill saw Uriel standing by a large tree next to the grave. Each one of them saw Uriel but kept it to themselves. They didn't want the others to think they were crazy. Bob had jumped in his car to drive over to the Chief's house when a young red-haired man who was dressed in a light gray suit knocked on his car window. He thought for a second the man looked familiar. Bob smiled and rolled his window down, "Can I help you, buddy?" He answered, "My name is Uriel. I was told you were looking for some good team players. Do you have some job openings?"

Bob handed him his business card. "As a matter of fact, I do have some job openings. Were you friends with Chief Saunhac?"

Uriel nodded. "Yes, the chief and I were very good friends. He told me that you were looking for some good people to work for you."

Bob nodded. "I tell you what, Uriel, why don't you call me for an interview and send me your resume. We'll see if you have the qualifications to be on our team. I have to ask, do you have a brother in St. Louis? Because there's a librarian there who could pass for your twin." Uriel smiled. "My father was an innovative creator and got around. What can I say, wherever he hung his hat was his home. Heaven only knows, he could be a relation. Thanks, Bob, you will be getting a call. I hope I pass the drug screening."

He chuckled and gave Bob a wave good-bye. Bob laughed and drove off thinking Uriel better pass that drug screening or he wasn't getting hired. It was a challenge to find good people you could trust but he had a good feeling about Uriel, especially if he knew the Chief. Bob drove to the reception. He knew Cordy needed all the support she could get.

The reception was held at the chief's house. Ash was wonderful and stayed to help. Later in the evening, Ash sat with Cordy on the porch outside under a full moon. On Cordy's lap lay Chief Saunhac's book containing her family's legacy. An open page showed the design of the Solomon Seal engraved on a ring.

Cordy asked, "Ash, where do we go from here?"

The Chief's Funeral

Ash looked at her. "I know what you mean. The chief told me the war was just starting and that a terrible man would try to gain the power of the universe. He was looking for all the objects of power because one of them will give the ultimate power over heaven and earth. No man can handle this power, but he didn't say a woman couldn't handle it. Solomon's ring was so powerful that the world could be destroyed by it or saved. I think we have some of the objects of power but not all of them."

Cordy fingered the chief's necklace around her neck. Solomon's seal was engraved on the ring that was on the chain he gave her before he died and on the crystal stone. Ash looked at Cordy and looked up at the stars. "The Pure of Heart are going to have to rise up for the biggest battle of the ages. I don't have anything better to do. Do you?"

Cordy held in her hand the crystal ball, and Ash placed the Ankh symbol for the Key of Life into the hole on the top. The crystal ball lit up, and Cordy smiled at Ash.

"I come from a family of great warriors. I'm here to witness the biggest conflict mankind and the earth has ever seen. Bring it on!"

Cordy let out the Mi'kmaq war hoop and Ash followed. Ash and Cordy heard the howl of a wolf-dog in the distance.

Epilogue

Cordy wasn't sure when she first met Ash what type of man he was, and he didn't disappoint her. Most men were still playing childish games. Ash was different. He had just been in a life and death conflict. He didn't hesitate to put his own life on the line to save the chief. To say he was the hottest guy she had ever met was an understatement, and now she felt herself drawn to him but for other reasons that she couldn't explain.

Ash started to walk toward her, and Cordy couldn't help but feel her heart start to beat faster. The palms of her hands started to sweat. For the first time in her life and for a split second, she thought is this true love? As he got up close, she panicked and grabbed him by the shirt and threw him up against the doorjamb. She leaned in and pressed her body up against his as if they were one body. She looked into his eyes and whispered, "You confuse me!"

She turned her head and snuggled next to his chest. Cordy could feel and hear his heart beating fast, and his chest started to move as if he couldn't catch his breath.

Epilogue

Ash was trying his best to be a gentleman, and then without warning, his animal instincts kicked in. His arms that were dangling at his side suddenly wrapped around Cordy, and he pulled her in even tighter. Now, he was taking deep rhythmic breaths, and Cordy could tell he was equally taken by her.

Without any warning, Cordy began to cry. She couldn't remember the last time she cried and never like this, with her whole body shaking uncontrollably. Ash could feel her chin quiver as she gasped for air, and he could feel his shirt start to get damp from the river of warm tears. Ash had never experienced anything like this before in his life. He wished he could hold her forever, but he knew this was not the true Cordy, the hard-as-nails woman he had admired from afar. He grabbed her shoulders, pulled her back and brushed off her cheeks with his two thumbs and smiled at her dark gypsy eyes. He knew his opportunity was at hand.

Ash said, "Damn, woman, if this is what happens when I confuse you, I would hate to see what would happen if I scared you or made you mad."

Cordy broke loose of his hold and with a small laugh said, "Anyone who scared me never lived to tell about it." She laughed again.

Bob was standing just outside in the next room and knew it was OK to come in. Cordy was wiping off the rest of her tears and started to smile. Bob instinctively knew not to comment on Cordy's appearance.

"Well, Bob, what can you do to cheer me up? I'm missing the chief already."

Bob had a grim and concerned look on his face. Bad news isn't easy to give to someone who is already crying, but he knew deep down Cordy had the strength to handle it.

"I'm sorry, Cordy, but I am afraid you had an emergency call from a Sister Agnes. It isn't good. She said to tell you that they are out to kill you. You need to trust her and go to the Knock Shrine in Mayo County, Ireland. It isn't safe for you to see her any more, and she was going to the old home. She said you would know where that is and then she hung up."

Ash looked relieved. "Thank God, I thought they were after me. It's you they're after."

Bob and Cordy's heads snapped over to look at Ash. Cordy looked at Ash intensely. "It's about time you brought us up to speed naked tomb robber. If you have something to tell us, Ash, last week would have been the time."

Ash blushed. "Well, I am afraid there is more to tell than I would like to admit."

Cordy looked pissed enough to kill.

"You see, one of the reasons I needed to see the chief was because of the Mi'kmaq hieroglyphs. It happens that on a photo shoot, I came across some artifacts that are quite unique. They have Egyptian and Mi'kmaq symbols on them. In today's archaeology world, if you find something new that doesn't fit, then the academic community's thinking is that they just bury it, and it never sees the light of day. A good example of this happened in the United States. The Kensington Runestone was found in Minnesota in 1896. On the stone, it stated that a group of North men were on a journey, and it was dated 1362. Christopher Columbus wasn't born until 1451. If the academics were to acknowledge this, then all American history would have to be rewritten. How could so many be wrong for so long? The heads of state and even the Pope don't like to admit they got it wrong. It's because any time something changes, it makes the masses question what they have been told over the years. And if they're wrong on this, what else could they be wrong about? It has to do with credibility."

Cordy put both hands on her hips. "So are you a tomb robber?"

Ash started stuttering, "No, well, well, I guess yes, in a way."

"In the Navy SEALs, we were taught to believe nothing you read or hear, half what you see and be ready to kill anybody you are not sure of. And right now, I am halfway to killing you, Ash."

Epilogue

Bob took two steps toward Ash, and Cordy reached out to stop him.

Bob questioned him further, "How did you get out of Egypt? And why didn't you get stopped?"

Ash answered, "By boat to Greece, and anyone can get in or out of there. The country is in turmoil."

Cordy looked at him intensely. "Is that all?"

Ash decided to tell them everything. "No, there's more. My real name is Asho."

Cordy looked at Bob exasperated. "Oh my God, Bob, we are looking at a truly one of a kind asshole."

Ash thought, here we go again. "I didn't say asshole, I said Asho, and it is spelled A-S-H-O."

Bob began to smile and then to laugh uncontrollably. Cordy cracked a smile, too.

Ash became defensive. "My father gave me that name, and my mother let me change it to Ash because of people like you. It is a proud name that has Persian origins. In Egyptian hieroglyphics, the meaning of Asho is 'Pure of Heart.'"

Ash glared back at Cordy and Bob. Cordy in an instant changed her demeanor toward Ash as she realized he was hurting.

Cordy quietly touched his shoulder. "That's why you were looking for Maggie on the Internet and you emailed me. Cordelia means 'Pure of Heart,' too."

Ash nodded. "Yes, and the fact that you had the necklace with the Mi'kmaq hieroglyphics on it in the video was the clincher."

"I don't know if we can trust him, Cordy. Let me kill him?"

Cordy shook her head. "Sister Agnes said I was going to meet up with more Pure of Hearts. Ash proved himself to me when he was willing to save the chief's life."

Bob backed off and looked at both of them. "Well, it looks like you two are off to Ireland. I'll get your private plane ready. Cordy and you will be flying out of Halifax. I have come up with an untraceable system to get you cash on the run. We are going

Keys of Life

to use prepaid gift cards, and Cordy knows where they have been hidden. Cordy, you have your two passports. We have a problem with where you will sleep. They will be looking everywhere, and you won't be able to use hotels so it could get very dangerous. You'll have to get creative. It sounds like your little asshole already has some experience running and hiding."

Ash was getting really mad. "Cut the crap, Bob."

Bob was thinking about hitting Ash. "You're lucky to be alive, you little asshole. There are two things to remember about me. One, never make me mad, and two, never make me mad!"

Cordy tried to lighten the charged atmosphere. "Now Bob, I think you're scaring Little Rabbit. You see, Ash, I do have feelings after all, and who knows, Bob, he may come in handy."

Ash countered back, "Yeah, Bob, I didn't see you jump out of the helicopter to save anyone."

Bob lunged at Ash and then stopped. Ash jumped back two steps instinctively but ready to fight.

Cordy spoke with a smile on her face, "Stop it, you two, or I will kick both your asses."

Ash had a thought. "I do have someone that can help us. She has ties to the U.S. diplomatic core, and we should have a safe haven in any port. She was just transferred to Ireland, so I'll give her a call. We worked together on my last photo shoot. Her name is Linda." Ash took out his cell phone.

"My guess is they're already trying to track you Ash. Give me that cell phone." He handed Ash one of two new cell phones. "They won't trace the numbers to these two. Just don't let them out of your sight. The CIA and Army are issued these." Bob handed one to Ash, and the other to Cordy.

Ash opened up his wallet and pulled out a small address book the size of a business card.

Cordy smiled, "I never saw a black book that size. I guess you like to have your numbers close at hand."

Ash shook his head. "It's not like that, Cordy. I have a lot of professional people I work with."

Epilogue

Cordy playfully said, "I understand all the working girls call themselves professionals today."

Ash chuckled. "Ha ha, very funny. If you only knew." Ash started to call Linda on his new phone and asked Bob how to turn the volume up. As he was looking, he pushed speaker by mistake. The phone was ringing, and Ash didn't think anything of it.

Linda picked up on the other end. "Hello. This better be good. Your number didn't come up on caller ID. I don't take calls from strangers."

"Linda, is that you? This is Ash."

"Ash, oh my God, I was just lying here thinking of you. I remember that day in the temple when you put your hand on me, it made me feel so exhilarated and scared. When we were done, I was exhausted but never felt better. I never did apologize for acting so aggressive in the truck that night. It wasn't like me. I hope I didn't scare you."

Ash was trying to get the phone off speaker, but the damage was already done. Cordy rolled her eyes at Ash.

Cordy started to walk away. "Come on, Bob, let the love birds have some privacy." Cordy grabbed Bob's arm, pulling him into the other room.

Ash finally got the phone off speaker. "Linda, stop talking about that day, and just listen. I am going to need some help. A close friend of mine and I are going to need a place to stay in Ireland. Can you help me make other arrangements to stay with some of your girlfriends?"

Cordy was listening in from around the corner. She heard Ash asking about arrangements to stay with other girlfriends.

Linda said, "I had so much fun working with you that day. I was anticipating what to do next so you could get the best photos. Ash, I would like to do it again sometime."

"Linda, I had a lot of fun that day, and you did a great job anticipating all of my needs. I got a lot of great pictures, and who knows, we may get to do it again sometime."

Keys of Life

All Cordy's mind registered was, he had a lot of fun, she anticipated all his needs, and he'd like to do it again sometime. Cordy was getting mad at herself. She couldn't believe Ash got her to drop her defenses.

Ash warned, "Linda, it could be dangerous. I want you to be extremely careful."

"Most of my friends in the diplomat core are in danger every day. Will you need protection from the U.S. military? How many will be with you? Are they physically fit? Sometimes you may have to gain entry to the estates by climbing a wall or a tree, especially if you don't want anyone to know you are there."

Ash answered matter of factly, "I don't like using protection. I know it can get messy. It will just be me and one other very physically fit woman. She has long legs and plenty of muscle that would get her on top of anything."

All Cordy heard was, he didn't like using protection, and he was expecting her to be on top. Cordy was thinking there was no way she was getting on top, and there was no way she was going to be in a three-way.

Bob walked over to Cordy. He was just getting off his phone. Cordy was still trying to eavesdrop on Ash, but Bob was too distracting.

Cordy looked at Bob. "Well, Bob, what did you come up with?"

Bob reached into the other room and motioned to Ash to come.

"Linda, I have to go. I will call you when we land in Ireland. Thanks!" Ash hung up the phone and looked at Bob. "Bob, what's the deal?"

Bob answered, "It's time for you two to get going. The plane will be ready when you get to the airport. That's the good news. The bad news is that the pilot said there is fog moving in. The pilot informed me if you aren't there in less than an hour you won't make it out tonight."

Ash was puzzled. "We are late already. We can't drive fast enough to make it."

Epilogue

"Cordy, are you sure this one is smart enough for you to hang with? The helicopter will be here in less than five minutes, Mr. Ash." Bob winked at Cordy and then chuckled.

Ash shrugged. "I never had my own helicopter, private boats, ship, or plane, so excuse me. I was born poor."

"Relax, Ash. I'm not used to it either. It wasn't until just recently that I came into a big, or should I say gargantuan, pile of money".

Bob smiled. "Oh yeah, by the way boss, that pile has already grown by five percent, and you have a lot of investments cooking already."

Cordy shook her head. "Bob, I don't really need any updates. I trust you with my life and my money, especially seeing how you did come to the rescue at just the right time." They could hear the sounds of the helicopter and now it was coming into view.

Bob grinned. "How did you do on the sleeping arrangements?"

Ash smiled. "We are all set. We have a bed waiting for us in Ireland as we speak."

Cordy looked at both of them. "You better hope there is more than one bed because your ass will be sleeping out in the car. If it's good enough for the homeless, well, let's just say it should be good enough for one on-the-run tomb robber. You can put any hopes of a three-way out of your head right now."

Bob and Ash looked at Cordy as if, where the hell did that come from, and then they just shrugged their shoulders. The helicopter was on the ground now, and two men came in and dropped off two black backpacks and two black duffle bags. Cordy picked hers up and started toward the helicopter. Bob pulled Ash to the side and gave him two Glocks with two additional clips for protection. Ash put one down his pants and the rest into the backpack.

Bob whispered, "A Glock 20 has the force to knock down anything. You may need them at the airport. The pilot told me they had two groups without identification go by twice. Someone is looking for someone or something. I don't know what the chief gave you, but it was worth dying for. I like my new job, and I like my new boss. The way you have been looking at her lately tells me you like her a lot more than me, lover boy, so don't let anything happen to her."

Ash shook Bob's hand and smiled. "I'll take good care of her." He ran to the helicopter. Cordy was sitting inside as Ash jumped in and sat across from her.

As the helicopter took off, Ash noticed Cordy's eyes fixated on his crotch. She was looking at the huge bulge in his pants. Little did she know the lethal Glock was there. Ash pulled up his shirt and Cordy could see that while most men had six pack abs, this one had an eight pack. They were like chiseled stone. Then he pulled out the Glock 20 from his pants. Cordy started to laugh. "I was wondering what you were packin', cowboy."

They both laughed before putting their war faces on.

Ash reached in his bag and pulled out the second Glock 20. "Bob said we might need these." They knew the danger and the grave circumstance that they were getting ready to embark on, and at the same time, they reached out and grabbed each other's hands.

About the Authors

Carolyn Schield and Tom Vorbeck are a unique brother and sister team who decided to write a thrilling, adventurous, and mysterious trilogy. The Keys of Life, the first book of the trilogy, brought them together after they had drifted apart over the years.

Carolyn writes articles for alternative media and international magazines. Some of her favorite topics are stories concerning the search for the Holy Grail, for which she has been interviewed on live radio. She lives in Texas with her husband and children.

Tom is an award-winning artist. His work can be seen at the Holocaust Museum in Washington, D.C. Carolyn and Tom hope to share with readers their passion and excitement for life.

For more information, visit www.facebook.com/urielsjustice.

To hear about new releases, sign up for the Keys of Life Newsletter.

All readers can visit our website at www.urielsjustice.com

You can buy Carolyn and Tom's books at most online retailers and bookstores. If your bookstore or library doesn't carry our book, sometimes they can order it for you.